SIXTY DAYS TO LIVE

Her Uncle Oliver, the distinguished astronomer, told
Lavina: 'It would be a pity for you to die without the
experience of marriage, my dear. A comet is due to hit
the earth on the 24th of June and none of us has more
than sixty days to live.'

Once the cat was out of the bag, things began to happen. A plot to overthrow the Government. Panic, riots,
street fighting. London under martial law.

Fire, flood and tempest: the world gone mad. Scene
after scene of breath-taking excitement, written with all
that vigour and suspense which has made Dennis
Wheatley's books so eagerly sought after all over the
world.

BY DENNIS WHEATLEY

NOVELS

The Launching of Roger Brook
The Shadow of Tyburn Tree
The Rising Storm
The Man Who Killed the King
The Dark Secret of Josephine
The Rape of Venice
The Sultan's Daughter

The Scarlet Impostor
Faked Passports
The Black Baroness
V for Vengeance
Come into My Parlour
Traitors' Gate
They Used Dark Forces

The Prisoner in the Mask
Vendetta in Spain
The Second Seal
Three Inquisitive People
The Forbidden Territory
The Devil Rides Out
The Golden Spaniard
Strange Conflict
Dangerous Inheritance

Codeword—Golden Fleece
The Quest of Julian Day
The Sword of Fate
Bill for the Use of a Body

Black August
Contraband

To the Devil—a Daughter
The Satanist

The Eunuch of Stamboul
The Secret War
The Fabulous Valley
Sixty Days to Live
Such Power is Dangerous
Uncharted Seas
The Man Who Missed the War
The Haunting of Toby Jugg
Star of Ill-Omen
They Found Atlantis
The Island Where Time Stands Still
The Ka of Gifford Hillary
Curtain of Fear
Mayhem in Greece

SHORT STORIES

Mediterranean Nights
Gunmen, Gallants and Ghosts

HISTORICAL

Old Rowley
(*A Private Life of Charles II*)
Red Eagle
(*The Story of the Russian Revolution*)

AUTOBIOGRAPHICAL

Stranger than Fiction
(*War Papers for the Joint Planning Staff*)
Saturdays with Bricks

DENNIS WHEATLEY

Sixty Days to Live

ARROW BOOKS

ARROW BOOKS LTD

178–202 Great Portland Street, London W1

AN IMPRINT OF THE HUTCHINSON GROUP

London Melbourne Sydney
Auckland Bombay Toronto
Johannesburg New York

First published by
Hutchinson & Co. (*Publishers*) Ltd 1939
Reprinted 1950, 1952, 1956
Arrow edition 1960
Second impression 1966

*Made and printed in Great Britain
by The Anchor Press, Ltd.,
Tiptree, Essex*

For

JOHN AND HILDA GARDNER

Because they are my oldest friends, because of the many happy hours I have spent with them and because, by a strange coincidence, John suggested that I should write a 'Comet' story one day last autumn when that very morning I had decided to write one myself.

CONTENTS

CONTENTS

1

AN OFFER OF MARRIAGE

Lavina Leigh paused for a second in the entrance of the Savoy Grill. The *maître d'hôtel* smiled, bowed and moved forward, upon which she made her entrance.

Lavina was good at making entrances. She was slim, very fair and, although she was not tall, her film work had taught her to make the best of her inches and she carried herself like a Princess.

Even in that sophisticated supper-time crowd, heads turned as she swept forward. Ace director Alfred Hitchcock, perched like Humpty Dumpty on the edge of a chair, gave her a little wave of greeting from one table; and B.B.C. chief Val Gielgud, looking very Russian with his little pointed beard, smiled at her from another.

The man who followed Lavina was in his late forties. He had a square face with a bulldog chin, but his features were redeemed from coarseness by pleasant brown eyes, a fine forehead and a touch of grey in his dark, smooth hair, over either temple.

Sir Samuel Curry was used to appearing in public with good-looking women. He was very rich and decidedly a connoisseur, but even so, on this night towards the end of April he was conscious of a little glow of pride in his glamorous companion as he followed her to their table and they settled themselves at it.

He did not ask her what she would have to eat but ordered for her, as they had been friends for some months and he knew all her favourite dishes. In less than a minute the waiter had departed to execute Sir Samuel's clear, decisive orders.

'You know,' he said, 'I never come here except with you. I much prefer the Restaurant.'

She shrugged. 'Don't be difficult, Sam dear. I know you millionaires always congregate there but the Grill's so much more interesting. Look, there's Gilbert Frankau and his pretty wife, with Leon M. Lion; and at that other table Doris Zinkeisen and her husband, Grahame Johnstone. You saw "Hitch", too, as we came in. The big man with him is Henry Sherek and the little woman is "Hitch's" clever wife who vets most of his scripts for him. Besides, all the big boys on the Press come here and that's immensely useful.'

Sam Curry smiled a little ruefully. 'Yes, I suppose it's part of your job to keep in touch with all these people, but I wish to goodness you'd be sensible and chuck it. You'll never make a film star.'

Her small, beautifully-shaped mouth opened on an exclamation of protest, but she suppressed it and lit a cigarette before she replied with calm aloofness: 'I am one already.'

'Oh, no, you're not,' he mocked her. 'You're only a starlet. No one's a real star until they've been given a Hollywood contract.'

Lavina lifted her heavy eyelids lazily. 'That doesn't apply any more, Sam.'

But in spite of her denial she knew that he was right. In three years she had done very well and, as she was only twenty-three, she still had a good film life before her. But, at times, she was subject to horrid doubts as to whether she would get much further.

Her acting was sound; she had a personality that attracted every man with whom she came in contact and, physically, she was about as nearly perfect as any woman could be, but, all the same, she knew quite well that her beauty was not of a kind best suited for motion-pictures.

It was of that fine, aristocratic type which is based on bone-formation and ensures for every woman who has it the certainty of still being lovely in old age. Her small, perfectly-chiselled Roman nose and narrow, oval face gave her great distinction; but her nose had proved an appalling handicap in her work, as in all but the most carefully selected angles it threw a tiresome shadow when she was being filmed under the glare of the arc-lamps. That one factor had already robbed her of several good parts and might well prevent her from ever achieving real stardom, unless she was willing to have her nose broken and re-modelled—which she was not prepared to do.

While they ate their *bligny* and the stuffed quails which followed they talked of the people round about them. One waiter refilled their glasses with Roederer '28. Another brought them fresh peaches. After he had peeled them and moved away, Sam Curry said:

'When are you going to present me to your people, Lavina?'

Little wrinkles at the corners of her eyes, which came from frequent laughter, creased up as she parried: 'Why this sudden question?'

'Because I'm old-fashioned enough to want to observe the custom of meeting your relations before I marry you.'

Her blackened eyelashes lifted, showing the surprise in her blue-grey eyes. 'Surely you don't mean that you would walk right out of my life if they disapproved of you?'

'Of course not. It's just a courtesy.'

'But I haven't said that I *will* marry you, yet.'

'You're going to, as sure as my name's Sam Curry.'

She shook her golden head in silent mockery.

'Listen, Lavina,' he went on. 'Even if you could become a real film star, it's a dog's life, and you know it. On the set at eight o'clock or earlier most mornings; often working the whole night through; and what little leisure you *do* get is wasted in acting a part all the time: opening bazaars, posing for photographers, endless fittings at dressmakers', showing yourself off in places like this because it's vital to get continuous publicity if you're to keep in the swim at all.'

'I like it,' she shrugged.

'Maybe. But in ten years, at the outside, you'll be worn out, finished, and no good to anyone. Already you're losing your eye for make-up and, if you go on this way, you'll become a hag before you're thirty. Get some of that paint off your face and look twice as beautiful. Cut out this film business and enjoy yourself, my dear, while you're still young and healthy.'

'I should be bored to tears doing nothing all day.'

'But you wouldn't be doing nothing,' he persisted. 'I've made enough to take things easy now, and we could travel. You'd like that, wouldn't you? There's the house in London. And we'd have another in the country; a big place where we could entertain. Think what fun it would be for you, with your artistic flair, to furnish and decorate it. Besides, you could do an immense amount of good with my money. I've been too busy to think of other people while I've been making it, but you must have lots of pet schemes you'd like to foster; and if running a couple of big houses, with frequent trips abroad, isn't enough, you'd find plenty to occupy you in really worth-while charities.'

'You think I'm a much nicer person than I really am. Actually, I'm extremely selfish and rather lazy.'

He looked her straight in the eyes. 'That's just one of your poses, Lavina, and if you stick on in the film game, it may become a permanent part of your nature. Instead, you're going to marry me and remain your own sweet self, and I suggest that as a first step you should introduce me to your people.'

'I've never confessed to having any.'

'True. You always pose as a "mystery woman", but I'll bet you've got some relatives tucked away somewhere. Of course, if they gave you a rotten deal, we'll leave it at that; but the chances are that they follow your career through the papers with tremendous pride, so it would be the decent thing to do just to go and see them before you get married.'

'As a matter of fact, they're very fond of me. But you might not like them.'

'Does that matter?' He smiled suddenly and his brown eyes twinkled. 'I'm not suggesting that they should come and live with us.'

'I'm afraid the squalor of my old home would quite appal you.'

'So the glamorous Lavina Leigh was dragged up in a slum?' he said meditatively. 'I find that surprising. You're an aristocrat to your finger-tips; but then, perhaps you're a love child.'

'No. I'm as certain as one can ever be that I'm not, but remember, it's marvellous what the film people can do when they groom a girl for stardom.'

'Voice, hair, beauty culture, deportment, clothes, I grant you,' he nodded, 'but they couldn't have given you those long, slender hands, your narrow wrists and ankles; or that princess-look that's so marked in all your features. The fact that you're a thoroughbred is stamped all over you. But, anyhow, what's it matter where you came from? My father was a foreman-mechanic and, if I wore the only old school tie that I'm entitled to, no one would know it outside Bradford. Are your people very poor, Lavina?'

'They struggle on, somehow, but they never quite know how they're going to keep the roof over their heads.'

'In that case I'd like to arrange to make things a bit easier for them in the future.'

Lavina laughed readily at every jest and was almost always smiling, either at something someone had said or at her secret thoughts, but now her eyes took on a serious expression as she said:

'You're a nice person, Sam, aren't you?'

'No. I'm hard as nails but it happens that I love you, so I'd like to do things for anybody with whom you're connected. Do your people live in London?'

'No.'

'In the provinces, then?'

'No. In these days I suppose you'd almost call it a suburb.'

'Whereabouts?'

'Well, if you *must* know, I'm a farmer's daughter and I spent most of my childhood in the country. But Surrey has been so built-over now that you can hardly call it country any longer.'

'D'you ever go and see them?'

'No. I haven't been home for three years, because Mother's dead and I quarrelled with Father about going on the films.'

'Then it's quite time that you made it up with him.'

Lavina half-closed her eyes as she drew upon her cigarette. Then she nodded slowly. 'Perhaps you're right, Sam. My father adores me really and I've been thinking rather a lot about him lately. Mind, I still haven't said that I'm going to marry you, but if you like I'll write and say that I'm prepared to bury the hatchet and ask if I can take you down there next week-end.'

2

AN INCREDIBLE ANNOUNCEMENT

On the following Saturday afternoon Sir Samuel Curry drove
down into Surrey with Lavina beside him. When they had passed
Dorking, with its outcrop of modern, jerry-built houses, she
directed him as he swung the powerful coupé through narrow,
twisting lanes towards the little village of Stapleton.

The previous night she had told him that he was to pack a bag,
as her father had written that he would be glad if she and her
friend would stay the week-end.

Sam was immensely intrigued to see what Lavina's home
would be like and had been visualizing some tumbledown old
farmhouse; so he was considerably surprised when she checked
him at a pair of great iron gates flanked by stone pillars, set in a
wall that hemmed in a belt of woodland.

True, the iron gates, which stood open, were rusty and one of
the stone lions holding shields, which crowned the pillars, had lost
its head. But, quite obviously, it was the entrance to a big estate.

'Where's this?' he asked.

'Stapleton Court.'

'Has your father got the home farm here, then?'

She smiled. 'I suppose you'd call it that, as it's the only one
that's left to us.'

He pulled up the car a couple of hundred yards along the drive
and turned to look at her. 'D'you mean, Lavina, that Stapleton
Court's your home?'

'Yes. And I don't think I told you that my real name is
Stapleton, did I? My family has lived here for centuries.'

'You little devil,' he laughed. 'You led me to suppose that your
father was just a poor farmer.'

'But he is, Sam. We had money once, lots of it, and owned
miles of country hereabouts; but a Stapleton, in Regency times,
gambled nearly everything we had away, racing cockroaches and
things. Now, farming doesn't pay any longer and the family's on

14

its beam-ends. You may have noticed that the Lodge is empty and the drive all overgrown. Of course, I pulled your leg a little bit, just for fun, but Daddy really is most desperately poor.'

'Well, perhaps we could rectify that.' He smiled as he let the clutch in again. 'Buy the place and let it to him for a peppercorn, or something.'

She quickly shook her head. 'For goodness' sake don't try to. He's as proud as Lucifer and determined to die here rather than sell the place, even if the roof literally falls in. He wouldn't accept a loan from one of his own relatives, so please don't even mention the word money.'

A quarter of a mile farther on they swept round the curve of a broad lake, beyond which lay a square, red brick Georgian house of moderate size.

There was no butler to receive them but Gervaise Stapleton came out himself with his brother, Oliver, who was also down for the week-end, and Lavina's elder sister, Margery.

Although Gervaise Stapleton had not seen his errant favourite daughter for just over three years, he greeted her as naturally as though they had only parted the day before. He was a tall, white-haired man nearing sixty, with the same aristocratic features as Lavina and the same magnetic personality.

Her Uncle Oliver was a less distinguished and more untidy replica of his elder brother. The best part of his life had been spent in the Royal Observatory at Greenwich and his stooping shoulders were the result of the countless hours he had spent poring over abstruse astronomical calculations.

Margery Stapleton was three years older than Lavina and seemed to have just missed all the qualities which made Lavina such an outstanding beauty. Her limbs were sturdier, her hair light-brown instead of natural gold, her mouth even smaller and a little thin; her nose more beaked and so too prominent in her otherwise handsome face.

It was soon clear to Sam Curry that only one portion of the house was occupied; but the bedroom to which his host showed him had a cheerful wood fire burning in its grate.

'We live very simply here, as Lavina will certainly have told you before she asked you down, so I fear you'll have to unpack and fend for yourself,' was Gervaise Stapleton's only reference to his lack of servants.

'I'm used to that,' Sam lied cheerfully. It was twenty years since he had done anything but use his brain and give orders to others, but his age, his arrogance and his habit of taking it for granted that every service should be performed for him seemed to have unaccountably disappeared from the moment he had entered the half-derelict Georgian mansion.

He felt almost a boy again and that it would have been more natural to accept a five-bob tip from Lavina's father than to offer him financial assistance. There was a strange, compelling dignity about the tall white-haired figure, although Gervaise Stapleton was not the least stiff and his smiling blue eyes showed whence his younger daughter had got her sense of humour.

On coming downstairs Sam found the family assembled in the library; a long, book-lined room furnished with an assortment of pieces from a dozen different periods, but all mellowed by time, so that nothing jarred. Gervaise loved his books and so had chosen it as the living-room when economy had compelled him to close up the others.

As soon as he had a chance to talk to Margery, Sam discovered that she was as different mentally from Lavina as she was physically. The beautiful Lavina could be hard, but that was a sort of protective armour, whereas Margery's hardness was a natural quality and, clearly, she was jealous of her younger sister.

It transpired that she ran the house and looked after her father with only the help of a woman in the kitchen and a farm hand who laid the fires, cleaned the shoes and did the other heavy work each morning. She made an unnecessary parade of busying herself and mildly sarcastic remarks about Lavina's proverbial laziness.

But Lavina, lolling in a big armchair, refused to be drawn and watched her sister with a faintly cynical smile as the older girl went off to lay the table for supper.

To his own surprise, Sam found himself offering to help and he could cheerfully have smacked Lavina for the openly derisive grin with which she favoured him; but Gervaise Stapleton would not hear of his guest lifting a finger and had just produced some remarkably fine Madeira in a dust-encrusted bottle.

'We have unfortunately used up all our old sherry,' he explained, 'but I trust you will find this a passable substitute.

Luckily, I still have a few bins of it. My grandfather laid it down.'

Sam made a rapid calculation. The dark golden nectar had been bottled in the 1840's or early '50's at the latest, then. He sipped it and found it marvellous.

A newcomer entered at that moment; a good-looking, fair man aged about thirty, in well worn tweeds; whom Gervaise introduced as 'our neighbour, Derek Burroughs'.

With a quick nod to Sam, Burroughs walked straight over to Lavina, took both her hands and smiled down into her face.

'So you're back at last,' he murmured. 'I was beginning to think you'd completely forgotten us.'

'I could never do that, Derek,' she smiled up at him.

Sam Curry's mouth tightened. The fellow was in love with her. That was as clear as if he had said so, and it looked as if she had tender memories of him. For the first time that evening Sam felt himself Sir Samuel, and his age—getting on for fifty. He didn't like the thought of this solid, good-looking ghost that had suddenly arisen out of Lavina's past but he comforted himself quickly. Burroughs was evidently a gentleman-farmer—a country bumpkin with little brain and probably less money. What if he had had an affair with Lavina in the past? Surely he could not hope to attract the sophisticated woman she had now become. Still, Sam admitted to himself, he would have given a good few of his thousands to be Derek Burroughs's age again or even to have his figure.

'Do you think I've changed much, Derek?' Lavina was asking.

'You're still the same Lavina underneath,' he replied slowly, 'but on the surface—well, you're a bit startling, aren't you?'

'D'you mean my make-up?'

'Yes. All that black stuff round your eyes makes them look smaller and somehow it doesn't seem to go with your fair complexion. I suppose it's all right in a film star but the simple folk round here would take you for—for . . .'

Oliver Stapleton had been quietly working at a desk in a corner of the room. He turned, and raising his horn-rimmed spectacles, looked across at Lavina under them. 'Go on, say it, Derek,' he urged with a dry chuckle. 'A scarlet woman. That's the classic expression, isn't it? She's remained quite a nice girl really, but she's still very young.'

Lavina sat up with a jerk. 'Uncle Oliver, you're a beast!' she laughed. 'Perhaps I have got a bit much on for the country but I'm so used to it.'

Sam Curry cut into the conversation with smooth tact and was rewarded by a little look of gratitude from Lavina which made his heart beat faster.

At dinner they waited upon themselves. The meal was simple but good, and over it the Stapletons and Derek Burroughs talked mainly of old times and friends whom Sam did not know, which left him rather out of it, although Gervaise Stapleton took pains to draw him into the conversation at every opportunity.

Afterwards they sat in the library again and Lavina told her family something of the joys and pitfalls that she had met with during her three years in the studios.

At half-past eleven Derek Burroughs reluctantly broke up the party as he had a sick mare that he wanted to look at before he turned in; but on leaving he said that he would be over again first thing in the morning and it was agreed that he and Lavina should go for a ride together.

Margery, Lavina and Sam went up to bed, leaving the two older men together. Oliver had a great pile of logarithm books and other astronomical impedimenta on the desk in the far corner of the room; and he settled down to do an hour's work before going to bed. But Gervaise Stapleton was, for him, un- usually restless. After reading a few pages of his book, he threw it down and addressed his brother.

'Well, what do you make of her, Oliver?'

The tall, untidy astronomer pushed his spectacles up on his forehead and turned in his chair. 'Make of whom?' he asked, vaguely.

'Why, Lavina, of course.'

'Oh—Lavina. I think she's looking very well. Older, of course, and a little hard; but that is only on the surface. The girl has character, you know, Gervaise. Always had. And that's doubtless stood her in good stead through any trouble. She laughs as easily as ever, which shows that she has come to no serious harm; but then, I never thought she would, and you may remember that I felt you were wrong when you so strongly opposed her going into the film business.'

Gervaise nodded. 'Yes. I think I *was* wrong but, from all one had heard, the film people seemed such a terribly mixed lot, and she was only twenty.'

At that moment Lavina came into the room again, looking very small and very young now that she had taken most of the make-up off her face and was wearing flat-heeled slippers and a dressing-gown.

She was an impulsive person, and feeling that she owed it to her father to have a heart-to-heart talk with him at the first opportunity, had decided not to delay it until the morning. The fact that her Uncle Oliver was there did not deter her, as the two brothers had no secrets from each other and, in any case, he had turned back to his calculations on her entry.

Going straight up to her father where he stood with his back to the smouldering wood fire on its great pile of accumulated winter ashes, she said softly: 'Well, dearest, am I forgiven?'

He put both his hands on her shoulders and smiled down at her. 'Of course you are, my princess. It is really I who should ask your forgiveness, for opposing you so bitterly three years ago that you ran away and cut yourself off from us.'

'I ought to have been more patient, darling, and waited another year as you wanted me to, but I can understand now just what you felt. You must have thought that all sorts of terrible things would happen.'

He shook his head. 'I should have known that with your personality you'd be all right, and I've blamed myself terribly since for not letting you go when you wanted to. Then you would at least have had our support in those early months when you must have needed it most.'

'They weren't so bad. Of course, there are bad hats in the film business just like any other; but I soon learnt how to deal with them when they became difficult, and most of the film people are wonderfully kindhearted. Many of them were absolutely marvellous to me.'

'I wish I'd known that at the time, because I'm afraid I did them an injustice and it would have saved me many a night of sleepless worry about you.'

'Poor darling! Never mind. It's all over now and we're together again.'

'Yes. And you've come back triumphant, a famous film star.'

'No, dearest, not really. I am a star by courtesy, but I've never made a really big picture. The trouble is that I'm not really photogenic and every picture I play in means endless extra trouble for the director and cutters before they're satisfied. What d'you think of Sam?'

Gervaise considered for a moment. 'He seems a nice fellow. Is he the Sir Samuel Curry who gambles for such big sums at Deauville and Le Touquet? I seem to remember seeing his name in a paper somewhere in that connection.'

'Yes. He's immensely rich and the few thousands he makes or loses at the tables are only a bagatelle to him. He wants to marry me.'

'So I supposed,' Gervaise remarked dryly.

'Why?'

'What man could know you and not want to marry you?'

'You always were a flatterer, darling; but what do you think about it, seriously?'

'Does that matter? My little princess always did have her own way in everything, so it's a bit late in the day for her to try to put her responsibilities on her old father now.'

'But it *does* matter what you think, darling. Because, you see, for once in my life I can't make up my mind. If I were convinced that I could become a really great star I'd stick to my career, but I'm afraid the odds are rather against it. Yet I like making pictures and all the friends that I've made are in the film world. Sam insists that, if I marry him, I must cut out the films entirely, but of course he can offer me everything that money can buy by way of exchange.'

'Surely the crux of the matter is, are you really fond of him?'

'Yes. I'm not passionately in love with him or anything of that sort, but I'm beginning to think that I never shall be with any-one, and Sam is the only man I've ever met who has all the qualities a woman could ask for in a husband. He's kind, generous to a degree, definitely good-looking, and has that force-ful personality which a real man should have.'

'On the other hand, he is a bit old for you, isn't he?'

Lavina nodded. 'That's just it. He's forty-six and I'm only twenty-three. I suppose that doesn't matter, really, if you're fond of a person, but I'm just a tiny bit frightened that in a few years' time I might fall for somebody younger and I'd hate to break up Sam's life by running away.'

Oliver had finished his calculation and was looking across at her. 'I don't think you need let that worry you,' he said quietly. 'I didn't mean to tell anybody, because it's a highly dangerous secret; but I think it a pity, Lavina, that you should die without going through the experience of marriage.'

Gervaise and Lavina turned to stare at him and she exclaimed: 'Oliver! What on earth d'you mean?'

He laid down a long Burma cheroot he was smoking on the edge of the ash-tray. 'Just this, my dear. A comet, which is not yet visible to the human eye, is approaching us at enormous speed. If it is a solid body, as we have some reason to suppose, our earth will be shattered into fragments when it hits us. It is now April 25th; the comet is due to arrive on June 24th and, in my opinion, none of us has more than sixty days to live.'

3

EVEN WORLDS SOMETIMES DIE

In her three years as a film actress Lavina had ridden on outdoor locations when her work required it, but it was many months since she had mounted a horse solely for pleasure. In consequence, it was with a special thrill that she cantered beside Derek Burroughs over the meadows surrounding her home, on the morning after her return to it.

After her three years' absence she was a very different Lavina from the girl of twenty who had run away to seek fame on the films, yet, to her, not a blade of grass seemed to have changed in the quiet Surrey landscape. The old Georgian mansion in which she had been born lay behind them down by the lake, with two-thirds of its windows dusty and shuttered; the green pastures curved away in front, broken by hedges, occasional coppices and the belt of woodland that bounded the estate, just as she had always known them.

On the crest of a hill she and Derek reined their horses in to a walk and he turned to smile at her.

'I see you haven't lost that splendid seat of yours.'

She laughed. 'Riding's like bicycling, isn't it? Once learnt, never forgotten. *You* ought to know that, darling.'

The endearment slipped out. In the film world she was so used to calling everybody 'darling', but she regretted having used that term to Derek. Time was when she had often called him 'darling', but that was long ago; and she feared now that he might attach a meaning to the word which she had not intended.

Before he could reply, she hurried on: 'Gervaise is looking well, isn't he? But keeping up this place must be an awful strain on him. Are things just as bad as ever, Derek?'

He nodded. 'I'm afraid so. He doesn't tell me much. You know how proud he is. If only he'd sell the place he could have a comfortable flat in London or a small house somewhere in the neighbourhood, but he's absolutely determined to hang on here. His income is just enough to keep the house going without servants but we poor farmers have been pretty badly hit, and I don't see much hope of permanent recovery.'

'You seem to take it very philosophically yourself.'

'Oh, I manage somehow. Selling a mare here and there and by sending all my stuff from the hothouses up to London. And I like the life; I wouldn't change it to be cooped up in an office, even if I could make ten times the money.'

She glanced at him swiftly from beneath lowered lids. His clear-cut features and the wavy brown hair she had so often stroked were as attractive as ever. Even the sight of him was enough to call up for her the smell of tobacco and old tweeds that clung to him and had once meant more to her than the perfumes of all Arabia. Giving herself a little shake she said:

'I think you're right. I can't see you mixed up in the turmoil of modern business. You'd hate it, Derek.'

'I should have thought you would have hated it, too. I've never been able to visualize the Lavina I loved rubbing shoulders with all the queer birds you must have met by this time.'

'Oh, I can look after myself. It's always the woman who makes the running, you know. A girl gets what she asks for and, if she takes a firm line to start with, all but a few outsiders are perfectly prepared just to remain friendly and let her alone.'

'You're glad to be back, though.'

'Terribly. It's like escaping from an orchid house, or rather from the heat and din of a ship's engine-room into the fresh sea air on deck.'

'Does that mean—' he hesitated, 'that there's a chance of your staying for some time?'

She shook her head. 'I'd like to, for Gervaise's sake. He's so very glad to see me. But I've come to a turning-point in my life and, whichever way I decide, I'll have arrangements to make which mean my going back to London tonight.'

'D'you mean that they've offered you a Hollywood contract and that you may be going abroad?'

'No. I may be giving up the films altogether. That's what I've got to decide.'

'By Jove! If you do chuck the films, once you've fixed things up we may be seeing lots more of you.'

'Yes. I shall never stay away so long again.'

'You might even come back to live here?'

'No, Derek, no.' She quickly quelled the hope that was so clear in his eager voice. 'If I decide to give up my career, it will be to marry.'

'I see,' he said slowly. 'So at last you've found a chap on whom you're really keen?'

'Sam Curry wants to marry me.'

'Curry?'

'Yes. Didn't you realize?'

'But, hang it all, he's old enough to be your father.'

'What has that to do with it?' Lavina looked away angrily. 'He has one of the best brains in England and he's incredibly nice.'

'Perhaps. But, if it comes to brains, I daresay Einstein has a better. I should have thought brains were one of the least important things when it came to a question of marriage.'

'Oh, don't be silly. I never said I was marrying him for his brains alone.'

'For what, then? His money?'

'Don't you think that you're exceeding the privileges of even a very old friend?' Lavina said, with dangerous quietness.

'Sorry,' he apologized. 'Let's canter.'

An hour later, when they got back to the house and Derek had handed the horses over to the groom he had brought with him, they found Gervaise Stapleton, his brother Oliver, and Sir Samuel Curry congregated in the library.

'One can't ignore Oliver's statement,' Gervaise was saying. 'After all, he's an astronomer, and if he says this comet is coming nearer to the earth than it ever has before, we must accept that as a fact.'

The three men turned as Lavina and Derek came into the room. 'Hullo,' she cried, 'we've had such a glorious ride that I'd almost forgotten about the comet. I see Sam's having it out with you.'

'I was just saying,' smiled Sam, 'that, although your uncle is no doubt right about this comet approaching, the universe being so vast, it doesn't follow that the thing will get drawn into our orbit and smash us up.'

'What *is* all this?' inquired Derek amiably.

'You'd better ask Uncle Oliver,' Lavina replied. 'He scared me into fits last night by saying that he didn't think any of us had more than sixty days to live.'

Oliver shook his dome-like, sparsely covered head, from the back and sides of which wisps of fine brown hair stood out untidily. 'You're a very naughty girl, Lavina. I told you this was a most dangerous secret and must go no further, yet the first thing you do is to tell Sir Samuel here, and then Derek.'

She blew him a playful kiss. 'Nonsense, darling. Sam's as deep as a well and Derek is almost one of the family. Besides, you as good as confessed, before I went up to bed, that you were joking. I only mentioned it to Sam after breakfast this morning because I thought it would be fun to see you pull his leg about it.'

'I'm afraid Oliver wasn't joking, dearest.' Gervaise spoke with quiet firmness. 'He only allowed you to assume that he was, so that you could sleep on it and this appalling thing shouldn't come as too great a shock to you.'

Her eyes widened. 'You mean—you really mean . . .?'

'I mean that Oliver seems to be convinced that a comet is going to smash our world to fragments on June 24th.'

'But—what do *you* think?'

Gervaise smiled a little grimly. 'My dear, what can any of us think, or do, except accept the opinion of an expert and make up our minds to face whatever is to come with what fortitude we may.'

Derek flung his riding crop on a chair and sat down. 'Surely, Oliver, you can't be serious? The idea that the world will come to an end in eight weeks' time is really a bit too much to swallow.'

'Naturally, it is rather an alarming thought at first,' Oliver replied mildly. 'But worlds do come to an end, you know, and there's no reason to suppose that ours should be specially immune from such a catastrophe. If you had witnessed some of the mighty flare-ups which have occurred in the heavens during the many years I have spent in Greenwich Observatory you would, I think, be more ready to accept my statement as a real probability.'

'I wouldn't dream of challenging your authority on such a subject, sir,' Sam Curry said politely, 'and you must correct me if I'm wrong, but I've always understood comets were mainly composed of gases. Even if one hit our earth, it would probably only destroy a portion of the population. In any case, there would be no cataclysmic collision such as one might expect in the case of two great heavenly bodies rushing together.'

Gervaise smiled. 'I expect you're thinking of H. G. Wells's fantasy, *In the Days of the Comet*. In that the gases only caused everyone to fall into a twilight sleep, from which they woke up as model socialists to develop a new and perfect world-state.'

Oliver shook his head. 'This comet may be composed only of gas and a great collection of small meteorites. Many comets are, but not all. There is, for example, the classic case of a comet which caused the great red spot on Jupiter.'

'What was that?' asked Derek quickly.

'Jupiter has a very dense, cloud-laden atmosphere which, as far as we know, was more or less uniform all over its surface until May 19th, 1664. It was then that the astronomer, Hooke, observed a huge red spot on its surface. That spot has been there ever since, and our modern instruments have shown us that it consists of fiery vapours like those of a vast volcano which pour out unceasingly right through the planet's thick cloud-layers. The only possible explanation for the phenomenon is that a solid comet of great size crashed into Jupiter in the seventeenth century with such force that it broke clean through the planet's surface making a rent which has never healed.'

'Well, even if that happened to us,' said Sam, 'it might mean great loss of life in one particular area but the rest of the world would go on much the same.'

'I fear that would hardly be the case,' Oliver disagreed, 'if it were a comit like the one that hit Jupiter. You see, Jupiter is over thirteen hundred times the bulk of our earth and its cloud-layer alone is estimated to be 6,000 miles thick. The rent that was torn in it is 7,000 miles broad by 30,000 miles long, so, if we came into collision with the same sort of body, the whole of our earth would be shattered into tiny little bits.'

'Still, it might not be as big,' Derek suggested hopefully.

'True,' Oliver agreed.

'And it might not be a solid meteorite at all,' added Sam.

'Quite,' agreed Oliver again. 'The chances are, in fact, somewhat in favour of its being no more than a great mass of cosmic dust, small meteorites and flaming gas. But, even if it is, should it actually come into collision with us, the disturbance caused by its arrival here would almost certainly blot out all life on our planet.'

'Oh, come!' exclaimed Sam. 'The earth has often passed through the tails of comets without the public even being aware of what was happening.'

'True. But the tails of comets are often tens of thousands of miles in length and such comets have always swept on their way without passing sufficiently near to be drawn into our sphere of gravity; whereas in this case, if my calculations are correct, we shall pull the solid body or the mass of flaming gas right in on top of us.'

'I gather, though, Oliver, that all your colleagues are not of the same opinion as yourself,' remarked Gervaise.

Oliver shrugged his bent shoulders. 'The comet is still so distant that it has been impossible up till now to estimate its track with any real exactness and some of us consider there is still a hope that it may pass us by. Until we reach agreement there is no point in alarming the public unnecessarily and that is why we have, so far, refrained from publishing anything about it.'

'That, too,' added Gervaise, 'is why I think it should be understood between us that no mention of the matter is made outside this house. You see, if the danger became generally known, it might lead to the most appalling panic, and even riots.'

'But your own opinion, Oliver, is that it's going to hit us?' Lavina's voice had a slightly hysterical note.

'Yes, my dear. When I spoke to you last night I had just finished an entirely new set of calculations by which I proved the matter to my own satisfaction and which I feel reasonably certain will convince my colleagues that I am right.'

'But hang it all!' Derek jumped up from his chair. 'I can't believe it! I suppose the world's got to end some time, but it's been going on for such millions of years. It just doesn't seem credible that it should come to an end almost without warning like this.'

'I'm afraid that's what most people will feel,' Oliver said

quietly. 'Perhaps I ought never to have mentioned it. You must forgive me if I've scared you all but when I spoke to Lavina I was a little over-excited by the success of my calculation.'

'Success!' Sam echoed, with a queer little laugh. 'Anyhow, you don't seem at all put out about the impending catastrophe yourself.'

'Oh, no, not at all. You see, as a scientist, I can only regard the ending of the world as an extraordinarily interesting phenomenon. In fact, I count it a great privilege to be living at a time when such a momentous event is about to take place and I hope to have the opportunity of making observations up to the very last moment. But, of course, you people having other interests are naturally inclined to take a rather different view. I'm so sorry if I've upset any of you by letting the cat out of the bag a little prematurely.'

Gervaise was not listening to his brother's rather vague apology for his pronouncement, which might well be calculated utterly to disrupt the even tenor of all their lives. He was studying the expressions of the people grouped about him.

Derek Burroughs' open face showed quite clearly that the full import of Oliver's words had not yet come home to him. Sir Samuel Curry's was veiled, but Gervaise felt instinctively that the millionaire believed Oliver to be a crank, although he was much too polite to say so.

Margery had entered the room while they were talking and she had also been present during the earlier part of the discussion, before the arrival of Lavina and Derek. Her father knew that, although for a long time she had given up going to church, she was still imbued with the rather narrow religious beliefs of her youth; and therefore regarded Oliver's prognostications with a somewhat similar disbelief to that displayed by the priests of the Middle Ages when Galileo declared the world to be round. He gave an inward chuckle at the thought that her reactions could almost be summed up with some such phrase as 'I'm sure God would never permit His creatures all to be wiped out, without warning, like that.'

Gervaise's eye then fell upon his younger daughter. Lavina, he knew, was a fatalist and she had unbounded faith in her uncle's scientific knowledge. The night before she had thought

that he was joking, but it was clear that she had now accepted
his prophecy of death for all mankind without further question.

Gervaise was not surprised when she laid her hand on Sam
Curry's arm and said, 'Well, if we've only got sixty days, darling,
I'll marry you just as soon as you like.'

4

A STRANGE PREMONITION

When Lavina had promised Sam Curry that she would marry
him just as soon as he liked, she had not meant that quite
literally; and the ten days that followed seemed to her one long
series of abominably crowded hours punctuated by intervals of
exhausted sleep.

At times he chaffed her, on the lines that, if the world was
really coming to an end on June 24th, why should she worry
herself about a hundred little things which would not matter to
anyone on June 25th.

As the passing days had not in the least shaken her belief in
the accuracy of her uncle's scientific prediction, she admitted
that many of her activities were really a waste of time; yet some
innate sense compelled her to put her house in order. She spent
hours with her agent, who thought her mad, wrangling about the
cancellation of future contracts; and further hours endeavouring
to placate irate film magnates. In addition, she had made up her
mind that, even if she was not going to have a big wedding, that
was no reason at all why she should not get herself a complete
trousseau, and her dressmakers claimed her constant attention.

Sam had not pressed her unduly about the date of the wedding,
as he did not believe for one moment that the world was coming
to an end on June 24th, but he got her to agree to marry him on
May 12th and in the meantime he was anxious that she should
meet as many of his friends as possible; for which purpose he
arranged a series of luncheons at his big house in St. James's
Square.

Most of these were large affairs but on May 8th he had a small
party consisting of Mr. and Mrs. Fink-Drummond, the Marchesa
del Serilla and Captain Rupert Brand. Conchita del Serilla was
an old friend of Sam's and it was he who had introduced her to
Rupert Brand, the ace airman. They had fallen for each other at
once and were now engaged to be married, which made Sam

rather pleased with himself. He was, therefore, particularly anxious that Lavina should get to know and like them.

Having called for Lavina at Aage Thaarup's and dragged her away from the collection of hats which that expert was making for her, Sam told her on the short drive back to St. James's Square something of the people whom she was going to meet.

'The Marchesa sounds most seductive,' Lavina smiled. 'I shall be diabolically jealous of her, though. I'm sure you know her much better than you're prepared to admit.'

'Oh, not really.' Sam looked a little self-consciously at his feet. 'She's a good-looker, of course, but she had a ghastly time in Spain. She was pretty badly beaten up by those swine in the Revolution and she just wouldn't look at a man after that—till she met Rupert. He's a grand chap and they're absolutely made for each other. Neither of them are children and I believe they've both fallen really in love for the first time. It's only when you've had plenty of experience that you recognize when a person's really worth while, you know.'

Lavina shot a swift glance at the greying hair above Sam's strong features. He had never concealed the fact that he had had plenty of experience.

'Does that apply to women, too?' she could not resist asking with just a shade of gentle mockery.

'Lord, no! Women are different,' he laughed, 'although Conchita must be thirty-ish.'

'What are the Fink-Drummonds like?' she inquired, to break the little silence that followed.

'Surely you know about them. He resigned from the Government about a year ago. Made a great song and dance about it. Thought he could split the Cabinet and force them to go to the country; but he didn't pull it off. He's not quite as clever as he thinks he is, but he's been mighty useful to me in a business way and may be again if a sudden twist of the political wheel brings him back into power. That's why I want you to be nice to him.'

'I see. He's the puppet and you pull the strings. How clever of you, Sam darling. But what about her? She was a famous beauty, wasn't she?'

'That's right. She's hard as nails and has had lovers by the score, but she still believes he'll be Prime Minister one day. She'd like to move into No. 10 Downing Street, and, through her boy-friends, she wields enormous influence. That's why they married and why they stick together.'

Over cocktails Lavina met the people of whom they had been talking. Fink-Drummond was a tall, dark man, with a pompous manner, a very prominent nose and a rather weak chin; his wife certainly had been beautiful in her youth and was beautiful still. Her large, rather tired blue eyes looked out of a pale, oval face, crowned by not too obviously touched-up golden hair. She was as slim as a sylph and as icy as a February wind. Lavina took an instinctive dislike to the Fink-Drummonds but, having Sam to consider, she used all her cleverness to conceal it.

Her view of Conchita del Serilla and Rupert Brand was entirely different. The big, dark eyes of the lovely Spanish Marchesa were friendly and sincere, while the strong, light-grey ones of the airman held courage and good faith. To anyone coming from Lavina's sophisticated world it was a joy to see two people who so obviously adored each other and made no bones about showing it.

It was after lunch when the servants had left the room that Fink-Drummond said:

'I heard an extraordinary thing this morning. Although I'm no longer in the Cabinet, I know everything that's going on. I've plenty of friends on the inside, still, who keep me well informed. Apparently, the P.M. is considerably disturbed about a comet that's coming our way. Of course, it's all very hush-hush, but the Astronomer Royal reported it some days ago, and it appears they're afraid now that somewhere towards the end of June it's going to hit us.'

'That seems a pretty tall story,' laughed Captain Brand, as Lavina and Sam exchanged a quick glance.

'It certainly seems so on the face of it,' Fink-Drummond admitted. 'I shouldn't have taken any serious notice of the story myself if it hadn't come from an impeccable source. I'm told, though, that some members of the Cabinet are seriously alarmed. They seem to think it may bring about the end of the world.'

'How absurd!' exclaimed his wife. 'And just the sort of stupid story which might create a panic. But perhaps that's the explanation. The P.M.'s clever. He's quite capable of using it to force a General Election in order to get the Government home again on a wave of hysteria.'

Fink-Drummond nodded. 'That occurred to me, but I don't think that's the game. I hear they're determined to keep it from the public as long as possible, so it looks as if they were genuinely scared.'

'What would happen if it were really true?' asked the Marchesa, in her deep, husky voice.

'I don't really know.' Fink-Drummond considered for a moment. 'Probably we'd have earthquakes, great tidal waves, and that sort of thing.'

Rupert Brand laughed. 'Then the only safe place would be in the air. My new plane, which is specially equipped for stratosphere flying, would be just the thing. Whatever happened down here, we'd be safe enough up on the ceiling; then we'd land again when the tidal waves had subsided.' He looked across with smiling eyes at Conchita.

'What a honeymoon,' she purred. 'Perhaps, when we came down again there'd be no one left alive on the earth, so we should have to start the world all over again, like Adam and Eve, in a new Garden of Eden.'

Mrs. Fink-Drummond smiled a little weakly. 'It sounds too enchanting, but I don't think being up in the air would help you much if this comet really crashed into us.'

'It won't,' her husband declared pompously. 'Comets are only composed of meteorites and gas, so there is no question of any actual collision.'

'Are you quite sure about that?' Lavina inquired politely. 'I was under the impression that some comets were solid.'

'Oh, no, you've been misinformed there,' Fink-Drummond contradicted her quickly.

Lavina considered her uncle a much better authority upon astronomical matters than the ex-Cabinet Minister, but she tactfully refrained from mentioning the source of her own information.

'I really can't believe there is anything in this story of yours, Finkie,' Sam remarked. 'The world has survived for such billions of years, with comets rushing about the heavens the whole time. It seems to be an incredibly long chance against one hitting the earth head-on during the infinitesimal span of time that constitutes our own lives.'

'Of course, there's nothing in it. Can't be,' Fink-Drummond

B

agreed. 'Anyway, no more than that a comet may pass within a few score million miles and appear as a big, bright new star in the heavens for a time.'

'That's about it,' Sam nodded. 'Just like the comet of 1811. I remember reading somewhere that people thought then that the world was coming to an end, and there were all sorts of demonstrations and riots in consequence.'

Beatrice Fink-Drummond screwed another cigarette into a long, jade holder. 'That is evidently what the Cabinet are worrying themselves about. They fear that ignorant people will get frightened without cause, and that somebody may play upon their fears to make trouble for the Government.'

Lavina saw Fink-Drummond's eyes suddenly narrow, as though an idea had just occurred to him. But he said nothing.

'Well, if there is any excitement,' Sam remarked, 'we should be back just in time for it. I wanted to do a trip round the world, but Lavina says, "Let's save that for the winter." '

'Yes, a month to five weeks is quite long enough now,' Lavina smiled. 'Then I want to get settled in my new home.'

'Where are you going?' Beatrice Fink-Drummond asked. 'Or is that a secret?'

'Goodness, no!' Sam cut in. 'But it's going to be about the queerest honeymoon that you could imagine for two people like ourselves. We're both a bit tired of city lights and crowds and dressing-up, so, after a few days in Paris, we're going south, to the Pyrenees. Once we get there, we're going to abandon Lavina's maid, my man, and nine-tenths of the luggage. Just take the car up into those lovely, sun-baked pine woods along the foothills of the mountains and lead the simple life. Stay at tiny places, do a bit of walking, and, in fact, get some real fun out of the one sort of holiday that neither of us has ever dreamed of trying before.'

'My dear, how primitive!' Beatrice Fink-Drummond made a pretence of being shocked. 'You really must love each other almost indecently if you're not afraid of getting bored with five weeks of that.'

'Either you love a person or you don't,' Rupert Brand took her up swiftly, 'and, if you do, those first few weeks alone together must be heaven. Most of us are such fools that we fritter away all our lives mixing with crowds of mainly stupid people most of whom we don't care two hoots about.'

Without waiting for a reply he turned to Lavina. 'Will you forgive me if I go now? I've got a flying appointment down at Heston.'

His departure broke up the party, and when Sam's guests had gone Lavina said suddenly:

'Well, my unbelieving love, what about the comet now?'

He shrugged. 'I don't see that what Finkie said changes the situation. We've never questioned your uncle's statement that a comet is coming our way, and, naturally, the Astronomer Royal would report that to the Cabinet. It doesn't follow that it's going to smash us up, though.'

'I must confess that there are times when I can't really believe that Oliver's right about the comet hitting the earth,' she admitted. 'The idea that we're actually going to witness the end of the world is too utterly fantastic. All the same, I'm sure the old boy believes it himself, and he's such a very brilliant scientist that somehow I don't think he can be mistaken.'

Sam took her hand and squeezed it. 'Don't worry your sweet head about it. If it comes, it comes. In the meantime, we're going to have five glorious weeks together and, personally, I don't care if the whole box of tricks does blow up after that.'

'Nor do I, Sam darling.' She lifted her face to his kiss and for a few moments they lingered together. Then, as he led her out into the hall, he said:

'By the by, Hemmingway got back last night and I gave him details of all the alterations that you want made to the rooms during our absence. I think you ought to go over them with him, though, in case I've forgotten anything, and anyhow, I want you to meet him.'

'Yes, I'd like to. He's your secretary, isn't he?'

'Hemmingway Hughes is something much more than that. I've come to regard him as my closest personal friend and he would have lunched with us to-day if he hadn't had urgent business in the City. He's half American, you know, and has just returned from a trip to the States where he's been conducting some secret negotiations for me, while ostensibly on a visit to his mother.'

'You must trust him a lot, then. How old is he?'

'He's only twenty-nine or thirty but he has the ablest brain for his age of any man I've ever met and he's extraordinarily knowledgeable about books and art and all sorts of other things outside business. I do hope you'll like him.'

'I hope so, too, although he sounds rather frightening.'

Sam took her up to the first floor and opened the door of a big room at the back of the house. A youngish man was seated there, behind a desk. As he rose at their entrance, Lavina saw that he was about six feet tall, and well-built without being unduly heavy. His dark hair, which curled slightly, had receded a little, which made his broad, high forehead a particularly outstanding feature; but it was his eyes which were most remarkable. They were dark, intense, and seemed to have a quality of wisdom and age about them far beyond the years of their owner.

'Hemmingway,' said Sam, 'I'm most anxious for you to meet my fiancée, Lavina Stapleton. Darling, this is my friend, Hemmingway Hughes.'

For a second Lavina felt as though those strange eyes of Hemmingway's were looking down into the most secret recesses of her mind; then his pale, young-old face was lit by a smile. 'It's grand to meet you in the flesh,' he said. 'I've often admired you as Lavina Leigh in your pictures.'

'That's nice of you,' Lavina smiled in reply. 'Sam tells me that you're his second self, so I shall be seeing lots of you, and I do hope we'll be good friends.'

'I'm sure we shall.' He extended a well-shaped, carefully manicured hand.

As she took it, Lavina was conscious of a horrible premonition that they were either going to be deadly enemies or something very much more to each other than just friends.

5

THE UNSCRUPULOUS EX-MINISTER

On May 12th Lavina and Sam were married. There had been no time to arrange the great social function which Sam would have liked to stage, in order to show off his lovely young film-star bride to his hundreds of wealthy acquaintances; and, although Lavina, having become accustomed, to the limelight during the latter part of her film career, would have raised no objection to a big show, she really preferred the idea of being married quietly from her own home in Surrey.

The initial difficulty had been the dilapidated condition of Stapleton Court and the fact that her father lived by such a narrow margin that he could not possibly afford even the few pounds it would cost to open up the house, much less give her a reception there; and he was far too proud to allow Sam to foot the bill for him.

Yet Gervaise Stapleton was not an unreasonable man. He was delighted at the thought that his daughter wanted to be married from her old home rather than from an hotel in London, and when she pointed out that her film earnings had left her with a considerable bank balance, from which she could well afford to pay for everything herself, he readily agreed that she should do so.

For the past week charwomen, french-polishers and menders had been hard at it, scrubbing and cleaning the reception rooms —which had not been open for nearly a quarter of a century— and mending their furnishings. So that on the morning of the wedding a firm of London caterers had had a clear field to prepare for the reception.

Only about a hundred people had been invited; Sam's more intimate friends, some of Lavina's film folk and a number of neighbours who had known her since her childhood.

Derek Burroughs was there, making a gallant attempt to hide

37

the gloom he could not help feeling. Conchita del Serilla, Rupert Brand and Fink-Drummond were among those who had motored down from London; but Mrs. Fink-Drummond was not present, as she had sailed the day before on a visit to friends in the United States.

Everyone agreed that Lavina, with her slight figure, thin, Roman-nosed, aristocratic little face and natural golden hair, made an enchanting bride; and that, in spite of his bulldog chin and greying hair, Sam did not really look old enough to be her father.

Gervaise, in an old-fashioned grey frock-coat and topper, dug out for the occasion, looked positively ducal, and Sam thought that Margery, as the only bridesmaid, looked younger and prettier than on any of the few occasions he had seen her.

Hemmingway Hughes, his pale, clever face smiling but sphinx-like, made an excellent best man and, without appearing to do anything very much, saw to it with his usual efficiency that all the arrangements worked smoothly.

One guest whom Lavina was particularly pleased to see after-wards at the reception was Oliver's son, her cousin Roy. He was the bad hat of the family and had spent the best part of the last ten years roving about in the Far East, earning a precarious living in a variety of rather dubious ways; but he was a good-natured, amusing person and Lavina had always been fond of him.

When he managed to get her to himself for a moment he laughingly congratulated her upon having been clever enough to find such a good-looking millionaire for a husband.

'You're over thirty so it's time you settled down yourself, Roy,' she laughed back at him.

'No one will have me,' he grinned.

'I don't believe it.' Her glance took in his bronzed, attractive face with the fair, wavy hair above it. 'You haven't lost your looks and you always *were* a devil with the women!'

'That's just the trouble. Each girl seems to find out about one of the others, and there's always a rumpus before I even get as far as popping the question. Besides, there aren't so many young women knocking around who have the cash and would be prepared to keep me.'

'You're still broke, then?'

'Absolutely stony. That's why I decided to come back to England. Things were getting too hot for me in the East. Too many writs flying about, and I thought I might induce the old man to kill the fatted calf and set me up in some sort of business here.'

'Poor Oliver's killed too many fatted calves for you already, my lad, and he's never had much money, so I shouldn't think you'll have any luck in that direction.'

He sighed. 'No. He was decent enough, but he's so wrapped up in his astronomy that it's almost impossible to get him to talk business. How about this wealthy husband of yours, though? He's got all sorts of interests. Think you could do me a turn, old girl, and get him to put me into something?'

Lavina smiled a little doubtfully. 'You've blotted your copybook so often, Roy, and I'd have to tell Sam the truth about you; but if you care to leave it like that, I'll ask him if he can do anything when we get back from our honeymoon.'

'Thanks. You're a darling. Always were. Don't blacken the old horse too much, though, and I really will put in man's time if you can persuade him to give me a job. You might tell him, too, that I approve the brand of champagne he's given us for this little "do". I'm going to knock off another bottle before I hit the trail for London.'

'Do, Roy. Two, if you like. And thanks for the compliment, because I chose the wine and am paying for it.'

He lifted an eyebrow lazily. 'Poor old girl. With his money-bags to draw on, you must be crackers! But you always were queer about that sort of thing. Anyhow, good hunting on your honeymoon!'

As some other guests came up he left her and, while she was talking with them, she noticed that Fink-Drummond had got Sam a little apart from the crowd, in another corner of the room.

Fink-Drummond was saying: 'Listen, Sam, I hate to drag you away from your friends at a time like this but I've a most important matter that I must tell you about before you leave England. I won't keep you long, but is there somewhere we could have a quiet word together?'

'Of course, Finkie, if it's something really urgent.' Sam glanced quickly round the room and added: 'Come along to the library.

The family use it as a living-room so it's been shut up for to-day. No one will disturb us there.'

When they reached the library, Fink-Drummond perched himself on the corner of Gervaise Stapleton's big desk and said impressively: 'Since I lunched with you the other day I've been doing a lot of quiet thinking. You may remember it was suggested that the Government might intend to use this threat of danger from the comet that is approaching as a means of panicking the public and getting themselves home again on a snap election.'

Sam nodded. 'Yes. But you said yourself that that could not possibly be their intention because they had decided to keep all knowledge of the comet from the public as long as possible.'

'Exactly. Fink-Drummond tapped Sam on the grey satin stock he was wearing, with a strong, slightly twisted forefinger. 'That is the whole point. If they're not going to use it, is there any reason why somebody else shouldn't?'

'I see.' Sam frowned slightly as his quick brain grasped the trend of the ex-Cabinet Minister's thoughts. 'You're suggesting that, when you've got your own followers organized, you should blow the gaff about the comet before the Government has the chance to do so? Accuse them of criminal negligence in failing to take such precautions as are possible against the danger, force a General Election and ride home to power yourself on a panic wave of popular indignation?'

'Precisely. And I'm certain it could be done.'

'Perhaps. But have you considered the risk of such a proceeding? To pull off a scheme like that you'd have to stress the danger sufficiently to create a state of national alarm. Once you do that, the masses might get out of hand. Riots, even revolution, might result from such a policy.'

'That is a risk, of course; but it could be dealt with. And look what you stand to gain. Since the arms race has been stopped by these new treaties, your steel plants must have been feeling the draught pretty badly. Once we get this thing going, they'll be working overtime again. It will be just like 1938, when the Air Raid Precautions business started. As a protection from the flaming gases of the comet shelters will have to be dug all over the country; thousands of tons of steel girders will have to be supplied; and, naturally, I should see to it that you got the lion's share of the contracts.'

'Very decent of you,' said Sam quietly. 'And what do you require as a *quid pro quo*?'

'Money, my friend. Without money I can't possibly fight an election. I shall want £100,000 for Press and election expenses. You put up the funds and leave me to do the rest. How d'you like it?'

'It requires a little thought; £100,000 is a pretty considerable sum to risk on an election gamble.'

Fink-Drummond drew his heavy brows together in a frown until they almost met over his big, fleshy nose. 'What's come over you, Sam?' he asked impatiently. 'Your love affair must have dulled your wits, I think. Surely you see that I'm not really asking you to gamble a single cent. You can make your money back time and again on the falling markets, quite apart from any question as to whether I go back to Westminster as P.M. and am able to push any contracts in your way, or not. If this scheme is worked properly, it'll be far and away the biggest thing that either of us has ever gone into. But if you have any doubts about it, I don't want to press you. You know quite well that I can get the money from half a dozen people in the City. I'm just making you the first offer, that's all.'

'Wait here a moment, will you?' Sam turned away. 'I'm just going to get Hemmingway. I always like to have his views on anything that's really big like this.'

'Is that necessary?'

'Yes. Lavina and I must leave in half an hour or we shall miss the Paris plane and, in any case, if I take it on, Hemmingway will have to handle the financial side of it while I'm away.'

When Sam returned a few moments later he had Gervaise with him as well as Hemmingway Hughes. He shut the door carefully behind him and said to Fink-Drummond:

'You've met my father-in-law. He knows all about this comet business, and I told Hemmingway of it myself the other day. I want them both to know about this proposition of yours.'

Fink-Drummond shrugged. 'Just as you wish. But it's most important that as few people as possible should know of our intentions until we're ready to launch our campaign.'

'I quite agree,' said Sam dryly, and, turning to the other two, he added: 'Gentlemen, Mr. Fink-Drummond has just put up to me the following proposition. The Government, as you know, are aware of the approaching comet but they have decided to keep any knowledge of it from the public as long as possible, in order to avoid unnecessary panic. Mr. Fink-Drummond has suggested to me that I should finance him, to the tune of £100,000, to promote that panic, in order that he may force a General Election and get back to power himself on a wave of national hysteria. In return, he offers me certain very large contracts, for steel to be used in dug-outs and so on, which his Government would order directly he became Prime Minister.'

'But such a thing is impossible!' exclaimed Gervaise.

'Not at all,' Fink-Drummond replied smoothly. 'If the Press campaign is handled properly, I should say the odds are a good five to one upon my being Premier by the second week in June.'

'I was not referring to the possibilities of your unscrupulous scheme, sir, Gervaise snapped, 'but to the impossibiilty of my son-in-law soiling his hands with such business.'

'Thank you,' said Sam. 'I was quite sure that was the way you would feel and it's the way I feel myself.'

Fink-Drummond drew himself up. 'I can only excuse Mr. Stapleton's ill-considered expressions on the grounds that, having lived here buried in the country for so long, he can have no understanding of the methods people like myself are sometimes compelled to use to bring about political necessities. Please be good enough to order my car.'

'I haven't finished yet.' Sam held up his hand. 'Mr. Fink-Drummond has also informed me that, if I refuse him the financial assistance that he seeks, he will endeavour to secure it elsewhere, and I have no doubt whatsoever that he will be able to do so, if not from British, then from foreign financiers.'

'But listen, now,' Hemmingway Hughes cut in, 'surely Mr. Fink-Drummond can't have fully considered the sort of situation which he proposes to bring about. For one thing, the stock markets will slump to zero directly he gets his Press campaign going.'

'What of it?' said Fink-Drummond coldly. 'Those of us who are in the know should all be able to pick up a fortune.'

Gervaise frowned. 'You do not seem to consider the misery

that such a slump might bring to thousands of small investors.'

'My dear sir,' Fink-Drummond turned towards him, 'it is quite clear that you know little of high finance. Small people make or lose money every day, but that is no concern of the professionals who control the markets.'

'But that's only the start of it,' Hemmingway Hughes cut in again. 'To put this thing over, you'd have to make people believe that their lives were in danger. There would be the most frightful panics, demonstrations, riots. You might throw the whole country into a state of anarchy.'

'There would naturally be a certain amount of trouble,' Fink-Drummond conceded, 'but we should proclaim martial law and with a good man at the War Office, we should soon get the unruly elements under.'

'What?' exclaimed Sam. 'You actually mean that to serve your own ambitions you're prepared to plunge the country into such a state of strife that there will be street-fighting and the troops will be called out to fire upon our own people? I've always known you were pretty unscrupulous, but this . . .'

'That's quite enough,' snapped Fink-Drummond. His face dark with rage, he took a quick step towards the door. 'You're behaving like a fool and later you'll regret it. Kindly send for my car.'

'One moment,' Gervaise said quietly. 'Since Mr. Fink-Drummond appears determined to go through with his plans, with or without your assistance, Sam, I think it would be as well to dicuss the matter further. We all seem to have got a little heated and I was surprised into a breach of good taste myself only a moment ago. To calm ourselves I suggest that we should drink a glass of wine together before we say anything more. I'll go and get a bottle.'

'Let me, sir,' Hemmingway offered.

'No, no, I can manage,' Gervaise replied. 'But please, all of you, remain here. I don't want this affair to reach the ears of any others members of the party.'

As Gervaise left the room it was on the tip of Sam's tongue to say that he did not think further discussion could serve any useful purpose, but as he had already conceived a great respect for his father-in-law's wisdom he remained silent.

When Gervaise returned he was carrying four full tumblers of champagne on a tray, which he offered first to Fink-Drummond.

The ex-Cabinet Minister took the nearest glass and smiled again. 'Let me congratulate you, Mr. Stapleton, on your good sense in suggesting that Sam should reconsider my proposition. He's a hot-headed fellow but I feel sure that when he thinks the matter over he will see reason. As he admits himself I could easily get the money elsewhere, but I would prefer to work with Sam because I know that I can trust him.'

Sam shrugged. 'Oh, if I came into this, you could trust me all right; but I'm not coming into it.'

'But why, my dear fellow? We've done many other deals together and some which, I think you will agree, certain people who know little of the inner workings of big business might, quite unjustifiably, consider questionable.'

'That's true. But I've done nothing that my competitors, who *do* understand such things, would not willingly have done, and for that reason I am not the least ashamed of our dealings. Big business, plus politics, plus finance, has its own code of laws and I've never gone outside them; but this is different, because it affects the happiness of the whole nation.'

'We all see that, Sam,' Gervaise reasoned mildly. 'But if Mr. Fink-Drummond is determined to do this thing, surely it's better for you to go into it with him than to permit somebody else to take it on who might prove—well, shall we say, much less scrupulous. Anyhow, here's your health once again!'

Sam looked at his father-in-law in surprise. It came as quite a shock to him that anyone so upright as Gervaise Stapleton should countenance his agreeing to Fink-Drummond's suggestion on any terms whatsoever; but he lifted his glass with the rest and they all drank the proposed toast.

'I don't like it,' Hemmingway Hughes exclaimed suddenly. 'I'm damned if I do! High finance may have its own code, as Sam says, but this is different. Why, even the armament racketeers don't go to the length of fermenting trouble which may cause bloodshed among their own people. Honestly, Sam, I wouldn't touch this thing with a barge-pole.'

'I've never had the least intention of doing so,' Sam said firmly.

'Perhaps you're right.' Gervaise set down his glass on a nearby table. 'It's difficult for me to express an opinion because I entirely lack experience in such matters, but I've always understood that some very queer things occur behind the scenes in politics.'

'They do,' Sam agreed, 'but there's a limit, and I should have thought anyone could see the misery that would be caused to countless innocent people if Fink-Drummond goes through with his scheme to unseat the Government.'

'I should be able to form a better judgment on that if Mr. Fink-Drummond would be kind enough to explain his plans to me in some detail.'

'By all means.' Fink-Drummond took another drink from his glass, straightened himself up and began to outline his proposed campaign. Rumours must be set going at once, he explained. Ten days should be sufficient for him to get his following in the House together. They would then launch a huge Press attack on the Government for having concealed the approaching danger.

Having got so far, Fink-Drummond passed a hand over his forehead as though to collect his thoughts. He then went on to speak of various measures that would get the public behind him and of special lines which his principal supporters would be instructed to follow. By that time he had gone deadly white and Sam noticed that he was slurring his words a little.

For another moment Fink-Drummond continued to speak but his words came with difficulty and it was clear that something was wrong with him. He broke off abruptly, exclaimed 'Sorry, I—I'm feeling ill,' and began to mop his face with his handkerchief.

Suddenly his eyes bulged, he sagged a little, rocked from side to side, choked and collapsed in a heap on the floor.

Believing that he was suffering from a fit, Sam ran to him and, kneeling down, undid his collar. Hemmingway Hughes moved forward, too, but towards the desk against which Fink-Drummond had been leaning. He picked up the ex-Cabinet Minister's half-empty glass and sniffed it.

Gervaise Stapleton's voice rang out like the crack of a whip. 'Put that glass down!'

Hemmingway turned to stare at him, and exclaimed: 'Good God! I thought as much.'

Fink-Drummond was now lying stiff and still upon the carpet. With a look of horror on his face, Sam glanced first at Hemmingway and then at his father-in-law. 'Heavens, man!' he cried. 'You'll swing for this. You've poisoned him!'

6

A PLOT TO SAVE THE NATION

'Yes,' Gervaise admitted quietly, 'I poisoned him.' There was a look of calm satisfaction on his aristocratic features and with one hand he smoothed back his fine crop of white, slightly wavy hair.

Sam jumped up from beside Fink-Drummond's still body. 'But hang it, man! You don't seem to realize what you've done. We can't conceal this thing—we'll have to call in the police.'

Hemmingway Hughes stepped towards the door. 'We must get a doctor—a stomach pump. There may be a chance of saving him yet.'

'That's it,' cried Sam, 'hurry! In the meantime, we'll try and think up some story to get my father-in-law out of this. If we keep our heads, we may be able to persuade them it was suicide.'

Gervaise barred Hemmingway's passage to the door. 'Thanks,' he said. 'It's good of you to be so concerned for me, but we don't require either a doctor or the police.'

'Don't be a fool,' Sam snapped. 'Of course I appreciate your motives. You were kidding us just now when you appeared to be persuading me to listen to his rotten scheme; just giving the poison time to work. You made up your mind from the beginning that the only way to stop the swine sabotaging the whole country was to kill him, didn't you? But that's no reason why you should sacrifice your own neck, if we can save it.'

'You're right about my motive, Sam,' Gervaise smiled, 'but I've no intention whatever of sacrificing myself.'

'If we can't get a doctor to pull him round, or fix a suicide story, you'll have to stand your trial for murder.'

'Not at all. It's true that I poisoned him but he's not going to die.'

Sam frowned. 'Then, why the devil didn't you say so?'

'You didn't give me much chance.' Extending his left hand, Gervaise pointed to the little finger upon which there was a large, old-fashioned ring. 'You see that? I bought it in Florence many years ago. There was still one man living then, a descendant of the old alchemists, who possessed the secret of some of the Medici poisons. The ring is hollow and he sold it to me with four little pills in it. The pills consist of a poison that is tasteless and odourless when served in wine. Two pills will cause death, while one will bring about a state of catalepsy within five minutes. I only put one pill in this rogue's champagne.'

'Thank God for that! But what do we do now? When he comes round there'll be hell to pay. And I don't see that having put him out for a bit is going to prevent him carrying through his Government-wrecking programme.'

'He won't come round for twenty-four hours at least, and by that time he will find himself a prisoner in the old nursery of this house. It's on the third floor, looks down on the empty stables where no one ever goes these days and has barred windows.'

'By Jove! You *are* a stout fellow.' Sam grinned at his father-in law with sudden admiration. 'I take it you mean to keep him a prisoner here until the trouble is over?'

'Until then, or, if my brother is right, until the world comes to an end on June 24th.'

'That's all very well,' remarked Hemmingway. 'It's a grand scheme as far as it goes; but there'll be a terrific hue and cry after he's been missing for a day or two. Ex-Cabinet Ministers aren't given to disappearing without leaving any trace of their whereabouts.'

'I can't help that,' Gervaise declared firmly. 'This man is a danger to the State. It is our duty to protect our fellow-citizens from such people at whatever risk to ourselves. I am prepared to take the whole matter upon my own shoulders if you wish but, if you're willing to co-operate, I shall be grateful for any help you can give me to cover his tracks.'

'Of course,' Sam agreed at once. 'Somehow or other we must think up a plausible reason to account for his sudden disappearance.'

'Could we use his wife in any way?' Hemmingway suggested. 'She sailed yesterday for the States. How about his going off in a private plane to overtake the ship and join her?'

'That's a grand idea,' Sam nodded. 'Then the plane disappears. His wife will radio that she knew nothing of his intentions, but we'll spread a story that he left for urgent private reasons. It will be assumed that something went wrong with the plane and that he was drowned at sea.'

'We can't keep him a prisoner for ever, though.'

'No, and he'll sue the lot of us for conspiracy directly we let him out. Just think what a scandal there'll be; and the case will cost us thousands. We may even be sent to prison ourselves for kidnapping.'

'We need not worry about that till the end of June,' Gervaise reminded them grimly. 'And, if the world is still in existence then, I'm prepared to face any prosecution that may result from this business.'

Hemmingway's shrewd eyes were veiled for a moment by the lowering of his lazy, eyelids. 'There won't be any prosecution. Fink-Drummond would never dare to bring one. We'd tell the whole story in court and show that none of us had benefited personally in any way by his disappearance. We might be fined a farthing damages but he'd be hounded out of the country. Let's get on with the job and think of a man we can trust who's got a plane. We ought to fake his departure this evening.'

'Rupert Brand will do that for us, said Sam. 'I'm sure we can rely on him and he's got a big private plane at his place down at Cobham. He'll have to disappear, too, for the time being and you, Hemmingway, must arrange to get the story of their sudden departure in to-morrow's papers.'

'That's easy. I can fix it through the usual channels we tap for special business, without anyone being the wiser.'

Gervaise pushed a cushion under Fink-Drummond's head, and said: 'We'd better get back to the others now. They must be wondering what on earth has happened to us. I'll lock this door and attend to our prisoner myself when all the guests and hired staff have gone. I can leave the rest to you two, I take it?'

Sam nodded. 'I'll tacke Rupert and he and Hemmingway can make all the other arrangements between them. If there were anything I could do that they can't, I'd put off my honeymoon; but, as it is . . .'

'My dear fellow, you mustn't dream of such a thing.' Gervaise patted him kindly on the shoulder and the three men left the room together.

In the hall Sam paused. 'You'd better find Rupert, Hemmingway, and bring him out here. If I go back into the drawing-room, I shall be surrounded by the crowd.'

As Hemmingway hurried off, Lavina appeared, with Margery beside her. 'Why, there you are!' she exclaimed, as she saw Sam and her father. 'Everybody's been wondering wherever you two had got to.'

Gervaise smiled. 'We've been having a little private celebration. I'm sorry to have robbed you of Sam but you see it's a new and very pleasant experience for me to have a son.'

She kissed him quickly. 'It makes me very happy that you like each other, darling. I'm just going up to change.'

'You'd better go up and change, too,' Margery admonished Sam. 'You mustn't keep the bride waiting.'

Sam gave her an amiable grin. 'It won't take me as long as it will Lavina, but I'll be up in a minute.'

The two girls had just disappeared round the bend of the stairs when Hemmingway returned with Rupert Brand.

'Listen, Rupert,' Sam plunged in right away, 'I'm going to ask you to do something pretty big for us. You may think us crazy but we want you to take that private plane of yours up to-night and disappear in it for six or seven weeks.'

'The devil you do!' exclaimed Rupert. 'To put it mildly, that's a most extraordinary request.'

'We're in an extraordinary situation and we're counting on you to help us. It's a matter which may affect the welfare of the whole nation. I really mean that.'

'Well, if you put it that way. Is this M.I.5, or something?'

'No. The three of us are acting absolutely unofficially. In fact, we're even risking prosecution for conspiracy and, later on, it's possible that you might be called on to answer some pretty tricky questions. But Hemmingway will give you the details and I think when you hear them you'll agree that this job has simply got to be done. I must go up and change now, and all I can add is that I do beg you to give us your assistance.'

Rupert brushed up his small, fair Guardee moustache with the knuckle of his first finger. 'Well, it's going to be hellishly inconvenient—and there's Conchita to be thought of; but I'm game to listen to anything Hemmingway's got to say.'

'Right,' said Hemmingway. 'Let's go out into the garden where we can't be overheard.'

Gervaise nodded. 'That would be best. I'll go back and look after our guests while you change, Sam.'

As they strolled up and down the newly mown lawn in the May sunshine, Hemmingway gave Rupert particulars of what had happened.

When Hemmingway had done, Rupert said slowly: 'I see the necessity for covering the disappearance of that swine, Fink-Drummond, all right. But there are a lot of snags to doing it the way you suggest.'

'Let's hear them.'

'Well, to start with, there's Conchita. We'd arranged to be married on the first of June. And to ask me to postpone our wedding is pretty tough on both of us.'

'That certainly is a nasty one,' Hemmingway agreed, 'but it's a purely personal matter and we're asking you to make this big sacrifice in the service of your country.'

Rupert grunted angrily. 'Damn it, man, you don't have to tell me that!'

'What I'm really concerned about,' Hemmingway went on smoothly, 'is how you're fixed officially. If you're committed to the Service in any way, you couldn't just flit off into the blue without obtaining leave. To do so would create immediate suspicion that the whole job was phony.'

'Oh, you needn't worry about that. I resigned from the Coldstream six months ago, so I'm my own boss these days. Of course, there's my job with the Akers Wentworth people. I'm testing the new Akers "Eagle" fighter, but there's nothing to prevent my taking on a private engagement to fly a man like Fink-Drummond out to catch a ship off the west coast of Ireland. If we left to-night, I should normally be back to-morrow morning and, if I failed to return, the assumption would be that the plane had crashed and we'd both been drowned at sea. That would be just too bad. But there's nothing that anybody could do about it.'

'Well, that's exactly what I want. And it takes a whale of a load off my mind to know you're free to do it.'

'That's all damned fine! But what about Conchita?'

Hemmingway considered for a moment. 'The best thing we can do is to call her in on this, and see what she's got to say herself. Let's go and get her.'

They turned back and walked quickly up the slope to the french windows of the long drawing-room on the south side of the house. Conchita was talking to some people by the buffet, but Rupert succeeded in getting her away, and, once the three of them were out in the garden, Hemmingway told all over again the story of Fink-Drummond's activities.

'I refuse to be separated from Rupert for all that time,' she said, when Hemmingway had finished. 'You see, for the first time in my life I'm really in love, and I couldn't bear the thought of being parted from him even for a week.'

Hemmingway shot her an anxious look. 'I know we're asking an incredibly hard thing of you, but there's so much at stake, and none of us know an airman we could trust with such an important secret, except Rupert.'

Her generous mouth twitched with amusement. 'I *do* understand how much is at stake, so therefore he shall go—but I intend to go with him.'

'Would you?' exclaimed Rupert, his face lighting up.

'Why not, darling? Do you not think it would be rather fun for us to elope?'

'By Jove! And to-night, as ever was.'

'To-night, my sweet. We will pass out of this so stupid social world, and go into hiding together for just as long as you like.'

Hemmingway smiled at her. 'Well, now, isn't that just splendid!'

'It'll be the most glorious adventure of my life,' Rupert cried 'and I've had a few already. But we're not out of the wood yet, by a long chalk. Where are we going to on this honeymoon of ours?'

'Anywhere you like,' Hemmingway said airily.

'That's not so easy. Surely you realize that planes are labelled and numbered, just like cars, these days; and my big beauty is a special model which plenty of air people would recognize on sight. We've got to land somewhere; and, whatever airport we chose, our landing would be reported. It would be known in England a few hours later, and that would upset the entire apple-cart.'

'Let me solve this difficulty,' Conchita suggested. 'Why should we not fly to my old home in Spain? It is an estate of many thousand acres, in La Mancha. My house-servants were loyal to me in the Revolution, and, even if they wished to talk, who could they talk to when the nearest city is Ciudad Real, fifty miles away? The house is in what you call here the back of beyond. We have no neighbours, only little peasant villages scattered over the Great Plain.'

'That's a grand idea,' Rupert agreed, 'as long as no officious person sees us landing.'

She laughed. 'My dear one, the peasantry are so ignorant that they're only just learning to read. How could they possibly know one aeroplane from another, even if they saw it? But few of them will do so, if we land at dawn. And then we will lock the plane away out of sight in one of the great barns.'

'It sounds good to me,' Hemmingway admitted. 'But, wait a minute! If it's a land-plane it couldn't come down on the sea; so you'd never have used it for taking Fink-Drummond to catch a liner. The air reporters will spot that as soon as the story breaks.'

'Fortunately, we're all right there. She's an amphibian, so we could come down equally well on land or water.'

'How about the distance, though? It's clear from what you said just now that to land at any place *en route* would give the whole game away. Can you make it in one hop?'

'It's under a thousand miles, and, fuelled to capacity, my new bus could cover three times that distance.'

'How long will it take you to get there?'

'About five hours.'

'Fine. I reckon that's a little longer than you'd need to over-take the *Falconia*, but not enough to matter. If you leave at one, you'd be certain of having the morning light to land by.'

'Yes, and I'd need that to spot the ship. It's important, too, that I should pass the Spanish military aerodromes while it's still dark; otherwise they might send up a plane to challenge me. I hope they haven't built a drome anywhere near your place, Conchita?'

'No. I am sure I should know of it if they had.'

'That's O.K., then, as I shall fly very high until we have to land.'

'Right,' Hemmingway nodded. 'Now, this is the drill. You go straight home from here, Rupert, get your plane ready, and tell your mechanics you're flying Fink-Drummond out to catch the *Falconia* off the west coast of Ireland. You're leaving at one o'clock, but you don't want to keep them up once the plane is ready. Say you're taking your fiancée with you, just for the trip, and that you expect to be back at—well, whatever you work out to be the normal hour to-morrow morning.

'I'll take Conchita back to London in my car. She must pack and tell her maids the same story. But, for goodness' sake, Conchita, don't take a lot of luggage, because you're only supposed to be staying up all night. It's hard to ask you to leave most of your things behind, but, strictly speaking, you shouldn't set off with much more than your beauty-box.'

'That I understand,' she replied gravely. 'But, as I am flying to my own home, I have no need to do so. For the simple life that we shall lead I have plenty of clothes out there.'

'Good. Then I want you to order a car from Daimler Hire to pick you up at midnight. You must make a special point of insisting that they supply you one which has blinds. Directly you get in the car pull them down, and tell the man to drive to Bryanston Square. You'll find me waiting by the garden railings opposite No. 102. That's Fink-Drummond's house. Luckily, I'm about his height, and dark. I shall be carrying a big suitcase as though for a journey, wearing an overcoat with a fur collar pulled up round my face, and a gangster hat right down over my eyes.

'Directly you drive up in the car I shall jump into it, taking care that the chauffeur doesn't see my face. You will then tell him to drive us down to Rupert's place at Cobham. When we arrive I shall get out with my bag and walk round the side of the house. You'll pay the man off, and tell him to drive back to London. Then ring the front door bell, and when Rupert's man answers it say to him, "Would you tell Captain Brand that we've arrived, and that Mr. Fink-Drummond is so anxious to get off that he's gone straight round to the plane."

'Rupert will be lurking in the lounge listening for your arrival. Directly he hears the butler go to open the front door he will come out into the hall dressed all ready for his flight. He should hear what you say to his man about Fink-Drummond being in such a hurry to get off, and greet you at once with the words: "In that case it's not much good my offering you a drink." He'll then join you on the doorstep, say good night to his man, and walk with you round to the hangar.

'I shall be there to give a hand with the plane, if necessary, and to see you off with my blessing. After which I'll have to do a cross-country walk of six or seven miles into Epsom, knock up a garage there, and hire a car to take me back to London. Is that all clear?'

The others agreed that it was, and he went on:

'Grand. Now, let's see how things will pan out from there on. I can fix it this evening that a small news paragraph appears in one or two of the leading morning papers, saying that, for urgent private reasons, Fink-Drummond has left England by plane to join his wife, who is on the S.S. *Falconia*, two days out, bound for New York. The midday editions of the evening papers will carry a more prominent story: "*Ex-Cabinet Minister's dash to join his wife on outward-bound Atlantic liner. Famous airman, Captain Brand, engaged at short notice to fly him out. Brand takes beautiful fiancée with him as passenger on trip.*"

'By midday your people, Rupert, will be getting really worried about your not having returned. They'll 'phone the Air Ministry and the balloon will go up. The late editions of the evening papers will carry a headline story: "*Ex-Cabinet Minister, ace airman, and fiancée reported lost over Atlantic.*"

'The *Falconia* will radio home that she is keeping a constant look-out, but has seen nothing of you. In the following mornings papers there will be a real hullabaloo, and I'm sorry to say we'll have to cost the country a whole packet of money sending up planes to look for you; but, of course, without result. After a day or two the excitement will die down, and it will be believed that all three of you have been drowned at sea.

'If any of Fink-Drummond's relatives feel that there is something queer about his sudden departure, and start to make inquiries, this is what they will learn. That he was last seen at Sam's wedding here, to-day. Then . . .'

'Wait a minute, though,' Rupert interrupted. 'How about the chauffeur in the car that brought him down? His man is bound to wonder what's happened when he fails to leave with the other guests.'

'Say! I'm glad you thought of that. I must fix it. I'll have a message sent him, when people start to go, that he's to drive home empty, as his chief is returning to London with the Marchesa del Serilla. That will tie up nicely with the rest of the story later on.

'Getting back to the investigation. The chauffeur will tell Fink-Drummond's relatives that he left here with Conchita. For a few hours Fink-Drummond disappears entirely, and no one will ever be able to find out what he did during that time, but that dovetails with this mysterious personal business on which it was so urgent that he should see his wife. The Daimler people will say that Conchita hired one of their cars to collect her at midnight, and specially insisted that the car should have blinds.

'Their man will tell *his* story: that, having picked her up, she pulled down the blinds in the car, and he then drove her to Bryanston Square, where they picked up a man whose face he did not see; but whose description will roughly tally with that of Fink-Drummond. And this man was carrying a large suitcase, as though for a journey. The couple were then driven down to Captain Brand's place at Cobham, where the lady paid the car off.

'Conchita's maid, when questioned, will say that her mistress arrived back from Sam's wedding, and said that Captain Brand was going to take her on a night-flying trip out over the Atlantic with Mr. Fink-Drummond.

'Rupert's mechanics will tell their story of how he returned from Sam's wedding to supervise their getting his plane ready for a special trip because he was going to fly Fink-Drummond to join his wife that night.

'And Rupert's butler will conclude the chain by informing inquirers how Conchita arrived at the house about one in the morning with Fink-Drummond, and told Rupert, in his presence, that Fink-Drummond was in such a hurry to get off that he had gone straight round to the hangar. The plane took off a few minutes later, and that is that.'

'Marvellous!' purred Conchita. 'You seem to have thought of everything; except for one small point. What if he has some important dinner to-night, a speech to make, or a banquet to attend? Will they not start to search for him prematurely when he does not return to his house or send any message?'

'That certainly is a snag to be got over. How would it be if

Rupert telephoned Fink-Drummond's secretary to cancel all his engagements because urgent business made it necessary for him to spend the late afternoon in the City; and, after that, his plans were so uncertain that he might not be able to get back to-night? The inference afterwards would be that he'd made up his mind to join his wife at the last moment, returned to Bryanston Square, let himself in, and packed his own bag as he was in too much of a hurry to ring for any of the servants.'

Rupert shook his head. 'The part about my telephoning's all right, but not your inference about his returning to pack his bag. Otherwise one of his bags with his brushes, shaving tackle, and so on, would be missing from the house; and we can't just wish them into vanishing into thin air.'

'Sure, sure.' Hemmingway passed a hand over his big forehead. 'Yes, we must better that. I'll tell you. When you 'phone, speak to his butler. That's less risky than the secretary, who might start asking awkward questions. Tell the butler to pack him a bag for a couple of nights away from home, then to take it to Grosvenor House, check it into the cloakroom there, and say that the Marchesa del Serilla will call for it.'

'Do you think the butler would take such instructions from me without any confirmation from his master?'

'You've been to Fink-Drummond's house, haven't you?'

'Yes. I've lunched there two or three times.'

'That'll be all right, then. It's not like asking him to let a lot of jewels or important papers out of his keeping, and he must know that you and Conchita are not the sort of people who'd enter into an elaborate plot to steal a week-end suitcase.'

'That's true.'

'Then Conchita will collect the bag from Grosvenor House around midnight, and instead of picking me up in Bryanston Square I'll be waiting on that quiet corner behind Grosvenor House where Park Street joins Mount Street.'

'That is much better,' Conchita conceded, 'except that everyone will think he ran away with me.'

Rupert laughed and squeezed her arm. 'Not as it's my plane you're both going in, my sweet. They'll just believe that, as I was flying him out and you were in the secret, you helped him in his trouble by running him around to places in your car and picking up his things for him so that nobody should know, outside us three, what sort of funny business he was occupied on or whom he saw during the evening, before he made his get-away.'

Hemmingway gave a sigh of relief. 'Well, thank goodness we've sorted that. I'm most terribly grateful to you both, and I know Sam will be, too.'

'Not a bit of it,' Rupert smiled. 'Let's go and drink the old boy's health in another glass of wine, before the happy couple depart for their honeymoon.'

'I'll have a drink with you later. As best man, it's up to me to see they've got all their things together before they go.'

Conchita and Rupert went back arm-in-arm through the french windows into the drawing-room, while Hemmingway entered the front door. For a few moments he was busy giving final instructions and seeing the pile of luggage loaded on to the car. Then Sam came downstairs and looked across at him inquiringly.

Hemmingway nodded. 'It's all fixed.'

'Good work,' Sam smiled. 'But if there's any trouble, you must cable me and I'll return at once to take responsibility.'

'Don't worry. I won't have to.'

They talked together for a few moments about business arrangements during Sam's absence, but broke off as Lavina and Margery came downstairs.

'I think I've got all your things,' Hemmingway said to Lavina, 'but you might just check them up. I know Sam's stuff but I'm not so used to yours.'

'Of course I will.' She went out with him on to the porch and together they ran over her pieces of luggage in the waiting car.

Margery, meanwhile, had turned in the other direction and was talking to Sam. From where they stood they were out of earshot of Hemmingway and Lavina but could see them just outside the open doorway.

At that moment Hemmingway held out his hand to Lavina and said: 'Well, I'll say good-bye now, before the crush surrounds you. Happy honeymoon.'

She looked up into those strange, wise eyes of his again and once more she had that sensation of vague fear. But Lavina was a courageous person and believed that the best way to conquer fear of anything was to face it boldly. This was fear of herself; not fear of him. And she knew that, since they would be together so much in the future, she must root it out now, once and for all.

To prove herself she smiled back into his eyes and said: 'Thanks so much for all you've done to-day, but isn't it usual for the best man to kiss the bride?'

'Not in the States, and I'm half American,' he laughed. 'I'm a poor hand at kissing people, too, unless I really mean it; and, if I did that, I'm afraid I'd make an awful hash of your make-up!'

It was said with such charming lightness that it was quite impossible for Lavina to take offence, but she was determined not to be side-tracked so she answered gaily: 'All right, then, I'll kiss you.' And, standing on tiptoe for a second, she gave him a swift kiss on the cheek.

Sam and Margery had witnessed the little scene from the distance. As he turned towards her to say something he saw that her face was strained and intent.

'May I give you a piece of advice?' she asked suddenly.

'Why, yes.' He lifted an eyebrow in surprise.

'Sack that secretary of yours.'

'Sack Hemmingway! Good Lord, why?'

'You'd better, unless you want your marriage broken up. He's young, extraordinarily attractive and the type that doesn't fall easily for women but, when they do, fall hard—and I know Lavina. All her life she's battened on admiration. She'll never rest until she's made him as mad about her as all the other men she's ever known for any length of time.'

'Margery!' Sam was really shocked. 'How *can* you say such a frightful thing about your own sister?'

Suddenly Margery turned away and burst into a violent fit of tears.

Sam cast an anxious glance towards the drawing-room, flung an arm round the weeping girl's shoulders and pushed her into the cloakroom nearby; pulling the door to behind them.

'For God's sake, don't make a scene!' he said angrily. 'Stop crying, now. Stop it! Or your tears will mess up your face.'

With an effort Margery checked her sobbing, dabbed her eyes with a handkerchief and, walking over to the mirror, pulled out her compact to make good the traces of tears left on her cheeks.

Sam was furious and he let himself go. 'You must be downright wicked to say such a thing to me on my wedding-day. Hemming-way's my best man and my best friend. I'd trust him anywhere with anything, and I'd trust Lavina to the limit, too. It's just your rotten, filthy imagination.'

She turned then, and faced him calmly. 'I'm sorry, Sam. Terribly sorry. I should never have said that but I did believe it at the time. It was something in their attitude to each other that I can't explain, and my wicked jealousy, I suppose. You see, Lavina's always had everything—everything I've ever wanted; even the rather second-rate boy-friends, whom she couldn't be bothered with but I would so gladly have had, all fell for her.'

Sam stared at her and realized for the first time that she was quite young, not more than twenty-six, and definitely good-looking. Not beautiful like Lavina, but very attractive in her own way; which must have made it all the harder for her that she had had to play the drudge's part while Lavina had all the fun.

Suddenly overwhelmed with a great wave of pity he put his arms round her and kissed her. 'You poor kid,' he said. 'I'm sure you didn't mean it. Let's never think of it again.'

7

INSIDE INFORMATION

The day after Sam and Lavina were married life at Stapleton Court resumed its uneventful routine. The big reception rooms were closed once more; the caterers had removed all traces of the wedding feast. Gervaise and his elder daughter, Margery, were once again in sole possession of the derelict Georgian mansion; unless one counted an entirely new and disturbing factor which had suddenly entered their quiet lives—the prisoner in the nursery.

After the departure of the wedding guests Gervaise had called in Derek Burroughs, told him of the events which had led up to the decision that Fink-Drummond must be kept a prisoner of the next few weeks and secured his assistance in putting the ex-Cabinet Minister to bed.

It was not until five o'clock the following afternoon that Fink-Drummond came out of his cataleptic state but as soon as he had recovered sufficiently to think and talk coherently he created a very pretty scene.

Gervaise had been sitting in the room reading a book while he waited for his prisoner to come round and he explained at once that, although he disliked Mr. Fink-Drummond very much indeed, he felt himself compelled, in the interests of national safety, to offer him his hospitality for some time to come. Neither arguments nor threats could induce him to take a refusal and he backed up his statement by producing an antiquated revolver that had seen service in the Boer War.

Fink-Drummond raged and stormed. He declared that all the forces of the law should be brought into operation the second he was free; that he would sue the lot of them for conspiracy and forcible detention and that they should see the inside of a prison.

Gervaise pointed out that, if the world came to an end on June 24th, none of them would have to bother themselves on that score. And, on the other hand, if it did not, Mr. Fink-

Drummond might possibly be induced to reconsider his decision when he was restored to freedom as, whatever penalties the Law might award against those who had detained him, prosecution and the attendant publicity could only result in his being hounded out of the country.

This gave Fink-Drummond furiously to think and Gervaise left him still thinking; although he took care to shoot the two bolts which he had fixed on the outside of the door that morning, before going downstairs to drink a glass of old Madeira in his comfortable library.

The nursery suite consisted of day-nursery, night-nursery and bathroom. The windows of all three were barred and looked out upon the deserted stable-yard, which was well away from the tradesmen's entrance; so Gervaise was reasonably confident that his prisoner could not escape providing a watchful eye was kept upon him in case he started taking up the floor-boards in order to break out through the ceiling below, or something of that kind.

There was, however, one possible danger. Fink-Drummond had to be fed and, although Gervaise intended to take every possible precaution when taking his food to him, in so long a period as six weeks the prisoner might well think of some subtle way in which to surprise, attack and overcome his gaoler. If that occurred since Margery was the only other person in the house, Fink-Drummond would have a free field for escape. In less than a couple of hours he would be back in London, beyond all possible hope of recapture, and free to develop his own schemes which might bring about untold misery and disaster.

Having considered this problem, Gervaise decided to call in Derek as a permanent Assistant Gaoler and, after dinner that evening, he strolled over to see his neighbour.

Derek was willing enough to co-operate but his farm and hot-houses were his livelihood and at such a season it would have caused him grievous loss to abandon them permanently. Had he been convinced that the end of the world was really approaching, he would have done so, but he did not believe in the predicted catastrophe for one moment.

However, he put forward a suggestion. Gervaise's nephew, Roy, was back in London doing nothing, and so hard-up that he could not do it with any enjoyment. Couldn't he be persuaded to come down to stay and help his uncle look after the prisoner?

Gervaise considered for a moment. 'That might serve us for a week or so, but by the end of that time I fear Roy would be so bored with the quiet life he would have to lead that he'd refuse to stick it any longer. Besides—I can be quite frank with you, Derek—although I don't suggest that he's a drunkard, Roy likes his liquor and from that point of view I'm afraid he's too expensive a guest for me to entertain for such a period.'

'I think we can get over that,' Derek smiled. 'As long as he's with you each time you take a meal up to Fink-Drummond that's all you really want him for.'

'True. The essential thing is that two people should be present whenever his door is unlocked.'

'Then for the rest of the time there's no reason why Roy shouldn't get out and about a bit. He's always liked the country. I'll lend him a horse to ride each morning and there's a golf club nearby at Dorking where I could make him a member. He can fish your lake and swim a bit if the weather's decent; so I don't think he'll be too bored.'

'How about the evenings, though?'

'Oh, I'll come over in the evenings to make up a four at Bridge, or take him down to the "George" where he can get a game of billiards. Roy's a lazy, shiftless devil, but he's a most amusing companion so I shouldn't mind looking after him. As for the drink question, I think we're old enough friends for you not to mind my sending you in a case or two of whisky to keep him going while he's in the house.'

'That's very good of you, Derek—very good of you indeed. I think I can manage the whisky, though, providing you're game to take him about so that he's not running me up a bill for a case of Scotch a week.'

'Right. Let's telephone him now, then, shall we?'

They got on to Oliver for Roy's address and managed to locate him at a small Bloomsbury hotel. It was impossible to explain over the telephone the real reason for his being required at Stapleton Court, but Roy's lack of funds brought him to the quick decision that a week or so in the country would be a welcome economy at the moment. With his usual optimism he was now considering Lavina's half-promise, that Sam might get him a job, as a certainty, so he had no intention whatever of looking for anything else in the meantime and had to hang out somehow until Sir Samuel and Lady Curry returned from their honeymoon. He therefore accepted his uncle's invitation at once and said that he would be down for lunch the following day.

It was so long since the nursery suite at Stapleton Court had been occupied that, apart from the bed which Gervaise and Derek had made up for Fink-Drummond, all the furniture was so dusty one could write one's name on it; so next morning Margery set about giving the rooms a thorough spring-cleaning.

Fink-Drummond had to resign himself to being locked in the bathroom meanwhile, but he did not protest as it was clear that his gaolers were doing their best to make him comfortable. Gervaise brought him up a supply of books in the afternoon and at the same time produced Roy, who had been told over luncheon of the real reason he had been summoned to the country.

Derek came in that evening and put up various suggestions for Roy's entertainment during his stay and the ne'er-do-well accepted the situation quite cheerfully; in fact, he found it rather novel and amusing, as his duties consisted of no more than accompanying his uncle up to the prisoner's room three or four times a day.

Fortunately, the weather was good so Roy was able to get out of the house most days for several hours, and as he was an excellent mixer he soon formed a little crowd of cronies with whom he played darts and exchanged bawdy stories at the 'local', on such evenings as Derek could not drive over and make up a table for Bridge.

The days drifted by, May passing into June quite uneventfully. An occasional postcard came from Lavina and Sam. They were somewhere in the foot-hills of the Pyrenees, staying at small places right off the beaten track and thoroughly enjoying themselves.

Hemmingway Hughes' scheme for covering Fink-Drummond's disappearance had worked entirely according to plan. There had been great excitement for a few days. Headlines in the papers, Royal Air Force squadrons fruitlessly searching the grey wastes of the Eastern Atlantic. Then, with amazing rapidity, other news had filled the papers; Fink-Drummond, Rupert Brand and the Marchesa del Serilla were assumed drowned.

Beatrice Fink-Drummond bought herself some very light widow's weeds on her arrival in New York and no one but their intimate friends gave them another thought.

It had been agreed that, in the event of Fink-Drummond's escaping, Hemmingway should be informed at once but, apart from occasional storms of abuse which grew less frequent as time wore on, the prisoner gave no trouble; so there had been no reason to ring up St. James's Square. On the 2nd June, however, Hemmingway telephoned to say that he would very much like to have a talk with both Gervaise and Oliver Stapleton; so it was arranged that he and Oliver should motor down and lunch at Stapleton Court the following day.

When Hemmingway arrived he appeared as calm and inscrutable as ever, but after lunch he disclosed the fact that he was extremely worried. The Government had, so far, succeeded in keeping from the public the news that a comet was approaching, but in the three weeks since Sam's wedding a constantly increasing circle of people had become acquainted with the fact. This was already affecting the markets and, as the rumours spread, it was certain that they would soon precipitate a really serious situation. Stocks were not slumping yet, as the general public were still buying, but many of the big financiers were unloading heavily with a view to buying in again at much lower levels during the panic which was certain to ensue directly knowledge of the comet's approach became general. In consequence, it was to be expected that when the small money was exhausted the markets would break and shares plunge headlong.

To protect Sam's interests Hemmingway could only do as the other big men were doing but he felt that a crisis, all unknown to the public, was rapidly approaching.

The situation abroad was much the same as at home. Hemmingway had learned through Foreign Office sources that conversations had been entered into on the subject of the comet with every foreign Government. By mutual consent all controversial problems had been shelved for the time being. This had caused a sudden lessening of international tension and was one of the factors which caused the little man to have a renewed feeling of confidence and so more readily support the markets.

The Governments had already reached agreement upon the point that no useful purpose could be gained by allowing the

C

danger to become known prematurely and, with the willing co-operation of their Press chiefs, were exercising a rigid censorship. They were now discussing the problem of mutual aid in the event of the comet's damaging one area of the earth's surface but leaving the others comparatively unaffected.

In fact, since the rulers of the world now took the approaching danger with extreme seriousness, it was rapidly bringing about a spirit of goodwill which had long been lacking from the international situation.

The great majority of the people in the know, however, still assumed that the comet was composed only of gas and meteorites. They believed that, even if it got drawn into the earth's orbit, it would do no more than cause grave disturbances among the terrified masses; which would quickly subside once it had disintegrated and its great shower of meteorites had embedded themselves in the earth.

That many of the meteorites would cause considerable destruction was unquestioned; but, according to Hemmingway, the Governments at home and abroad were allaying their own fears by the supposition that no more havoc would be caused through this heavenly bombardment than might be expected from an intensive but brief aerial attack brought about by the major nations going to war with each other. In view of the fact that for some years past they had all been prepared to face intensive bombing for days, if not weeks and months, they were not unduly perturbed at the thought of showers of meteorites descending for an hour or two.

Many buildings would be wrecked, large casualties were to be anticipated, their heaviness depending upon the size of the meteorites. If some of these were as large as the largest which had struck the earth in historic times, the shock of each might devastate the country for miles around the spot where they fell. But there seemed good reason to suppose that, once the ordeal was over the dead would be buried, the buildings would be erected again and life go on much as before.

Numerous astronomers of various nationalities were of Oliver Stapleton's opinion that the comet was a solid one and the probability was that it would shatter the earth altogether; but, as 'hope springs eternal in the human breast', the majority of the national leaders refused to accept this view, realizing perhaps that even if it were correct there was nothing whatsoever that they could do about it.

When lunch was over and they were gathered in the library, Hemmingway, having given his own news, asked Oliver the result of his latest observations; upon which the untidy astronomer lit one of his Burma cheroots, drew upon it, and replied:

'I'm sorry to say I've found no reason whatever to change my opinion. Of course, if the various Governments choose to hide their heads in the sand like ostriches, that is their affair. But the spectroscope does not lie; and there are certain shadings in the analysis of the comet which now convince me absolutely that it is solid. A number of my most distinguished colleagues here and abroad entirely agree with me. A greater number do not do so openly and, in my opinion, are giving their Governments false hope. Their reason for doing so doubtless is that, if they are proved wrong and the world is shattered to bits, there will be no one left to accuse them of being false prophets afterwards; whereas, if they admit that the comet is solid now and it proves not to be so after all, they will have to live on with reputations which have been seriously damaged.'

'Are you quite sure, though, that the thing will be drawn into our orbit?' Derek, who had also been invited to the lunch party, inquired.

'Oh, yes. There's no longer any question about that. The comet's track is so exactly plotted now that we are all agreed that it can't possibly avoid coming well within the sphere of the earth's gravitational influence.'

'And June 24th's the jolly day,' Roy laughed, a little uncertainly, and took the opportunity to help himself to another ration of the old Madeira that Gervaise had got up for the others before lunch. 'What time does the balloon go up, honoured father?'

Oliver's mild blue eyes turned towards his flippant son. '10.55 p.m., my boy. That, of course, is the time at which the comet is actually due to impinge on the North Pacific; but we may well be dead long before then.'

'What'll we have to fear before the crash?' Hemmingway inquired.

'All sorts of unpleasant things. As you probably know, the crust of the earth is thinner, by comparison, than the skin of an orange. Its whole interior is still a molten mass with, we now believe, a solid core at its centre. Directly the comet is near enough for the earth to feel its influence, the centrifugal values of the earth are bound to change. The solid core, if it exists, will respond to the pull of gravity and, instead of continuing to rotate on a constant axis, will revolve on one moving in an increasing spiral following that part of the earth's surface which, as the earth turns, is nearest to the approaching comet. In any case, the mass of molten matter under the earth's crust is bound to be affected, which will cause many volcanoes to become active. There will be terrific eruptions and almost certainly major earthquakes long before the comet hits us.'

'At all events, we may console ourselves with the thought that Britain is well away from the earthquake zones,' Gervaise remarked.

'True,' Oliver nodded, 'but these seismic disturbances will give rise to other serious happenings. Britain is hardly likely to be affected by the first shocks but, as the earthquake belt passes from Iceland through the Azores and thence to the more southern of the West Indies, we may anticipate great upheavals under the sea which will cause tidal waves to pile up on both sides of the Atlantic. It is even possible that they might be so vast as to sweep right over Great Britain.'

'Another flood,' interjected Hemmingway.

'Exactly. You may remember the legend of *The Lost Atlantis*. Most scientists regard that as a myth but during the last century many myths have been proved to be race-memories of actual occurrences. It is said that a great island continent, as large as France and Germany put together, once occupied the centre of the Atlantic and that it was submerged with all its people about 11,500 years ago in one terrible day and night of tempest, earthquake and flood. Such a cataclysm might well have been caused by a comet coming very near the earth, or as some people believe, a comet actually colliding with it, and it's quite on the cards that a similar fate might overtake us.'

'Personally, I'm quite convinced that the submergence of Atlantis is an historic fact,' Gervaise declared. 'Anyone who has an extensive knowledge of ancient religions can hardly fail to see that. It was the destruction of Atlantis which gave rise to the Biblical account of the Flood and similar stories which are to be found in the literature of all ancient peoples living on both sides of the Atlantic. But, of course, the flood was local, and by far the greater portion of the human race survived.'

'I still can't believe it'll happen,' Derek said suddenly. 'I'm sorry, Oliver, but the whole thing's too fantastic.'

Hemmingway drew slowly on his cigarette and looked across at him. 'I felt that way, too, when I was first told of this business but, knowing as I do how the national leaders of practically every country in the world are reacting, I can't escape the conviction that something pretty frightful is coming to us. It's that which decided me to have this talk with you all to-day. I wish I'd done it sooner, but I wasn't quite convinced before. Now I am, I want to know what our chances are. The big question is, will the whole earth go to pieces or have we only to face a major catastrophe in which there's a chance for some of us to survive?'

'That none of us can tell until the 24th of June,' Oliver said quietly.

'Then there *is* a hope that some people may manage to see the party through?'

'Certainly. Although I consider it a very slender one.'

'Still, in that case, it's surely up to us to use every ingenuity we have to provide ourselves with the best possible chance of survival?'

'Yes, that's only reasonable. But such a huge tidal wave as we may expect would sweep everything before it; so I don't think there's much that any of us could do with any real hope of saving ourselves.'

'I'm pretty hot on mountaineering,' Roy grinned. 'If I can raise the cash to get across the Channel, I shall go and sit on top of Mont Blanc.'

'No,' said Gervaise decisively. 'If there's going to be a second Deluge, our best hope is to build another Ark.'

8

RUMOURS AND A REFUGE

'An Ark,' Roy repeated with a grin. 'Uncle Gervaise would make
a splendid Noah but he has no sons and only one son-in-law. If
Derek and I play Ham and Japheth, may we each bring along a
girl-friend?'

Derek smiled. 'I'll leave that to you and Hemmingway; but
I'm pretty good with animals so I'll superintend the "they
marched in two by two" business.'

'Shut up, you idiots!' frowned Margery. 'Can't you see this
is serious?'

The other three ignored their flippancy and Oliver inquired:
'What sort of Ark had you in mind, Gervaise?'

'The best thing, I suppose, would be to charter a medium-
sized, well-built sailing ship. We should then be independent of
coal or oil; which it might be impossible to obtain after our first
supply had run out if we chartered a steamer. Unfortunately
though, I'm in no position to do so myself, because I lack the
money.'

'Sam's got plenty. So have I, for that matter,' Hemmingway
said quickly, 'and it's my job to do anything I think Sam would
wish while he's away. I feel now that we should not delay another hour in taking what steps we can to survive if possible,
and Sam will naturally want his wife's people to be in on anything we may decide to do. As he's absent, it's up to us to make
some sort of plan, and I'll be responsible for finance, whatever
the amount may be.'

'Wouldn't it be better either to buy or build a life-boat?'
Margery suggested. 'In a rough sea it would keep afloat longer
than any larger craft and be much easier to manage. Besides, you
could man a life-boat yourselves, whereas, if we charter a ship,
we'd have to take on a crew and in the kind of upheaval that
seems likely a crew might give us all sorts of trouble.'

Hemmingway looked at her with fresh interest. 'That's certainly a very sound idea, Miss Stapleton.'

'Margery, please,' she smiled. 'It's rather pointless to be formal with each other if we're going to sink or swim together.'

'Sure, Margery then, and I'm all for a life-boat. We'd get one of the very latest type, too, like they're making now in the States. It's not an ordinary boat at all, but a huge round ball with a platform circling its outside, just as the rings encircle the planet Saturn. In a very rough sea the ball can roll to practically any angle but, since it's water-tight once the doors are closed, it can be swamped; and it can't be sunk except through a collision or being flung on the rocks. Meanwhile, the spherical chamber inside is kept level, however much the outer sphere rocks, by means of a system of gyroscopes.'

'That's right,' Roy added. 'I saw it on the movies in a news film when I was in Singapore.'

'It sounds the very thing, but is there time to import one?' Gervaise objected. 'To-day is the 3rd of June, so we have only just over three weeks left to work in.'

Hemmingway stubbed out his cigarette. 'It's too late to ship one over but, if we hustle, I reckon we could build one.'

Oliver looked dubious. 'I don't see how, in such a limited time. Such a device must contain many scientific mechanisms, some of which are certain to be patents. Even if you could get permission, presumably there's no model in Britain from which you could have them copied. I doubt, too, if you could get the parts manufactured here.'

'Plans can be sent by radio, these days,' Margery said quietly.

'Exactly!' Hemmingway threw her another appreciative glance. 'That's what I had in mind. Once I get the cables working I'll soon trace the company that's making these things in the U.S.A., and, whatever it may cost, I'll buy the British rights in their patents. As to manufacture, Sam's factories will rush through the parts, if I say they've got to. The next point is, where'll we build it?'

'Somewhere in Wales,' Derek suggested, 'on the highest hilltop the workmen can get the parts up to.'

'No.' Gervaise shook his grey head. 'If we did that, a great wave might roll it over and smash it before it could get properly afloat. It would be much better to construct it on a lakeside and launch it so that it is actually floating when the time of the emergency arrives.'

'Then why not build it on the lake here?' Margery put in.

'Why not?' Hemmingway agreed. 'This place is within easy reach of London for when we have to get out; but it's so shut away that we're unlikely to be interfered with by crowds of terrified people. It's an ideal spot from every point of view.'

'What about the chappies you'll have to send down to build it?' Roy asked. 'When they know what it's for, won't they want to come, too?'

'We ought to take them with us if we can,' Gervaise said at once.

Hemmingway's broad forehead wrinkled. 'I'd like to, but there won't be room. It wouldn't hold more than eight or ten people if we're to take the stores we'd have to carry to keep our-selves going for any length of time. Goodness knows, I'd like to take every man, woman and child in Britain if we could, but I'm afraid the engineers who construct this thing will have to take their chance with the rest when the time comes. To prevent trouble later we'd better not let them know what we're up to. After all, it won't look like any kind of boat, so our best plan would be to say it's some sort of scientific experiment in which Mr. Oliver Stapleton is interested. He'd better come down here to stay, and pretend to superintend things.'

Oliver frowned. 'It's asking a lot of me to leave Greenwich just now. Naturally, I'm intensely interested in all that is taking place at the Observatory.'

'When will the comet become visible to the naked eye?' Derek inquired.

'Not for ten days or more yet. You see, it is approaching along a track which passes within three degrees of the sun so, until the last phase, the sun's glare will make it invisible in daylight except to those using special instruments. At night you should be able to observe it, if the weather is good, from about the 18th, first as a tiny pin-point of light and later as a fiery ball; but, even then, it will only be visible very low in the heavens for a short time, as it passes under the horizon eleven-and-a-half minutes after sunset. My only regret is that so many of us wish to observe the comet at Greenwich each evening now that we have to take our turn and I get much less time at any of the telescopes than I could wish.'

'I'm afraid we couldn't get a telescope anything like the size of those at Greenwich,' Hemmingway smiled, 'but I'm game to buy you the biggest that can be procured in London; so that you could install it down here and have it all to yourself. How would that be?'

'A very generous offer, I'm sure.'

'Not at all. But we need your presence here to give colour to the building of the Ark. If a big telescope is being erected at the same time, that will help a lot in persuading the mechanics the Ark is only some new invention to do with your astronomical research.'

'In that case I'm quite agreeable. As it happens, one of my colleagues died only about ten days ago and he had a very fine telescope in his private observatory. It would take some moving, of course, but if we could buy it off his widow I could get it set up in a steel scaffolding, which would serve for temporary purposes, in the course of two or three days.'

'Good. That's the drill, then. Get in touch with the lady at once. See her this evening if possible and make it a cash transaction. I'll supply the funds and men to start dismantling it first thing to-morrow.'

'How long do you think such a flood would last?' Gervaise inquired, looking across at Oliver.

The astronomer shrugged his sloping shoulders. 'Who can say? If the comet is as big as I fear, there will be no flood but total disruption. If it's a smaller body the Rockies and the Andes should protect us from any great tidal wave it may create in the Pacific. Short of annihilation our danger will be from a wave created by sympathetic eruptions in the central Atlantic. Unless the earth bursts, one can hardly visualize a local disturbance of sufficient magnitude to send out a wave which would wash right over the mountain chains of Britain. It's more likely that although high land would be swept by the first onrush only valleys and low-lying land would be flooded for any length of time. But, even that, would mean the submergence of practically every city and town in the country; and weeks, if not months, before the waters finally drained away.'

'Say we took enough provisions to last us two months then?'

'Yes, that should certainly suffice. In such a local flood we should probably be washed up somewhere within a few days. But our trouble then would be to reach an area which had not been flooded at all. You see, the wave would wash right over all but the highest ground destroying everything in its path.'

'You mean that we might find ourselves marooned on an island for several weeks,' said Hemmingway, 'and, maybe, one where we'd have to rely on such stores as we brought with us?'

'Exactly.'

'How about if the comet caused a permanent rise in the ocean level? Britain would be converted into an archipelago, wouldn't it?'

'That is certainly a possibility.'

'Then we might find ourselves stuck on our particular island for good?'

'Yes, that too might quite well happen.'

'We'd look a pretty lot of fools if we escaped the flood and died of starvation in a stretch of isolated fields two months later, wouldn't we?'

'We could eke out our supplies with roots and fish,' Gervaise interjected.

'Maybe,' agreed Hemmingway. 'In fact, we'll have to chance being able to do that as the storage space of the Ark will be limited. But it seems to me we ought to ensure ourselves against such an emergency by preparing to meet it properly. As far as space permits we ought to take all the things we'd be most likely to need if we were deliberately going off to found a new settlement.'

'Books,' said Gervaise.

'Seeds and roots to ensure ourselves future crops,' said Margery.

'Scientific instruments,' said Oliver.

'Engineer's stores,' said Derek. 'I was at an Engineering College till my father died, so I could give you particulars of the most useful things in that line.'

'Fine,' said Hemmingway. 'Let's make some lists, shall we?' Upon which they spent the next hour jotting down all the less bulky items they could think of which might prove invaluable to them if chanced to be stranded.

When they had done it was agreed that they should divide the

labour of ordering the goods and have all accounts rendered
to Hemmingway. He then smiled round at the others and
said:

'I'd best be going now. It's still only a little after midday in
New York, so I'll get busy with my cabling the moment I'm back
in London and with any luck we'll have the plans of the new
life-boat coming through by radio some time to-night. Whoever
the firm is that makes these things, they'll know Sam's good for
the money, whatever price they ask.'

Soon afterwards Oliver and Hemmingway returned to London
but the following morning the centuries-old peace of Stapleton
Court was shattered; and fate had decreed that it should never
again be resumed.

A party of surveyors, sent by Hemmingway, arrived with instructions to prospect the lake-shore for the best site in which
to lay down a slipway on which the spherical Ark could be built;
and later in the day he telephoned to say that, although it had
cost Sam a small fortune, he had secured plans of the Ark from
the States.

Gangs of workmen then put in an appearance with lorry-
loads of rubble, sand, bags of cement and dredging apparatus.
On the 5th a huge truck arrived bearing Oliver's new telescope
packed in sacking, and other lorries loaded with the tubular
steel scaffolding which was to form its temporary support.

Soon the lawn running down to the lake was hardly recognizable. Wooden hutments, dumps of material and deep ruts cut
in its grass by the wheels of the heavy lorries all disfigured it;
while the roar of concrete-mixers, the din of hammering and the
shouts of the workmen shattered the stillness of the tree-girt
park. Even at night the pandemonium never ceased as the men
laboured on under the glare of great arc-lamps, but the work
progressed with amazing rapidity.

By June 7th a great concrete platform, the size of a tennis
court, had been constructed at one end of the lake and Oliver's
telescope had been erected on the higher ground near the house,
so that he could now observe the comet again, without interruption, at every favourable opportunity.

Derek, convinced now by the sight of these activities, more
than by all the arguments he had heard, that the approaching
danger was a real one, had abandoned his own affairs to play

the part of Oliver's assistant in superintending the work; a rôle for which he was much better fitted than the older man owing to his early training as an engineer. His easy manner enabled him to collaborate with the professionals without giving offence and, while he interfered as little as possible, his presence was valuable in that he was able to fend off awkward questions about the true purpose of the constructions on which they were engaged. Margery suggested that she should clear out a bedroom for him and from the 8th he took up his permanent residence at Stapleton Court.

Gervaise continued to be responsible for Fink-Drummond and Roy assisted him as before. The prisoner appeared resigned to his captivity but was curious about the din which now drifted without cessation round to his side of the house. Gervaise refused to satisfy his curiosity but Roy, who on further acquaintance found the ex-Cabinet Minister an extremely interesting person, had formed the habit of sitting with him sometimes and, under pledge of secrecy, saw no harm in giving him particulars of the projected Ark.

Hemmingway now motored down from London every evening to see how the work progressed. He reported that the casting of the curved steel sheeting for the outside of the Ark, its floor and struts had presented no difficulties but he was having trouble with some of the smaller parts of its mechanism as similar objects had never before been manufactured in Britain.

Each night Hemmingway brought the latest news from London. The gradual decline in the markets was accelerating to a steady fall as the small investor, who still knew nothing of the comet, was now suspicious of this slow but definite depreciation in share values, when international relations were infinitely better than they had been for many years.

Yet, underneath the surface, the foreign Governments were by no means so fully agreed as they had been the previous week. Many of them felt that they were no longer justified in concealing the approaching danger from their people, and the heads of religious bodies, who were in the know, were urging them to disclose the facts.

Moreover, where knowledge of the comet had previously been confined to a few score astronomers, national leaders, their advisers and financiers, it had gradually leaked out, so that most well-informed people all over the world now knew a comet was approaching and that there was some risk of its endangering the earth. It was clear, therefore, that the secret could not be kept from the general public much longer, as constantly spreading rumours would do more harm than a plain official statement.

By June 12th it had been decided to adopt half-measures and that the papers should carry the story of the comet without implying that there was any chance of its hitting the earth. Certain sections of the Press were in favour of telling the whole story and appealing to the public to face the danger bravely; but in the world-wide emergency that had arisen they loyally accepted the request of their Governments and the first official news of the comet appeared only as small paragraphs in the evening papers of that date.

The following day many special articles appeared, but mainly upon comets in general and accounts of historic comets which had caused great excitement in their time but swept harmlessly on their way into space.

When Hemmingway came down to Stapleton on the evening of the 14th he said that in London the news had been accepted by the public better than the Government had anticipated. Everyone was talking 'comet' now, but taximen and bus conductors were joking about it and the great majority of people considered it only as an interesting event which would provide them with a little mild excitement in nine or ten days' time. Stocks had made a slight recovery, as now the man-in-the-street knew the reason for their recent decline he had found renewed faith and was buying again, confident that the markets must take a turn for the better before very long.

One piece of good news Hemmingway brought was that he had at last succeeded in getting the more delicate parts of the Ark manufactured satisfactorily and that the engineers could now go ahead with its construction.

Meanwhile, Sam and Lavina remained in blissful ignorance of the agitated cipher cables which were flashing round the world from Government to Government; of the increasing tension on the Bourses where the brokers were growing more worried with every fresh rumour they heard from important clients, in spite of the fact that they were making fortunes out of the terrified buying and selling that was in constant progress; and of the gradual feeling of unrest and uncertainty that had been spreading during recent weeks among the peoples of the world.

The fact that a great comet was hurtling earthwards at many thousands of miles an hour was stale news to them and for weeks past they had known the worst possibilities that might have to be faced when it came flaming downwards from the heavens; yet they rarely spoke of it. Even on June 13th, when the world's Press released the first official statements, they were so far off the beaten track that they did not see a paper or even hear the matter mentioned at the little inn where they were staying.

Their honeymoon had proved a great success, largely owing to their wise decision to break away from the type of luxury resort that they both knew well into an entirely new life which they had never sampled.

At first it had seemed a little strange to stay at small unpretentious places where there were no cocktail bars and members of the proprietor's family were the only servants. But the rooms of the French inns were bright and clean, and although the cooking was plain it was almost always excellent.

For the first few days it had not been easy for either of them to adjust themselves to the idea of having nothing in the world to do and nowhere to go for either work or amusement; and stranger still to have to go to bed soon after sunset. But the utter rest did them an immense amount of good. The sunshine tanned their bodies to a golden brown, and the less they did the less they wanted to do except just laze about and talk to each other.

Sam had travelled in many parts of the world, whereas Lavina had never been outside England, except to Paris and for brief holidays to a few of the most famous Continental bathing beaches since she had become a film star. On the other hand, her education was very much better than Sam's. Gervaise had seen to that and, without ever having consciously studied or been forced to sit for wearisome examinations, she had accumulated a great store of miscellaneous information on history, literature, religions and art. Sam knew the political game, the inside of all the major moves that had governed international relations in the last ten years, and he had met innumerable famous people. But he was a townsman, born and bred. Lavina knew nothing of such things and few people outside the film world, but she had lived nearly all her life in the country and was at home with all the wild life they met when strolling across the wooded mountainsides; the habits of birds and beasts, the names of flowers and trees were nearly all familiar to her. In consequence, as both were good listeners, they had an immense amount to talk about.

It was not until the morning of June 14th that the proprietor of the little inn where they were staying brought a copy of the previous day's paper over to Sam just as he and Lavina were sitting down to their *vermouth et syphon* before lunch.

With a stubby forefinger the Frenchman pointed to a four-column article on comets and their peculiarities. He did not seem the least perturbed at the announcement that a large one would shortly become visible and in ten days' time pass comparatively near the earth; but pointed out the article as a matter that might be of interest. It was one of the many little courtesies by which he sought to retain the goodwill of his wealthy English visitors.

Sam thanked him and, as he moved away, looked across at Lavina. 'So it's out at last. I'm rather surprised that Hemmingway didn't say anything about it in his letter that came in this morning. He must have known they intended to break it to the masses when he was writing.'

Lavina puffed lazily on her cigarette. 'He's hardly said anything in any of his letters except that business has been going as well as could be expected and that they've been having good weather in England. I think it's rather decent of him to have taken everything on his own shoulders and not worried you with a single thing while we've been on our honeymoon.'

'Yes. That's like him. He's a good boy and not afraid to take responsibility.'

A faint smile twitched the corners of Lavina's beautifully modelled little mouth. Hemmingway was seven years older than herself so it had never occurred to her to regard him as a boy, but Sam, of course, was some sixteen years older than his gifted secretary. She bent over her husband's shoulder to read the heavy black print of the French article on the comet and, after a moment, she remarked:

'They don't tell the whole story. There's no suggestion that the comet may hit us or anything of that kind.'

'No, they're breaking it gently, I suppose. Or maybe your Uncle Oliver wasn't right, after all.

'I doubt that. Anyhow, we shall know if he's still of the same opinion in three days' time.' She tapped the date on the paper with an unvarnished finger-nail of moderate length. After a few days in the wilds she had taken a quarter of an inch off the long, pointed, decorative claws of which she had been rather proud, and had ceased to enamel them.

'This is yesterday's paper,' he said.

'Why, so it is! Then we'll be leaving here to-morrow.'

It came as quite a shock to realize that their honeymoon was almost over. Days and dates had meant nothing to them in the last five weeks, but they had all their reservations booked for the homeward journey on which they were due to start next day.

When they arrived in Biarritz to catch the Paris express they found everyone talking of the comet. The papers were now full of it, but there was still no indication in any of them that there might be cause for alarm.

On the evening of June 16th they were back in London. Hemmingway was at the station to meet them and he dined with them in St. James's Square that night. They already knew from a guarded statement in one of his first letters that Fink-Drummond's disappearance had been accounted for satisfactorily, but he had plenty of other things to tell them about, including the construction of the Ark.

Sam at once approved everything he had done but, somewhat to Lavina's disappointment, instead of going with her round the rooms which had been redecorated according to her wishes in her absence, the two men went into a huddle over business after dinner.

They discussed finance and the international situation exhaustively, yet it seemed that there was nothing further that could be done. Hemmingway had already taken every possible precaution to protect Sam's interests. He had sold many blocks of shares at good prices before the decline set in and bought again at lower levels for delivery on June the 30th. If the world came to an end on June 24th, the prices of stocks would no longer matter to anyone, but, if it didn't, Sam would reap enormous profits.

Nevertheless, many of the directors in Sam's companies had been pressing Hemmingway to recall him for well over a fortnight and, although Hemmingway had steadfastly refused, it was clear that Sam would have to meet them at the earliest possible moment.

For the next two days he was kept frantically busy with such appointments. The shares of his own companies were falling with the rest, and his co-directors wrangled with him interminably at hastily called board meetings as to whether they should support their own shares with their private means or let them slump to any level.

It was not until the evening of the 18th, the second after their return, that Sam could find time to go down to Stapleton Court, and Lavina, who had been impatiently waiting for him to do so, accompanied him filled with curiosity about the Ark.

When they reached Stapleton, just after seven, they were amazed to see the upheaval that had taken place along the lakeshore in front of the house. The lawn was cut to ribbons; cranes, sheds, stacks of concrete blocks, steel girders and other building materials littered the place for two hundred yards round the flat surface on the lake-edge where a huge steel ball, over thirty feet in height, now stood.

Gervaise and the rest came out to greet the visitors at the entrance of the house, and both parties were unaffectedly glad to see each other. Margery held out her hand to Sam but he gave her a rather boisterous brotherly kiss, as he wanted to show her that he had not allowed any memory of her strange outburst on his wedding-day to rankle.

Meanwhile, at the sight of Lavina, Derek had caught his breath.

'What is it?' She laughed, as she saw him staring at her. 'Has marriage changed me so much that you don't recognize me any more?'

'No—oh, no!' he muttered hastily. 'But you're looking twice as beautiful.'

Lavina accepted the compliment and knew the reason for it. Her nails were enamelled bright red again and her golden hair was done with her usual meticulous care; but her eyebrows were now brown instead of black, she had given up using kohl on her eyelids, her lashes were suitably darkened but not heavy with mascara and she was wearing only a moderate amount of lipstick.

The change was due to Sam's gentle insistence, that being so blessed with natural loveliness, her slavish adherence to the heavy make-up favoured by less fortunate women only detracted from her looks. She had not really believed that, but to please him she had cut it down while she was abroad; and now, Derek's bewildered admiration at last convinced her Sam had been right.

As Hemmingway had remained in London, Derek took Sam and Lavina over the Ark and explained its workings to them. Its interior mechanism was not yet completed, but he said that the engineers hoped to launch it on the 20th.

'The sooner the better,' Sam remarked. 'We're passing now through the calm before the storm because the bulk of the people still have no idea what we may be in for. I doubt if the Government can hold up the facts much longer, though, and once the cat's out of the bag the work-people may throw their hand in.'

After drinks in the house Oliver took them out on to the terrace. It was nearing sundown and, as the weather was fine, he was able to promise them their first view of the comet.

As it was now sufficiently near to be discernible to the human eye, diagrams of the section of the heavens in which it appeared were being printed in all the papers and, just after sunset, they had no difficulty in picking it out as a faint new star low on the horizon.

When Lavina remarked how tiny it seemed for such a terrible menace, Oliver chuckled and, promising a surprise, led them over to his telescope.

In turn they lay back in an adjustable chair like those found in dentists' surgeries and focused the eye-piece above them according to Oliver's instructions. The powerful lenses in the big tube seemed to bring the comet right down on top of them. It appeared as a huge, reddish mass which wobbled slightly at the edges. Oliver said that was to be accounted for by great waves of flame, hundreds of miles long, flickering out from its circumference, and that its tail was not visible owing to the fact that it was heading almost directly for the earth.

Sam had just had his turn of gazing at this terror of the heavens when Margery came out of the house and called to him.

'Sam, you're wanted on the telephone.'

He left the group by the telescope and went inside. When he returned a few minutes later his face was grave.

'Hemmingway promised to ring me here if anything fresh was decided at this evening's Cabinet Meeting,' he said slowly. 'It's just been announced that the Prime Minister is to broadcast to-morrow night, and, according to Hemmingway, he intends to tell the nation the whole truth.'

9

THE LAST DAYS OF LONDON

'In that case I think the time has come when we should release our prisoner,' Gervaise suggested. 'By Jove!' Sam swung round. 'I'd almost forgotten all about him. How's poor old Finkie been taking his captivity?'

'He was a little troublesome at first. He tried to batter his bedroom door down with some of the furniture; but the doors here are old and solid and I'd taken the precaution of putting extra bolts on. I had to tell him that, unless he stopped that sort of thing, I should be compelled to put him on bread and water. He's been very little trouble since.'

'I wonder he hasn't gone mad from boredom,' Lavina said. 'Just fancy, he's been cooped up with not a soul to talk to all these weeks while Sam and I were enjoying ourselves in France.'

Gervaise shrugged. 'It hasn't been quite as bad as that. I dislike the fellow so much that I really couldn't bring myself to exchange more than the necessary civilities with him, but Roy is more broad-minded—or shall we say charitable. Since Fink-Drummond settled down, Roy has spent quite a lot of time with him.'

'Yes. He's not at all a bad sort, really,' said Roy, 'and extraordinarily interesting to talk to. Whenever the weather isn't very good and I'm a bit bored myself, I go up and sit with him.'

'Isn't that a bit risky? He might have taken you by surprise one day and laid you out. Then, if he'd got the key off you, he could quite easily have escaped.'

Roy laughed. 'No fear of that. Uncle Gervaise locked the two of us in each time I decided to spend an hour or two in his room.'

'It's too late for him to do any damage to the Government now, as the Prime Minister's going to tell the country the truth tomorrow night,' said Sam thoughtfully, 'but I don't think we should release him yet. We shall have quite enough on our hands during the coming week without the additional bother he'd be certain to cause us if we freed him.'

'But are we justified in detaining him any longer now that he can't harm the nation?' asked Gervaise doubtfully.

'Perhaps not,' Sam smiled, 'but I think we will, all the same.'

Gervaise still looked a little dubious, but at that moment Margery came out again and called them all in to supper, which Derek had been helping her to lay. It was a cold meal and they waited on themselves, but, the comet temporarily forgotten, they laughed a lot and it was late when Sam and Lavina got back to London.

On the following morning the comet was front-page news again, and large headlines informed the world that the Heads of Governments were to make a statement about it that evening to their respective peoples.

When evening came the streets of London were almost deserted. Everyone who was not actively employed upon some unescapable duty was listening-in to a radio set.

The Premier opened with a brief résumé of the new spirit of conciliation and friendship which had entered into international relations during recent weeks, and went on to say that the reason for this was that all Governments had received reports from their official astronomers that a comet, of which mention had been made in the Press during the last few days, was approaching the earth. They were unable to disguise from themselves that such a visitation might cause disturbances of a serious nature and had therefore co-operated to prevent the premature spreading of any, possibly baseless, alarm.

There were, however, certain eminent astronomers who considered that there was a far greater danger than that arising through panic on the comet's passing close to the earth, since these gentlemen believed that it might actually come into collision with us. Governments had therefore found themselves in a somewhat difficult situation.

If these eminent astronomers proved wrong in their calculations—and many of his colleagues were with him in thinking that they might well be so—any official statement based upon their findings might have caused the most appalling fears to destroy the mental balance of innumerable people; and when the comet did not hit us after all, that distress and terror, affecting perhaps millions of lives, would have been brought about without any justifiable cause.

On the other hand, by suppressing all news of the possible danger, Governments took the risk of being abused afterwards for having concealed the truth and for not having taken such precautions as might be possible to protect those for whom they were responsible.

For his own part, he had cheerfully taken that risk, and the Heads of foreign Governments had done likewise, since it was so very evident that, if the comet was about to come into collision with us, no human ingenuity could prevent its doing so; whereas, if it passed us by, an immense amount of distress would have been averted by concealing the danger.

If the worst happened, he went on, even the most eminent astronomers were far from agreeing as to what the effect would be. Some thought such a calamity might bring about the end of the world, but he considered that to be exaggerated pessimism. Others declared that it would only affect one portion of the earth's surface and, if this were the case, arrangements had already been entered into between Governments for immediate succour to be sent to the afflicted area. Other astronomers, again, postulated that, owing to the apparent size of the comet, a good half of the earth's surface would be bombarded for the space of an hour or so by a great hail of meteorites. In this latter case the danger could be regarded as no greater than that of a brief although severe enemy air attack, and as in no sense so dreadful as a European war.

Many of the Heads of foreign Governments had held the view that, in order to minimize apprehension to the shortest possible space of time, no statement of the full possibilities should be made until the last moment; but here they had met with opposition from the heads of their respective Churches.

These gentlemen felt it their duty to take the gloomiest view and had urged upon their Governments the necessity for giving their peoples at least a week to prepare themselves spiritually for the ending of the world, or possible death if they happened to be in an area seriously afflicted by the comet.

While practical considerations had, therefore, swayed the Governments to withhold this information concerning the more terrible eventualities which might have to be faced, the spiritual could not be lightly disregarded, so it had been mutually agreed that the Heads of all Governments should make this announcement to-night.

In making it he could only stress the fact that, although the danger could not be ignored, whether it would be fatal to humanity, or even serious, was still highly problematical. Science had brought many benefits to mankind, but before each definite achievement it had made many blunders. Even to-day scientific theories were constantly being proved inaccurate as the result of further research. And if this were so with things which scientists could place under their microscopes or experiment on by trial and error, how much more was it true of theories about incalculably remote heavenly bodies rotating in space which, in itself, must for ever remain a problem insoluble to man.

Our knowledge of everything outside the confines of our own earth was still almost entirely theoretical. Therefore, the eminent astronomers might be completely wrong in their theories as to what would occur if the comet hit us. It might well be only a great mass of gas, small meteorites and dust, which would provide us with a splendid display of shooting stars but not damage us at all.

In any case, the Government had already taken such precautions as were possible by deciding that three days before the comet was due the schemes for the evacuation of women and children from the highly populated areas which had been worked out as a war measure, should be put into operation, thus ensuring that a minimum of life would be sacrificed should large meteorites fall upon cities causing fires and considerable destruction of property.

Finally, he begged that in the approaching crisis the nation would show that sense of order and discipline for which the British people had always been so remarkable. He and his colleagues would leave no stone unturned to protect the population and essential services from destruction. There need be no fear of any food shortage as their ample war reserves could be brought into use if required; but they must all be prepared to face whatever might befall them with that calm and courage which had ever marked the people of these Islands in great emergencies.

'Damned good speech,' said Sam, who had been listening-in

with Lavina and Hemmingway at St. James's Square. 'The old boy's been clever, too. He's drawn the teeth of the Opposition—who'll naturally have a crack at him for having withheld the truth for so long—by throwing doubt on the astronomers' infallibility; and he's evaded criticism from the die-hards who think he ought to have concealed everything up to the last moment, by pushing the responsibility for telling the nation now on to the Archbishop.'

'Yes,' Lavina agreed. 'And, although he told them the worst, he gilded the pill very prettily by as good as saying he didn't think it would happen. I wonder how the public will take it?'

'Fairly well, I should say,' Hemmingway remarked. 'His speech was by no means alarmist and it was very well timed. We've got five days to go, which leaves two days for people to make their arrangements before the evacuation starts. During the next forty-eight hours they'll be kept pretty busy preparing for it. Let's go up to the roof and have another look at the comet. It's a nice night again and it must be visible just about now.'

The three of them went upstairs and stared towards the west at the heavenly terror which was rushing towards the earth. It was no longer a pin-point as it had been the night before, but the size of a major star, and in the clear summer night it winked at them, red and evil.

Lavina felt a strange tremor run through her and some instinct made her reach out to take Hemmingway's arm; although Sam was standing equally near her on her other side. Next moment Hemmingway's free hand had closed over hers, gripping it tightly, and they stood so until the comet had disappeared behind some chimney-pots, upon which, with a self-conscious glance, he released her hand and they drew quickly apart again.

Next morning Britain woke to find herself under martial law. The Government was taking no chances. There were troops in the streets, tanks parked in the Squares, and on the roof-tops machine-gun nests by which main thoroughfares and Government buildings could be covered.

The papers carried the Premier's speech in full, but as practically everybody had heard it, their major news line was 'MARTIAL LAW—MOBILIZATION—PARTIAL MORATORIUM.'

Under their emergency powers the Government had introduced a Finance Bill by which all writs for debt were indefinitely suspended, and during the ensuing week the banks were only allowed to pay out to their customers the average amount which they had drawn per week for the last three months. This ensured the payment of wages and that the public could secure cash for its necessities, but prevented a run on the banks which might have caused financial chaos. The Stock Exchange was closed by order and all dealings in shares forbidden.

The Fighting Forces and Reservists were called up, and a warning issued that on June the 22nd the Civil Defence Forces would also be mobilized. All A.R.P. Chief Wardens and Heads of Fire-fighting and Nursing Units were instructed to remain within reach of their posts and to make a thorough inspection of their equipment forthwith, so that any deficiencies could be made good immediately.

The B.B.C. announced these measures over the wireless and, interspersed with light musical numbers, gave appeals for the maintenance of order, anti-alarmist talks belittling the comet's possible effects, and religious services. They also issued news bulletins of events abroad, and, with a view to reassuring the public, every one of these was designed to suggest that foreign populations were taking the crisis seriously but calmly.

In Parliament that afternoon the Prime Minister faced his critics, but the Opposition behaved well and gave him no serious trouble, since they realized that in such an emergency they must think of nation rather than Party. The only new point that emerged from the debate was when a Member suggested that the gravest risk from the comet would probably be big fires in the cities, caused by the intense heat setting light to inflammable materials.

This, the Home Secretary agreed, was a serious danger, but the number of buildings to be protected was so great that it would have been impossible to roof them all with asbestos sheeting, even if they had had ten years in which to do it. As against this, the Government had already commandeered all supplies of asbestos and vast quantities of sand, with which key-points were to be rendered immune from fire as far as possible.

It was stated that at a zero hour, to be announced later, everyone remaining in the cities was to go to ground in the A.R.P. shelters that had been prepared for war, taking their gas masks with them; and that all the shipping in the Thames had been commandeered so that if serious fires in London got out of control, that section of the population which had not been evacuated could take refuge in it.

Great crowds congregated in the streets that evening; particularly in the West End, round Trafalgar Square, Buckingham Palace and the Houses of Parliament. The police found it necessary to divert all traffic from the main thoroughfares, as the strolling masses slowly perambulated Piccadilly, Whitehall and The Mall. Except that there were no flags or decorations in evidence, it was almost like the night of a Coronation or Royal Wedding. The events of the day had caused considerable anxiety, particularly to parents who had young children, but that did not prevent the bulk of the people deciding to come out and see any fun that was going.

On his return from the House to Downing Street, the Prime Minister was loudly cheered, and when the King came out with the Royal Family on the balcony of Buckingham Palace he received much more than the usual loyal ovation, for it had just been announced that, although His Majesty was sending his family to Windsor, he and the Queen had decided to remain in London to face the approaching crisis in the midst of their people.

Lavina would have liked to have gone out and mingled with the crowds, but she could hardly do so alone, and both Sam and Hemmingway were much too busy that evening for either of them to take her.

From early that morning Sam's co-directors and the principal executives of his many companies had been in constant communication with him to discuss what steps might be taken to protect their employees and the companies' properties.

There were constant comings and goings and telephone calls at St. James's Square, but none of the people concerned could offer any original suggestions. All the factories had their A.R.P. schemes which had been worked out to the last detail, and these would automatically be put into operation. The Government's evacuation measures took care of the women and children in the congested areas as far as it was possible to do so, and the same fire precautions were to be adopted as if an enemy air raid was expected.

There were, however, innumerable detailed decisions which

could be taken to render the factories less vulnerable. Stocks of inflammable material could be moved out into fields; temporary wooden structures could be demolished; coal and oil stores could be emptied of their contents, and so on; and it was the making of such decisions which kept Sam and Hemmingway busy with a succession of works managers and Trade Union officials far into the night.

Soon after breakfast next morning Derek Burroughs arrived from Stapleton to report that the Ark had been completed and launched the previous afternoon, and that the engineers who had constructed it were now packing up to return to their homes. He said he had decided to come up and report in person because he did not think it wise to give any particulars over the telephone as, if the fact that they had constructed an Ark down in Surrey once got out, any number of terrified people might make their way to it, in the hope of using it as a means of escape.

Sam agreed that he had been wise, and suggested that he remained at St. James's Square to keep Lavina company; as Hemmingway and he would be frantically busy all day continuing their arrangements and inspecting such of his factories as were near London.

'How about the servants here?' Lavina asked. 'We can't possibly leave them in the lurch.'

'We can't take them in the Ark,' said Derek. 'There just isn't room for more than the eight of us. It's going to be a pretty tight squeeze as it is, if we have to remain in the thing for any length of time. So much space has had to be given up to the food, oxygen cylinders, and all the emergency stores we have collected.'

'I was thinking of the servants when I went to bed last night,' Sam replied. 'I only wish we could take them, but since it's impossible I suggest that we should only retain the new Rolls here, pack them in the other three cars, and send them all off to Wales.'

Derek nodded. 'Tell them to find the highest mountain that they can, get up there and sit on it until the party's over, eh?'

'That's the idea. I laid in a whole lot of tinned stuff as an emergency ration in the event of war—enough to last the household at least a month. They can take that with them so that they'd be independent of anyone else; and, short of sacrificing ourselves, sending them off with plentiful supplies seems the best we can do for them.'

'In that case, the sooner they get off, the better,' Lavina suggested. 'The general evacuation takes place to-morrow, so if they start this morning they'll be able to get well ahead of the crush.'

'Clever girl. That's just what I was thinking,' Sam grinned. 'And until we can get down to Stapleton ourselves, I take it you'll manage to knock up any meals we may want.'

Lavina made a face, pulling down the corners of her mouth and the tip of her little Roman nose. 'I've got all sorts of attractions, but I'm a rotten cook. We'd much better feed at the Berkeley Arms.'

Sam shook his head. 'No time to spare even to go that far. You'll have to do the best you can for us.'

'I'll help you,' Derek volunteered. 'I'm a dab at scrambled eggs and, until we decided to shake the dust of London from our feet, I've got nothing else to do.'

'That's settled, then.' Sam stood up. 'I'll leave you to talk to the servants, darling, and see them safely off. Say good-bye to them and wish them luck for me. I wish I could do so myself, but I've got to get down to Brentford with Hemmingway now, to inspect the Mayo-Thompson works.'

'Will you be back to lunch?'

'I'm afraid not, my sweet. I've got a whole round of inspections to make to-day, just as a check-up on what's being done. Actually, I don't think there's much more that we can do, but at a time like this the workpeople will expect me to put in a personal appearance and say a few words to them.'

When he had gone, Lavina sent for the butler and asked him to assemble the servants in the drawing-room. She then explained to them the plans that Sam had suggested for his staff and added that, if any of them did not wish to go to Wales, they were perfectly free to join their own families or go anywhere else they liked.

Several of them offered to stay on, and Lavina thanked them but said that as she and Sam would shortly be going to the country they were closing down the house and, after a brief consultation, all but two of the staff agreed to Sam's proposals that they should pack up and leave at once for Wales.

The cars were brought round from the garage, the tinned provisions and baggage of the staff were loaded on to them, and then the servants all came in to say good-bye to Lavina.

She did not know any of them well enough to be really distressed at the thought that she might never see them again, but it was a queer little ceremony to be shaking hands and wishing good luck to all one's domestics dressed in their best clothes in the middle of the morning.

A few of the younger women seemed a little scared, but the second footman, who appeared to be the jester of the household, kept cracking jokes with the others, as they piled into the cars, about the adventures that might befall them when they pitched camp upon their Welsh mountain-top; and at half-past twelve Lavina and Derek waved them all good-bye from the front door-step.

When they were inside again, they found the great house strangely silent after the continuous hustle which had been going on all the morning. At first they thought of lunching out, but everything seemed so unsettled that they decided against it.

Derek mixed some cocktails and Lavina turned on the radio. A lecture on fire-fighting was in progress, so she promptly switched it off again as she never listened-in unless she could get dance music. As she was passionately fond of dancing she had a big selection of the latest dance-band records, and picking eight of her favourites she put them on the gramophone-attachment instead.

For about ten minutes they wandered restlessly about the room, glasses in hand, while negroes crooned at them and trumpets blared. Somehow, there didn't seem to be anything to talk about except the comet and both of them wished to avoid that subject if possible. It was also the first time they had been alone together since her marriage.

Suddenly Lavina set down her glass and started to kick back the Persian rugs.

'Come on,' she said, 'we can't gloom about like this eternally. Let's dance.'

Derek sank his cocktail and smiled. He was a good dancer, as she remembered well, and something of his old attraction for her came back as he put his arm round her and they moved slowly up and down the parquet floor in well-timed rhythm.

'Remember the last time we danced together?' he asked.

'No,' she lied. 'Years ago we danced together so often.'

'Then I'll tell you. It was at the Hazlitts'; a party they gave for Hugh's coming-out.'

'Was it?'

'Yes. I can even tell you the dress you wore. You had on a lovely thing made of golden satin which went wonderfully with your fair complexion and golden hair. It was a slinky sort of frock and much too old for you, but, all the same . . .'

'Oh, shut up!' she exclaimed, digging her nails into his arm and giving him a little shake. The next second she had left him, flung up the lid of the radiogram and switched it off.

When she turned again her grey eyes were dark and angry. 'It's rotten of you, Derek, to dig up those old memories. That's all past and done with and I'm happily married now.'

'Of course you are.' He thrust his hands deep in his pockets and smiled at her. 'But what's all the excitement about? I wasn't making love to you or anything.'

'No?' she regarded him doubtfully. 'It sounded suspiciously like it, and I warn you I'm not having any. Since we've been thrown together again like this it's best we should forget what we were to each other. If Sam suspects that you're still in love with me it will make things abominably awkward for all of us.'

Derek lit a cigarette. 'You needn't bother your little head about Sam. I'm not given to poaching other men's coverts, but asking me to forget the past is an altogether different matter. I loved you then, and you loved me. I love you still and I believe, if you told the truth, you still love me a little bit. Anyhow, I'm quite certain that you're not in love with your husband.'

'You're wrong there. I . . .'

He held up his hand. 'One minute. I'm not saying that you won't be loyal to him; and, please believe I haven't the least intention of trying to break up your marriage.'

'You couldn't if you tried.'

'I know that; but when the smash comes a lot of us may get killed. It's even possible that the whole social order as we know it may go down the drain and that money and position won't mean a thing any more to those of us who come through.'

'Well, what of it?'

'Simply, that we'll just be men and women, without any trimmings. You might as well know now that if anything happens to Sam, but you and I survive to live on in a strange new world, you're going to be my woman.'

10

A TERRIFYING EXPERIENCE

Lavina's eyes narrowed and her under-lip drooped a little. Normally she was a very gay, good-tempered person but quick to follow her emotional impulses, and although her anger never lasted any length of time, it could be surprisingly intense and it showed now in every line of her slender body.

'You fool!' she snapped. 'We're not living in the Dark Ages. If the two of us were marooned on a desert island I wouldn't let you even kiss my hand unless I wanted you to.'

'But you *would* want me to,' he said quietly.

As she looked at his firm, sunburnt face, square shoulders, and strong, healthy body, she knew that he was right. Ever since she was seventeen she had been having love affairs, although she had never really been in love, except, perhaps, with Derek, and she was quite certain now that her love for him was as dead as last year's roses; yet she liked being kissed and she knew that, if she were marooned with any attractive man, she would not be able to resist the temptation.

'I don't think we need discuss it,' she said more soberly. 'The chances are we'll all be killed or all survive together. In the mean-time you'd better not try to start anything, because, if you do, there'll be trouble.'

'Are you inferring that if I did you'd tell Sam what I said just now?'

'Good Lord, no! I've always handled my own affairs and the last thing I'd do would be to run screaming to my husband.'

'Well, you needn't worry. I'm much too fond of you to cast the least shadow on your married bliss. I was only saying that, if anything happened to Sam, I should enter the lists again. That's fair enough, isn't it?'

'Oh, perfectly. But, even then, you wouldn't get anywhere by trying to be possessive. Let's go down to the kitchen and try to rake up a meal, shall we?'

'By all means.' He smiled again. 'I'll cook you some of those scrambled eggs I was boasting about.'

By the time the eggs were sizzling in the pan, the emotional tension had eased and they were back once more on their normal friendly footing.

Lavina's slender hands were not made for work and she was a past mistress in the art of getting other people to do things for her. While Derek cooked the eggs, and at the same time endeavoured to prevent the toast from burning, she sat perched on the edge of the kitchen table idly swinging her legs and puffing lazily at the twenty-fourth cigarette she had smoked that morning.

After the meal they went upstairs again and played the gramophone until three o'clock. Lavina then said she thought she would go and look through her things to decide what she would take when they left London.

Derek read for a bit, dozed a little in a comfortable armchair and, rousing up about half-past four, went down to the kitchen to make tea.

He carried a cup up to Lavina and found her in her bedroom, surrounded with trunks and enough hats, shoes, dresses and *lingerie* to fill a small shop.

'My dear! What are you up to?' he laughed aloud. 'You won't be able to take one-tenth of that lot.'

She opened wide her grey eyes and stared at him. 'Why not? I must have clothes, whatever happens to us.'

'Yes, clothes, but not a film-star's trousseau; some serviceable tweeds and your warmest fur coat, a pair of trousers, perhaps, some woollies, gum-boots if you've got them, and a few changes of underwear. That's all you'll need for this trip. We're not carrying a jazz band in the Ark so there won't be any dancing after dinner.'

'Silly of me. I hadn't thought. Oh, well,' she smiled resignedly, 'I think I'll take my new grey satin, though. If I'm fated to die I'd like to meet Death looking my best.'

'I believe you'd even tempt Saint Peter into giving you a special place in Heaven if you had the chance.'

'Derek, you're horrid.'

'No, darling. It's only that I know you rather well.'

Eventually he managed to persuade her to confine her packing

D

to one cabin-trunk and two large suitcases, after which they went downstairs.

At six o'clock they turned on the radio to get the news, and both their faces became grave as they heard the first item. That morning one of the worst earthquakes ever recorded had occurred in Tokyo. For over three hours tremors had shaken the city. Huge crevices had appeared, engulfing houses, buses, cars and hundreds of people. Two-thirds of the buildings, other than those made of steel and concrete, were reported to be in ruins; and great fires were still raging in many parts of the city. The loss of life was not yet known, but it was estimated already at over a hundred thousand.

Lavina switched the wireless off. 'I don't want to listen,' she said. 'It's too terrible.'

Derek put his arm round her shoulders in brotherly fashion. 'Don't let it get you down, old girl. I've a sort of conviction that we're coming through it.'

'Oh, but it's not us,' she moaned, as she leant against him. 'I'm not afraid for myself, but just think of those poor people.'

'Try not to.' He squeezed her hand. 'We'd help them if we could, but we can't, and we must do our best to carry on as cheerfully as possible. That's all there is to it. I'm going to mix you a cocktail.'

Sam and Hemmingway returned soon afterwards. They were hot and tired after their long day of dashing from factory to factory, and neither of them had eaten since breakfast. Without a word Lavina suddenly disappeared. Ten minutes later she returned with cake, fruit, sandwiches and drinks for them.

They had just settled down to their picnic meal when the knocker on the front door sounded. Derek went to answer it and found Roy on the doorstep.

'What's brought you up here?' Lavina inquired, as soon as he had greeted the little gathering in the lounge.

'Your especial safety, dear friends,' he grinned. 'Uncle Gervaise sent me. Apparently, the world has started to blow up already so he's anxious you should come down to Stapleton as soon as possible.'

'You mean the Japanese earthquake?' said Derek quickly. 'We heard about it on the radio. Pretty ghastly, isn't it?'

'That, and other things.' The grin left Roy's face. 'Oliver was

on the telephone to Greenwich this afternoon and heard about
the Tokyo business before it was announced over the wireless.
Of course, the announcer said afterwards that the 'quake had no
connection with the comet, and, as they're always having earthquakes in Japan, most people will accept that; but we know
better. The fools ought never to have announced it at all, but
they've had orders now to suppress all news about the other
eruptions.'

'There have been others, then?' Hemmingway inquired.

'Yes. There's been a bad one in northern India and another
in Brazil. Lots of volcanoes, too, are reported as showing unusual activity. That's why Gervaise is so set on it you should
leave London to-night. If the shocks get worse, we're going to
feel them here. Then people may lose their heads and in the
stampede you may not be able to get out of London at all.'

'Sorry,' said Sam, 'I can't go down to-night. I've got to go
over a big factory out at Hendon this evening, and I've another
two that I must visit to-morrow; but that's no reason the rest of
you shouldn't go.'

'I'm not leaving London without you,' Lavina said quietly.

'Nonsense, darling.' He squeezed her arm. 'I was going to
suggest that you got away to-night before the evacuation starts,
in any case. You needn't worry about me. I must see my job
through, then I'll get to Stapleton under my own steam.'

'I'm not leaving without you, Sam,' she repeated.

'Now, be sensible,' he urged. 'I'll be much easier in my mind
knowing that you're safely out of it.'

'I'm sorry, but I've no intention of being parted from you at a
time like this.'

Sam had known Lavina long enough to realize how mulish
she could be when she had made up her mind upon a thing, so
he did not press her further; and after a short silence Derek
asked Roy:

'How did you find things on your way here?'

Roy depressed the corners of his mouth. 'Down the line
everyone's hard at it digging trenches and sand-bagging their
houses and that sort of thing, but London's pretty mouldy.
Squads of soldiers and police are patrolling the streets and
breaking up any crowds that try to gather. The shops are all
shut, of course, which seems queer, with so many people about.

A woman threw herself under my train as we steamed into Waterloo, but apart from that I didn't see much hysteria.'

'The churches are doing a roaring business, though,' Sam added. 'They're in perpetual session and packed to suffocation. I even saw some people kneeling on the steps of St. Martin-in the-Fields as I passed it. There are a good few drunks about, too. But, by and large, people are still taking things pretty calmly. There are no signs of any riots yet, anyway.'

'Then let's go out this evening,' Lavina suggested. 'I'm sick of sitting here doing nothing, and I've been cooped up in the house all day.'

'I'd rather you didn't, darling,' Sam said quickly.

She gave him one of her most bewitching smiles. 'I shall be perfectly all right, sweet, with Derek and Roy to look after me.'

'Where would you go?'

'Oh, I don't know. But we may be living in the last days of London, and I'd like to see how its people are behaving.'

'Well, if I let you, will you promise to set off for Stapleton first thing to-morrow morning?'

'When do you expect to get there yourself?'

'To-morrow evening at the latest.'

Lavina nodded. She was not really an unreasonable person and was excellent at making compromises. 'In that case, I'm game to play. What time will you be back to-night?'

'It's difficult to say. I tell you what, though. As you've agreed to leave first thing to-morrow, there's not really much point in my coming back here at all. You see, my first visit in the morning is Edmonton and, as the evacuation will be in full swing, the traffic congestion going out of London is sure to be appalling. If I pack a bag, I could get a bed in my manager's house at Hendon for to-night and then go across country to Edmonton to-morrow without coming back into London at all. That'd save me so much time I might even be able to get down to Stapleton by the afternoon.'

'Then although I hate the thought of being parted from you even for a single night, that's clearly the thing to do, darling. Roy and Derek will take care of me and we'll all meet again at Stapleton to-morrow.'

'I'd better pack a bag too, then,' said Hemmingway.

Sam shook his head. 'No. One of us must sort out all the private papers here and, since I'm not returning, that'll be your job. I can manage quite well without you for these last factory visits. While the others are out on the spree you'd better go through the safe and sling all the contracts and important stuff into a suitcase. I shall have to take the Rolls but you've got your own car and Derek's got his so one of you can take Lavina and the other Roy down to Stapleton first thing to-morrow.'

When Sam had packed and gone, Hemmingway disappeared to his room while Derek went round to get his car, which he had left in the garage at the back of the house. Lavina and Roy were waiting for him outside the front door and the three of them set off on a tour of the West End.

There was not much traffic about as most people who had private cars were now on their way to the country, feeling that they would be safer there than in London where big fires were liable to break out. Turning into Piccadilly, they saw a line of vans outside Burlington House into which porters were loading works of art for removal to places of safety. There were vans, too, in Bond Street, as many of the luxury traders had decided to evacuate their stocks of furs, jewels and *objets d'art*; but most of the shops were closed and shuttered.

The streets were fairly full of people strolling aimlessly, or gathered in small knots on corners arguing together. But it was by no means a typical West End crowd. Most of them seemed to have come in from the poorer districts, judging from their clothes.

Apart from the small squads of police and troops who were patrolling the streets, the most unusual sight was the activity which was going forward on nearly every roof-top. As they turned west along Oxford Street, small figures were silhouetted against the evening skyline busily placing layers of sand-bags on roofs as a protection against the smaller meteorites.

At Marble Arch the crowd overflowed into the roadway, as the Park, having been turned into a supply depot, was closed; and the Hyde Park orators had set up their stands round the Arch itself. The political speakers were, as usual, denouncing the Government but their audiences were poor ones. The religious preachers were having it all their own way as they urged the packed throngs to 'repent in time,' and some people were even kneeling on the pavements before them. A policeman signalled

Derek down a side-street so, turning the car round, they ran slowly back towards Tottenham Court Road.

On reaching Charing Cross Road they turned south and came into the theatre district, which again was crowded. In order to keep things as normal as possible, the Government had decreed that the places of amusement should be kept open, but there were no pit queues although it was just past eight. On the other hand, the pubs were doing a roaring trade. There was not enough room in the bars to hold the customers and many of them had carried their drinks outside, where they stood arguing over them in the sultry, windless air.

The majority of the people seemed calm and expectant, just waiting for something—they didn't quite know what—to happen; but it was clear that two schools of extremists had arisen. A strong religious revival was gaining many adherents. Street preachers had taken up their position on corners and outside some of the theatres. In raucous tones they were proclaiming the Second Coming and large, earnest audiences were gathered in front of each of them.

The other school consisted of those fatalists who were thronging the public-houses, determined to follow the old exhortation, 'Eat, drink and be merry, for to-morrow we die.' Many of them were already drunk and some were dancing with the women on the pavements.

Slowly Derek edged the car down as far as Trafalgar Square, where more meetings were in progress. Whitehall had been closed so the Square was packed with humanity and the car was once more turned back by the police.

'We could get into Piccadilly *via* Leicester Square,' Derek suggested, 'then I think we'd better go home. After nightfall the streets will be more crowded than ever, and even if the police don't close them to traffic, I don't want to take the risk of running down a drunk.'

'Oh, don't let's go home yet,' Lavina cried. 'I want to see things.'

'I tell you,' exclaimed Roy, 'what about the cause of all the trouble—the old comet? Sunset should be in about an hour and it's only for a short spell after sundown that one can see it.'

'There's not much chance of our seeing anything of it from central London,' remarked Derek.

'What about running up to Hampstead Heath, though? We'd get a splendid view from there.'

'Yes, let's!' cried Lavina enthusiastically.

Derek had already turned the car round. Yard by yard they crawled up St. Martin's Lane, across Oxford Street and along Tottenham Court Road. It took them over half an hour to get as far as the Euston Road but once they had crossed it the drifting crowds no longer overflowed into the roadway. Derek was able to put on speed and another ten minutes brought them to the south-east corner of Hampstead Heath.

Here they parked the car and set out along the track past the ponds, up Parliament Hill. Quite a crowd of people were moving in the same direction and several thousand more were already massed up there on the highest spot overlooking London.

Mingling with the crowd, they managed to find a place well up the slope from which they could gaze across the million roof-tops of the mighty city. Right across the valley on another hill-top in the distant south-east, the two towers of the Crystal Palace were faintly discernible. More to the south the dome of St. Paul's and the tower of Big Ben stood out clearly; while to the south-west rose the twin chimneys of Battersea Power Station.

But no one was now interested in picking out these famous landmarks. They were all gazing westward into the setting sun. Most of them had smoked glasses or pieces of coloured mica to prevent the glare hurting their eyes and, apparently oblivious of the fact that they possibly had only three days to live, hawkers were moving among the crowd doing a brisk business in such wares.

Derek bought three pairs of cheap smoked glasses for Lavina, Roy and himself, then they settled down on the grass to watch the heavenly phenomenon which threatened the doom of the world.

The comet was only three degrees in elevation above the sun and a little to its left; so, even through smoked glasses, it was difficult to get any clear impression of it while daylight lasted. But the menace in the heavens at least appeared to have brought a spell of exceptionally fine weather. The sky was cloudless and the opportunity for getting a good view of the comet remarkable for London.

The sun sank like a great yellow ball behind the horizon and, normally, twilight would have followed, lasting about an hour, until darkness supervened and the stars came out. But now a dull yellow-orange light became slowly perceptible above the spot where the sun had gone down. The light grew in strength until it suffused the whole scene, changing it weirdly, and the multitude were able to gaze their fill upon the concentrated blotch in the heavens from which it came.

The comet was now far bigger than any star and had a diameter about one-fifth of that of the moon. But, unlike the moon, it had no clear-cut edge or cold brilliance.

Even seen through smoked glasses it had no regular outline but wobbled slightly, having the appearance of a large red nebula; a ball of fire that twinkled fiercely.

Daylight had gone, yet the Heath, the great crowd upon it, and the nearer portion of the city below were still clearly visible; but as an eerie landscape bathed in a strange, baleful, reddish light. The sight was most uncanny and the evil radiance seemed to affect the crowd on the hillside in an alarming manner.

A woman near Derek began to laugh hysterically. Another began to sob. The eyes of the men glinted strangely. A great wave of excitement suddenly seemed to surge right through the watching thousands. In a moment, from stillness the whole human mass began to pulse with a weird, unnatural life.

A great murmur went up. A mingling of shouts and wild laughter. Two men just in front of Lavina began to fight. Another suddenly thrust his way through the crush towards a pretty girl, seized her in his arms and, in spite of her struggles, began to kiss her avidly.

Derek felt an overpowering desire to do the same to Lavina. He was standing just behind her and his arms positively ached to reach out and draw her to him. He fought it down, but suddenly she swung right round and flung her arms about his neck.

For a good minute their mouths were locked together; then, with a little moan, she wrenched her head away and began to hammer on his shoulders with her fists.

Roy had pulled a large flask of whisky out of his hip-pocket and was gulping down its contents as though they were only water.

The baleful rays from the big splodge of reddish-yellow light near the western horizon seemed to have raised the basest passions of the whole multitude. Parliament Hill was now a scene of indescribable confusion. People were fighting, kissing, struggling, rolling on the ground either in the grip of uncontrollable hate or passionate desire.

The comet set twelve minutes after the sun. With its disappearance the shouting died. The red glow faded, giving place to a pink-twinged twilight sky.

People were now coming to their senses as quickly as they had lost them ten minutes earlier. They were apologizing to each other on every side and helping their late antagonists up from the ground. Almost at once the great crowd began to disperse, moving down the hill's sides to the roads that led into London.

Derek took Lavina's arm. 'Come on,' he said gruffly, 'let's get back to the car. What happened to us all, God knows! For a few minutes we must have been out of our senses.'

Lavina put a hand over her eyes. 'Extraordinary, wasn't it. The thing seemed to exercise a malign influence on everybody. But we aren't responsible; we only behaved like all the rest.'

Roy followed them, lurching slightly. His breath was coming fast and his eyes were bulging a little from the amount of neat spirit he had consumed in gulp after gulp.

'That's all very well,' he muttered. 'But if it can do that sort of thing to us now, what effect is it going to have on us in a day or two's time, when it gets a bit nearer?'

11

'EAT, DRINK AND BE MERRY . . .'

Distinctly sobered by this strange experience they regained the car and drove back towards London. Derek took the quieter streets and as they were passing through St. John's Wood Lavina broke a long silence by saying:

'Where are you heading for now?'

'Back to St. James's Square,' Derek replied promptly. 'Surely you've seen enough for one night, haven't you?'

'Yes. But I was thinking of dinner. Where are we going to feed?'

'Oh, we'll knock up something.'

'Why should we, when the restaurants are still open? It's getting on for ten o'clock and I feel extraordinarily hungry. Let's stop on the way back and get something to eat somewhere.'

'All right,' he conceded, a trifle reluctantly. 'Where would you like to go?'

'Let's try the Dorchester. We can get there without going through the most crowded parts of the West End.'

'We'll have to cross Oxford Street.'

'We'd have to do that anyway, unless we go right round Hyde Park, *via* Notting Hill and Kensington.'

'That's true. And I can avoid Marble Arch by going down Park Street. The Dorchester let it be then.'

'That's O.K. by me,' Roy muttered from the back, 'as long as one of you has enough cash to pay for the feast. I'm stony.'

Derek smiled. 'The meal, if we can get one, is on me. I drew fifty quid out of the bank last week in case of emergencies.'

At Baker Street they came into the crowds again so Derek turned right, into Gloucester Place, then back through Portman Square into Orchard Street. They were hung up for a quarter of an hour at the Oxford Street crossing and in the distance could see masses of people jamming the roadway right up to Marble Arch. But the crowd was good-tempered and eventually they managed to get through; reaching Park Lane at last, and their destination, by way of Deanery Street.

To their surprise, they found the Dorchester packed to the doors. The lounge was as crowded as a railway terminus before a Bank Holiday week-end, and waiters were having difficulty in securing a passage through the crush to bring drinks to those people who had been fortunate enough to obtain tables.

Every table in the Grill Room was also taken but the head waiter, who was standing in the doorway, recognized Lavina.

'You seem to be doing marvellous business,' she smiled at him.

He gave her a worried look. 'It is not good, madame. Many of our waiters have failed to report for duty and many of the kitchen staff are also gone; yet we have to cope with all these people. And we do not like this crowd. Very few of them are our usual patrons and they make unpleasantness for the guests who are still staying in the hotel.'

'We were hoping to get some supper here,' she said, 'but it looks as though that's impossible.'

'In the Grill, yes, madame,' he spread out his hands, 'but I may be able to get you a table in the Restaurant.'

'But we're not changed.'

He shrugged. 'Temporarily, that rule is no more. People made us withdraw it when they overflowed from the Grill, and old customers like yourself we could not refuse.'

Turning, he forced a way for them through the press and as there was not a single table vacant in the Restaurant he had one set up on the already diminished dance-floor.

They were lucky in getting a bottle of champagne almost at once, but it was a good half hour before the caviare rolled in smoked salmon, which they had ordered as a first course, appeared; and during their wait they had plenty of time to study the people about them.

It was quite clear that very few of them frequented the Dorchester in normal times. Only a handful were in evening dress. Many of the women were exotic-looking ladies, obviously from the streets round Piccadilly, and the bulk of the men were flashily-dressed foreigners of the type that usually haunt the Soho bars.

At nearly every table people were drinking champagne but, although appearances are often deceptive, something about the types which formed many of the groups made Derek wonder vaguely if they meant to pay for it or would try and slip away before their bills were brought to them. He wished now that he had insisted on taking Lavina straight back to St. James's Square, but she was in excellent form and Roy, his rather weak but attractive face wreathed in smiles, was entertaining her with a series of limericks in Pidgin-English which he had brought back from China.

The band, reduced to half its usual number, was doing its best but it was almost drowned in the babel of voices. The dance-floor was crowded with a solid mass of perspiring humanity. One look round the great room was enough to see that the people in it were the very antithesis of those who were praying in the churches. They typified the wilder elements of the Metropolis whom the possibility of being struck down in three days' time had released from all normal restraint. Their set faces and harsh laughter suggested a fierce determination to get everything possible out of life while it was still in them.

Perhaps as a result of their recent experience on Hampstead Heath Lavina and her two escorts found themselves unusually thirsty. Between the three of them their bottle of champagne was finished before their *hors-d'œuvres* arrived, and Derek ordered another.

Twenty minutes went by but it did not appear, and Roy was grumbling about the delay when a big man with a bald head and bushy eyebrows, who was wearing a horse-shoe tie-pin in a striped cravat, leant across from the next table proffering a magnum.

'Here have some of ours, old boy, till yours turns up,' he leered. 'It's all on the house to-night so what's the odds?'

Roy held out his glass at once and Derek, although he would have liked to refuse, followed suit because the big man looked as if he might resent a refusal and it would have been the height of folly to start a row at such a time on a point of ethics.

'And some for the little lady,' said their new acquaintance.

When Lavina's glass was full the big man picked up his own. 'Well, here's to you all! Happy days and three nights of bliss before the old comet hits us!' He gave a special smirk in Lavina's direction.

As they were about to drink, a Spanish-looking woman at

his table irritably claimed his attention so for the moment they were relieved of his advances.

In spite of the crush Lavina wanted to dance, so Derek took her on to the floor; but when they returned to their table neither their second course nor the second bottle of wine had appeared and it seemed, on looking round the room, that the waiters had given up the unequal struggle.

'It's nearly half-past eleven,' Derek remarked, 'and it doesn't look as though we're going to get our omelette. I think we'd better go home.'

'Don't be silly,' Lavina shrugged. She was staring out under lowered lids, over the cigarette she was constantly puffing, at the jammed mass of dancers. 'I'm enjoying myself watching all these queer people.'

'Maybe, but things are going to get pretty tough here soon, unless I'm much mistaken.'

'Well, I'm not going,' she said, with sudden firmness. 'It's just like a gala night, only the most extraordinary one I've ever seen.'

At that moment a man in a check suit pushed his way past their table. He was carrying four bottles of champagne in his hands and others were wedged under his arm-pits.

'By jove!' exclaimed Roy. 'That chap's been raiding the cellars. I'm in on this. Hang on here, and I'll get a few bottles.'

'You can't do that,' Derek protested.

'Why not?' Roy got to his feet. 'If the waiters won't serve us, why shouldn't we help ourselves?' He left them abruptly.

That he was right in his surmise that looting had started was soon clear as other men in lounge suits, quite obviously not employed by the hotel, came thrusting their way through the crowded entrance of the Restaurant clutching bottles of champagne, brandy and whisky.

The new supplies of drink were soon in circulation and gave an added fillip to the already irresponsible assembly. Someone else had thought of raiding the hotel's supply of carnival favours. Coloured streamers, balloons and puff-balls began to be thrown from table to table; paper hats appeared on the heads of the dancers; tin whistles and klaxon horns were thrown from hand to hand and added their noise to the already incredible din.

Roy returned flushed and laughing, with a couple of magnums

of Louis Roederer. He gave one to the big man with the horse-shoe tie-pin at the next table and opened up the other for his own party.

'You should just see the crowd in the cellar,' he grinned. 'This little beano's going to cost the hotel a packet. Some of the chaps down there are too tight to move already and others are sitting on the floor lapping it up out of the bottles.'

Derek stood up. 'Come on, Lavina, I've had enough of this. I'm going to take you home.'

'Don't be an idiot, darling!' She smiled serenely. 'I've already told you I'm thoroughly enjoying myself.'

A few tables away a man had a girl pulled back across his chest and was kissing her neck. At another, two men were attempting to fight, while a flaxen-haired young woman screamed drunken curses at them as she endeavoured to pull them apart.

Lavina could see perfectly well what was going on around her and knew that she ought not to remain there any longer; but she was now a little tight herself and in one of her pig-headed moods in which she was capable of almost any folly rather than submit to anyone else's dictation.

'Come on,' said Derek. 'If we stay here, we'll get mixed up in some rough-house or other.'

She impatiently shook off the hand he had laid on her arm, and stood up. 'I'm not going I tell you. Let's dance.'

'No,' he said firmly. 'I'm taking you home.'

'All right. I'll dance with Roy, then.' She swung round and held out her arms to her cousin.

Roy was a little unsteady on his legs from the considerable amount of whisky and champagne he had consumed and his mouth hung slackly open, but he pulled himself together. Before Derek could say anything further, the two of them had glided off together into the crush.

Derek wished now that he had begged Lavina to come home instead of trying to order her to do so, and determined to try persuasive methods directly she got back to the table. In the meantime, he followed her golden head with an anxious eye as far as he could among the bobbing jam of people.

She and Roy had very nearly completed the circuit of the restricted dance-floor three times—but were hidden from Derek for the moment—when a dark-complexioned, tight-lipped man jumped up from a table and laid a sinewy hand on her shoulder.

'I want to dance with you,' he said. 'My name's Finnigan and any of the boys'll tell you that I'm an ace-high picker of good-looking women.

Lavina met his insolent stare with a glance that would have shrivelled most men, but it had no effect whatever on the forceful Mr. Finnigan. With his left hand he gave Roy a violent push in the chest and with his right he wrenched Lavina round to face him.

'Take your hands off me,' she snapped, white with rage; but Finnigan only grinned at her.

'I like a girl with spirit,' he said, and, grabbing her small waist, jerked her to him.

She was not in the least frightened, but absolutely beserk with rage. Her eyes became hooded—mere slits in her pale little face —and the corners of her small mouth turned right down at a sharp angle. Raising her right hand she smacked Mr. Finnigan with all her force across the face.

As he jerked back, surprise gave place to black anger in his dark eyes; but before he could do anything further Roy had recovered and hit him an ineffectual blow which grazed his cheek.

In a second, Finnigan braced himself, swung round, and struck out with deadly precision. His fist took Roy under the chin and he went sprawling to the floor among the dancers.

Someone laughed hysterically, a woman screamed, but Finnigan took no notice. Completely unruffled, he turned back to Lavina and said smoothly:

'Now that's settled, we're going to dance, and I'll teach you how to smack people a bit later on this evening.'

As Finnigan grabbed her again she looked wildly round for Derek but could not see him. Then, on her right, she suddenly caught sight of the big bald man with the horse-shoe tie-pin.

'Half a minute! What's all this?' he exclaimed, advancing on Finnigan.

'You keep out of this, Harris, or I'll put my boys on to you,' snapped the Irishman. 'This little floosie's my pigeon.'

'Oh, no, she's not,' declared Harris. 'As for the boys, there's plenty of mine here, too.'

Finnigan still had hold of Lavina by one wrist but Harris

put an arm round her shoulders from behind. Pulling her to him he gave her a sloppy, wet kiss which landed under her right ear.

'Oh, no, she's not,' he repeated. 'We're acquainted already—been neighbours all the evening. I've only been waiting my chance to have a dance with her until the party got going.'

'Stop it, both of you!' Lavina's voice came hoarse and unnatural. 'Let me go! I don't want anything to do with either of you.'

So many quarrels over women were now taking place that the squabble for Lavina had passed almost unnoticed. Everything had happened so quickly that Roy was still sitting on the floor dazedly fingering his injured chin, while the dancers continued to jig all about them.

Suddenly Finnigan released Lavina's wrist, thrust his hand under his arm-pit and withdrew it clutching a razor; the sharp edge uppermost across the back of his knuckles.

He made one slash at Harris but the big man was extraordinarily agile. Thrusting Lavina aside, he ducked; and next second he had also whipped out a razor.

Both men began to shout at the top of their voices and almost immediately their respective adherents came charging through the crowd towards them.

Within a moment a gang battle was in full progress. The dance-floor became a scene of wild confusion. Screaming women fought their way from it between the nearest tables. Bottles and glasses were being hurled; blood was flowing from ugly razor slashes. Lavina missed one right across her face only by inches and another in the neck because she tripped and fell.

Derek had jumped to his feet directly the shouting started. Using his elbows indiscriminately on men and women, he forced his way forward until he saw Lavina. As the floor cleared of non-combatants he made better progress and began to hit out savagely at any of the men who barred his path.

Roy had staggered to his feet again but he was still half dazed. Harris and his men were getting the best of the battle. Finnigan and his boys were being driven back. Derek was still some distance off, fighting with a fleshy, hook-nosed Jew.

In a gallant attempt to save Lavina, Roy plunged into the whirling mêlée. In doing so, he blundered into Finnigan from behind and threw him off his balance. With a blasphemous curse the Irishman fell to the floor.

Stooping, Roy grabbed Lavina and dragged her to her feet. Finnigan was up again, but in his fall he had dropped his razor. Reaching behind him, he snatched up an empty champagne bottle, and, raising it aloft, he brought it down with all his strength on the back of Roy's head.

At that moment Derek reached them. As the blow fell he lashed out with all his force and, catching Finnigan full under the jaw, sent him flying backwards among the tables.

Whipping round, Derek stared at Lavina. She was kneeling again now and held Roy in her arms. The whole of the back of his head was shattered and blood was pouring from it all over her light summer frock.

The mêlée of gangsters had swayed away from them. Derek knelt down beside her and saw that she was weeping hysterically.

'He's dead,' she moaned. 'He's dead. And it's all my fault. Oh, how wicked I was to insist on staying here.'

A fresh din of shouting was now coming from the lounge outside. A moment before, the Restaurant doors had been jammed by a solid mass of people trying to escape from the gangsters' razors. Now they had turned and were streaming back into the room, yelling as they came: 'The Police! The Police!'

Derek realized at once that the hotel management had at last succeeded in getting aid from the authorities to clear the place. One drunken man was lying on the floor nearby, apparently oblivious to all that was going on except for the presence of the equally drunken woman in his arms over whom he was slobbering. But others, wounded, unconscious, dead, were strewn about the floor among the broken glass. The rest were clambering over the chairs and tables in a desperate attempt to escape by way of the windows.

A phalanx of police, pressed shoulder to shoulder, burst their way through the crowd in the doorway. Their batons were drawn and they were in no mood to be trifled with. Several had lost their helmets and others had cuts upon their faces from missiles that had been thrown at them as they had fought their way through the hall.

For a moment Derek thought of trying to get Lavina out through one of the windows; but, although poor Roy was dead, his blank eyeballs upturned and protruding, they could not leave him.

The gangsters had ceased their fighting and turned upon their common enemy. Those who had not already fled began to hurl bottles and chairs at the advancing police, but scores of Specials were now pouring into the room behind the shock column of hardened regulars.

At a sharp word of command, their formation broke into two wings, each of which swept sideways, encircling great batches of the riotous crew. People were now stumbling back through the windows, driven in by more squadrons of police who were lining the pavements outside. The gangsters were being forced into corners and beaten to their knees.

Suddenly a big Sergeant, with an angry eye, charged across the floor and, seizing Derek by the scruff of the neck, shouted:

'Come on, you!'

At the same moment a young Special grabbed Lavina with a yell of 'Keep your claws down or I'll have to hurt you.'

Before they had time to exchange a word they were hauled to their feet and dragged in opposite directions.

12

DEREK DOES HIS DAMNEDEST

'Steady on, Sergeant!' gasped Derek. 'I haven't been throwing any bottles.'

'You can tell that to the magistrate in the morning,' the big man panted. He had an ugly bruise over one eye and no cause whatever to feel tolerant towards the rioters.

'I didn't assault you and I'm not drunk. You've got no right to arrest me.' Derek struggled to free himself from the iron grip of his captor.

'Oh, yes, I have—participating in riotous assembly; and I'll add "resisting arrest" to that if you're not careful.'

'All right, then. But hang on a minute.'

Lavina had been pulled a dozen yards away by the young Special. She was still weeping hysterically and making little resistance, but Derek pointed with his free hand anxiously towards her.

'Listen, Sergeant. That lady I was with—she's Lady Curry. For goodness' sake don't separate me from her at a time like this.'

'I don't care if she's the Duchess of Dartmoor,' grunted the Sergeant with heavy humour. 'Men one way and women the other. That's the order.' He gave Derek a violent shove towards two constables. 'Here! Keep your eye on this one. I found him kneeling beside a chap who'd had his head bashed in.'

A number of the police had now formed two lines. Behind one they had penned a large number of their male captives and behind the other, at the far side of the room, the women. They were rapidly sorting out the rest of the mob and clearing the centre of the ballroom.

Derek found himself among a motley crowd that now looked less than ever like regular patrons of the Dorchester. Most of them were drunk, many had cuts and bruises, torn clothes, ruffled hair and blood upon their faces.

On glancing down he saw that his own hands and shirt-cuffs were bloodstained from having raised poor Roy's battered head off Lavina's lap. He peered anxiously between the shoulders of two stalwart Specials but could see nothing of her.

A few moments later the police began to march their prisoners off in batches. Craning his neck, Derek caught one glimpse of Lavina. She was being hustled along in the midst of a group of drunk and cursing women. At that moment she looked across and, with a shrill cry of 'Derek! Derek!' made a desperate attempt to run towards him; but a policeman firmly thrust her back and she was forced to leave the ballroom with the others.

When the women had all gone, the men were shepherded out in groups of about a dozen. The lounge was now clear except for little knots of police and some harassed-looking members of the hotel staff. Outside the entrance of the hotel a line of small Ford vans was drawn up. Derek and his companions were hustled into one. The doors were slammed, locked, and the van drove off.

It was completely dark inside. Some of the drunks were jolted off their feet and the others were badly jostled, but their drive was a short one. When the van came to a halt, and its doors were unlocked, Derek tumbled out of it to find himself standing on grass in the fresh night air. After a second he recognized the lights of Grosvenor House and the skyline of Park Lane, above the trees in the distance, and realized that he was in Hyde Park.

On looking round he saw that they were outside a barbed-wire encampment, which was guarded by soldiers in khaki. There were many police and military about, but Derek did not have long to observe them as he and his companions were hurried into a large wooden hut just by the entrance of the barbed-wire enclosure.

Inside it a Guards Captain was seated behind a trestle table. Beside him was a Corporal, busily writing upon a stack of forms. Two or three orderlies stood near, besides a double row of policemen who had participated in the raid on the Dorchester.

One by one the men in Derek's group were pushed forward, and when particulars of each had been taken down by the Corporal, they were handed over to the military and marched outside again.

When it came to Derek's turn, the Captain asked: 'Name?'

'Derek Burroughs.'

'Address?'

'The Old Mill, Stapleton, Surrey.'

'Charge?' The Captain looked interrogatively towards the group of policemen, and the big Sergeant stepped forward.

'Riotous assembly, sir. And would you add to that—when arrested, was kneeling beside the body of a fair man, aged about thirty, who had had his head bashed in.'

The Officer nodded and signed to Derek to move away so that the next prisoner could come forward, but Derek stood his ground and said quickly:

'Look here, this is all an awful mistake. I was in the Dorchester having supper.'

'I know,' interrupted the Captain wearily. 'They're all saying that.'

'But listen,' Derek insisted. 'I'm not drunk. I was with Lady Curry but we were separated and I've simply got to find her.'

'Sorry,' The Guards Captain fingered his small, dark moustache. 'I'm afraid I can't release you because, you see, you've been charged. We'll have to hold you with the rest until the morning.'

'But I'm not a rioter. We got mixed up in this affair,' Derek protested.

'Well, that's your fault, isn't it? The Government has appealed to everybody to stay indoors so as to prevent this sort of thing happening. Anyhow, you've no need to worry. They'll probably let you off with a caution to-morrow.'

'But, don't you see, it's not myself I'm worried about,' Derek cried in desperation. 'It's Lady Curry. God knows where they've taken her and she was lugged off among a lot of drunken women.'

The Officer shrugged. 'I can't imagine how any decent woman got mixed up in a show like this and, for all I know, you're just trying to put one over me. Any number of people are to-night. I'm really very sorry but I can't give you any more time. Take him away.'

The wretched Derek was pulled from the table, thrust out of the hut and handed over to a Corporal, who passed him in through the iron gates of the barbed-wired prisoners' cage.

He looked gloomily round him. There was no moon but it was a fine night and the stars gave enough light to see by. In the

big encampment there were hundreds of men standing, sitting or
lying on the grass. On speaking to some of them he soon discovered that comparatively few had been brought in from the
Dorchester. Most of them had been rounded up from other
hotels, restaurants and bars, as, apparently, the riot in the Dorchester was only symptomatic of the sort of thing that was
happening all over London that night wherever supplies of drink
could be got for the taking; and the police were now systemati-
cally clearing and closing down such places.

There were no troops in the encampment but plenty of sentries
outside it and, after walking a little way round its rim, Derek
saw that he would not stand the least chance of getting away
even if he could have wriggled through the eight-foot-high
mesh of barbed-wire which fenced in himself and his fellow
prisoners.

He was acutely worried about Lavina. The shock of seeing Roy
killed before her eyes was quite enough to have sent such a
highly-strung girl out of her mind. Again and again he cursed
himself for having allowed her to remain there among such a
crowd when they were so clearly boiling up for trouble. Yet so
strong a personality animated her slender body that he doubted
if anyone else would have succeeded, where he had failed, in
persuading her to go home before she wanted to.

As he let his imagination race over the possibilities of her
present situation, he groaned. He had just got to get free himself
and find her somehow.

Retracing his steps to the gate, which was some twelve feet
wide, made of steel bars and hinged on two great posts, he
peered through it. The sentry remained as though dumb and ignored his questions but, after a little, Derek managed to attract
the attention of a Sergeant-Major and, beckoning him over,
offered him a cigarette. The Sergeant-Major took it through the
bars of the gate with a polite 'Thanks, old chap.'

'What chance is there of getting out of this place?' Derek
asked.

'Not an earthly, until you've been before the Court in the
morning,' the man replied, with a friendly grin.

Derek then told his story of Roy's murder and how Lavina had
been dragged off by the police.

The Sergeant-Major was sympathetic, but unhelpful. 'Hard

luck, that,' he nodded, 'but I'm afraid there's nothing I can do about it.'

After a little hesitation Derek produced his note case. It had about £50 in it and, opening it up so as to make certain that the Sergeant-Major could see its contents, he said:

'I'm not trying to bribe you but I'll make it very well worth your while if you can help me. The girl I was with must be in a shocking state and I've absolutely got to get to her somehow.'

'It's no good, sir,' the Sergeant-Major shook his head. 'I'd help you gladly if I could, but I can't. The sentries on the gate have their orders and no one's to be let out unless an officer signs a written form releasing them.'

'Couldn't you talk to one of the officers for me, then?' urged Derek.

'Yes. I might do that, though I doubt if it will do much good. They're a pretty decent lot in the ordinary way but just now being so overworked makes 'em a bit abrupt and disinclined for conversation. Still, when the Lieutenant does his rounds I'll wait my chance and have a word with him.'

'Thanks—thanks most awfully,' Derek muttered. 'Look, take this on account and drink my health with it to-morrow.' He thrust a couple of pounds into the Sergeant-Major's hand.

'Very good of you, I'm sure.' The notes disappeared into the Sergeant-Major's pocket. 'I can't promise anything, though, and the Lieutenant won't be round for another three-quarters of an hour or so. If I have any luck with him, where'll I find you?'

'I'll be about here. My name's Derek Burroughs. If you give a shout, I'll hear you.'

'Right-o, sir.' The Sergeant-Major gave a perfunctory salute and moved away into darkness.

As Derek turned, he bumped into a tall, thin, bony man who had been standing with a group of others just behind him. The tall man muttered an apology and went on talking to his cronies, a rough-looking lot in caps and scarves who looked as though they had been rounded up from some public-house.

For a few moments Derek stood still, then he began to walk up and down making a detour here and there to avoid little groups or some of the drunks, who were now huddled, snoring, on the grass; yet he hardly noticed them, his brain was so occupied with the thought of Lavina.

Where had they taken her? To Holloway? No, that would be full to overflowing. Much more probably it would be to some municipal building converted into a temporary prison or a barbed-wire cage for women in some other part of the Park. Anyhow, wherever she was, she must be in a most desperate state. Derek knew her well enough to realize that the toughness she sometimes displayed was not even skin-deep; it was only a sham armour of silver paper by which she deceived people so that she could force her will upon them. Underneath, she was just a rather fragile, delicately-nurtured girl, with quick sympathies and a special horror of any form of uncleanness.

As he thought of her, cooped up somewhere with a lot of prostitutes, drunks and the riff-raff of the streets, he seethed with rage at his inability to help her. The fact that she was at least indirectly responsible for Roy's death would certainly have driven her half out of her senses with distress and remorse. All his old love for her had surged up again during this long day they had spent together. As he had told her in the afternoon, now that she was married he had every intention of suppressing it and, at the time, he had felt himself quite strong enough to do so; yet now, as he paced up and down, he would have given anything in the world to be able to get to her, put his arms round her, and comfort her.

The three-quarters of an hour he had to wait seemed absolutely interminable and, although he kept the gate in sight, each time he turned about he walked a little farther away from it. He had just covered his maximum distance so far and was about to turn again when somebody tapped him on the shoulder.

Looking up, he recognized the tall man who had been near him when he was speaking to the Sergeant-Major.

'You're Derek Burroughs, ain't yer?' the tall man asked in a husky voice.

'Yes,' said Derek quickly.

'You was torkin' to the Sergeant-Major 'alf an hour ago, wasn't yer? Well, 'e's lookin' for yer.'

'Is he?' Derek started forward towards the gate but the man gripped him quickly by the arm.

'Not that way, mate. The Serg' says to me as 'ow I was to find you and, when I did, bring you to the far side of the camp where there ain't so many people 'angin' around. I think 'e's got some idea in 'is noddle for gettin' you out of this.'

'Thank God,' breathed Derek, and, without further hesitation, he began to stride beside the tall man towards the less crowded section of the encampment.

The barbed-wire cage enclosed an oblong space running north and south, several hundred yards in length. The gate was at the southern end and comparatively few of the prisoners had bothered to move far from it after being ordered inside.

As they advanced, the sleeping forms scattered over the grass grew fewer and by the time they had covered two hundred and fifty yards the last of the prisoners had been swallowed up in the darkness behind them.

Suddenly Derek felt a vague sense of apprehension. There was a rustling in the grass at his rear. Glancing swiftly over his shoulder he saw that three men were padding softly on his heels.

He had just time to avoid a blow that one of the men aimed at his head, by springing aside, and all three were upon him.

In an instant he saw the trap into which he had fallen. The tall man had overheard his conversation with the Sergeant and seen him produce his wallet with the wad of notes in it. His treacherous guide and the three evil-looking thugs who had suddenly appeared now formed a circle round him. He had been lured to a quiet part of the camp so that they could attack and rob him.

The odds were heavy, but in his day Derek had been a runner-up for the Public Schools boxing championship. He was still under thirty and a healthy outdoor life and kept him remarkably fit. But he did not mean to rely on that. Lavina's rescue from the purgatory she must be suffering now depended on his own escape. There were plenty of people within call.

He lashed out, giving one of the men a crack on the jaw that sent him reeling, and at the same moment opened his own mouth to shout for help. But at that very second the tall fellow struck him a savage blow on the head from behind. His shout was never uttered; instead, his back teeth clicked and his front teeth bit into the tip of his tongue, causing him almost to screech with pain. Instantly all four of his attackers flung themselves at him.

He was borne down, kneed a man in the stomach and, wriggling free, staggered to his feet again. With the strength of desperation he hit out right and left, the image of Lavina ever in his mind;

and many of his punches got home, as he knew from his smarting knuckles.

Suddenly the tall man landed a brutal kick on his shin, another of them got in a heavy blow on his ear and a third, charging him head downward, butted him in the midriff. With a gasp he was sent flying to the ground, the man on top of him.

For the next few moments he suffered indescribably. Heavy boots thudded into his ribs. One of the men jumped upon his stomach. Kneeling beside him, they wrenched out his pocket-book and delivered blow after blow on his face wherever he was unable to guard it. A vicious kick on the back of the head caused him to see red lights stabbing the blackness before his eyes; then he fainted.

As consciousness left him, his last coherent thought was that these devils had robbed him of all chance of getting free to find Lavina.

13

HELL IN HYDE PARK

When Derek came round he was one mass of aches and bruises. With infinite caution and considerable pain he lifted his hand to his head. It felt the size of a pumpkin and as though the soft matter inside was gently surging to and fro, each beat of his heart propelling it backwards and forwards in great waves of pain.

At first he did not know where he was or what had happened to him, but gradually his thoughts became coherent and he remembered how he had been attacked and robbed by some of his fellow prisoners.

With a great effort of will he sat up and began to examine himself all over. His shin hurt abominably where he had been kicked and his ribs pained him every time he took a breath, but he did not think that any of his bones were broken. There was a lump on the back of his head and another on his jaw. One of his eyes was half-closed and from the sticky crust which had formed on his upper lip he knew that his nose had been bleeding.

It struck him then that the sky was much lighter. He must have been out for a long time, as dawn was approaching. He began again to wonder miserably about Lavina and in what wretched state the new day would find her.

Looking round him, he saw that nearly all his fellow-prisoners were lying on the ground asleep. There were many more of them than there had been when he was put in the cage. Evidently the police had been rounding up fresh batches of rioters and interning them all night. There were now several thousand men in the great oblong barbed-wired encampment. Vaguely he began to wonder if he would be able to find his assailants and charge them, but he had seen the tall, bony man only by starlight and the others had been no more than whirling figures in the semi-darkness. With such a vague memory of his face, to look for the tall man among all these hundreds of prisoners would be like searching for a needle in a haystack.

Slowly he got to his feet and, limping painfully, made his way to the gate of the enclosure. About fifty men were congregated there; recent arrivals, who were still telling each other of their exploits during the night and how they had been captured.

Clinging on to the bars of the gate for support, Derek peered through them and called to the sentry. The man took no notice but, after a few moments, Derek managed to attract the attention of a passing Sergeant.

'What do you want?' asked the Sergeant gruffly.

'I've been attacked and robbed,' muttered Derek.

'Been in a rough house trying to rob people yourself more likely.' The Sergeant stared unsympathetically. 'Plenty of your kind brought in to-night.'

'No. It was here in the camp, a few hours ago. Some thugs beat me up and stole my money.'

The soldier peered a little closer in the uncertain light. 'You do look a bit of a mess,' he granted.

'I'm pretty well all-in,' Derek mumbled. 'For God's sake get me a doctor, can't you.'

'All right, then. You'll have to wait your turn, though.'

'My turn?'

'Yes. The doctor's been busy on casualties all night. He's still got a dozen or so in that hut over there waiting to be patched up.' The Sergeant nodded in the direction of a fair-sized wooden building some distance away then, turning, called a Guardsman out of the guard hut nearby.

The gate was unlocked and, taking Derek by the arm, the Guardsman led him over to the doctor's quarters.

Inside a small ante-room two lines of men were sitting dejectedly on wooden benches. Some were already roughly bandaged with blood-soaked rags, and all had injuries received in fighting. One was sobbing quietly in a corner and another moaned monotonously. Derek took his place upon a bench and waited.

It was over an hour before his turn came to go inside and, in the meantime, other casualties had been brought in to replace those who had been treated.

The doctor proved to be a fat, bald, sharp-eyed little man

wearing the uniform of a Captain. No nurses were present but he had two Orderlies in white overalls as assistants and one of them was dressing an arm wound for the last patient as Derek entered.

'Well, what's your trouble?' the Doctor asked sharply. He had been working all night without respite and was in no mood to exchange idle pleasantries.

'I was attacked and beaten up,' Derek said briefly.

'All right. Better strip, then.'

The other Orderly helped Derek in the painful process of getting off his clothes. He was then told to lie down on a bare, hard couch in the centre of the room and the doctor gave him a swift examination; some of the spots on which he pressed firmly with his thumbs causing his examinee excruciating agony.

'Not much wrong with you,' he said after a moment. 'Nasty bruise on your shin but no bones broken. A day or two in bed will see you fit—when you can get there; but you're not a hospital case. I can't spare beds at St. George's for anyone who's not seriously injured.'

The Orderlies came forward and dabbed the worst of Derek's bruises with some soothing ointment. As they produced some bandages he said slowly:

'I'll be all right, but what I'm worried about is getting out of here. You see, I was with a girl last night and we were separated. I've simply got to find her.'

'I'm afraid there isn't much chance of your being able to do that. The orders are that anybody who's been arrested is to be kept inside until the trouble's over.'

'What?' Derek sat up with a start, felt a stab of pain and sank back with a moan. 'But they can't do that—it isn't legal.'

'My dear man, under its emergency powers the Government can do anything and, to my mind, they're behaving very sensibly. Nearly all the lawless elements of the city were out on the spree last night and that gave the police just the chance they wanted to collar them. By keeping them behind barbed wire we'll be able to stop a great deal of looting.'

'But I'm not a crook. I wasn't even drunk when I was arrested.'

'That's just your bad luck, then. But, if you were mixed up in such a crowd, you asked for it, and evidently you're an irresponsible person.'

'I'm nothing of the kind; and the girl I was with is highly respectable, yet she was lugged off with a lot of drunken street-women.'

'Perhaps, but the very fact that you were involved in a riot justifies the Government in arresting you both for your own protection.'

When the Orderlies had finished bandaging Derek he was told to dress while another casualty was brought in. But when he had struggled back into his clothes, he made one last effort.

'Look here, I've simply got to find this young woman I was with somehow. Couldn't you possibly get me an interview with an Officer?'

'No, I couldn't,' the doctor replied irritably. 'There aren't enough Officers in the whole battalion to listen to one-tenth of the people who're asking to see them. Here, drink this up; it'll take your head away. Then get out and have a good sleep on the grass.'

Derek dutifully drank up the potion he was offered and, leaving, was led back to the barbed-wire enclosure.

The people in it were rousing up now and he began to look round with a vague hope of finding the tall man who had trapped him, but he could not see him anywhere.

Half an hour later the gates were opened. Some lorries drove in and the Troops who were with them lined up the prisoners in long queues to receive their breakfast ration. It consisted of a mug of coffee—which had to be drunk on the spot and the mug passed on to the next man in the queue—a hunk of bread with a slice of bully, and an orange.

Derek carried his portion away to the far side of the camp, where it was less crowded, and slowly began to chew this sustaining but not particularly appetizing breakfast. His jaw hurt him every time he moved it and he wasn't feeling at all like food, but he decided that he ought to eat it if he could do so, to keep up his strength as much as possible.

As he ate he thought of Lavina again—probably receiving a similar ration in some other encampment with hundreds of women. Somehow he had simply *got* to escape and find her. At the worst, he had expected to be brought before a magistrate or military tribunal that morning and dismissed with a caution or a fine; and he had assumed that the same would happen to Lavina.

Even if he had failed to locate her while she was still a prisoner, he had anticipated that she would make her way back during the morning to St. James's Square and that they would then be able to set off together down to Stapleton.

But now it seemed all prisoners were to be detained for the next three days, which meant that, unless he could escape, both he and she would still be captives when the comet either singed or hit the earth. He had been banking more than he realized on the Ark proving their salvation, however great the catastrophe, and now they were both to be robbed of their chance of surviving in it.

Wearily he turned the problem over in his still aching brain. Bribery was no good, now that he had lost his money. As it had appeared impossible to break out of the cage the night before, it would be even more difficult in daylight. Perhaps if he could find the friendly Sergeant-Major again and get an interview with an Officer, he might still be able to persuade them to release him.

Almost unconsciously he turned over on his side and pillowed his head upon his arm. For some reason he was feeling extraordinarily drowsy. Perhaps the doctor had put something in the headache draught he had been given—something to make him sleep. But he mustn't sleep. He mustn't let himself go to sleep, whatever happened. Yet a moment later he had fallen into dreamless slumber.

When he woke it was already evening. He felt considerably better than he had done in the morning. His head pained him less and his shin was not throbbing quite so agonizingly; but as he moved he gave a groan, for he was almost as stiff as if he had been imprisoned in a strait jacket.

By easing his muscles cautiously he gradually got back the use of his limbs, and on looking round he saw that the encampment was now more crowded than ever. Evidently, fresh batches of prisoners had been brought in during the hours he had been sleeping. There was now hardly a vacant patch of grass in the whole enclosure.

He glanced across at a round-faced little man who was seated near him and asked if he knew what time it was. The man produced a large gold watch.

'Ten to seven, mate,' he said. 'That's a nasty eye of yours. How d'you get it?'

Derek gingerly felt his swollen left eye, which was now almost entirely closed. 'Here, last night,' he said. 'Some toughs set on me and robbed me of my wallet.'

'That was a bit hard,' the man grinned cheerfully. 'Where did the cops pinch you?'

'At the Dorchester.'

'They pinched me at the 'Bunch of Grapes' in the Strand. Cor, it was a beano, and no mistake! My name's Alf Wilkin. What's yours?'

'Derek Burroughs. D'you think there's any chance of getting out of this place?'

'Not much, with all these khaki boys around. But who cares? It's bin a nice day in the sunshine and there's some talk of their issuing us blankets to-night. The grub's not bad, either, and it's free. We might do much worse than sit around here for a few days.'

Derek did not go into details with Mr. Wilkin as to why he was so frantically anxious to regain his freedom but, pulling himself together, nodded good-bye to the little man and made his way towards the gate.

Knowing now that it was no good trying to talk to the sentry, he waited till a Corporal came along and inquired for the Sergeant-Major.

'He's out on duty,' the Corporal replied. 'They're mopping up down Limehouse way this evening.'

'When will he be back?' Derek asked.

'How should *I* know?'

'Then d'you think you could get hold of an officer for me?'

''Fraid not. It isn't for me to go worrying the officers with prisoners' grievances.'

'Oh, hell!' Derek exclaimed, as he turned away dejectedly.

'What's wrong, old chap?' asked a friendly voice nearby.

The speaker was a youngish man dressed in a suit of overalls and a flying-helmet. He offered a packet of cigarettes, and Derek took one gratefully as he began to give a brief version of his plight.

'You've certainly had a raw deal,' the young man remarked when Derek had done, 'and I can sympathize because, as a matter of fact, I'm here on account of a girl myself.'

'Was she arrested, too?' inquired Derek.

'No. I haven't seen her for six weeks. That's just the rub. My name's Babforth and I live up at Hull. By my girl's a Londoner; her home's in Kilburn. We met at the Butlin Holiday Camp at Skegness last year, had a grand time and absolutely fell for each other right away. We're not engaged exactly, but we write to each other twice a week and I've managed to get up to see her half a dozen times in the last ten months. When I heard the Prime Minister's speech on the radio the other night, I got anxious about her.'

'Naturally,' agreed Derek.

'So I made up my mind to come up to London on my motorbike, with the idea that whatever happened we'd be together. If I'd only got here yesterday things would have been all right, but, apparently, when the evacuation started this morning they not only closed all roads to incoming traffic but they've got police posts everywhere which are turning back pedestrians as well; in fact, they won't let anybody into London now who hasn't got a permit.'

'I see. And I suppose you tried to gate-crash?'

'That's it,' Babforth nodded. 'Wouldn't you have done the same? Hang it, I'd come all that way to be with my girl and I was worried out of my wits about her. I tried four different roads but I was turned back every time so I abandoned the old bike and climbed over a garden wall. But they've got a ring of police and Tommies the whole way round London, and a Special spotted me. I gave him a run for his money all right and when he *did* collar me I knocked him down; but he whistled up a couple of his pals and they put me in a van and sent me here. Where I was a fool was to hit the officer. If I hadn't done that, they'd only have turned me back again. Then, if I'd waited till to-night, I'd have been able to get through the police cordon easily in the darkness.'

'Yes, that's where you slipped up,' Derek agreed, 'although I expect I should have done the same myself. Anyhow, as we're both in the same sort of mess we must put our heads together and think up some scheme for getting out of here. How's the evacuation going?'

'Pretty well. As they've cleared the roads of all incoming traffic, it's just one steady stream of cars and buses going out; although, of course, I didn't see what was happening in Central London.'

For a little time the two of them discussed their rather slender

E

prospects of escape. Derek was still feeling weak and ill but having a decent fellow like Babforth to talk to cheered him up considerably.

At half-past seven the gates of the encampment were opened and the food lorries drove in again. As Derek had been sleeping when the lunch ration was issued, he now felt hungry and, with Babforth beside him, managed to get a fairly good place in one of the many queues.

To his disappointment he found that supper consisted only of tea, cheese and biscuits, a more solid meal of stew and plum-pudding having been issued in the middle of the day. But there was a liberal supply and when he told the Quartermaster who was superintending operations that he had missed his lunch he was given a double portion without argument.

In the gentle light they sat on the grass nibbling their cheese and biscuits. Babforth had fortunately provided himself with several packets of Players on his way down from Hull so they had an ample supply of cigarettes and, having decided that it was useless to attempt anything until darkness had fallen, they lay side by side smoking while they waited for night to come.

Unlike the previous evening, the sky was overcast so they could not actually watch the sun sinking, but by 9.40 the outline of Park Lane to the east had become blurred in semi-darkness; while the colour was rapidly fading from the trees to the west in Kensington Gardens.

Then, almost imperceptibly the sky there took on a different hue; a reddish tinge, as though a great fire was burning somewhere in the far distance. The men in the camp began to stir uneasily. At one moment a good two-thirds of them had been lying or sitting on the grass. The next, they were all standing on their feet. Derek felt a strange, unaccountable glow of exultation run through him and he saw that Babforth's eyes had taken on a glassy stare.

As the sky reddened in the west a low murmur went up which gradually increased to an angry roar. The prisoners were all in movement now. Some had started to quarrel over portions of unconsumed rations. Others began to move from all sides, as though by a common impulse, towards the gate.

Derek, too, instinctively turned in that direction and Babforth strode along beside him. Soon they were wedged in a struggling, yelling mass and found themselves shouting aloud like the rest.

Fortunately, they had been some distance from the entrance of the compound when the mob began to converge upon it; otherwise they might have been crushed to death. As it was, they could hear the agonized screaming of the men a hundred yards in front who were now being pressed flat against the iron bars of the great gates.

Suddenly, under the enormous pressure, they gave; and the mob surged forward fighting and struggling to get through them, as though they had been trapped in a building where there was a raging fire.

The jam was so great that Derek's damaged ribs suffered severely. He kept his arms pressed down to his sides to give them some protection, but after a few minutes he thought his heart would burst and a scream was forced from him. Then the pressure eased. He caught a glimpse of the barbed-wire entanglements now on his right rear and knew that although he had not even seen the gates he had been carried through them.

Those prisoners who had already succeeded in escaping were racing across the Park in the direction of Park Lane and, despite his pain, Derek felt a thrill of elation at the thought that he, to, was now once more a free man. But next moment the man in front of him tripped over the body of one of the poor wretches who had been crushed in bursting open the gate and Derek pitched forward on top of them.

Stretching out a hand, Babforth grabbed Derek's elbow and for a second he regained his feet; but Babforth was swept on by the swirling stream of prisoners who were still stampeding through the gate, and a violent thrust behind sent Derek spinning to the ground once more. He felt a heavy boot descend in the middle of his back and the mob came surging over him.

Instinctively he threw up his arms to protect his head. It seemed quite certain that he would be trampled to death. For the second time in twenty-four hours he was kicked, bashed, stamped on. As he was far from recovered from his first flailing the second was even more painful, yet now he was at least face down and the blows that rained upon him were not deliberate.

After what seemed an eternity the human herd had passed. He lay still for a moment, half-stunned and breathless. Then he managed to raise his head again and saw that the red glow in the western sky was fading. Dimly he realized that very soon the troops, whom the comet must also have affected, would regain their senses and start rounding-up such prisoners as they could. He must get away at once or he would be recaptured.

All about him lay the bodies of crushed and trampled men. Some of them were now sitting up groaning over their injuries; others lay still where they had fallen, never to rise again. In the distance a number of the escaped prisoners were still running towards Park Lane.

Aching in every limb he swayed to his feet and set off at a drunken run; several of the fallen, who had not been too badly trampled, were also staggering up and running with him.

When they reached Grosvenor Gate a trickle of escapers was still passing through it but behind them angry shouts to halt told them that the soldiers were already giving chase. The great iron gates of the Park had been burst by the same method as those of the encampment. The bodies of more dead and injured were strewn in the roadway outside. Derek did not pause to look at them but lurched on down Upper Brook Street into Grosvenor Square.

The comet had now set and full night was come. Police whistles were shrilling from both behind and in front as Derek ran. Ahead of him, on the Carlos Place corner of Grosvenor Square, he saw a body of police heading back the escapers, so he turned on his track and ran down South Audley Street.

Except for the prisoners, who had scattered in all directions, the street was empty. Every shop was in darkness and the blinds of most of the houses were drawn. As he reached the *cul-de-sac* which ends in Mount Street Gardens he noticed that the windows of the wine-merchant's shop on the corner opposite Grosvenor Chapel had been smashed. At the same moment he saw some police coming round the corner of South Street just ahead of him, so he halted, turned abruptly, and scrambled in through the broken window of the wine-merchant's.

The place had been looted; it was a shambles of broken bottles and spilt liquor. Feeling his way forward in the darkness, he found some offices behind the shop. Entering one, he closed the door behind him, tripped over something, and fell upon the carpet.

For a moment he was so exhausted that he could not move but lay panting where he had fallen. When he got his breath back a little he lit a match from a box that Babforth had given him. The thing he had tripped over was the dead body of a man.

The match having burnt down to his fingers he did not light another, but remained sitting on the floor with his back propped against a desk. Apparently, the police had not seen him enter the shop or they would have followed him already, so he felt that the best thing he could do was to remain there until the excitement had subsided.

A quarter of an hour later he lit another match and peered round him by its feeble light. Apart from the dead man, there was nothing unusual about the office. The looters had evidently contented themselves with drinking or smashing the bottles on the shelves in the shop outside during their drunken orgy. At one side of the room there was a mahogany cupboard, the top of which formed a tasting table, and, above it, shelves backed by mirrors with glasses upon them.

Crawling to the cupboard, he opened it and found some bottles inside. Picking one up he poured himself a drink without bothering to find out what the bottle contained. On sipping it he found it to be sherry and swallowed a couple of glasses one after the other.

The generous wine restored him a little, so leaving the office, he went out into the shop and peered through the broken windows. As there was no one about he slipped out into the street again and set off, at a walk this time, towards St. James's Square.

He could hardly see from the pain that racked him but he managed to find his way somehow down Curzon Street, through Lansdowne Passage and up Berkeley Street.

Normally the walk from South Audley Street to St. James's Square would not have taken him more than fifteen minutes, but he was so exhausted that he had to go very slowly. The street lamps were only on at half-pressure and there was no traffic except for an occasional police car or military lorry. There were a few pedestrians hurrying along here or there and a certain number of police patrolling in couples, but wherever Derek saw these he avoided them by crossing to the other side of the road.

He instinctively felt like a hunted criminal and, in any case, his state might have caused them to ask questions.

Crossing Piccadilly, he turned down St. James's Street, along King Street and at last entered St. James's Square. Staggering up the steps of Sam Curry's house, he rang the bell and banged violently with the knocker. Almost at once the door was thrown open and Hemmingway stood there framed against a dim light in the hall.

'Good God!' he exclaimed, as Derek clutched at him and fell forward on the mat; and, hauling him to his feet, he went on angrily: 'Where the devil have you been, man? I've been waiting here all day for you.'

'I—I got caught—arrested by the police,' Derek muttered. 'I've only just escaped.'

'Never mind that. You can tell me about it later. What have you done with Lavina?'

'I've lost her,' Derek moaned. 'She's imprisoned somewhere but I don't know where.'

A strange light suddenly leapt into Hemmingway's eyes. 'You fool!' he breathed, with menacing quietness. 'If I can't find her I'll break your neck for this.'

14

HEMMINGWAY GOES INTO ACTION

Derek suddenly slumped forward and catching him as he fell, Hemmingway saw that he had fainted. Pulling one of the unconscious man's arms round his neck he heaved him up in a fireman's lift across his shoulders, carried him into the lounge and gently lowered him on to a sofa.

At first, in the dim light of the hall, Hemmingway had not fully grasped the shocking state Derek was in but it was now clear that he had been through a terrible gruelling.

His suit was so torn, bloodstained and dirty that it would have disgraced a tramp. His collar was gone, his tie a rag knotted round his neck; even his shoes were cut and filthy. Sweat, dust and congealed blood matted his light-brown, wavy hair. His left eye was closed and the swollen flesh all round it had a horrid purplish hue. Cuts and abrasions disfigured his regular features and his hands were as grimy as if he had been crawling across a ploughed field.

Crossing the hall to the downstairs cloakroom, Hemmingway picked up a jug to fill it with hot water but as he turned the tap he suddenly remembered that the boilers in the house were out. He himself had had to make do that morning with a quick splash in a cold bath—a thing he hated. Filling the jug with cold water and collecting a couple of towels, he carried them back to Derek and, kneeling down, began to sponge some of the grime off his injured face.

After a few moments Derek began to groan.

'It's all right, old chap. You're safe enough now,' Hemmingway comforted him.

'Lavina,' muttered Derek, coming round. 'Lavina——'

'Yes, I know.' Hemmingway's face darkened. 'But we'll go into that in a moment.'

Walking over to a side-table he mixed a stiff whisky-and-soda.

'Here, drink this,' he said, propping Derek's head up on one arm and holding the glass to his lips.

Derek swallowed some of the whisky, choked a little, and sat up. 'God knows where she is,' he murmured, 'but we've got to find her.'

'Sure.' Hemmingway continued his ministrations with a towel and water. 'But I want to get you cleaned up a bit first, otherwise the dirt will get into those cuts and inflame them. Here, take the towel yourself and do what you can, while I go and put on some hot water.'

Going down to the kitchen he filled the largest kettles he could find and put them on the stove. When he returned, Derek had finished his drink but was lying back on the sofa, evidently too weak to be able even to bathe his wounds.

'Now, d'you think you can tell me your story?' Hemmingway said, sitting down beside him. 'I'm afraid you're pretty done, but I must know what happened before I can go into action.'

Derek nodded weakly and gave a more or less coherent account of what had happened since he had left St. James's Square with Lavina and Roy the previous evening. Hemmingway listened without making a single comment. He was not particularly distressed when he heard of Roy's death, as he only knew him very slightly and had not been at all favourably impressed with what little he had seen of him. With Derek, on the other hand, he was furiously angry. Derek had been responsible for Lavina and it was not his fault that she had not had her brains bashed out by that bottle descending upon *her* head. As it was, they did not know if she was alive or dead and it was going to be the devil's own job to trace her. Hemmingway knew that, if he had been in Derek's shoes, he would have taken Lavina out of the Dorchester no matter what she said—even if he'd had to yank her out by the scruff of the neck—long before the trouble had started. But he did not allow the least sign of his inward feelings to show in his face as he listened to the injured man's story.

When Derek had done, Hemmingway left him again, carried the kettles of hot water up to his own bathroom, got out a clean suit of pyjamas and turned down his bed, which he had re-made himself that morning.

On his return to the lounge Derek asked weakly: 'What had

we better do now? Is it any good trying to telephone anywhere before we set out to try and find her?'

'You can leave all that to me,' Hemmingway replied briefly. 'You're going to bed, my boy. Come on, up you get!'

'But I can't. I've got to , . .' Derek began to protest.

'You're going to do as I tell you. You're about all-in, my friend; and in your present state instead of a help you'd be a hindrance. I doubt if you could walk another hundred yards and you couldn't run if your life depended on it.'

Without further argument he hauled Derek to his feet, supported him up the stairs to the bathroom and began to undress him.

Derek knew that Hemmingway was right as, in a mist of pain, he allowed himself to be stripped and bathed like a child in the luke-warm water to which Hemmingway had added a good ration of disinfectant.

Actually, Hemmingway grudged every moment of the time he was giving to his self-imposed duties as Derek's nurse. The stupid fool deserved all he had got and was lucky to be alive at all, was what he was thinking. But Derek was much too weak to look after himself and Hemmingway had not the heart to leave him, perhaps for many hours, uncared for; so he put a cheerful face on the business and got through with it as quickly as he could.

At last when Derek was rebandaged, his cuts and bruises eased by a liberal application of healing ointment, and safely tucked up in bed, Hemmingway said to him:

'You've lost your own car, I suppose?'

'Yes, we left it outside the Dorchester.'

'Well, fortunately mine's still in the garage at the back of the house. Now get this clearly before you go off to sleep. I'm going out now to try and find Lavina. It's impossible to say how long I'll be, but we've still got the best part of forty-eight hours before the balloon goes up. If I run her to earth I shall bring her back here and we'll all go down in the car to Stapleton together. But if I don't return, you'll know I've had no luck. In that case, after two nights and a day in bed you'll be fit enough to walk down to Stapleton, if need be. Don't wait for us any longer, as we may not get back at all, but start out on your own early in the morning on the day after to-morrow. You ought to make it in about eight hours, allowing for plenty of rests, or less if you can manage to get a lift part of the way. But in the meantime, if you feel fit enough to get up you're not to leave the house because, if I *do* find Lavina, I'll want to get her out of London without the least delay. Have you got that?'

Derek nodded feebly. 'Yes. I wish to God I could come with you, but I can hardly lift a finger. Best of luck!'

'Thanks. I'll need it.' Hemmingway smiled with a friendliness he was far from feeling as he switched out the light and closed the door behind him.

On coming downstairs that morning he had naturally assumed that Lavina, Derek and Roy had returned from their previous night's joy-ride after he had gone to bed and were somewhere in the house still sleeping.

Having made tea, put some eggs on to boil and banged loudly on the gong to let them know that breakfast was nearly ready, he had expected that they would come down in dressing-gowns. When none of them appeared, he had visited their rooms and, finding them empty, realized at once that something very serious must have happened to keep them out all night.

His first thought was to telephone Scotland Yard and the hospitals, but the exchange informed him they were now only working on skeleton staffs and that since six o'clock that morning they had had to refuse all private calls in order to devote the lines exclusively to Government business. They also refused to take any telegrams, which prevented him from communicating either with Sam—who was by that time presumably at the Edmonton factory—or with Stapleton Court to try and ascertain if Lavina's party had, for some reason unknown, decided to drive down there direct during the night after their trip round the West End of London.

He had contemplated personal visits to Scotland Yard and some of his friends in various Government Services; but felt that, with the evacuation of London in full swing, they would all be far too busy to give him any help in a private inquiry where there was so little to go on except the bare fact that three people in a motor-car had failed to return to their home the night before. In addition, he feared that if he once left the house they might turn up in his absence which, if he was not there to set off with them, would further delay their departure to the country.

In consequence, he had decided that the only thing to do was to wait in the house in the hope that they would either come back to it or manage to send him some message to let him know what had happened to them.

He had made several more attempts to use the telephone but by midday the exchange no longer answered him and he could not even get the ringing tone, so now, having attended to Derek, he wasted no time in trying to get through to anybody.

Instead, he went to his private sitting-room, took a large automatic from a drawer, loaded it and put a handful of spare ammunition into his pockets. From another drawer he took a torch and fitted it with a new battery. He then unlocked the safe and, taking out all the money he could find, proceeded to distribute it about his person; some in his pockets for immediate use, but the larger amounts he placed in his shoes where he could not easily be robbed of it.

Downstairs he hunted round till he found a motoring map of London and the Home Counties and filled a flask up with brandy which went into his other hip pocket to balance the gun. He then descended to the basement.

In the scullery he found just what he wanted: a length of stout clothes-line and a bundle of firewood. Picking out the biggest pieces from the bundle, he knotted the rope securely round them so that when he had done he had a line about twelve feet long with the pieces of wood projecting at right-angles to it roughly twelve inches apart. Having removed his coat, he wound the whole contraption round his body and, proceeding to the odd man's room, he took a steel case-opener from the tool chest, stuffed it inside the rope and put on his coat again.

Returning upstairs, he selected a crop from a rack of sticks and sporting impedimenta that belonged to Sam. It was one that Sam had used in the War, made of bamboo covered with leather. The end of it was a fat Turk's-head filled with lead, and with the thong round one's wrist it made a most formidable weapon.

While he was making these preparations Hemmingway was half inclined to laugh at himself; but he had not the faintest idea where he would have to go or what he might have to do during the next twenty-four hours, and although the authorities were still maintaining an outward semblance of control, Derek's experiences showed that London was no longer a law-abiding city. Hemmingway simply wished to ensure his being able to bribe, fight, break in, or face any other emergency with which he might be faced, under the best possible conditions.

Leaving the house and the semi-darkened square, he proceeded east across Lower Regent Street and the Haymarket. The restaurants were all closed now and each had a police guard outside it to prevent looting of its stocks of drink. There were few people about and no traffic, except for patrolling police cars; and it was not until he got down to Trafalgar Square that he saw any considerable number of people.

Religious meetings were still in progress there although, owing to the evacuation, the lateness of the hour and the fact that all public transport services had now been cancelled until further notice, the crowd was nowhere near as large as that which had packed the square the night before. The audiences consisted mainly of those pig-headed citizens who had refused to leave their homes and a certain number of local A.R.P. wardens, fire-fighters, etc., who had come out for an airing while remaining near their posts.

There was no drunkenness or fatalistic jollification among the crowds now. Every public-house in London had been closed by order and the police, who had been issued with revolvers, had received instructions to shoot looters if they made any attempt to resist arrest.

Whitehall was open again but troops were mounting guard over all Government buildings and the entrance to Downing Street was closed by a wooden barricade; yet the lights were burning in nearly all the windows showing that the harassed authorities were still hard at work controlling the evacuation.

Hemmingway turned left towards Scotland Yard and its annexe, Cannon Row police station, but here he found the pavements blocked by a solid jam of people. Only the roadway was being kept open for traffic by the police.

He saw at once that he was not the only person who had come to inquire for friends and relatives. There were several hundred in the two queues before him, all of whom, anxiously silent or quietly sobbing, were in search of missing dear ones.

If he took his place in the rear of one of the queues it was clear that he would have to wait hours before he got anywhere near the police station; so, abandoning that idea, he walked round to the Embankment entrance of Scotland Yard. There was a small queue there, too, but in a few moments he had reached the police sergeant who was dealing with inquiries.

Knowing that Sam's name would carry more weight than his own and gambling on the fact that Sam was not known to the sergeant, he announced boldly:

'I'm Sir Samuel Curry. Would you be good enough to ask Colonel Hodgson if he could possibly spare me a moment?'

The sergeant looked dubious. 'The Assistant Commissioner's frantically busy, sir. I doubt if he can spare time to see anyone.'

'I know. He must be having a gruelling time just now. But, as I'm a personal friend, I think he'll see me if you send my name up.'

'Well, I'll do that, sir, although we don't like to bother him more than we have to. Just wait here a moment.' The sergeant spoke to a telephonist in a small lodge nearby, who put the call through.

An answer came back almost at once and the sergeant reported: 'The Assistant Commissioner says he'll see you, sir, but he may have to keep you waiting a little time. The constable, here, will take you through.'

Suppressing a sigh of relief, Hemmingway passed inside and was led by the constable down a succession of long stone corridors to a bare-looking waiting room. He sat there for some twenty minutes and was then summoned to the Assistant Commissioner's office.

Colonel Hodgson was a shrewd-eyed, wiry-haired man nearing fifty. He looked very tired as he had been working almost continuously for the last week, snatching only an hour or two's sleep in the building when nature absolutely demanded it, but his manner was still calm and cheerful.

'Hullo! You're not Sam Curry,' he said at once, as Hemmingway entered the room.

'No, sir,' Hemmingway apologized, 'but I'm his confidential secretary and I'm acting for him. I know you're a friend of his so I used his name to get in.'

The Colonel nodded. 'All right. Since you're in, let's hear what's brought you. But for God's sake don't waste my time on trifles.'

As briefly as he possibly could Hemmingway gave particulars of Lavina's disappearance.

'I'm sorry Sam's young wife's got herself into trouble,' the Colonel said, when Hemmingway had finished. 'She deserves a lesson, though, for going out at a time like this. Respectable people ought to set an example and aid us rather than hinder us in this hellish mess we've got to handle.'

'I know that, sir. But what's done is done, and it's up to me to find her.'

'I'm afraid I can't help you much there. Thousands of women have been brought in; far too many for us to keep any sort of register.'

'I see. But surely you can tell me where your people would have taken her?'

'She'll be in one of the encampments for women. As she was arrested at the Dorchester, the one in the grounds of Buckingham Palace is the most likely.'

'Then I'll try that first, and the others afterwards if necessary. Perhaps your secretary could give me a list of them?'

'Yes. There are seven altogether, but it'll be like looking for a needle in a haystack and, even if you do find out where she is, you won't be able to do anything about it.'

'I want to take her to the country and I imagine, sir, that you'd have no objection to giving me an order for her release?'

A telephone buzzer sounded on the Colonel's desk. He picked up the instrument and was talking down it for the next few moments. When he had done, he turned back to Hemmingway.

' I'm sorry, but that's impossible. Of course, the great majority of the people who have been rounded-up are only drunks; but hundreds of lives have been lost in these riots, property's been destroyed and goods stolen. If the comet doesn't hit us, every one of the prisoners will have to go before a tribunal; some will be charged with manslaughter, others with looting, and so on. But as we have no particulars of what any individual will be charged with yet, it's quite out of the question for us to release anyone.'

'But Lady Curry's not a thief or a murderer.'

'Of course not, my dear fellow, but she must have been arrested for something; even if it was only participating in a riotous assembly. And, until she's been charged and either proved innocent or guilty, we've got to hold her. You must see for yourself that we can't make exceptions.'

'But, Colonel, her cousin was killed before her eyes last night. She's probably half off her head with worry.'

'I'm sorry. But, if she's a hospital case, she'll receive medical attention. Anyway, she'll fare no worse than thousands of others and they're all being fed and looked after. They'll be as safe in the open parks as anywhere. That's why we put them there. They'd be no better off in the open country. Now, I really can't give you any more time.'

Hemmingway saw that it was useless to argue further so he thanked the Colonel for seeing him, obtained from his secretary a list of the women's encampments in the London area, and left the building.

The encampments were scattered far and wide. One was on Wimbledon Common, another in Greenwich Park, a third on Hampstead Heath. The garden of Buckingham Palace was the only one anywhere near West Central London and, as Derek had been taken straight to Hyde Park, it seemed almost certain that Lavina would have been taken to the Palace grounds rather than to one of the more distant camps.

It was getting on for one in the morning as Hemmingway set out at a good pace across Parliament Square and along Bird-cage Walk. Outside the Palace, where great multitudes had congregated on the previous nights, there was now only a small crowd of about fifty people. They stood in a ragged line, staring through the railings at the scene that was proceeding in the court yard.

There, long rows of closed vans were drawn up, numbering, Hemmingway estimated at a rough guess, well over a couple of hundred. Khaki-clad troops were moving about among them and the driver on the box of each was a soldier.

As Hemmingway halted outside one of the main gates it was thrown open and six of the vans drove out. Almost immediately afterwards another fleet came round the corner, from Constitution Hill, and drove in at the other entrance.

'What's going on?' Hemmingway asked one of the onlookers.

'They're evacuating the women,' replied the man, laconically.

'Hell!' Hemmingway exclaimed. 'D'you know where they're taking them?'

'Not for certain. They do say, though, that they're loading them on to ships down at the Docks because they reckon they'll be safer out at sea. Why? Have you lost your wife or something?'

'Yes,' Hemmingway agreed, to avoid entering into long explanations.

'Thanks very much,' he added, and made off quickly.

This new move on the part of the authorities further complicated his problem. Evidently, the decision to evacuate the women prisoners had been made during the last hour or two and Colonel Hodgson, having been busy upon other matters, either knew nothing about it or had forgotten to mention it. The odds were all in favour of Lavina's having been taken to the Palace garden after her arrest; but was she still there or was she in one of the vans on her way to an unknown destination?

If the latter was the case, Hemmingway knew that his chance of finding her would be rendered almost impossibly slender. His one hope now lay in the fact that the Colonel had said there were several thousand women in the garden. It would take some hours to evacuate them all and, if he could get into the garden at once, there was just a possibility that he might discover her before she was carted off in one of the vans.

The next thing was to get into the gardens. He knew that he stood no chance at all of penetrating to them by the front way, through the Palace Courtyards. The sentries would never let him pass without credentials. He had got to make his way in, therefore, by some illegal method.

The grounds of the Palace formed a rough triangle, with the Palace itself making a blunt apex at the eastern end. The south-eastern side of the great walled enclosure was occupied by the Royal Stables, which were certain to be policed, so there was little prospect of getting in there. The north-eastern side ran parallel with Constitution Hill, up to Hyde Park Corner. A narrow belt of railed-off park, only a few feet deep, lay between the roadway and the wall of the Palace garden. As the belt had trees in it, that would certainly provide the best cover for any attempt to scale the wall but, for that very reason, it was almost certain that a chain of police would be keeping every foot of it under observation.

The third side of the triangle ran north and south the whole length of Grosvenor Place, and here the garden wall abutted on the pavement. There was no cover of any kind for anyone who tried to climb it, but the fact that the whole length of the wall was exposed to view rendered it much less likely to be heavily guarded; so Hemmingway decided to make his attempt from that direction.

Turning right, he set off up Constitution Hill and he saw at once that his surmise, that this side of the Palace grounds would be well watched, had good foundations. He encountered six policemen between the Palace and Hyde Park Corner and he doubted if a cat could have got over the railing—let alone the wall—without having been spotted by one of them.

Rounding the corner of the grounds he proceeded south, down Grosvenor Place, which formed the longest side of the triangle. A shabby woman shambled past him, then the broad pavement stretched away empty as far as he could see, except for two small figures in the far distance.

As he walked on he saw that they were two policemen who were advancing towards him. A long line of lorries, coming up from the direction of Victoria, rumbled past just as he came level with the officers. They took no notice of him and he covered another hundred yards which brought him about half-way down the western base of the triangle with the Palace almost opposite to him at its apex.

Pausing, he looked round and saw that the policemen were walking slowly on. He guessed that when they reached Hyde Park Corner they would turn and come south again; so he had no time to lose. The road was now empty of traffic and he could not see any casual pedestrians on its far side. The street lamps were burning only at half-pressure and every twenty yards the trees growing out of the pavement, being in full leaf threw a good patch of shadow.

Halting beneath one of them, he rapidly unwound his length of clothes-line, with the wooden struts knotted across it, from beneath his coat. At one end he formed a loop; then he ran softly forward to the wall.

If it had been designed for the special purpose of helping un-authorized persons to get over it easily it could not have been better planned. True, it was some twelve feet in height but, instead of having broken-glass on its top, it had a long, iron rail running a foot above it from which spikes protruded in all directions. Originally, perhaps, the spikes had been intended to revolve so that no weight could be attached to them, but many years of rust and coats of paint had now made them immovable.

At the second cast the loop at the end of Hemmingway's line caught over one of the strong, iron spikes. Blessing himself for his forethought in having brought this rough scaling ladder he grabbed at the pieces of firewood nearest above his head and swarmed up to it.

Just as he gained the top of the wall and was negotiating the iron rail to which the spikes were attached the policemen reached the end of their beat, turned, and saw him.

'Hi, there!' they shouted in unison. The shrill blast of whistles shattered the silence of the night and they both began to run; but Hemmingway, now perched on the iron rail, unhurriedly drew up his rope-ladder.

Panting and flushed, the policemen arrived below him. 'Come down off there,' bellowed one.

Hemmingway laughed in gentle mockery.

'Come up and get me,' he replied, knowing perfectly well that he had them on toast. They could not reach him except by one of them clambering on the other's shoulder and, if they attempted that, he could slip down on the far side of the wall; while, as there was no gate into the garden for at least five hundred yards in either direction, by the time they got inside he could easily have lost himself among the trees.

'Come down at once!' shouted one of the policemen angrily.

Hemmingway shook his head. 'Please don't excite yourselves. I've no intention of trying to assassinate the King or rob the Palace. I'm just looking for a young woman who's been brought into the encampment. I think, for your own sakes, your wisest plan would be not even to report that you've seen me.'

Having let his rope down on the garden side of the wall, he waved the police a cheerful good night and lowered himself to the ground. A flick of the wrist detached the rope from the spike by which it hung and he re-coiled it round his body in case it might come in useful again later on. He then buttoned his double-breasted jacket about him and set off at a brisk pace through the night-enshrouded garden.

On the west side of the grounds there were many trees, so he had to flash his torch here and there to see where he was going, but he found a path and soon afterwards came upon two of the women prisoners.

They were lying side by side under a tree, each wrapped up in a blanket and with their heads upon small, hard pillows such as those which are issued to troops in barracks.

A beam of the torch showed that neither of them was Lavina, so Hemmingway passed on; encountering more and more of these sleeping figures as he advanced.

Here and there couples or groups, still wakeful, sat talking together in low voices and, as his torch picked them out, a few of them called to him; asking the time or just cursing him for flashing his light in their eyes. But, assuming that he was one of the detectives in charge of them, they took no further notice when he did not reply.

Owing to the darkness it was impossible for him to estimate how many women were being kept captive behind the high walls of the huge, rambling garden which covered an area as big as St. James's Park; but the farther he penetrated, the more numerous the women became. As he flashed his light from side to side on each group in turn his progress was slow, but he gradually made his way round the north side of the lake and came out on to the open slope which runs down to it from the terrace at the back of the Palace. Many of the windows at the back of the Palace were still lit and the light they gave was sufficient to disclose a sight that made his heart sink with dismay. The whole great lawn was covered for as far as he could see with figures rolled in blankets.

In the distance, towards its southern end, he saw that there was considerable movement and, picking his way forward among the sleeping forms, he advanced up the slope; still flashing his torch from side to side in the hope of spotting Lavina as he went.

He found that the movement was concentrated round two large marquees where tea and food were being served to any of the women who wanted it in the groups that were being quietly rounded-up for evacuation by a number of Tommies.

Batches of about a hundred prisoners were being roused at a time, passed through the marquees and thence into the south-eastern courtyard of the Palace where Hemmingway could just discern some vans.

No one took any notice of him as, in the constantly shifting throng, there were a number of plain-clothes men among the uniformed police, troops and herds of women. Pocketing his torch, he slipped inside one of the marquees, knowing that the light in it would enable him to see more women at one time than he could by flashing his torch about on the people outside.

Behind a long trestle-table a number of well-dressed but tired-looking women were handing out cups of tea, bread and butter and buns to the dejected-looking captives before them. Some of them were bandaged for wounds they had received; the faces of others were tear-stained and drawn with anxiety. All of them were dirty and dishevelled.

In vain Hemmingway searched for Lavina's golden head. She was not among them. Leaving that marquee, he crossed the intervening space and entered the other. The scene was the same; a low murmur of voices, tear-stained and dejected faces. But Lavina was not there either.

It was just as he was going out that the face of one of the ladies behind a tea-urn struck him as familiar, and a second later he realized that it was the Queen. Of course, he thought, since she and the King are remaining in London, she would be here. How tired she's looking, but how splendid.

As he left the tent the batch of captives in it were quietly moved on towards the courtyard. He turned in the other direction and began to flash his torch again among the new groups of women who were being roused for their journey. Nobody questioned him, as many of the officers and police were also using flash-lamps. Now and again his light flickered on golden hair, raising his hopes only to disappoint him, as haggard face after haggard face came for a second into the torch's beam.

He had realized from the beginning that it was useless to ask if anyone had seen her. The only thing he could say was that he was searching for Lady Curry, a slim, good-looking girl of twenty-three, with golden hair and aquiline features. To inquire for her as Lavina Leigh would have been little better as, after her thirty hours as a prisoner, she could hardly now be recognizable as the beautifully-groomed film star.

Again and again Hemmingway ran his eye over fresh batches of women as they were brought into the marquees. In between whiles he returned to the crowded lawn or penetrated as far as the courtyard where the women were being shepherded into the vans. Hundreds of the prisoners had been removed during the time he had been searching, yet only the eastern end of the lawn showed signs that the evacuation was making any progress.

Glancing at his watch, he realized that he had been in the grounds for three hours already and it would take hours yet before the whole great garden could be cleared of the thousands of prisoners.

His main hope now was that Lavina might be sleeping in a far part of the garden so that daylight would have come before she was collected into one of the batches. He knew that in the semi-darkness by the marquees he must be missing scores of women as they were led away, however frantically he looked to right and left; whereas, once dawn came, he would be able to scan each batch as it was shepherded into the courtyard. Tired and dis-spirited by this constant searching, which necessitated his turning his head first one way and then another without intermission, he began to fear that his task was completely hopeless.

At a quarter past four he visited the courtyard again. Another line of closed vans had been drawn up. The women were being helped into them by the soldiers and as each van was filled its door was locked behind them so that they could not jump out when the vans had left the Palace yard.

Suddenly, as the last van in the line of six was being loaded, he caught sight of a slim, golden-haired girl being helped up into it. Although he only glimpsed her for a moment, he felt certain it was Lavina and, all his depression gone in a second, he rushed forward. As he reached the van the last woman scrambled into it; a Guardsman slammed-to the door, an Officer locked it and handed the key to a Sergeant.

'Stop!' panted Hemmingway. 'Lady Curry's in that van. I've been searching for her all night.'

The Officer gave him a surprised glance. 'Who're you? What are you doing here?' he asked quickly.

'I've just told you. I've been searching for Lady Curry and I've only just spotted her. Please unlock that door again.'

'Sorry.' The Officer shook his head and signed to the Sergeant, who saluted and turned away. 'It's too late now. My orders are to get these women out of here with the least possible delay.'

'But please,' Hemmingway pleaded, as the right-hand van in the line began to move. 'It won't take you a minute to get the key back and unlock that door. She's ill from shock and I've got to get her down to the country.'

'Sorry,' the Officer repeated. 'I couldn't release her, in any case, without an order.'

'Then at least let me speak to her.'

The second and third vans were now moving towards the outer courtyard. The fourth was just about to follow.

'No time now,' the Officer said firmly. 'You can see for yourself the convoy's moving off.'

'Then, for God's sake, let me go with her.'

As Hemmingway spoke the fifth van ran forward and the sixth followed. The Officer shrugged helplessly but, now he had sighted it, Hemmingway was determined not to lose his quarry. Darting past the Officer, he raced the moving van and leapt up on to the box beside the driver.

'What the hell?' exclaimed the soldier as Hemmingway subsided, panting, beside him.

'It's all right,' he gasped. 'A friend of mine's inside your van. There was no time to get her out so the Officer said I could come along with you.'

'Oh, in that case—' the driver shrugged. 'Got a cigarette on you?'

Hemmingway produced his case and, as his van followed the convoy out of the front courtyard of the Palace into the Mall, the man took one.

From Trafalgar Square they turned into Northumberland Avenue and headed for the Embankment. As they ran smoothly through the almost deserted streets Hemmingway was considering his next move. Everybody seemed to have a definite order that none of the prisoners were to be released without a written sanction. If he waited until the van got to its destination the probability was that another Officer there would refuse Lavina her freedom. Was it possible to bribe the driver to halt the van on the way down and get her out before they arrived at the place they were bound for?'

'D'you want to earn a fiver?' he asked the man quietly.

'Does a monkey like his nuts?' replied the driver, with a grin.

'Then, it's easy money for you,' Hemmingway went on. 'My girl-friend is inside and yours is the last van in the convoy. Pull up when they turn the corner under the Bridge into Queen Victoria Street as though you'd had engine trouble. Unlock the van so that I can get my girl out, and the fiver's yours with my eternal blessing.'

'No go, Guv'nor,' said the soldier regretfully. 'I don't suppose

they'd miss her. What's one piece of skirt in all these truck-loads?
And I'd be happy to oblige you, but I haven't got the key.'

'Who has, then?'

'The Sergeant, who's riding on the leading van.'

'Well,' said Hemmingway, thinking of the steel case opener
under his coat, which was digging into his ribs now that he was
sitting down, 'I shouldn't imagine the lock's very strong. We
could break it open.'

'Maybe we could, but we're not going to. Think I'm going to
be crimed for busting His Majesty's property and helping
prisoners to escape? Not likely!'

'I'll make it a tenner,' Hemmingway offered.

The driver shook his head. 'Sorry, mate, but it can't be done;
not if you made it fifty. In ordinary times I might have chanced it
for ten or twenty quid—staged a little plot about you knocking
me out or something—but in these days it just isn't worth it.
They court-martial people for as little as blinkin' an eyelid;
though, mind you, with all the trouble they're having and no
sleep or anything, I don't blame 'em. But I'm not taking any
chances of being pooped in a cell because I want to be free to
run for it when the old comet arrives.'

Where he proposed to run to he did not specify, but, seeing
that further attempts to bribe him were quite useless, Hemmingway had to contain his impatience as well as he could for the
rest of the journey.

They ran on past the Mansion House, down Cornhill, Leaden-
hall Street and Aldgate, to the East End. In the Commercial
Road Hemmingway noticed that many of the shops had been
looted; but all was quiet now except for patrolling squads of
police and an occasional armoured car rolling by on its solid
rubber wheels.

At last they veered south and, a few minutes later, passed
through the gates of the West India Dock. Crossing railway lines
and bridges, they wound their way between Customs sheds and
dark out-buildings until they eventually pulled up on a wharf-
side to which a big ship was moored. There were a dozen other
vans there besides those of the convoy with which Hemmingway
had come, and the women from the earlier arrivals were already
moving slowly up the gangways under big arc-lights into the ship.

Hemmingway got down, said good-bye to the driver, and

waited patiently at the back of the van until the Sergeant came along and unlocked it. The van was pitch-dark inside and a blowsy woman fell out when the doors were opened. As she was helped to her feet she let out a stream of blasphemous curses.

'Steady there,' said the Sergeant. 'Letting fly at us won't do any good.'

An officer who had come up added: 'For your own sakes, as well as ours, please don't make a fuss. We're going to put you in this ship, where you'll be well fed and taken care of. As soon as you're all on board it will take you out into the estuary of the Thames.'

'Little trip to Southend, eh?' said a fat old woman jovially.

'That's it, mother,' laughed the officer. 'We're giving you a holiday for nothing and we want you to make the best of it. You'll be much safer out there in the ship, too, than you would be in London.'

Hemmingway was standing just behind the officer, craning his head to catch the first glimpse of Lavina as she scrambled out of the van. The arc-lamps suddenly glinted upon golden hair. It was a natural blonde, but a second later, he saw the blue-eyed, haggard face beneath it; and his heart seemed to sink into his boots. It was not Lavina.

15

THE GREAT EVACUATION

Although at times Hemmingway felt things very deeply, he was not given to showing his emotions freely. He had learned in adversity that it is only waste of time to lose control of one's feelings, for, like many successful people, he had had a hard struggle in his early days.

His father had been one of those old-fashioned professors who coupled a brilliant brain with a congenital disability to make or keep money. Even when the Professor had left his native city of Cardiff to take up the Chair in Mathematics which he had been offered at a minor American University, and so passed to what was for him comparative affluence, he had consistently fallen a prey to every rogue in the matter of his small investments; and he had an incurable habit of lending money to people who never paid him back. In addition, instead of marrying one of America's ten thousand heiresses, he had married one of America's ten million nice girls who have no money at all.

That she, too, had brains and could write interesting little monographs upon such subjects as Ming porcelain and the use of cosmetics in Ancient Egypt did not materially help the family budget.

In one respect Hemmingway's inheritance was remarkably rich; as he had not only derived a remarkable flair for figures from his father but also a wide knowledge and love of all things beautiful from his mother. But in the material sense they had been able to do practically nothing for him at all.

His parents had been vague, kindly, untidy people, living in a world of ideas that far transcended any sort of social round or even the calls of their own kitchen. They had lived mostly on tinned foods, grudgingly served by a succession of hired helps who despised them for their lack of practicability and robbed them unmercifully, although they never knew it. No one ever came to the house except visiting intellectuals, and when money ran short they just sacked the hired help, barely noticing the difference, and pigged it on their own until they could afford to engage a new one.

In consequence, Hemmingway's childhood had been an exceptionally lonely one. He never went to parties or played with the neighbours' children, so by the time he went to school he had not acquired the common basis upon which most youthful friendships are formed and was already something of a mystic. Added to which, he was mentally so far in advance of the other children of his age that they either disliked or were vaguely frightened of him. Only the fact that he was physically strong saved him from serious bullying, and after a time his schoolfellows were content to leave him to himself.

On the other hand, this isolation had its advantages; since, if his parents neglected him in other respects, they watched and tended the development of his brain with all the loving care that any horticulturist ever lavished on a black tulip.

Fortunately for all concerned, he loved reading and took to learning like a duck to water; so that during those countless hours when he should have been playing Redskins or Robbers with his contemporaries he was mastering subjects which few boys study until they have reached the University. He took scholarship examinations as a joke, so his education was little strain upon his thriftless parents; but it was after he had passed out of the University that his real troubles began.

It is one thing to have brains and quite another to convert them into money. He was a lanky, untidy youth in ill-fitting clothes. He lacked every social grace and had not even attempted to master the simplest sports. Moreover, he had not a single friend in the world who could be counted on to assist his advancement, except those connected with the scholastic profession; and that, with the example of his father before him, he was determined not to enter.

Although his reading had covered a multitude of subjects by no means all of them had been of a learned nature. Through autobiographies and magazines he was just as familiar with the social functions of a London Season as he was with the quantum theory; and, quite definitely, he wanted to qualify by means of money, personality and achievement for a place among the ruling

classes of the Anglo-Saxon world. Yet, how to set about it he
had not the faintest idea.

Having no money, he decided to travel; which may sound a
paradox, but is certainly not so in the case of a young man
brought up in the United States. For two terms he slaved as a
junior usher—a job he hated—at a local day school; but it
enabled him to save enough to pay his fare to Europe, and during
the next eighteen months he hiked through a dozen countries.

He found it intensely interesting to see the historic places of
which he had read. Contact with people of various nationalities
broadened his views immensely, and it enabled him to get into
true perspective the political theories that he had formulated.
But at the end of that time he suddenly woke up to the fact that,
although tramping from city to city and doing odd jobs for a
week or two here and there in order to earn his keep provided an
excellent appendix to his magnificent education, it simply was
not getting him anywhere at all. He was just as far from a seat
in the Houses of Parliament or on the Board of the Bank of
England as he had been two years before on leaving his University,
and certainly no nearer to the Royal Enclosure at Ascot.

After a spell of work as translator for a German publisher in
Bremen he had made enough to pay his passage home, and he
settled in New York with the determination to carve out a career
for himself just as millions of young men had done before him.

Yet that was far easier determined than accomplished. Apart
from physical labour, teaching and translating seemed to be his
only marketable assets. He wrote some short stories and a novel,
but no one would take them. It seemed that he had not that kind
of mind. He made few friends, although he gradually bettered
his appearance and was quick to pick up social mannerisms on
the rare occasions when he was able to mix with moneyed people
of culture.

For three years he maintained a bitter struggle, taking job
after job to keep himself alive, but he chucked one after the
other directly he realized that each was nothing but a blind alley
and had saved a few weeks' rent.

Towards the end of that time he took a job as a professional
guide to a New York tourist agency. He knew the city well by
then, and few people could have done better justice to the Art
collections and antiques in its museums. In taking the job

he had hoped that he would at least come into contact with a number of interesting people and, perhaps, improve himself by going about with them; but he was bitterly disappointed.

Nine out of ten of the visitors whom he had to take round were idle, stupid people with more money than sense. The magnificent Egyptian collection in the Metropolitan Museum bored them to tears. Most of them did not know a Van Dyck from a Reubens, and when he took them to the Indian Museum, where treasures can be seen from the whole American continent which have no counterpart in any European collection, they grumbled bitterly because it was six miles from the centre of the city and they considered the time involved in a visit practically wasted.

All that most of them wanted to see was the view from the top of the Empire State Building, the great cinemas and stores, and, particularly, the night haunts. Both women and men kept him up taking them to places until the small hours of the morning, so that he found himself jaded and exhausted when he had to report to the office to take on another sightseer at 10 o'clock the following morning.

He made up his mind to chuck that too as soon as he had saved enough in tips—which was practically all he got out of it—to lay off for a little and look for something else. But, all unknown to him, his lucky star was just about to appear above the horizon.

Sir Samuel Curry had been in New York on a business trip. Negotiations had hung fire owing to the illness of an American steel king and were not completed until 'Sam' had missed his boat by a couple of hours; so he had found himself in New York with nothing to do for three days until he could leave for England on the next.

He had often visited New York before but it occurred to him now that it might be rather an idea to see something of the place outside its social life, which he already knew well. He decided that, anyhow, he would devote a day to looking round; the other two could easily be passed with the host of hospitable Americans who had only to be rung up and would be delighted to entertain him.

The hotel had a tie-up with the agency with which Hemmingway worked, so he was sent along to report to Sam and they spent the day together. Sam was not really a brilliant man. His success was due to clear-headedness, honesty in his business dealings, a colossal capacity for hard work, and a flair for employing people in the right places who were more gifted than himself.

When they parted that evening Sam had not rung up any of his American friends with the idea of filling in his next two days. Instead, he told Hemmingway to report again the following morning. He had been struck by the unusual way in which Hemmingway quite casually assessed artistic trends and ancient customs in terms of money.

Having found, for once, an interested listener, he explained, while taking Sam round the museums, how changes of climate had made or wrecked historic markets; how fortunes had been made by modern designers who were clever enough to study and adopt ancient fashions; how the germ of every modern invention had preceded it by hundreds of years, but remained undeveloped through lack of initiative or capital. But always there was that quiet preoccupation with finance applied to encyclopædic knowledge—the kind of knowledge that not one financier in a thousand possessed.

On the second night Sam kept Hemmingway to dine with him at the Ritz Carlton, and they talked upon a multitude of subjects which did not ordinarily come into the sphere of a professional guide. By that time Sam was absolutely convinced that in this tall, wise-eyed young man he had got something; and details never mattered to Sam once he had made up his mind about a thing. When they parted that night he said:

'Tell the agency to-morrow morning that you're leaving. I'll pay them compensation if necessary. Here's a thousand dollars to pay any bills you may have and buy any odds-and-ends you want. Pack your bags and meet me here at 8 o'clock to-morrow night. The *Normandie* sails at 10 and I'm taking you with me to Europe.'

Hemmingway's big chance had come. He asked no questions, neither did he give way to the immense elation he felt and pour out a spate of jumbled thanks. He just gave that sudden radiant smile of his and said:

'Thank you, sir. I'll be here.'

From that moment Hemmingway was made. On the voyage back Sam saw that he was no young man to put into an ordinary job, however good. He was so vastly knowledgeable, so sound in all his views, that he would be infinitely more valuable as an ideas man and an assessor before whom to place all sorts of knotty problems for a fresh, clear, logical opinion.

When Hemmingway arrived in London he stepped into another world—the world he had dreamed of for years. Sam installed him in St. James's Square, introduced him to his friends, and taught him the intricacies of his many businesses. Soon Hemmingway was formulating a score of new schemes for investing Sam's surplus profits, and Sam found himself never taking any major decision without talking it over with him first.

Very wisely Sam never made him a director of any of his companies, as he did not want Hemmingway's energies dissipated in the tiresome routine of board meetings. He worked alone in his room at St. James's Square and remained, outwardly, no more than Sam's private secretary; but within a few months he had mastered the essentials of Sam's innumerable interests, and in the following seven years he made him another million.

His salary was princely and, with the handsome presents that Sam made him after every successful deal they pulled off together, he now had many thousands of pounds' worth of investments of his own. That Sam would do nothing without him was known in big business circles; so, in spite of his lack of official position in any of the companies, he had power, influence and prestige.

Hemmingway never forgot that he owed it all to Sam, and that was why he was so intensely worried about Lavina. He liked her personally for a variety of reasons. She was beautiful to look at, which pleased his artistic eye; and, although he had really seen very little of her, he had already discovered that she was much better read than most young women. Further, he had soon discerned that under her gay and almost flighty manner she possessed real character.

Some people had shaken their heads when they heard that Sam was marrying a beautiful girl nearly twenty-five years younger than himself, but, as soon as Hemmingway had had a chance to sum Lavina up, he had come to the conclusion that Sam's friends had no real cause to worry. Whether the marriage would prove lasting it was impossible to say, but he felt quite convinced that Lavina was intrinsically a decent person. Whatever she might do later if Sam proved incapable of holding her affections, she would not make a fool of him or get herself talked about behind his back; and that to Hemmingway was the really important thing about modern marriage.

His may have been a cynical view, but it was based upon the only principle to which he had ever adhered: that it didn't matter very much what people did providing they never betrayed a trust or let each other down.

That was what troubled him so as he stood gloomily on the dockside in the early hours of the morning. Derek and Roy might be considered as the people really responsible for getting Lavina to Stapleton, but, since one was dead and the other *hors de combat*, that responsibility had, he felt, devolved on him the previous night.

Sam so patently adored his young wife and Hemmingway knew him so intimately that he felt it would absolutely break him up if Lavina could not be found before the arrival of the comet. In his failure to trace her he was letting Sam down, and it was Sam who had given him everything for which he had always longed.

The convoy of vans was now empty and the last of the women from them were making their way up the gangways of the ship. Should he get a lift on one of the vans, if they were going back to the Palace, or should he remain there at the docks watching the new arrivals? If he went back, he might pass Lavina in one of the numerous convoys which must be on their way to the East End at the moment. The journey back, too, meant wasting precious time when he might be scanning faces in the hope of finding hers; from that point of view it seemed better to remain where he was. On the other hand, it was improbable that all the convoys were arriving at the West India Dock. Many of them would doubtless be dispatched to others and he could not be at half a dozen docks at once.

It was a horrible dilemma, but another convoy was already arriving, and with every batch of women that he could see there came another chance of spotting Lavina, so he walked over at once to the place where the new arrivals were unloading.

As he reached them a big Buick drove up alongside of him. Its chauffeur was a naval Petty Officer and a naval Staff Captain jumped out of the back immediately it drew to a halt.

Hemmingway's face suddenly brightened. Here, at last, was somebody he knew, and he called out excitedly:

'Renshaw! Renshaw!'

'Why, if it isn't Hemmingway Hughes!' exclaimed the N.O. 'What the devil are you doing here?'

'I'm in the hell of a fix.' Hemmingway grabbed him by the arm. 'Sam Curry's wife was arrested two nights ago because she happened to be at the Dorchester when a riot started. God knows where they've taken her! But I've got to find her somehow and get her down to Sam, who's expecting us both in Surrey.'

'I see.' Captain Renshaw rubbed his nose thoughtfully with one finger. 'D'you know where she was taken after her arrest?'

'No. But, presumably, Buckingham Palace, as that was the nearest camp for women prisoners. I've spent the best part of the night in the grounds, but there's such thousands of women there that I couldn't have seen more than one in ten. Then I thought I spotted her being put into one of these vans and came down with the driver on the box. But it turned out to be the wrong woman.'

'I wish I could help you, old chap, but I don't see how I can.'

'Are you in charge of things here?'

'The Admiralty's taken over all shipping and are responsible for this evacuation by water of the women in the camps. My job is to see the Buckingham Palace lot safely off.'

'Are they all going from this dock?'

'Lord, no! We're using every dock in London.'

'But not at the same time, surely?'

'Oh, no. As soon as we fill a ship we direct the convoys by wireless to another dock.'

'Then, at least you know where they'll be embarking the women from the Palace when they've finished here.'

'Yes.' Renshaw shuffled some papers and looked at a list. 'We're filling the S.S. *Halcyon* in the East India Dock next. As soon as I've finished here you can come with me if you like.'

'Thanks. That's darn good of you.'

For the next ten minutes Hemmingway stood aside while Renshaw received reports, checked lists, and signed documents. Then the two of them got into the Buick and drove round to the East India Dock.

On the way Hemmingway said: 'There's another thing. If I *do* find her, she'll still be under arrest. Is there any way I can persuade the authorities to release her?'

Renshaw laughed. 'My dear fellow, once the women are handed over to us by the Military on the dockside, I'm the authority concerned; so there won't be any trouble about that. If she's committed a murder or anything, I may be called on to answer for her afterwards, but I hardly think Sam's wife would have done anything of that kind, so I'm game to chance it.'

'Well, that's a load off my mind,' Hemmingway sighed. 'The next thing is to find her. If only she hasn't been shipped off before I got down here.'

At the East India Dock more vans were already arriving and scores more women, some dumb with distress, others screaming protests, were being embarked on another ship. There was a chance that Lavina might have been sent on board, but Captain Renshaw dealt with that possibility by walking over to a police car which had a loud-speaker attachment on its top.

After a few words with the Inspector who was in it the loud-speaker began to boom: 'Lady Curry! Lady Curry! Will Lady Curry report to this car at once if she is on S.S. *Halcyon* or on the dockside.'

When the loud-speaker had been calling for a little time without result they came to the conclusion that Lavina was not on board, or else too distraught by her experiences even to be conscious that someone was searching for her.

More and more convoys arrived, and as each was unloaded the loud-speaker blared its message again. For half an hour Hemmingway stood beside Captain Renshaw watching the embarkation; and then, at last, his heart gave a sudden thump of excitement. A slim, golden-headed figure detached itself from the crowd and came walking slowly towards them.

'Lavina!' he cried, as he ran to meet her. 'Lavina!'

She did not increase her pace. Under the arc-lamps he saw that her face was deadly pale and that her footsteps dragged wearily. As he reached her she halted, extended both her hands, gave a faint smile and suddenly collapsed upon his chest, weeping hysterically.

He half-led, half-carried her to Renshaw's Buick and, getting her inside, began to pat her hands and soothe her as well as he could.

F

'It's all right,' he murmured. 'It's all right now we've found you. You're with friends, and you've got nothing more to worry about.'

'Oh, Hemmingway!' she sighed, recovering a little. 'I can't tell you how glad I am to see you. I've had a frightful time, simply frightful! And poor Roy was killed. Did you know?'

'Yes, yes. Derek told me all about it.'

'Is he—is he all right?'

'Yes. They took him to a camp in Hyde Park where he was half-murdered and robbed; but he managed to escape when everybody went wild just after sunset last night. I put him to bed when he got to St. James's Square and came out to look for you myself.'

'Oh, bless you!' She turned a pathetic, tear-stained little face up to him, and her eyes seemed much larger than usual. 'Sam always said that you were a wonderful person and now I know it's true. I can't think how you managed to trace me, but it's heaven to see that big forehead of yours and those queer eyes you've got, again.'

'I almost gave up hope when I started to hunt through that huge crowd in the grounds of Buckingham Palace,' Hemmingway smiled.

'You were there, then?'

'Yes. I got in over the wall, but I couldn't find you. Actually, we have to thank Captain Renshaw that you're here with me now. We have to thank him, too, for having promised to release you from arrest.'

Renshaw, who was standing by the open door of the car, touched his gold-braided cap and grinned. 'I hope I'm not compounding the escape of a felon. You haven't pinched the Crown Jewels or anything, have you?'

She smiled at him and held out a slender hand. 'No. I was only one of the drunks and disorderlies. If you'll let me off, I'll promise never to do it again. I'm most terribly grateful to you.'

'Oh, it's nothing,' he took her hand and pressed it. 'I'm delighted to have been able to help you, Lady Curry. Sam's an old friend of mine. But may I ask what you mean to do now?'

'Sam's down at Stapleton, Lady Curry's old home near Dorking,' Hemmingway said. 'He must be half-frantic by this time from not knowing what's happened to her. Somehow or other I must get her down to Stapleton just as soon as I can.'

'I wonder if that would be best?' Renshaw said thoughtfully.

'God knows what this comet's going to do to us! I'm not in the habit of getting the wind up, but I did after sundown last night. We don't often see an Admiral kissing his lady secretary before all and sundry; but that's how it was. And when the telephone started to ring I picked it up and smashed the bally thing myself. Just couldn't help it. I simply had to. They'll dock it off my pay, I expect. But it's a pretty unnerving business and, in my opinion, the safest place to see this party through would be in a ship.'

'What d'you suggest, then?' Hemmingway asked.

'Well, anything might happen to you between here and Dorking, so, in my view, your best plan would be to take Lady Curry on board the *Halcyon* right away. She'll be sailing in half an hour, and out in the estuary of the Thames you'll be as well placed as anywhere when the comet does its stuff. I'll see the Captain, if you like, and the N.O. who'll be officially in command. We'll fix it that they give you the best accommodation that's to be had.'

'But I must get back to Sam,' said Lavina quickly.

Hemmingway nodded. 'Yes. That's the trouble. And, as a matter of fact, we've got a sort of Ark down at Dorking—one of the new spherical life-boats that they've been using in the States. Our chances ought to be as good in that as anywhere; and I just can't think what Sam might do if his wife was still missing when the party started.'

'In that case,' Renshaw agreed, 'the sooner you get there, the better.'

'Then we'll be moving.' Hemmingway disentangled himself from Lavina, and she followed him out of the car.

They thanked Renshaw again, wished him luck, and began to walk towards the gates of the dock.

It was now half-past five in the morning and dawn was breaking. Having found Lavina, and found her sane, Hemmingway was much more cheerful; but, as they advanced, he was aware that only the last shreds of her courage were keeping her from collapsing. Although she was clinging to his arm her feet faltered as she walked, and it was only with an effort that she could raise her head.

'Did you get any sleep at all?' he asked after a moment.

'I don't know. I think so, in between whiles. But I couldn't get the sight—the sight of Roy, lying there dead on the floor of the ballroom, out of my mind. I've lost count of time entirely. I don't even know what day it is. I didn't cry, you know—not even once—until I saw you. Somehow I couldn't. And now I have, I'm feeling better. But I'd give the earth just to tumble into bed.'

Her utter exhaustion provided Hemmingway with a new problem. There was no public transport running by which he could get her back to St. James's Square, and no possibility of hiring a car; yet she was quite incapable of walking such a distance. The only solution seemed to be the finding of some accommodation where she could get a few hours' sleep while he went to St. James's Square and collected his car.

He thought of the Salvation Army Hostel outside the West India Dock, but Lavina's footsteps were faltering, she was dragging on his arm, and the Hostel was a mile away; so even that seemed too far off. Coming out of the dock gates they turned left along the East India Dock road, and on a corner he saw a little hotel called the 'Main Brace'. Its principal business was obviously done through its bar, but it had a sign hanging outside announcing 'BED AND BREAKFAST.'

He did not like the look of the place at all, as it was only the sort of water-front dive where, in that district, sailors of all nations normally congregate. But Lavina was now weighing on his arm so heavily that she obviously could not go much farther.

The hotel was shut and no one was about, so Hemmingway went to the side door and rang the bell. He kept on ringing for some moments and was beginning to think that the publican had taken his family out of London and left the place untenanted; but at last there was a shuffling inside and a corpulent man in a greasy dressing-gown threw open the door.

'Can you give this lady a bed for a few hours?' Hemmingway asked. 'She's been through a great deal and I must leave her somewhere to get some sleep while I go and collect my car.'

The fat man nodded. 'She can have six beds if she wants 'em. The 'ouse is empty except for me and the Missis, now.'

'One's enough,' Hemmingway smiled. 'But let it be the best you've got; and I'll make it well worth your while to see that she's not disturbed till I get back.'

'Oh, she'll be orl right,' the man shrugged. 'Nobody's goin' to interfere with 'er. Why should they? Two-and-six is the charge, pay in advance—unless she wants breakfast, and that's another bob.'

Comforted somewhat by the man's apparent honesty, Hemmingway produced a ten-shilling note. 'You can take this on account,' he said, 'and there'll be another like it if the lady's had a good sleep by the time I get back.'

'Thanks, guv'nor.' The publican thrust the ten shilling note into the pocket of his dressing-gown. 'Follow me, will yer?' He turned and led the way upstairs.

The hallway smelt of stale cabbage. The stair carpet was threadbare and the paper on the walls faded with age. But the landlord led them to a room on the first floor overlooking the street, which, while unpretentious, looked reasonably clean.

A big, old-fashioned, brass bedstead occupied nearly half of it while a marble-topped washstand with a jug of water and coarse-looking towels was wedged in one corner, Hemmingway noted with satisfaction that the door had a key on the inside. The second Lavina entered it, she collapsed upon the bed.

'Poor lady's in a shockin' state, ain't she?' said the landlord. 'Like me to get the Missis up an' give 'er a nice cup o' tea or somethin'?'

Hemmingway shook his head. 'No, thanks all the same. All she needs is sleep.'

The man nodded, and shuffled out of the door. 'So long, then. Tell 'er just to give a shout if she wants anything. You can find yer own way out an' I'll let you in again when you get back.'

As the publican closed the door behind him, Hemmingway looked down at Lavina. Dark circles showed under her eyes and her eyelids were blue, as though she had made them up, but actually from exhaustion. She was certainly all-in.

He shook her by the shoulder. 'Look here, we'll have to set off for Stapleton directly I get back from St. James's Square with the car. It's no good just flopping down like that with your clothes on. You must undress and get into bed so as to get as much real rest as possible out of the short time you've got.'

Lavina blinked up at him wearily. 'I can't, Hemmingway. I'm too tired. I can hardly stand up.'

'Now, do be sensible. It won't take you a moment to slip out of your things.'

She raised herself on one arm. 'All right. If you'll help me.'

Hemmingway was not used to undressing young women. He was not in the least a prude but his complete lack of social life and his preoccupation with learning when young had kept him right out of the sphere of the girls in his own home town. While he had been struggling to earn his living in New York he had had an unfortunate affair with a girl who had let him down extremely badly; and it had gone so deep that for a long time afterwards he had studiously shunned all feminine advances. Since then, although he had met many pretty women in Sam's company, his whole heart had been in his work. He and Sam travelled a certain amount but, even in the luxury resorts they sometimes visited, there were always big deals in progress, cables to be decoded, long-distance telephone calls coming through and schemes to be thought out for the development of this or that business, and Hemmingway never found himself particularly attracted to the elegant, but so often empty-headed, young women that he met in such places.

Women, too, were a little frightened of him; yet, had they known the truth, he was much more frightened of them when they did attract him; so, while he was not actually cold, he had fallen into the habit of never attempting to go further with them than casual friendship. The fact was that he no longer thought about women as women and was so absorbed in Sam's affairs that he had more or less drifted into the same sort of celibacy as that of a worldly priest who has fought and conquered all desire.

Lavina caught the rather queer look on his face and, exhausted as she was, could not repress a flicker of amusement at his shyness. Her three years on the films had long since accustomed her to acting, often in the scantiest of costumes, before crowds of technicians and lookers-on. She was very proud of her beautiful body and rather liked to show it off whenever she could do so without positive immodesty; so it had not even occurred to her that Hemmingway would be embarrassed by helping her shed her outer garments.

His hesitation was only momentary. As she slid off the bed and, crossing her arms, plucked at the hem of her frock he quickly took hold of it and pulled it over her head. Then, as she sank down again, he unlaced her shoes, took them off and helped her roll down her stockings.

'Thanks. That'll do,' she murmured. 'I'll wriggle out of my

body-belt somehow when you've gone; my chemise will have to do as a nightie.'

He pulled out his gun and showed it to her. 'Ever handled one of these things?'

She nodded. 'Yes, often in my film days but only with blanks.'

'Right. It's fully loaded. Just in case someone starts something while I'm away I'll leave it with you; and you'd better lock the door. Don't open it to anyone until I get back. The landlord seems a decent guy, but you never know in a place like this.'

Turning his back to her he went over to the mantelpiece and scribbled a note on an odd piece of paper from his pocket. It ran:

'I didn't want to scare you unnecessarily but accidents are more frequent than usual these days. If it's after midday when you wake and I'm not back you'll know I've slipped up. In that case give the landlord his other ten shillings, go along to the docks and get your-self taken on one of the ships. There were so many prisoners that they're certain to be still evacuating people then. I'll have to be a hospital case or in the can myself before I fail you; but, if I have to, best of luck! H.H.'

He laid the message and a little wad of pound-notes under the automatic. When he turned again Lavina had already crawled between the sheets and was just dropping off to sleep, but he roused her up and made her get out of bed for a moment to en-sure her locking the door after him.

'Happy dreams!' he said with a smile. 'I'll be back in less than a couple of hours and we'll be off to the country.'

'Bless you!' she said, and closed the door behind him.

Out in the street Hemmingway set off at a brisk pace west-ward. Although he had been up all night, finding Lavina had acted as a tonic to him and, after the frowsty atmosphere of the public house bedroom, the fresh morning air lent him new strength.

Outside a church a hoarding which bore the legend, IF YOUR KNEES KNOCK TOGETHER KNEEL ON THEM, caught his eye and he took off his mental hat to the stout-hearted parson who was sticking to his ship with such an appropriate slogan nailed to the mast. Except where they were still evacuating cases from the East End Maternity Hospital few people were moving in the streets and the Commercial Road seemed interminable, but at last he reached Whitechapel High Street and there he saw an event which gave him furiously to think.

One of the very few private cars he had seen that morning was coming down it, moving east, when a group of toughs ran out into the roadway in front of it. The car slowed up. The people in it, who appeared to be a middle-class family, were unceremoniously pulled out and, piling into it, the six or eight roughs drove off, leaving its owner cursing in the gutter.

It was quite understandable that East Enders should be just as anxious as anyone else to get out of London to the greater safety of the countryside but a little disconcerting to find that some of them were using such high-handed methods. He might be faced with the same sort of trouble himself when he drove back to pick up Lavina; so he determined that directly he entered the East End he would ignore all limits and lights. The police were much too occupied to bother about motoring offences and it was better to risk a crash than the loss of the car.

In Cannon Street he was lucky enough to strike a convoy of food lorries proceeding West which had just collected a supply of fish from Billingsgate, and seizing his chance as the last one rumbled by he ran out into the roadway, caught the tailboard and pulled himself up on to the load of boxed fish.

The lorries turned right, east of St. Paul's, into Newgate Street and rumbled through Holborn, so Hemmingway guessed that they were probably heading for Hyde Park. As they passed the top end of Bond Street he dropped off and, with renewed energy after his free ride, strode out down it towards Piccadilly.

It was five to seven when he arrived at St. James's Square. Letting himself in with his key, he went straight upstairs to his bedroom to rouse Derek; but directly he opened the door he saw that Derek was no longer there.

He was not in the bathroom either, and his clothes had gone; so, after having visited the kitchen and called his name loudly several times, Hemmingway concluded that he must have left the house.

Derek was a countryman and used to early rising; moreover, he had passed most of the previous day asleep in the Park. Evidently he had woken about six, found himself much better after his night in bed and felt too restless to remain indoors; but

Hemmingway was justifiably annoyed, because he had definitely told him that he was not to go out.

Now he had, it meant either waiting for his return, which would delay picking up Lavina and getting away into the country, or having to leave him behind.

It was on coming up from the kitchen that Hemmingway noticed a letter addressed to himself propped up on the hall table. He tore it open and read:

'I'm still feeling pretty groggy but better after a good sleep. I can't stay here doing nothing, though, as I'm so terribly worried about Lavina. I'm going out to see if I can find her and, if I don't have any luck, I'll get back this evening round about ten o'clock. If you haven't had any either, we'll consult then as to the best thing to do; but, if one of us has run her to earth in the meantime, we can all drive down to Stapleton to-night. D.B.'

Hemmingway rarely gave way to temper but, as he tore the note slowly across, his eyes were narrowed and his teeth were clenched. If Derek had been there he would have hit him, his annoyance was so intense. The whole wretched muddle had been Derek's fault in the first place, for not having been firm with Lavina at the Dorchester two nights before; and now he had messed everything up again.

If Hemmingway was not back at the 'Main Brace' by midday and Lavina woke to find his note, she would at once assume that some accident had befallen him and, leaving the pub, go down to the docks where all trace of her would be lost again.

There was only one thing for it. Lavina was the person who mattered; not Derek. He must darned well take care of himself; it was his own funeral now how he got out of London. Going into the lounge, Hemmingway wrote a brief note himself:

'I have found Lavina but I had to leave her at a pub in the East End. If I'm not back there by midday with the car, she'll read a note I left, think something has happened to me and, according to instructions, go off on her own. If you had remained here as I told you to, this mess-up would not have occurred. As it is, I'm afraid you'll have to get down to Stapleton on your own as best you can. H.H.'

He propped it up on the table in the hall, where Derek's note had been, collected the satchel of private papers from his room and, leaving the house, went round to the mews at the back to get his car.

As he pulled out his key to unlock the garage door he noticed with sudden apprehension that the lock on it had been broken. Pulling the door open, he saw that the car had gone. Scrawled in chalk on the inner side of the door were the words: '*I hope you don't mind, I've borrowed your car. Derek.*'

Mopping his brow with his pocket handkerchief Hemmingway damned Derek to all eternity.

16

LAVINA SHOOTS TO KILL

It was still only a little after seven so Hemmingway had at least the consolation that he had plenty of time to get back to Lavina before midday, even if he had to walk the whole distance.

His stolen lift on the lorry coming up had enabled him to do the journey in just under an hour and he could cover the six odd miles back on foot in two hours, or less if he hurried; but the problem now was, how the devil was he going to get Lavina to the country without a car?

Any attempt to hire one was out of the question. All the hire companies and taxi-cabs had been taken over by the Government for the purposes of the evacuation, while practically everybody who had a private car and was not detained in London on some official duty had used it to get his own family away; so, apart from vehicles in use by the various Services, London now was virtually stripped of motor transport.

Yet Hemmingway knew that he could not expect Lavina to walk the thirty odd miles from the East End of London to Stapleton. She was a healthy girl and, although she was much too lazy and uninterested in sport to make a fetish of exercise, the activities demanded by her film work had kept her fit, so that in normal circumstances she might conceivably have made the journey; but definitely not right on top of the strain and exhaustion of the last two days.

Like those modern military experts who are sometimes haunted by the thought of their entire forces being immobilized by a petrol shortage, Hemmingway pondered for a moment on the possibility of finding horses, only to realize immediately that all horse-drawn vehicles had also been pressed into service to aid in the evacuation. Fortunately, however, he possessed a sense of humour, and the mental picture of himself driving a hansom cab down to the East End did much to mitigate his mounting exasperation.

There was only one thing for it. Derek had borrowed his car so he must borrow, or rather steal, somebody else's. He did not like the idea a little bit, although it was not the moral aspect of the matter that troubled him. In such an emergency he considered that he would be perfectly justified in doing all sorts of things that he would never have dreamed of in normal times.

What did perturb him was the fact that, having evacuated the Capital, the Government's principal concern now was to prevent looting. He had listened-in to the stringent regulations issued over the wireless on the previous day. As the country was under martial law, any persons discovered attempting to break into enclosed premises, or in the act of looting, were to be summarily dealt with by courts martial and, if they attempted to resist arrest, the police and troops had authority to fire upon them.

If he endeavoured to steal a car and got caught in the act, that would be the end of any hope of collecting Lavina and getting her down to Stapleton. Yet he saw that he must take the risk.

The next thing was, where was there any likelihood of there being a car which he might annex? He could go to one of the Government depots, try bluffing the people in charge into believing that he was an A.R.P. warden and, perhaps, get a car in that way; but the odds seemed pretty heavy against such a scheme succeeding, and, anyhow, he didn't like it. The idea of stealing a Government vehicle which might later be needed for saving lives went too much against the grain.

Every motor showroom and public garage had already been cleared of its contents, so the only other line seemed to be a car which somebody might have left in a private lock-up. Such vehicles, he knew, were now very few and far between but there must be some which their owners still had under lock and key either because, like himself, their departure had been delayed or because they happened to have been out of England when the crisis had arisen.

He realized then that the most likely place to find such a laid-up car was right in the mews where he was standing. In ordinary times, at this hour of the morning, the chauffeurs would have been just getting up and starting to clean their cars for the day's work, but there wasn't a single person stirring in the mews at the moment nor any sound proceeding from the flats above the garages. In nearly all of them the blinds were drawn and there

was little doubt that most of the chauffeurs and their families
had left London with their employers. Yet only the very rich can
afford to live in the mansions of St. James's Square and very rich
people nearly always possess several cars. Sam, for example, had
four. It was, therefore, quite on the cards that one of the neighbours might have left behind at least one of his cars.

Hemmingway promptly began to hunt round in his mind for
the person in the block whose garage would offer the best prospects for raiding. On the right lived Lord Allenfield, the great
newspaper magnate. His legion of secretaries and hangers-on
would have seen to it that all his cars were utilized for some purpose or other. The next house was empty. On the left lived Char-
lotte, Countess of Duffeldown, an old lady of eighty. Her only
vehicle, Hemmingway was almost certain, was an incredibly
aged Rolls and he had seen her drive away in it, with mountains
of luggage, two days before. But the next one on the left offered
much better prospects. It belonged to Julius Guggenbaum,
the South African millionaire. He had been in South Africa
for the last three months and, as he was a bachelor, the house
had been shut up on his departure; so there seemed a really
good chance that he might have left one or more cars laid up in
his garage.

Hemmingway looked anxiously up and down the mews and
stood listening intently for a moment, but the silence of the early
morning remained unbroken.

Pulling the steel case-opener from under his rope-ladder
belt he inserted it under the hinge of the padlock on Mr. Julius
Guggenbaum's garage door. Forcing it down he threw all his
weight upon it and wrenched out the screws.

He had hardly done so when a voice called: 'Hi!'

Turning, he saw two policemen entering the north end of the
mews. His impulse was to run, but the mews was not a long one
and the policemen were only about a hundred yards away. Even
if he could outdistance them they would blow their whistles as
they gave chase. It was almost certain that before he could elude
them in the deserted streets he would be headed off by police
arriving from other directions. With an effort of will he controlled
his impulse and, turning, walked towards the rapidly-advancing
constables.

'Well! What is it?' he asked sharply.

'That garage door,' said one of the officers. 'We observed you breaking the lock.'

'Yes. What about it?'

They were a little taken aback by his self-assurance but the other man braced himself and said firmly:

'You know the emergency regulations. It's a serious matter breaking into places these days. We shall have to take you into custody and hand you over to the Military.'

Hemmingway laughed, although he did not feel at all like laughing. 'You'll look a pretty couple of fools if you do. There's no law to stop a man breaking into his own premises, is there?'

'Well, of course, that's different,' conceded the spokesman of the pair, 'but you'll have to satisfy us that this is your garage.'

'Certainly,' Hemmingway smiled. 'Actually, it's Sir Samuel Curry's; but I'm his secretary. Sir Samuel left for the country yesterday but I had to stay behind to sort out his papers.' He held up the fat satchel. 'Unfortunately, he was so busy when he left that he forgot to hand over the key of the garage, so I've had to break it open to get out my own car.'

'I see. That sounds all right. But you won't mind our asking, sir, just in the way of duty, to give us some proof that you really do belong here.'

'Not a bit. The best proof I can offer you is to suggest that you come round to the house with me and have a drink. I dare say you chaps could do with one, now you're on duty day and night like this.'

'That's very kind of you, sir.' The constable glanced at his companion. 'We're living in strenuous times these days so we don't mind if we do.'

Hemmingway led them back to the house; praying as he did so that it would not occur to them to count the number of garages in the mews and tumble to it that the Curry mansion did not back on to the garage that he had been caught breaking into.

Having let them into the house he filled two glasses two-thirds full of whisky and added a splash of soda to each. Then, with his back to his guests, he mixed himself another in almost the opposite proportions. He had entertained police officers before on a few occasions, and had a fair idea of their capacity. He was not disappointed. Both of them swallowed their drinks without turning a hair.

When they had emptied their glasses he asked them if they would like another, but they both shook their heads, so he said cheerfully:

'Well, if you're satisfied about me now, I must be getting along.'

'Yes. Everything's O.K., sir, and many thanks for the drinks,' replied the spokesman. Both now appeared in an excellent humour.

At the front door Hemmingway hoped he would be able to rid himself of them; but it wasn't going to be quite as easy as all that. With their long, unhurried strides they accompanied him back to the garage and, as he put his hand on the door to open it, a sudden, appalling thought struck him. What was going to happen if there was no car inside after all?

Taking a deep breath, he pulled the door open. To his immense relief a big Rolls and a Ford were inside; but both of them were chocked up and all their metal work was protected by sacking.

The senior constable gave Hemmingway a suspicious glance 'You don't seem to have used either of your cars much lately, do you, sir?'

'No.' Hemmingway plunged in boldly again. 'We keep half a dozen, and the ones in regular use have already gone to the country. They've landed me with the job of getting one of these going. I only hope to God they've left me some petrol.'

The suspicions of the police were apparently allayed once more and, to Hemmingway's inward amusement, the two constables set to with a will helping him to prepare the car he was about to steal for his journey.

On the old principle that one might just as well be hanged for a sheep as a lamb, he had selected Mr. Guggenbaum's Rolls rather than the Ford. In twenty minutes they had the big car out in the mews, unwrapped from its sacking and with its tyres pumped up. To Hemmingway's relief, he had discovered some spare tins of petrol and oil at the back of the garage. They filled the tanks, he got into the driver's seat and prepared to depart. Just as he was about to do so a last bright idea occurred to him.

'Can either of you chaps drive?' he asked.

'I can,' volunteered the younger constable 'Why, sir?'

'Well, I can't lock the garage up again and it's a pity to leave the Ford there at a time like this when it might come in useful to somebody. It would probably be stolen if I did, anyhow; so I

suggest that you drive it round to the nearest A.R.P. authorities
and hand it over to them with Sir Samuel Curry's compliments.'

'That's a very good idea,' agreed the senior policeman, and,
with a wave of his hand, Hemmingway drove away in the
luxurious Guggenbaum Rolls.

His journey to the East End was uneventful. After he had
passed through the City he found that there were more people
about than in the West End. Most of the women and children
had been evacuated, but quite a number of the male population,
having no place in the country to go to, had had perforce to
remain in London. A few food shops were open, but no other
business was in progress, and here and there groups of men were
standing talking on the street-corners.

According to plan, he drove all-out down the Commercial
Road, with his hooter screaming, to prevent a possible hold-up.
Angry looks were cast at him here and there from the groups on
the pavements as he whizzed by; and he was loudly booed by a
crowd outside the Catholic Church. At the crossing by Limehouse Town Hall a policeman waved to him to halt, but he
ignored the signal, swerved violently and raced on. As there was
little traffic, and no children were playing in the gutters, he reached
the 'Main Brace' without accident.

Pulling up, he saw half a dozen tough-looking men in caps and
scarves standing outside on the pavement. They immediately
began to eye the car with an interest that Hemmingway found
disturbing. With the memory of the hold-up he had seen earlier
that morning fresh in his mind, it seemed to him quite on the
cards that, if he left the car to go into the pub and rouse Lavina,
and if any of them were capable of driving, they might quite well
steal it.

Looking up at the window of the room on the first floor in
which Lavina was presumably still sleeping, he plied his klaxon
for all he was worth in the hope of rousing her, but, as it was only
8.30 and she had been in bed under three hours, he felt certain
that she must still be sunk in exhausted slumber.

Next door to the 'Main Brace' there was a small greengrocer's
which still had a little stock for sale, and, propped up on the pavement, were some baskets of potatoes. Taking a half-crown out
of his pocket, Hemmingway slipped out of the driver's seat, ran
across the pavement, threw the half-crown towards an astonished-

looking young Jewess who was seated inside the shop, and grabbed up two handfuls of the potatoes.

The men on the pavement had now stopped talking and were watching his unusual procedure with amazement. Before any of them had moved he was back beside the car. Raising his arm, he hurled one of the potatoes straight through Lavina's window.

The crash of glass roused the men into sudden activity. As the pieces fell tinkling on the pavement one little runt of a man stepped forward, crying: 'Oi! Wot's the gime?'

Hemmingway smiled disarmingly. 'The woman, the dog and the walnut tree, the more you beat 'em, the better they be,' he quoted cryptically.

'He's loopy!' said a brawny-looking fellow in a checked cap.

'No, I'm not,' Hemmingway grinned, 'but my girl's asleep up in that bedroom and I wanted to wake her. Nice little surprise for her. Treat 'em rough, and they think more of you.'

' 'E *is* loopy!' declared the man in the checked cap.

'Bin seein' too many films, that's wot it is,' remarked another. ' 'E thinks 'e's Errol Flynn or somethink.'

At that moment Lavina, blear-eyed and dishevelled, thrust her golden head out of the window. 'Oh, it's you!' she murmured, still half asleep. 'What a shock you gave me!'

Hemmingway looked up. 'Never mind that. Get your clothes on and come down at once.'

The little man who had first spoken turned to leer at Hemmingway. 'Nice bit o' skirt you've got there, mister.'

'Oh, she's all right,' Hemmingway consented casually.

'Nice car, too,' the little man went on, with a wink at his friends.

'Yes. I wish it were mine.'

'Ain't it, then?'

'No, I've borrowed it.'

'Fancy, now!' The tough looked round with a smirk. 'Queer, ain't it? Wot would you say if I told you me and my pals had been thinkin' of borrering it ourselves?'

'I should think it was your unlucky day,' said Hemmingway genially.

'Oh, you would, would yer?' The little man ducked suddenly and came charging at Hemmingway to butt him in the stomach.

But Hemmingway was ready for the attack. During the whole

of the conversation he had been leaning against the car with his right hand behind him gripping the end of his loaded crop which lay on the driver's seat. He side-stepped neatly and, bringing the crop round, landed the little man a swift crack over his bullet head with it.

As the leader of the roughs went sprawling in the gutter his friends charged in. Hemmingway dodged round the back of the car. With loud shouts three of his antagonists followed. The other two came round the front of the bonnet, so that he was caught between two fires.

The big man in the check cap was one of the two who had come round by the front. As he appeared to be the most formidable of the troop Hemmingway leapt straight at him, bashing the leaded head of the crop into his ugly face.

The man staggered, screamed and fell, but his companion caught Hemmingway off his balance with a blow on the side of the ear, which sent him reeling. Next second the three in his rear rushed at him and he had fallen fighting to the roadway with the whole pack on top of him.

He kneed one in the belly and struck another in the eye, causing him to shriek with pain. Then, with a desperate wriggle, he freed himself, staggered to his feet and dashed back to the pavement. But they were on him again before he had time to get his back to the wall. One of them kicked him in the stomach, another hit him in the mouth and he fell once more.

Meanwhile, the little man had picked himself up, climbed into the driver's seat of the Rolls and got the engine going.

'Come on, boys!' he yelled. 'Finish 'im off an' jump in before the cops turn up!'

Those were the last words he lived to utter. There was a sharp report, his head jerked up, an ugly splodge of red appeared just below his temple; without a moan he sagged and collapsed in a silent heap.

The men who were on top of Hemmingway sprang up in panic. Gasping from the pain in his stomach he rolled over. Framed in the side-entrance of the public-house he glimpsed Lavina. Her face was white as a sheet, but his automatic was clenched firmly in her hand and a trail of blue smoke still drifted from its barrel.

The roughs were staring at her. It takes a brave man to stand his ground when threatened with a loaded automatic; particu-

larly when the person behind it has already demonstrated that
he is prepared to kill with it. When that person is a woman, to
take such a risk is no longer bravery, but madness. Hemmingway's attackers turned and fled; the two remaining thugs picked
themselves up out of the gutter and took to their heels with equal
swiftness. In less than a minute after the shot had been fired
Hemmingway was standing on the pavement alone, with Lavina.

'God!' he panted, looking again at the tumbled figure on the
driver's seat of the car. 'You've killed him!'

'I'm sorry,' said Lavina in a small voice. She seemed a little
stunned but not particularly upset. 'You know, it all happened so
suddenly. I'd only just got my dress on when I heard the shouting
and when I looked out of the window I saw them all attacking
you. I simply grabbed up the gun, rushed downstairs and shot
him. Funny, wasn't it?'

The fact that she had killed a man did not strike Hemmingway as at all funny. The little rat was probably no better than he
should have been but, all the same, he was a human being and if
Lavina was caught all sorts of unpleasant complications might
ensue. The thugs had stopped farther down the street and were
shouting. The Jewish girl had rushed out of the greengrocer's
shop. Other people were running up the street from both directions
to see what had happened. The fat landlord appeared in the doorway of the pub and after one look at the dead man in the driver's
seat of the Rolls, began to blow shrilly upon a police whistle.

Lavina still held the gun and Hemmingway yelled to her:

'Don't let him grab you but throw him his money for the bedroom!' Then, turning to the car, he opened its door and dragged
the dead body out on to the pavement.

Lavina held out one of the pound-notes that Hemmingway
had left with her, but the landlord stopped blowing on his whistle
to exclaim: 'I wouldn't soil me 'ands with it.'

It was no time to argue. Hemmingway was now in the driver's
seat. As he called to her, she slipped round to the far side of the
car and jumped in beside him. He let in the clutch and the big
Rolls slid forward.

The roughs and a lot of other people were now barring their
passage a hundred yards along the street, but Hemmingway sent
the car charging straight at them. One flung a stone which starred
the window, but when they saw that he was prepared to run

them down they leapt aside and scattered. A moment later their shouted curses were fading in the distance.

'By Jove! That was a nasty business,' Hemmingway muttered.

'Horrible!' she agreed. 'Of course, I didn't really mean to do it.'

'You knew my gun was loaded.'

'Yes. But, except for the other night at the Dorchester, I don't think I've ever seen men fighting in earnest before. In a way that I can't quite explain, I felt as though I was back on a film set and we were all putting on an act. I was quite surprised myself when I saw that I'd killed him. I wonder if you can understand that?'

'I think so,' Hemmingway said slowly. 'My hurling that potato through your window had only just woken you from a deep sleep. I suppose you must have felt that the whole thing was a sort of nightmare.'

'In a way I did. But if I'd been fully conscious I believe I'd have shot him just the same.'

'What?' Hemmingway turned to stare at her for a second.

She nodded, and went on with that inexorable feminine realism which takes no count of ethics: 'You see, it was us or them, wasn't it? You were on the ground and it looked to me as though they were going to murder you, but I was scared that I might shoot you if I fired in that direction. The little fellow had started up the car and, if he had got away with it, I knew we'd both have been sunk. It just came to me in a flash that if I shot him that would scare the others out of their wits; so I aimed at his head and pulled the trigger.'

Hemmingway was quite staggered by the logic of her simple and effective reasoning. He knew there must be a catch in it somewhere but he couldn't argue about it, and she was probably right in believing that she'd saved his life; or at least saved him from serious injury. His laugh was a little uncertain as he said:

'Well, it was darned good shooting, anyhow.'

'Oh, no,' she demurred modestly. 'I was only about six feet from him; the poor little wretch didn't stand a chance.'

Hemmingway had turned south, into the Blackwall Tunnel, and was now running through it under the Thames. He was thinking what a mighty good job it was that there had been no police about; otherwise Lavina would certainly have been arrested for manslaughter in the first degree—and they were by no means out of the wood yet.

Fortunately, as it affected their situation at the moment, no private calls had been taken by the London telephone exchanges for the last twenty-four hours so that neither the landlord nor one of his neighbours could ring up the police, but the matter was certain to be reported as soon as they arrived on the scene. A description of themselves and the car would be given, and Mr. Guggenbaum's luxurious Rolls would be a very easy car to trace. Hemmingway wished now that he had contented himself with the Ford.

The question was: would the police be too occupied with other matters to wireless their speed-cars on the south side of the river to keep a look out for the Rolls? They were certainly much too busy to bother about ordinary motoring offences, but to shoot a man dead and leave his body on the pavement was a very different business. He did not mention to Lavina his gloomy speculations about possible trouble to come. Instead, he asked her how she was feeling.

'Pretty mouldy,' she shrugged, 'and I must look like the wrath of God. I lost my bag days ago in the riot at the Dorchester so there's not a trace of make-up left on my face and I didn't even have a chance to wash when you fetched me out of bed just now. D'you think we could pull up somewhere where I could buy a comb and some powder and a lipstick?'

'No,' replied Hemmingway, 'I don't. And it doesn't matter much what your face looks like, anyhow. It's how you're feeling in yourself that I'm worried about.'

'Then you don't know much about women, my friend,' Lavina said with some asperity. 'A girl feels good or ill to exactly the extent she sees her face looking in a mirror. I caught one glimpse of mine in that lousy bedroom and I feel like Methuselah's wife dug up out of her grave.'

'Well, you'll feel better when you get down to the country.'

They had left the Tunnel, crossed Greenwich Marshes and were passing the Naval College when Lavina suddenly exclaimed:

'I say, what's happened to Derek?'

'I haven't the faintest idea and I don't damned well care,' Hemmingway said bluntly. While they sped on through South Street, across the main Blackheath road and uphill towards

Lewisham, he proceeded to tell her of the extreme inconvenience which Derek had caused him.

'You don't like Derek, do you?' she said quietly, giving him a quick look from beneath half-lowered eyelids.

'I've no objection to him as a person but I don't suffer fools gladly at any time and I just hate having them around when I have to handle an emergency.'

'Poor Derek,' she sighed. 'And he's so good-looking, don't you think?'

'I've never even looked at him from that point of view. All I know is that he landed you in this mess and has given me one hell of a job to get you out of it.'

'Why did you bother?'

'Because you're Sam's wife, of course.'

She smiled a little acidly. 'Thank you. That's quite the nicest compliment I've had for a long time.'

'Oh, come,' he shrugged impatiently. 'I didn't mean it that way, but Sam's been more than any father to me for the last seven years. I'd be selling pea-nuts in the streets of New York, or something of that kind, if it hadn't been for Sam. You're his wife, so it was just up to me to find you and get you down to Stapleton somehow.'

'With a neat label round my neck, I suppose: "In good order and untouched".'

'That's just the way I hope it'll be,' he agreed, refusing to rise to her baiting.

There was very little traffic about and few people; and Hemmingway was anxious to place a good distance between themselves and the East End as soon as possible; so, on entering the broad tree-lined streets of Rushey Green, he let the car rip. In Catford, as he slowed down to enter a narrower turning, sign-posted TO THE CRYSTAL PALACE, Lavina remarked thoughtfully:

'You're rather an extraordinary person, aren't you, Hemmingway?'

'No. I wouldn't say that,' he smiled. 'My mental attainments are a good bit better than most people's, if that's what you mean; but otherwise I've ordinary feelings and only one head and a couple of legs like everybody else.'

'I wasn't thinking of you mentally or physically, but as a person.

It's so unusual to find anyone these days with such unquestioning loyalty.'

'I don't think so. Look at Sam. You couldn't find a more loyal man than Sam anywhere.'

'He's your hero, isn't he?'

'Yes. If you like to put it that way, I suppose he is.'

'And now you've saved his wife from worse than death!' she mocked him. 'It might have come to that, you know. I probably shouldn't have awakened till the evening, and if I'd still been on my own in the East End just after sunset the sight of me might have given lots of unpleasant people funny ideas.'

'Well, let's say that I was lucky enough to get you out of what might have proved a pretty sticky corner.'

'And I saved your life; or, at least, saved you from being beaten unconscious by those thugs.'

'You certainly did.'

'That's lovely. Then, we're all paladins together. But tell me, what sort of effect does the comet have on you?'

'It makes me feel very queer. I was in the house last night waiting for you and Roy and Derek to turn up and . . .' he hesitated.

'Go on,' she said.

'Well, if you ever get back to St. James's Square you may find out.'

'Don't be a pig! Do tell me?'

'All right. But you must remember that at the time I was completely abnormal. I'm afraid I used up all your scent.'

'My scent! I thought you smelt rather nice.'

'Oh, afterwards I naturally did my best to get the damned stuff off me but I suppose some of it's still lingering in my hair. Sorry to have robbed you, and how the idea came to me, God knows. But I just couldn't resist going up to your room, sitting down at your dressing-table and dabbing myself all over till the bottle gave out. Extraordinary, wasn't it?'

'Very,' agreed Lavina, smiling at her toes.

They had run up Perry Hill, entering a poorer district in Lower Sydenham. As they mounted the steeper gradient of West Hill, towards the Palace, they saw that a small crowd had collected about half way up it where the road narrowed to cross a railway bridge above Sydenham Station.

Hemmingway put on speed again. He did not mean to be held

up now that he had at last got away with both Lavina and the car and had every hope of being out in the open country in under half an hour; but a moment later his brows drew together in a frown and he checked the car.

As the group in the roadway parted he saw that they had stretched a number of thick wires across it, between two and six feet from the ground, and were flagging him to pull up.

For a moment he contemplated charging the barrier; but the wires were almost cable size and he knew that even the weight of the Rolls would not be great enough to snap them all. He would only succeed in forcing them back like bow strings and might even turn the car over.

'Lord, help us! It's the police,' was the thought that flashed into his mind. 'They must have telephoned through already and, knowing we'd killed one man, thought we'd take a chance on running others down if only we could get away. They've fixed these wires to make certain of halting us here.'

But, as he brought the car to a standstill, he saw at once that there was not a single policeman in the crowd. It was another gang of roughs.

'Give me that thing,' he cried to Lavina, snatching the automatic that lay on the seat between them as the ugly-looking mob surged round the car. Yet a second glance at the yelling crowd convinced him of the folly of either threatening them with it or attempting to use it. There were at least fifty men in the mob and their faces showed them to be desperate. He felt certain that if he even produced the gun Lavina and he would be dragged out of the car and kicked to death.

'Come on!' shouted a man in a red tie, who seemed to be the leader of the roughs. 'Out you get! We want that car!'

Hemmingway hesitated, but only for a second.

'Out you get!' repeated the man. 'And no argument, unless you want a beating-up!'

Discretion was unquestionably the better part of valour. For Lavina's sake as well as his own, Hemmingway saw that peaceable surrender was the only policy.

'It's no good,' he said, with a wry grin at her. 'We can't tackle this lot. We'll have to get out.' And, picking up his satchel of papers, he helped her down into the road.

The gang appeared to be organized and, having fixed up their car-catching apparatus, were taking their turns to get away in each private car they could waylay as it came along.

The man in the red tie gave an order. The barrier of wires was lowered. A flashy little Jew climbed into the driver's seat and drove the Rolls over it; after which about eight of the other men, laughing and joking, packed themselves into the car.

Taking Lavina by the arm, Hemmingway led her over to the pavement. As they had given up the car peacefully, nobody attempted to molest them; but with bitterness in their hearts they watched the wire barrier raised again and Mr. Guggenbaum's beautiful Rolls drive smoothly away.

17

CRAZY DAY

'Damn'!' said Lavina forcibly. 'What the hell do we do now?'

'We can either stay here, join the crowd and try and muscle into one of the cars they pull up, or start walking out of London.' Hemmingway's voice was quite dispassionate.

'We might wait here till doomsday,' she sniffed. 'It's really a sort of general post that's going on. They're simply turning one lot of people out of a car so that another lot can get away.'

'Sure. But there were only two of us in the Rolls and about ten of them packed into it before it drove off. If they manage to hold up a lorry or two, we might quite well get places. I'm game to walk myself but I'm afraid you'd just hate it, so in this case I'm leaving the choice to you.'

The question was unexpectedly settled for them. Three vans came streaking up the road from the direction of Forest Hill. They pulled up just in front of the barrier and a score of policemen tumbled out. Evidently one of the local police had seen what was going on and had succeeded in getting assistance.

Some of the roughs in the crowd began to hurl bricks and bottles. Hemmingway grabbed Lavina's arm and dragged her back into the shelter of the Station doorway. Striking out right and left with their batons the police drove the mob back. In two minutes it was all over: the organizers of the hold-up broke and scattered.

A few men whom the police had collared were bundled into one of the vans; they removed the wire barricade, coiled it up and put it in another; then they drove off again.

'What filthy luck that they didn't come on the scene ten minutes earlier!' Hemmingway muttered. 'Anyway, we've no option now; we'll have to walk.'

'Hell!' Lavina glanced at her feet. 'Anyway, thank goodness I had day shoes on when I left St. James's Square. Let's go then.'

They set off up the hill past the two towers of the Crystal

Palace on its summit and entered Church Street, Upper Nor-
wood, where the road sloped down again. Rather to her surprise,
after they had been going for about half an hour Lavina felt
better. Although she had only spent three out of the last forty-
eight hours in bed, she had been sitting or lying about in the
grounds of Buckingham Palace for more than half that time and,
whenever her brain had been too tired to wonder any more about
what was going to happen to her she had dozed quite a lot; so
that her exhaustion when Hemmingway had found her had been
much more mental than physical, and the walking was doing her
good.

The day was overcast so they could see neither the sun nor the
comet, which had now approached sufficiently near the earth
to have been visible, even in daylight, if the clouds had not
intervened. But the day was warm, dry and windless, so walking
was pleasant enough even on the pavements of the suburbs
through which they passed, now that there were no shopping
crowds to impede their progress.

Although it took them a little to the east of the shortest cross-
country course to Dorking, Hemmingway had decided to by-
pass Croydon from fear of becoming involved with other lawless
mobs in that densely populated area and the few people they met
were hurrying along on their own concerns. Cars and vans, all
on their way south, passed from time to time, but their drivers
ignored Hemmingway's signals, so eventually he realized that it
would be hopeless to try and cadge a lift until they were farther
out of London. As they walked on Lavina gave him her version
of the affair at the Dorchester and details of her internment.
Then he retailed to her an account of Derek's adventures and
ended with his own exploit in getting away with the stolen car.

She laughed a lot at the way he had fooled the police into
helping him to prepare the Rolls and, as Hemmingway's one
idea was to keep her mind occupied so that she should not tire
too quickly, he began to tell her some amusing episodes of the
days when he had been struggling for a living in New York.

The vague antagonism that had arisen between them before the
hold-up had now entirely disappeared and for the first time they
were really discovering each other as individuals. Each found
the other had more in them than they had previously supposed.
Lavina displayed a practical streak in her views on people and

affairs with which Hemmingway would not have credited her; and from having considered him as an almost monkishly seriously minded man she revised her opinion and decided that he was really a very cheerful and amusing person.

It was 8.30 when they had careered away from the 'Main Brace' in the Rolls and by 11 o'clock they were passing through Shirley. Neither of them had yet breakfasted and they both discovered suddenly that they were extremely hungry; so they began to look about for a place where they could get something to eat.

Here in the more distant suburbs there were more people about, as such districts had not been evacuated and comparatively few of their inhabitants had gone off on their own to the country. Most of them were either attending services at the churches or remaining in their own homes, killing time to the best of their ability until they could learn their fate.

In the shopping centres there were ration queues here and there in front of the food dealers who were now being supplied by the Government organization that had been set up; but most of the other shops were closed, no buses were running and there were very few cars about.

Inquiries of people in the queues soon informed Hemmingway that he would not be able to get meat, fish, bread, butter or milk without having a ration card; but, although the grocers' stores had been sadly depleted in the last few days, they still had a certain amount of stock. At one Hemmingway managed to buy a tin of oxtail soup; at another some biscuits and potted shrimps; and at a third a tin of cherries.

To Lavina's joy they also found a chemist's shop that was open so she was able to get a comb, mirror, face cream, lipstick and powder; while Hemmingway added aspirins, a bottle of Evian, a bottle of lime-juice and two collapsible drinking cups to their store. Just as they were leaving she joked him about his confession to having used up all her scent the night before, so he promptly bought her the most expensive bottle in the shop.

Having no tin-opener and being unable to buy one, Hemmingway had got the chemist to open the tins for them and, as it would have been awkward for them to carry the open tins far, they turned into the first field that they came to on their way to Selsdon.

It was quite a small field—just a plot that had never been

built on—between two fair-sized houses with long gardens. Crawling through a hole in its broken fence, they sank down gratefully in the long grass and began their picnic.

They had to eat out of tins and spread the shrimps on the biscuits with their fingers but after their long night out and the exertions of the morning the food tasted heavenly, and they both agreed that it was the best meal they had had for years.

'I think we're entitled to a bit of a rest now,' Hemmingway said when they had done.

'My dear,' she smiled, 'I don't think you'll ever get me on my feet again, anyway. I haven't walked so far for ages.'

'You'll have to walk much farther yet, unless we can get a lift from somebody. We've only covered about five miles so far and, if I possibly can, I mean to get you down to Stapleton tonight.'

'How far is it?'

Hemmingway got out his map and studied the country. 'About fifteen miles as the crow flies; that means at least twenty by the highways.'

'Twenty miles?' gasped Lavina.

'Sounds tough but it's not too bad, really. It's just past midday and if he started now an athlete could get down there by teatime. Even walking without effort one can cover three miles an hour so, for us, it would be about a seven hour trudge. Say we give ourselves two hours' rest and start at two o'clock, if we could keep going all the time we'd be there by nine. Let's allow fifteen minutes in every hour for a breather and we should still be able to make it at the latest by eleven. Think you can do it?'

Lavina yawned. 'I don't know, but I'll try.'

'You're a good guy when one gets to know you,' he smiled appreciatively. 'Say we don't reckon to get in till eleven, we'll only have to average just over two miles an hour. You ought to be able to do that if you can only keep the old feet going one in front of the other.'

'You're a good guy too—once one gets to know you—and I'm getting to know you fast,' she laughed in reply. 'I expect I'll manage it somehow. But how about our waking up at two o'clock? If I sleep now I shall probably lie here like a log till midnight.'

'Don't worry, I'm pretty good at that sort of thing; trained myself when I was a kid and I've found it mighty useful ever since to be able to drop off anywhere and wake again at will. As I've been up all night it's a bit of a risk, but I'm going to chance it. A couple of hours' sleep now will set me up again for quite a time but if I don't have it I'll be too beat to get you over the last lap this evening.' They lay down among the long grass and wild flowers and were conscious only for a moment of their perfume in the heat before dropping off to sleep.

When Hemmingway woke it was a quarter past two and he felt that his gift had not let him down too badly. He roused Lavina and, after she had tidied her hair and attended to her face, they set off along the road towards Selsdon. It was pleasant walking at a leisurely pace through Addiscombe Woods and they took their first rest on the top of the hill there.

It was then that they first noticed something queer about the sky. The clouds, which were of the pale-grey summery variety, had taken on a faintly pink tinge. Neither of them commented on it but both wondered with vague alarm if the comet, now being so much nearer, was about to produce its strange effect in spite of the fact that there were many hours yet to go before sundown. Everything was very still; not a leaf rustled in the windless air and it was so hot that most of the people they saw were walking in their shirtsleeves with their coats over their arms. Hemmingway followed their example and began to curse the weight of the satchel of papers he was still carrying.

With the slowly-reddening sky in mind they kept a close watch on themselves as they went on their way through Sanderstead, but experienced nothing unusual except a spontaneous gaiety that caused them to laugh a lot even at the most stupid things. At last they reached the main Brighton road and turning left along it through Purley tried once more to get a lift by hailing each of the few south-bound vehicles that passed them but, failing, they left it by a right-hand fork about a mile south of the town and, walking along some roads lined with substantial houses, at last reached more or less open country.

Hemmingway was much happier now that they had got clear of London. A thin trickle of refugees was still moving along all the roads that led out of the capital but if they could avoid populous places there seemed little risk now that they would run into mobs from which they might suffer violence. At their fourth halt Hemmingway reckoned they were more than half-way, having walked another eight miles, making thirteen in all since the morning; but Lavina was going well and he had a reasonably good hope that they would manage the remaining twelve miles which they still had to cover before nightfall.

As they went on again the pinkish-red of the sky gradually grew deeper and the atmosphere more sultry. Suddenly, without in the least intending to do so, Lavina began to sing. Hemmingway joined in and for a mile or more they marched along singing all the choruses they could think of together. Only the fact that their throats became parched through the stifling heat put an end to their impromptu concert and caused Lavina to suggest that they should try to get a cup of tea somewhere.

They were now going through narrow, twisting, hilly lanes; real country that might have been a hundred miles from London. There was not a soul about and even the scattered houses were hidden from them by high hedges. At a break in one they saw a garden gate and turned in through it; but a large dog rushed at them barking furiously. Hemmingway was only just in time to push Lavina out of the gate and slam it behind them; then the angry beast, its jaws slavering, scraped upon the woodwork with its claws in a frantic endeavour to get over it and attack them.

They had no means of knowing if it was just an ill-tempered brute kept by its owner to drive off tramps or if the red glow from the skies had turned its brain; but the dog showed all the signs of madness so it was certainly not worth risking its attacking them by trying to get up to the house.

At the next house they were more fortunate. It was hardly larger than a cottage but had a garden gay with flowers and in front of the porch they observed an old gentleman skipping. Approaching, they asked if they might buy a cup of tea from him. He panted out that they were very welcome to one and could make it for themselves but that he must not pause until he had done another hundred skips.

Leaving their strange host they went into his kitchen, made tea and carried him out a cup; but he only shook his head, so they retired to drink their own in his comfortable sitting-room. While they were there the floor suddenly seemed to move slightly beneath them and the tea rocked in the cups. It was an earth tremor and Lavina looked at Hemmingway apprehensively; but it was over in a moment and gave them no further cause for alarm.

On going outside they found their host red-faced, pop-eyed and gasping, but still skipping; and no argument which Hemmingway could produce would induce him to stop, except for a few moments from time to time to regain his breath. So, although they feared that he would have a heart attack if he kept it up till sunset, they had to leave him there still labouring in the grip of his strange mania.

Both of them were tired now but somehow it no longer seemed quite such an urgent matter that they should reach Stapleton that night. The reddish glow pervaded everything, changing the colours of the landscape so that it seemed strange and unreal. They felt as though, instead of tea, they had been drinking absinth and were slightly drunk upon it; their perceptions were hypersensitive, sharpened to every sound and feeling; yet they were filled with a delicious lassitude.

As they strolled side by side down a steep, hedge enclosed lane, Hemmingway suddenly realized with a little shock that he was holding Lavina's hand. He did not let go, however, because he felt that that might draw attention to the fact that he had been holding it; and it was a very nice firm little hand with long, graceful fingers, as he had previously noticed. They were heading for Tadworth but Hemmingway had not consulted his map for some time and evidently they had taken the wrong turning somewhere as, on entering a village, which sprawled along a wider road, they found that it was called Burgh Heath.

Roused now from his pleasant lethargy Hemmingway saw that it was nearly eight o'clock and his map showed him that although they had covered fourteen miles since lunch time, having gone out of their way, they still had another eight to do. That meant that, even if they did the last lap of the journey without resting at all, they could not hope to get in before eleven; but if they didn't rest it was certain that Lavina would crack up, so it looked now as though they would not reach their destination before midnight.

As it was, when he suggested that they ought to try and make up time by increasing their pace she insisted that they must find somewhere in the village where she could sit down for a little, and pointed to a cake shop, some distance down the broad street which appeared to be open. When they reached the shop they found that it had been broken into and the dozen or so people who were in it were mostly refugees like themselves who were snatching a free meal from such food as remained there.

The behaviour of the people in the shop was, to say the least of it, peculiar. One man was gobbling down stale buns as though he was trying to win a bet. Another had apparently raided the till and was counting the money in it over and over again. On the floor in one corner a couple were lying sound asleep in a most affectionate embrace; and, strangest of all, a cadaverous-looking man, dressed in women's clothes but with his trouser-ends projecting beneath a short skirt, was preening himself before a mirror. These antics did not strike Lavina and Hemmingway with quite so much surprise as they would have done normally and their only reaction was to laugh uproariously.

Hungry again after their long tramp since luncheon, they seized on a Madeira cake, hacked it in pieces and began to eat it almost ravenously. Between mouthfuls they exchanged remarks with some of the other people, which mainly concerned the distance each of them had tramped that day, where they were making for, whether the comet would kill them all, and wild rumours about an impossible invention with which the scientists intended to attempt blowing the comet up before it got much nearer.

They had just finished the Madeira cake when a nice-looking young man entered the door. No sooner did his eye light upon Lavina than he rushed at her, seized her in his arms and began to kiss her violently.

Hemmingway grabbed him by the neck and hauled him off; upon which he turned and struck out like a maniac. He was a well-built, powerful fellow and obviously dangerous, so Hemmingway, who was doing all he could to protect himself from a spate of blows, was compelled to snatch up his loaded crop and knock his attacker over the head with it.

Instantly the whole place was in confusion. The young man now lay spreadeagled, unconscious, on the floor and some of the people began to shout that Hemmingway had murdered him, while others declared that he had been perfectly right to protect his girl-friend; upon which they all joined issue with fists, chairs, cups, saucers, cakes and anything else that came handy.

Hemmingway managed to push Lavina behind the counter

G

and, filled with a fighting spirit which suddenly seemed to have got hold of him, lashed out right and left with his crop. But the riot was brought to a sudden and unexpected conclusion.

Without the least warning a 'quake shook the floor beneath their feet. They staggered, lost their balance and righted themselves. But the tremor came again. The woodwork of the counter creaked, some lumps of plaster dropped from the ceiling and the whole building trembled.

At the first shock the fighting had ceased. White-faced and scared the whole party rushed out into the street, Hemmingway and Lavina among them. Gripped by panic, the little crowd scattered, shouting with terror as they ran. The shocks continued; a chimney-pot leaned crazily, hovered a second, and fell; glass was tinkling down from some of the windows; the inhabitants of the village were tumbling helter-skelter out of their doorways. Grabbing Lavina by the wrist Hemmingway dragged her along after him towards the outskirts of the village, but they had not covered a hundred yards when she screamed and fell.

He pulled up with a jerk and lifted her from the gutter. She was not badly hurt, only having bruised her knees, but the heel of her shoe had caught in a grating, causing her to trip, and in her fall she had wrenched it right off.

The tremors eased as she sat on the roadside lamenting her ruined stockings but, actually, the tearing off of the heel was a far more serious matter as they had no means of nailing it on again and there was still an eight-mile walk before them. The only thing to do was to look for a shoe shop or the village cobbler.

With Lavina hobbling beside him Hemmingway turned back along the village street. It had been emptied as though by magic of the panic-stricken crowd and the people who had rushed out of their houses, but the village did not appear to boast a shoe shop and it was some time before Hemmingway could find anyone to ask where the cobbler lived.

In the churchyard a black-clad man was digging as though his life depended on it. He had already turned up three mould-covered coffins and was furiously shovelling away the earth from round a fourth. At Hemmingway's question the man turned towards them a haggard face down which the sweat was pouring in rivulets, shook his head angrily, and returned to his gruesome task.

A hundred yards farther on a skinny, middle-aged woman who was seated on a grassy bank busily plaiting a daisy chain, directed them; and they found the cobbler's cottage just outside Burgh Heath on the Epsom Road. As they turned in at its gate a fat, freckle-faced woman came rushing out of it.

'Go away! Go away!' she shouted excitedly, waving them off with her hands.

'What's the matter?' Hemmingway asked.

'My 'usband,' panted the woman, ' 'e's got a screw loose, poor dear. 'E's orl right with us but 'e's started shootin' at strangers. It's this filthy sky that's done it.' She pointed upwards at the heavens which were now a deep reddish-orange and added pathetically: 'It's got us all one way or another. Round five o'clock I started pickin' the flowers in the garden and I just can't stop.'

They noticed then that although she had a well-filled herbaceous border there was hardly a flower in it. Lupins, delphiniums, Canterbury bells, sweet-william, stock—all were gone—and, suddenly kneeling down, she began to pluck a few pinks that had escaped her previous forays.

At that moment a wiry, red-haired little man popped out of the cottage. Waving an old sporting gun he cried wildly:

'Enemy spies! Enemy spies! They can't deceive me. I know them,' and he proceeded to level his fowling piece at the intruders.

Hemmingway thrust Lavina before him through the gate and pulled her down under a bank at the roadside just as the gun went off with a loud bang.

The shot rattled through the hedge above them. Fearing that the mad cobbler might give chase before he blazed off with his other barrel, they jumped up and ran a couple of hundred yards to put a bend of the road between the cottage and themselves.

'Phew!' Lavina exclaimed, coming to a halt. 'That was a nasty one!' But suddenly they began to laugh uproariously and for minutes on end they stood there rocking with mirth, absolutely unable to control themselves.

Their laughter ceased only from lack of breath, and when they had at last recovered Hemmingway said:

'I can't think why we're laughing; it's no joke really because you can't possibly walk another eight or nine miles with the heel off one of your shoes.'

'I don't think I could anyhow.' Suddenly she leant against him. 'Oh, God! I'm tired.'

'I know, darling—I know.' He used the endearment quite unconsciously and she did not seem to notice it. 'But we've got to try and make Stapleton somehow. Come on, we'll go slowly.'

With her arm through his and their hands clasped again, they set off back through Burgh Heath to the main Reigate road. They were now moving south, about half-way between those two great southern traffic arteries, the Brighton and the Portsmouth roads, and the country had remained unspoilt except for an occasional row of modern dwellings.

When they passed through Burgh Heath again it was just on nine o'clock and they still had another eight miles to go. Both of them were incredibly foot-sore and weary, yet both were still buoyed up by the extraordinary mental exhilaration which came from the red glow in the sky and it was without any horror, but rather with an excited interest, that they came upon the body of a dead man at the forked roads half a mile south of the village.

He was lying on his back on the grass at the side of the road and his battered head showed that he had been attacked and murdered. His clothes were good but flashy and he was wearing a pair of lemon-coloured shoes.

As Hemmingway's eye fell upon the body he suddenly had an idea. The shoes would be much too big for Lavina but wearing them, stuffed with grass, might be more comfortable for her than hobbling along with one heel-less shoe.

Kneeling down, he took the dead man's shoes off and told her his idea. The shoes were so big round the instep that even stuffed with grass they were by no means comfortable; yet they certainly made an improvement as she was at least able to take even steps again.

A weird, uncanny light lit the scene and, glancing down, he caught his breath at the exquisite contours of her face, the splendid but easy poise of her head upon her shoulders, her supple, beautifully-modelled limbs. A frightful craving seized him to take her in his arms and press her to him; to hold her next to his beating heart so that he might protect her with his body and his life blood. She was not looking at him and he brushed a hand across his eyes, knowing that he, too, was going mad from that eerie red radiance that was all about them. Next moment they

entered the shelter of a tree-lined stretch of road and his sanity
returned to him.

It was just before they reached Tadworth that they noticed a
new change in the heavens. Before them to the south the clouds
had broken, revealing patches of livid sky. By the time they had
passed the crossroads south of Tadworth, leading on the right
to Walton-on-the-Hill and on the left to Kingswood, nearly half
the sky was clear. But as they mounted the hill a little farther on
Lavina's strength began to fail her. She staggered on for a little
along the open road across a desolate heath sprinkled with clumps
of gorse and silver birch; then suddenly she turned, clutched at
Hemmingway and burst into tears.

'I can't go on—I can't,' she wept. 'I can't go another step.'

They had walked over twenty-one miles that day; a splendid
effort at any time for people unused to walking. Coming on top
of the strain they had previously undergone it had been too much;
they were both now at the end of their tether. During the previous
night Hemmingway must have walked an additional ten miles
while he was searching for Lavina so he was almost as exhausted
as she was; yet they now had only five miles to go to be safe
among their friends and he still hoped that with frequent rests
they might get in, even if they only covered a little over a mile an
hour and reached their destination about two o'clock in the
morning.

Among the heather beside the road there was a pile of last
year's bracken. Picking up the sobbing Lavina in his arms, he
scrambled with her over the ditch and, laying her down on the
heap of dried fern, collapsed beside her.

After a few minutes she stopped crying and asked in a small
voice:

'Must we go on? Can't we possibly stay here tonight?'

He sighed. 'I wish we could, but Sam will have been half out
of his wits about you. We're on the last lap now and we'll rest a
lot, but I think we must do our damnedest to make it.'

It was just as he had finished speaking that the full glory of the
setting sun and its strange, malevolent neighbour burst upon
them.

The reddish clouds had drifted northwards and the whole
world was suffused with radiant light. The comet now looked
as big as the moon and its red rays, mingling with the yellow

ones of the sun, lit the whole landscape with a strange, unearthly glory, changing the colours of the trees and moorland so that they looked like the work of some mad artist.

Both of them felt a sudden renaissance of their strength. Their tiredness was forgotten. Their veins were filled with fire instead of blood.

They turned on the bracken and stared at each other hungrily. Hemmingway stretched out a hand and grasped Lavina's shoulder. Her voice came huskily:

'I'm sorry about Sam, but he's old and I'm young. I love you darling, and I've never really loved a man before.'

As he took her in his arms she was still choking: 'I love you— oh, I love you.'

18

THE LAST DAWN

Hemmingway lay on his back among the bracken, Lavina's golden head pillowed on his chest; clasped in a tight embrace they both slept the sleep of utter exhaustion, but they were not destined to sleep out the night.

Shortly after three in the morning a violent tremor shook the earth, the pile of bracken wobbled, the leaves of the trees rustled loudly, and there was a dull explosion somewhere in the distance. Instantly they both started up wide awake.

Two more tremors followed in quick succession, making them feel sick and giddy, then the earth was still again.

Lavina sat up and stared down at Hemmingway. He was lying on his side propped on one elbow, gazing up at her. Each could glimpse the outline of the other but the starlight was too dim for them to see each other's features.

Suddenly Lavina brought her hand up to her mouth to smother a little cry.

'What is it?' he asked. But he knew already. She was thinking of the way they had awakened in each other's arms and of those mad moments between the time when the full glare of the comet had beaten down upon them and the final fading of its after-glow as they had drifted off to sleep. That had been a glorious hour. Their tiredness forgotten, they had been like drug addicts, hypersensitive to every touch and sound and perfume; translated for a little time to the status of a pagan god and goddess in the Elysian fields, the past had ceased to have a meaning and the future was without significance.

Now they were sober and sane again, back in the cold pre-dawn world of inhibitions and commitments; conscious of shame and guilt; harrowed by remorse and horror of their weakness.

'Oh, I hate you!' cried Lavina suddenly.

'Do you?' Hemmingway's voice was bitter. 'I doubt if you hate me as much as I hate you.'

'How *could* you do what you did!' she went on quickly. 'After all your talk about your devotion to Sam. You're a fine friend, aren't you! Pretending to take charge of his wife and then making love to her at the first opportunity.'

'It wasn't that way—and you know it!' Hemmingway contradicted her angrily. 'You're a born man-snatcher. It's in your blood. The very first time you set eyes on me you made up your mind to get me, didn't you? Then, at your wedding—yes, even on your wedding day—you tried to make me kiss you. Last night was your big opportunity, and you took it.'

'That's a lie,' Lavina flared. Her own misery had made her want to hurt him and the fact that she now realized that there was just a vague sub-stratum of truth in his accusations about their early meetings made her want to hurt him even more.

'I was in your care, exhausted, utterly done in, terribly wrought up about poor Roy's death and all this frightful business. In such a state any woman would be easy money. But a man's different. Men don't suffer from hysteria or become so overwrought that they don't know what they're doing. No decent man would take advantage of a woman on the verge of lunacy. He'd know she didn't mean a thing she said or did and have the strength of mind to control himself. Instead of thinking for us both, you just let yourself go without the least hesitation. Oh God, how I loathe you!'

'I loathe myself,' Hemmingway murmured bitterly. 'But that doesn't let you out. It's no good pretending you're a precious little innocent—sweet seventeen, never been kissed and all that. We were both under the influence of the comet, of course, but the fact that you were tired out isn't any excuse. I had a much more tiring night than you did before we started to walk out of London; and as a grown woman you were just as capable of resisting your feelings as I was.'

After a moment he went on more calmly. 'As I see it, the effect of the comet is simply to release people's inhibitions and destroy all their sense of values. If they're murderers at heart, they go out and kill someone; if they're quarrelsome, they quarrel; if they've a yen to make daisy-chains or skip, they just go to it; if they have a subconscious desire to make love to somebody, out it pops. Call it propinquity in our case, if you like. If you'd been here with Derek, for example, or I'd been with some other girl, the same thing would probably have happened. Don't flatter yourself that I'm in love with you, because I'm not; and I don't imagine for one moment that you're the least bit more interested in me than you would be in any other healthy young man who happened along. But last night we just felt that way about each other and the responsibility is entirely mutual. That's all there is to it.'

'How flattering!' she sneered. 'To be dismissed like any trollop you might have picked up for the evening. I never thought any man would do that to me.'

'Then it's extremely good for your vanity.'

'You swine!'

'I see. I'm a swine now, because I'm not begging for some more of your remarkably good brand of kisses, am I? You'd like to continue the affair, it seems.'

'I'd like to beat your face in with a hunting crop. Above all, I'd like a bath to try and wash the very touch of you away from me. I feel like a leper at the moment.

'Don't worry! I wouldn't touch you again if you paid me; but since, apparently, you're not prepared to try and forget the whole thing, what's the alternative? 'D'you want to tell Sam about it when we reach Stapleton?'

'Good God, no!' Lavina's voice suddenly changed to a note of anxiety. 'You won't, will you?'

'Of course not. I've nothing but contempt for people who kiss and tell. What good does it ever do except make some other person miserable?'

'Yes. I've always felt that, too.'

'All right, then, let's declare an armistice. What's done's done, and there's no sense in continuing a slanging match. I'm prepared to take your word for it that you didn't really mean to tempt me, if you'll take mine that the comet absolutely overcame all the decent instincts I've ever had and the principles of a lifetime. Naturally, we're hating each other at the moment, because we're normal again and we've both got certain standards which the other caused temporarily to be thrown down the drain; but we've got to try our damnedest to get back to the natural friendly footing we were on yesterday round about midday.'

She nodded slowly. 'Yes, you're quite right. It won't be easy, and how I'll be able to look Sam in the face I can't think. But

I'm sure now that you couldn't help what happened. I've said awful things to you and I'm sorry.'

'I don't know how I'll face Sam again either. But I'm equally sorry about all the nasty things I said to you. I'm sure you know I didn't really mean them.' For the first time that morning he smiled, and he held out his hand.

She took it and with a firm hand-clasp they made their peace.

'How are you feeling?' he asked after a moment.

'Pretty mouldy. How about you?'

'Hardly at the top of my form. Still, I think we ought to get a move on.'

She stretched her arms and yawned. 'Wouldn't it be better to get another hour or two's sleep and set out in the dawn?'

'No. We'll be safe while darkness lasts.'

'Safe?' she echoed.

'Yes. But that's just as long as we will be,' he answered grimly. 'This accursed comet's so close to us now that even when the sky's cloudy its rays come through. You saw that for yourself from about four o'clock yesterday afternoon, and to-day it's certain to be much stronger. If we don't reach Stapleton by the time the sun gets up we'll be liable to go off the deep end again, just as we did last night.'

'I see. Then we'd better start at once.'

He laughed.

'I didn't mean to be rude or anything,' she added quickly, 'but we mustn't let that sort of thing happen again.'

'Well, we've only got about five miles to cover so we ought to be able to make it,' he said standing up.

They had nothing to pack so they set off at once, side by side, down the steep hill towards Pebble Combe.

When they reached the village, about half an hour later, Hemmingway happened to glance towards a villa standing quite close to the road. In the faint light he saw that there was a shed beside it and that the door of the shed was ajar. Touching Lavina's arm, he said:

'Wait here a moment,' and turned in up the garden path.

His luck was in. As he had half-hoped that there might be there was a bicycle in the shed. Quite unperturbed by the thought that he was stealing, he wheeled it out and back to the roadway. If he had been called upon to justify his act he would have defended it on the grounds that it was essential for Lavina and himself to get to Stapleton before sunrise and that, barring accidents, the bicycle would ensure their being able to do so.

Having adjusted the saddle he got on to it and Lavina mounted the step.

Everything went well until just after they had crossed the main Dorking-Reigate Road. When they were on the outskirts of Betchworth another earth-tremor ran across the night-shrouded land.

The bicycle wobbled violently. Although Hemmingway applied the brakes he could not control it as it swerved to the side of the road and they both fell off, landing in a ditch.

Having picked themselves up they sat there for a few moments, while fainter tremors continued to agitate the earth.

'With this sort of thing going on here,' Hemmingway said, 'God knows what must be happening in the volcanic zones—places like the West Indies and Peru.'

'Thank goodness we're out in the open anyhow,' Lavina sighed. 'At least we won't be killed by bricks falling on our heads, or be buried alive under a building.'

When the tremors had ceased they mounted the bicycle again; but they proceeded very cautiously as here and there they came upon cracks in the tarmac of the road's surface, some of them as much as two or three inches wide, which made the going difficult.

In Betchworth a number of people were endeavouring to cope with the effects of the recent 'quake. A water main had burst at one end of the street and was flooding the roadway, while a little farther on there was a strong smell of escaping gas and they knew that at any moment there might be a nasty explosion. Just outside the village they saw that a jerry-built cottage had subsided and some men were dragging the victims from its ruins; but there was a faint greyness now in the eastern sky so, knowing that dawn was close at hand, Hemmingway pressed on.

Another two miles and in the greyish light the gates of Stapleton Court at last came into sight before them. They ran along the moss-grown drive and past the lake up to the old Georgian mansion. As they dismounted before the front door Hemmingway glanced at his watch and saw that they had done the last stage of their journey in just an hour.

The house was in darkness; its inmates apparently sleeping or else, perhaps, already on board the Ark. Lavina was just moving towards the front door when Hemmingway touched her arm.

'One second. I hadn't thought about it before but d'you mean to tell your uncle how Roy died?'

She hesitated. 'Perhaps it would be kinder not to.'

'Sure,' Hemmingway nodded. 'Let him think Roy got separated from you with Derek and that they may both turn up here at the last moment.'

'Derek—' she drew in her breath quickly. 'For the moment I'd forgotten that you'd left him behind.'

'On the contrary,' Hemmingway's voice was sharp. 'It was he who stole my car and left us in the lurch. He may be here already, in which case he's probably told your uncle about Roy. But if he hasn't made it, and does so during the day, one of us can tip him off not to say anything.'

'But you wouldn't have known about me if Derek hadn't escaped. And if Roy had still been alive the two of them would have been imprisoned and escaped together. How can we get over that?'

'We'll just say Derek said he lost Roy in the excitement and didn't know what had happened to him after he'd escaped himself. It's better for your uncle to imagine that Roy is still alive and has an equal chance with everybody else when the balloon goes up to-night, than to know that he's dead already, don't you think?'

'Yes. I hate having to lie about anything, but poor Uncle Oliver would be terribly cut up if he knew the truth.'

They were looking at each other, not at the house door, so they did not see it open a crack as Hemmingway said:

'Well, this is just one of those cases where we've got to do a bit of lying for the sake of sparing somebody else's feelings.'

Out of the corner of her eye Lavina glimpsed a faint line of light coming from the slightly open doorway. Turning at once she ran to it and cried:

'Hullo, there! It's us. We're here at last.'

The moment she moved, the door was swung wide open and Margery stood outlined in the dim light of a solitary candle which she had left on a table farther down the hall.

'So it's you!' she exclaimed. 'I heard voices so I came to see.'

'Oh, Margery!' With unaccustomed abandon Lavina flung

herself into her sister's arms. 'I *am* so glad to see you. We've had a simply frightful time.'

'There, there!' Margery patted her back and kissed her affectionately. In spite of her jealousy she was really very fond of Lavina. 'We've been most terribly anxious about you—all of us—and we had to lock Sam up to prevent his going back to London to look for you yesterday.'

'Then, he got here safely! Thank God for that!' Lavina breathed, and, turning, she added: 'You know Hemmingway, don't you?'

Hemmingway stepped forward into the candlelight. 'Margery entertained me quite a number of times down here while you were on your honeymoon.'

It was as though the word honeymoon had rung a bell in Margery's brain. Hemmingway sensed a sudden hostility in the tensing of Margery's figure and as her eyes switched for a second to Lavina's face he felt sure that she had heard those last words of his outside the front door about lying for the sake of sparing people's feelings, and was putting a wrong interpretation on them. He tried to persuade himself that it might only be his own guilty conscience that had suggested it, but he could have sworn that Margery had guessed there had been something between him and Lavina. In a second, however, she recovered herself, smiled at him and said:

'Of course. Hemmingway was best man at your wedding. He's an old friend of the family now; but where are Roy and Derek?'

'We're a bit worried about them,' Hemmingway confessed. 'It's rather a long story so perhaps we'd better keep it until the others can hear it as well, but we're hoping they'll get down here some time to-day. By-the-by, where are the others?'

'Getting up, I hope. I called them half an hour ago.'

'Why this early rising, darling?' Lavina asked. 'It's not half-past four yet.'

'It's on account of the comet,' Margery explained. 'You know that beastly red light it gives out that affects everybody so strangely? Oliver says that, even if it's cloudy to-day, the light will come through quite strongly almost directly after sunrise and get worse as the day goes on. Sunrise is at 4.43, and the comet will be over the horizon twelve minutes later; so it was decided that we ought all to be in the Ark before five o'clock.'

'Won't it affect anyone in the Ark, then?' Hemmingway inquired.

'It would in the ordinary way, but for the last few evenings Oliver has been experimenting with micas of various colours and he's found one which will neutralize the rays. Yesterday afternoon he and Daddy covered the port-holes of the Ark with it and they think we won't be affected if we sit in there all day.'

'I *must* go up and see them,' cried Lavina. 'Where's Sam?'

'He's in the nursery. They lured him in there by a trick and locked him up when he wanted to go back to London to try and find you.'

'What, they locked him up with Finkie?' Hemmingway laughed. 'Poor old Sam! You might at least have put them in separate cells.'

'Oh, but Mr. Fink-Drummond went days ago,' Margery said quickly. 'Didn't Roy tell you?'

'He said nothing about it when he arrived at St. James's Square.'

'Well, it was the evening before he left.' Margery looked a little uncomfortable. 'You know Roy drinks rather a lot, and I think he'd been at the bottle. Anyhow, he went up to have a chat with Fink-Drummond that evening and next morning he confessed to Daddy that he'd been sorry for our unwelcome guest and let him go.'

Hemmingway shrugged. 'Well, as it was much too late for Finkie to have done any harm, it doesn't really matter. In any case it wouldn't have been fair to leave him a prisoner with the chance that an earthquake might bring down the house, so we'd have had to free him before taking to the Ark ourselves.'

Margery nodded. 'You'd better run up and let Sam out yourselves. It'll be a glorious surprise for him. I must hurry and get breakfast ready because the others'll be down in a moment.'

Up in the nursery they found Sam. He was sitting, still fully dressed, hunched up in a chair with his head between his hands, and it was clear that he had not been to bed that night.

The second he saw Lavina he sprang up and, absolutely choking with relief, seized her in his arms; then, immediately his first excitement had subsided a little, he gripped and wrung Hemmingway's hand as though he would never stop. For the last hour Lavina and Hemmingway had been dreading that meeting but, when it came, Sam carried them both away by his intense, infectious joy at seeing them again. In a moment all three of them were talking at the same time; babbling out the hopes, fears and anguish through which they had passed during the last forty odd hours. As they went downstairs Gervaise and Oliver joined them. There were more kisses, embraces, hand-shakes. It was almost as though Hemmingway and Lavina had returned from a war or a journey to the North Pole.

Breakfast was a hurried meal as time was flying; but, as they ate, Lavina gave a carefully expurgated account of her adventures and Hemmingway helped her out when she was questioned about Derek and Roy.

On Sam's asking about the private papers which Hemmingway was to have brought down he had to confess that, having dropped the satchel containing them behind the counter in the tea-shop at Burgh Heath when the fight started there, the ensuing earth-quake had caused him to forget all about it.

The loss of the papers was such a little thing compared to Lavina's safety that Sam only laughed about it; but the fact that they had been left behind reminded Lavina that the bags she had packed were still at St. James's Square and she had little hope that if Derek did arrive he would bring them with him.

Fortunately, she had left many of her older garments at Stapleton when she had run away three years before, so, taking Sam with her, she dashed upstairs to her old room. Spreading the coverlet from the bed on the floor they hastily pulled any of her clothes that they could find out of drawers and cupboards, flung them on the coverlet and made it up into a big bundle. By the time they had done, the others were shouting to them from the hall to hurry.

Everything except last-minute articles had been loaded into the Ark already so apart from Lavina's things there was little for them to carry down to it. After a last look round the house they crossed the lawn and walked along the edge of the lake to the landing stage beside the slips from which the Ark had been launched.

It was almost daylight and the sun was on the point of rising as they settled themselves in a big, flat-bottomed punt, and Gervaise and Sam began to pole them out to the centre of the lake where the Ark floated. The summit of the huge, steel sphere stood over sixteen feet above the water, as it was ninety feet in circumference and a little less than half submerged, with the two-foot-wide landing stage, which ran round its equator just clear of the lake's placid surface.

Ten minutes were occupied in poling the heavily laden punt out to the centre of the lake. Except for a few small fleecy clouds the sky was clear and they had covered only half the distance when the sun came up over the distant tree tops. As they reached the Ark the sinister pinkish light which heralded the rising of the terror of the heavens was already colouring the sky to the east.

Quietly but quickly Gervaise opened the steel door in the curved side of the Ark and, ducking their heads, they scrambled through into its interior. Having hitched the painter of the punt to the landing-platform, in case they might need it again later, he followed them inside and closed the steel door behind him. As he did so, the others were gazing from the port-holes of the Ark in silence and awe upon what was, perhaps, the dawning of the last day of the world.

PREPARE FOR DEATH

Lavina and Hemmingway had seen the Ark when it had been
nearing completion but not since it had been fully equipped and,
on looking round them, they marvelled at the manner in which
every spare inch of space had been made use of.

Its main deck was on the same level as the landing-stage that
ran round its equator and its upper part was divided into five
compartments.

One half of the upper part—a quarter of the whole sphere—
was fitted up as a living-room, having a maximum length along
its partition wall of 30 feet and a breadth, from the dead centre
of the sphere to its rim, of 15 feet; which gave a semi-circular
floor-space of approximately 350 square feet—roughly that of a
rectangular room measuring 20 by $17\frac{1}{2}$.

The other half of the upper part was divided into four segments,
two large and two small. The larger each had approximately 105
square feet of floor space, and the smaller 62 square feet, being
the equivalent of rectangular rooms measuring, roughly, 12 by
9 and 10 by 6 respectively. Where the segments met there was a
tiny hallway, measuring 4 feet by 3 feet, cutting off their points
but enabling separate doors to lead into each of them. The
two biggest consisted of a men's cabin and a kitchen; the two
smallest, of a women's cabin and a bathroom with the usual
conveniences.

The height of the segment rooms at their inner ends was 14
feet, which, allowing for the ceilings curving gently down to the
outer extremity of the sphere, still gave room in the men's cabin
for two sets of three bunks above one another on the partition
walls; but the smaller, or women's, cabin had one set of two
bunks only. At eye level in the curved walls there were twelve
thick port-holes, now covered with mica shades to neutralize the
rays of the comet; six in the living-room, two each in the men's

cabin and kitchen, and one each in the women's cabin and bath-room.

A trap-door in the centre of the living-room led downwards to a lower deck which was also divided into segments. Below it, where the bilge of an ordinary ship would have been, the space was utilized as a fuel tank; as the Ark had a keel which could be lowered to give it direction and an engine which would propel it although, owing to its shape, only in a calm sea at a few knots an hour.

The lower deck housed the engine-room, the electric-light plant, the heating plant and a number of storerooms which at the moment were chock-full of supplies. In addition to food, which Hemmingway had estimated would last the passengers in the Ark for a couple of months, most of their purchases of seeds and implements and a collapsible canvas boat were packed away there; as well as a number of oxygen cylinders for use in the event of the Ark's having to remain sealed for any considerable length of time and the air inside it becoming foul. Below decks there was also a baggage room for their spare clothes. Fortunately Hem-mingway had had the fore-thought to send his down in advance and those of Derek and Roy had been stored there against their arrival.

Margery immediately took charge of the kitchen, Oliver began to potter among his scientific instruments, Gervaise busied himself adjusting the ventilators, while Sam went below to test the engines out once more. They had counted on Derek as their engineer but on his non-arrival Sam had spent several hours running over them, as his knowledge of engines was sufficient to enable him to take over at a pinch.

Now that they were on board the Ark, Lavina and Hemming-way felt the reaction from the strain of the previous days come suddenly upon them in all its strength. They were deadly tired and could hardly keep their heads up. There was nothing which required the urgent attention of either of them, so, at Gervaise's suggestion, they retired to their cabins to go to bed.

'Look! Look!' exclaimed Oliver, and Gervaise joined him where he was staring through one of the living-room's port-holes. In the east the sun was now well up and below it, just above the distant trees, gleamed the red monster. It was bigger than the sun and flamed so fiercely that it would have been impossible to have looked at it without some protection for the eyes, but the mica screens provided that; although, even allowing for their colour distortion, it could be seen that the whole park was now transfused with a horrid, unnatural light.

'We shall find the suspense of the next sixteen hours very trying, I fear,' Gervaise remarked.

His brother nodded. 'I suppose you will but to me, of course, the whole thing is quite enthralling. Think of it, Gervaise, the millions of years that this world has been in existence; the æons of time it took to form the rocks. Even the life on our planet is a comparatively modern growth. Then, the great ages of the glacial periods and, coming nearer home to the sort of spans we can appreciate, the rise and fall of the great civilizations; Egypt, Mesopotamia, China, Mexico, Peru, Greece, Rome—the Christian era—a mere flicker of the eyelid in time, but so long to us. This might have occurred at any moment during all those countless years, yet it just happens in our time and we are to have the privilege of witnessing the end of it all at 10.55 to-night.'

'If it does come to that, I shan't mind for myself.' Gervaise shrugged. 'There is very little left in this modern age of cheap-jack bluster that appeals to me and, in spite of some difficulty in preserving my own standards, I have managed to have a not unpleasant time; but it's hard on the younger people who are just beginning their lives and can accept change more readily. Yes, it's hard on them and I'm hoping, still, that we may escape.'

Sam, who had just come up from the engine-room, remarked: 'We wouldn't stand an earthly if it were really coming slap at us as it appears to be at present; but since it's not due to hit the earth until long after sunset I think we've got a sporting chance.'

'I doubt it.' Oliver lit one of his long, strong-smelling cheroots. 'Even though the actual point of impact will be in the north-eastern Pacific some hundreds of miles west of Southern California, the shock will be so terrific that I cannot see how the earth can fail to disintegrate.'

They turned away then and went about their work again; but Sam refused to be depressed. He had reached Stapleton himself, as he had promised Lavina, on the afternoon of the 22nd. When he had failed to find her there he had spent an evening of ever increasing anxiety and sat up all night frantic with worry. To occupy his mind Gervaise had persuaded him to spend the morning of the 23rd overhauling the engines of the Ark, in case Derek failed them; but by midday Sam had been so distraught that he had declared his intention of returning to London. Feeling that if they allowed him to set off in search of Lavina his chances of finding her would be incredibly remote; and that if she arrived after all, as she still might at any time, she would become equally distraught at not finding him there; they had decided to lock him up for his own protection.

His fifteen hours' imprisonment had seemed to him like fifteen days, for during them he had conjured up every sort of harrowing vision in which the most frightful calamities had overtaken her. But now that she had arrived, tired yet safe and well, to relieve him of the frightful mental torture he had been suffering for the best part of two days, he felt that the worst positively must be over; that whatever happened he could not suffer like that again and that it would be a rank injustice on the part of Fate to destroy them both within a few hours of their reunion. Yet with him, too, the reaction from strain was setting in and Gervaise persuaded him also to go to bed for a few hours.

As Sam left them Oliver tried out the wireless but the atmospherics were so bad that they could not get a coherent reception from any station.

At ten-past eight there was another violent earth tremor. From a placid sheet of water the lake was suddenly broken into a small choppy sea with wavelets swishing up on to its banks, while the Ark began to rock and pull upon its anchors.

As the Ark consisted of two spheres, one within the other, its inmates hardly felt the shock. The gyroscopes kept the deck steady but they could judge the violence of the tremor by the way the outer sphere gave to it and its portholes oscillated over those of the inner sphere, temporarily making it impossible to see out of the Ark because the two sets of port-holes were no longer directly opposite to each other.

From that time onward lesser quakes occurred with increasing frequency until eleven when there was the worst upheaval they had so far witnessed, but after it the earth became quiet again. The sun and comet were now blazing from a brazen sky. It was intolerably hot and stuffy so that, although the ventilators of the

Ark were fully open, Gervaise and Oliver sat perspiring in their shirt-sleeves and could breathe only with difficulty.

At Sam's wish, and with the willing consent of the others, Gervaise had been elected captain of the Ark and at midday he decided to release oxygen in order to revitalize the atmosphere.

Margery, sweltering in the kitchen but with her usual sense of duty to be done, insisted on cooking them a lunch; but no one except Oliver could do justice to it. Hemmingway, Lavina and Sam, having slept through the morning, were roused for the meal and appeared in dressing-gowns; but all of them were so tense with excitement that they could hardly manage to swallow a few mouthfuls of the food that Margery had cooked.

After the meal they tried the wireless again but it still gave out only a nerve-racking hotch-potch of unintelligible sounds. Then Sam helped to clear away. With a smile at Lavina, he said:

'Hadn't you better give Margery a hand in washing-up?'

She did not return his smile, and it was the first time Sam had known that happen since they had been married. Instead, she almost scowled, glanced down at her beautiful, slender hands, and replied quietly:

'If Margery wants any help she can call me; but if I've got to become a charwoman I rather hope the comet does hit us.'

She would have performed any menial task without complaint for a person she loved, providing it was not expected of her as a daily drudgery, but she saw no reason whatever why she should do anything of the kind when there was somebody else to do it for them. Margery was used to such things, and didn't mind them, so Lavina considered that Sam had been extremely tactless in drawing attention to her own laziness.

In the early afternoon there was another series of earthquake shocks, and, when the outer sphere of the Ark had righted itself again after one which was particularly severe, they were alarmed to see that the level of the lake was lower, and its waters appeared to be seeping away into some invisible chasm below it; but another shock restored the situation as a humped waterspout, about four feet high, suddenly appeared in its centre, and the waters came bubbling back to their original level.

It was shortly after this that they observed a group of people running across the meadows towards the southern shore of the lake. Through binoculars it was as easy to study them as though

214 SIXTY DAYS TO LIVE

they had been at comparatively close quarters. All of them were pouring with perspiration, and clad in the scantiest garments. On reaching the lake-side both women and men tore off their remaining clothes, and plunged into the water.

'It's the heat,' said Oliver, tapping the dial of a thermometer which registered the temperature outside the Ark. 'It's over 120 degrees in the sun out there, as hot as in the Sahara. They're trying to cool themselves by taking refuge in the water.'

'Poor wretches,' sighed Lavina. 'Can't we possibly take some of them into the Ark? It's too awful to see them suffering like that.'

'We've only got two spare bunks—those that Roy and Derek should have occupied,' Sam replied doubtfully.

But they were not called upon to make any such terrible decision as to whether they should overcrowd the Ark or leave the distraught people to their fate. Another tremor churned up the waters of the lake and, staggering to its banks, the terrified bathers dashed away stark naked over the meadow.

' "Those whom the gods wish to destroy they first make mad," ' quoted Gervaise, 'and it seems that a merciful god is intervening in this instance. The comet's rays must be so strong now that everyone exposed to them is probably quite ignorant of what he is doing.'

Lavina caught Hemmingway's eye but they both looked quickly away from each other again.

'That's it,' agreed Sam, 'and if they have been driven mad they'll at least be saved from this awful suspense or any real understanding of what's happening when the last phase occurs to-night.'

Sweltering still, they lay about in the easy-chairs while one or other of them continued to keep a look-out through the port-holes. It was about half-past four when Margery suddenly cried:

'Look! There's a car coming.'

They jumped to their feet and peered out in the direction of the drive, which was visible for some distance until it was hidden where it curved up to the house. A low, long-bonneted car was streaking along it.

'By Jove, it's mine!' exclaimed Hemmingway.

'Derek!' cried Lavina. 'Derek's got here after all!'

The car suddenly swerved from the drive, apparently out of control, and came charging down the bank towards them. Leaving the grass it plunged into the water, sending up a great sheet of spray, and wallowed to a halt, half-submerged and with its tyres bogged in mud, about ten feet out from the bank. Its driver was thrown violently forward across the wheel and remained there sagging over it.

'Quick! We must get him!' cried Sam, as Gervaise sprang to the door of the Ark.

The second he opened it a blast of hot air surged in, searing them like the breath of a furnace. But the men of the party all scrambled into the punt and started to propel it as swiftly as they could towards the water-logged car. Running to the door the girls watched them as they dragged Derek's limp body from the wreckage and, having lain it in the bottom of the punt, began to pole back as though all the devils of hell were after them.

When they reached the Ark perspiration was streaming from them; their shirts were soaking with it and all of them, temporarily affected by the comet's rays, were laughing or cursing insanely. Gasping, swearing, staggering about like drunken people, they pulled Derek into the Ark and slammed its door shut again.

It was several moments before the rescuers recovered physically or mentally from their brief adventure, but the two girls carried Derek's unconscious form into the men's cabin, bathed his face, undressed him and got him between the sheets in one of the bunks.

Ten minutes later Gervaise, his handsome, aquiline features unusually grave, came to look at Derek and, after a brief examination, declared that he was suffering from concussion through his head's having hit the windscreen of the car so hard as he was thrown forward. They did what they could for him and tucked him up; but Gervaise thought it probable that he would not come to for several hours and feared that, when he did, he might have lost his sanity from having been exposed for the whole day to the comet's rays.

Unnoticed by them while they had been looking after Derek, the sky had started to cloud over. Great, dense, sharp-edged, thunderous masses were rolling up from the east and the wind was rising.

By six o'clock both the sun and the comet had been blotted out and the force of the wind had become terrific. They could not hear its screaming as the Ark was now sealed again, but watching through the port-holes they could witness the effect of the gale.

With greedy insistence the wind was tearing at the leaves of the trees and shrubs in the park. Small branches were being broken off and carried bouncing away across the grass. Many of the smaller trees were bent right over in sharp curves. A great elm was torn up by its roots and crashed to earth. The wind increased to hurricane violence, bushes were uprooted and blown like pieces of paper across the unkempt garden. Tree after tree snapped under the terrific strain.

The sky was still black but by the discoloration of the mica over the port-holes they knew that the awful red light must still be shining through it. Another 'quake came and then the rain.

It streamed down with tropical fury, in such a spate that they could not see a yard beyond the port-holes, and it seemed that the very heavens had opened, just as in the Biblical account of the Flood.

By seven it had eased a little and great jagged streaks of lightning flashed almost continuously from the pitch-black sky. Even the fact of the Ark being sealed did not prevent the crash of the thunder reaching them. In peal after peal it rolled through the heavens like the echoing broadsides of great guns. The lake was churning like an angry sea and the outer sphere of the Ark was rocking wildly; but its internal platform was still held steady by its gyroscopes and its anchors prevented it from being washed up on the lake shore.

'The house!' cried Gervaise suddenly. 'The house!' And through the murk they saw a red glow up the slope in the distance. Stapleton Court had been struck by lightning and one side of it was burning fiercely.

A quarter of an hour later the rain ceased and they watched the fire as it ate up the old mansion. Gervaise seemed heartbroken. It had been his home for so many years. He had resorted to so many shifts to keep it out of the clutches of mortgagees; exercised so much ingenuity to preserve it and its parklands from the hands of vandals. Even so sober a man could not quite grip the fact that a roving comet might really destroy the whole earth in a few hours' time. Somehow he had always felt that after a brief sojourn in the Ark he would return to that beloved home, and now, whatever might befall, that could never be; it was being consumed before his eyes by flames.

Sam began to mutter useless words of comfort but Lavina promptly stopped him; she knew better than any of them, even Margery, what her father was feeling in those moments.

The lake had overflowed its banks, flooded by the terrific downpour. On one side it now stretched for half a mile across low-lying meadows, on the other it had risen half-way up the sloping lawn below the house. From time to time earth tremors made it sink or rise with startling suddenness and agitated its waters until they became like a rough sea, while on its shores oaks and elms crashed earthwards.

By eight o'clock the house was a flaming pile, more than half-consumed; but without warning another cloudburst shut it out from them and the spate of water was so solid that when the torrent eased, just about nine, they saw that it had extinguished the fire in the burning mansion.

From what little they could see through the still sheeting rain the tempest raged without abatement. The lake was half full of shattered trees which had been blown into it and were now being thrown about upon the heaving waters. Earth tremors shook the land almost without cessation; fork-lightning streaked the skies; earsplitting thunder boomed and reverberated overhead; the fury of the elements was indescribable.

From the time that they had rescued Derek the inmates of the Ark had thought of nothing but watching the incredibly terrible spectacle which was occurring before them. Hour after hour they had remained by the port-holes peering from them at every opportunity; nobody had even thought of suggesting an evening meal; they had forgotten the time and the fact that the chronometers might be ticking out the last minutes of their lives.

It was Oliver who recalled them to the probability of their impending fate by saying quietly:

'In case any of you wish to make last-minute preparations, I think I ought to warn you that it is now 10.45. We have only ten minutes to go.'

They left the port-holes then and looked at each other. It seemed that there was nothing to say, nothing to be done but to commend themselves to the mercy of the Father of all things.

Oliver alone remained near his instruments checking and recording. Margery went a little apart and, kneeling down, bowed her head in prayer. Sam's instinct was to follow her example but Lavina stood beside him holding his hand and he did not like to withdraw it. Gervaise had never made his daughters follow a conventional religion. Since Margery liked going to church he showed his tacit approval because he recognized that such devotions took the place of other things for certain types of women but when, at the age of sixteen, Lavina had told him that she did not wish to go to church any more because it bored her, he told her that, in that case, the church had ceased to serve any useful purpose for her. Lavina had never gone again but she was supremely confident that there was a God who would deal justly with her if she died, without her kneeling down to mumble set phrases or personal pleas for assistance.

She stood there with her chin up, staring with unseeing eyes at the wall of the Ark. Sam was beside her and Gervaise, on her other side, put an arm gently round her shoulders. Hemmingway sat down in an armchair opposite them and lit a cigarette. He had decided, quite dispassionately, that she was superbly beautiful and as he gazed up at her face the artist in him took a curious delight in the thought that, if they had to die, that living masterpiece was the last thing he would ever see.

Those last minutes seemed to drag interminably. The lake outside was still like a storm-tossed sea. The terrific downpour continued. Earthquake shocks were still felt through the buffer of the surrounding waters.

Sam was thinking over and over again: 'It can't happen. It can't happen—not to us.' Gervaise, that this was the greatest adventure that anyone could ever set out upon; either they would be blacked out in a few minutes or be re-born into a strange new world; Lavina, that she had had a lot of fun in this life and that it wouldn't be her fault if she didn't have a lot of fun in the next. Hemmingway was wondering vaguely if death would take them instantaneously or if they would first be called on to face awful torments and, in the meantime, gazing enchanted at the perfection of Lavina's face. Margery was hypnotizing herself with a rapid repetition of whispered words.

The tense silence was shattered by Oliver's voice as he announced quietly: 'By Greenwich Mean Time it is now 10.55.'

20

THE COMET STRIKES

For a moment nothing happened—nothing at all. They stared at each other waiting, wondering, holding their breath, tensing their muscles in an agony of suspense.

Suddenly the Ark began to rise. They could no longer see what was going on outside, but it felt for a second as though they were in an express lift soaring upward.

There was a terrific jerk. Both the cables had snapped as the huge sphere was flung sideways right out of the water. It hovered in the air for a second then came plunging back into the lake. The electric lights flickered and went out. The mechanism of its gyroscopes was constructed to counter roll; not to withstand violent shocks. The floor tilted. Instantly the whole cabin was in confusion. Oliver fell backwards from his instruments; the others staggered, lost their balance and pitched forward on their faces. The chairs slid sideways, bumping into one another. Books, boxes, binoculars and a score of other things crashed to the floor and rolled about it as the Ark, its gyroscopes broken, lurched heavily from side to side in the frightful upheaval.

Terrified, gasping, they scrambled to their knees and clung to its solid fixtures to prevent themselves being flung backwards and forwards. Gradually the deck steadied a little and they were able to get on their feet again. Gervaise found the switch of the emergency lights and turned them on.

The outer port-holes no longer oscillated above the inner ones as the sphere rolled and, staggering to them, they were able to peer out. Almost with surprise they saw that, except for the fact that they had been carried a hundred yards nearer to the north shore of the lake, the scene remained unaltered. The lake was still a tossing sheet of spray. The rain still sheeted down and through it, by the jagged flashes of lightning that still lit the sky, they could see that the landscape of lake-shore, trees and ruined mansion was just the same.

With a shout Sam seized Lavina. 'We've come through, darling! D'you understand—we've come through! We're going to live now.'

Gervaise drew a deep breath. 'Yes, we've passed through the Valley of the Shadow and come out the other side.'

'I wonder what sort of a world is left to us, though,' Hemmingway said gloomily.

Margery felt sick and ill from the buffeting they had sustained but was thinking of the home in which she had lived all her life. During the last ten years much of her time had been spent in household drudgery but she had not really disliked it, and now the house was a burnt-out ruin. She had never altogether brought herself to believe in the comet, even though she had seen it, because she had a life-long habit of ignoring facts if they were unpleasant ones.

The business of preparing the Ark had been to her rather like getting ready a temporary home in which whey were all going to live for a while, but she had never visualized its being flung into space or smashed to pieces. Instead, she had definitely persuaded herself that, having taken refuge there for a few hours, or days at the most, they would land again and she would take up her household routine just where she had left it off. But now there was no house and, for the first time, she really began to worry about what was to become of them all.

Now it seemed that their lives were out of danger Gervaise, too, was thinking of the house. The home that he had clung to for so long, through every financial difficulty and all the attempts which his friends had made to persuade him to sell it in order to ease his situation, was now gone—or most of it. He peered again through the sheeting rain and waited till another flash of lightning lit the building. The southern half of it was still standing and he said with relief:

'Some of the rooms may still be habitable and, anyhow, I think the stables have remained intact.'

The Ark was now adrift and the wind-swept waves drove it to the east side of the lake where it gently grounded on the mud some twenty yards from the shore. Another earthquake tremor, now impinging directly on it, suddenly flung them all off their feet and for a few minutes afterwards the Ark pitched heavily from side to side again making their stomachs rise, in the case of

Margery and Sam to such an extent that they had to disappear.

'I expect the 'quakes will go on for some time,' Oliver said, when the Ark had steadied and the more hardy members of the party had settled themselves once again. 'The ferment caused by the penetration of the earth's crust by a foreign body is certain to cause terrific agitation.'

'Is that what you think has happened?' Hemmingway asked.

'I imagine so. The comet was certainly solid or we should not have felt the shock; but it couldn't have been as big as I feared. As it came down in the north-eastern Pacific the depth of the waters there would have proved a buffer to some small extent but the crust of the earth isn't very thick and the forward curve of such a spherical mass would almost certainly penetrate the rock-layers; even if the back half of it is now standing up out of the waters like some huge new island continent.

'How's that going to effect us?'

'It's impossible to say. The comet may have been the size of the Isle of Wight or the size of Australia, but I doubt if it could have been as large as the Dominion or it would almost certainly have shattered the earth to pieces.'

'It may have formed a new continent for us, then?' murmured Hemmingway speculatively.

Lavina laughed nervously. 'Are you already thinking of planting the Union Jack there and annexing it for Britain?'

'Hardly,' he smiled. 'There are probably plenty of people who took refuge in cellars and have survived like ourselves, but hundreds of thousands must have died or gone mad, so I should think those of us who have come through will have all our work cut out to get *this* country running again before bothering about any others.'

'Since the moment of impact the comet may no longer be a solid mass,' Oliver went on. 'There is a theory, which some geologists believe, that another comet hit us many millenniums ago and broke into thousands of pieces which we know to-day as the South Sea Islands. They say it caused the flood which submerged Atlantis. In any case, I shouldn't think that anyone has been left alive in western North America, and the Far East must have suffered severely, too. Tidal waves as high as mountains will have swept everything before them on both coasts of the Pacific.'

The Ark had grounded again and the storm outside seemed to be abating a little although a minor tremor still occasionally agitated the waters of the lake.

'How long d'you think it'd be before any tidal wave could reach us here?' inquired the persistent Hemmingway.

'Tidal waves travel at great speed,' Oliver replied. 'If a sympathetic disturbance has taken place in the Atlantic earthquake zone and the resulting wave is great enough to sweep over western Britain it might reach us in three hours. Say we allow a margin of a further two hours; if nothing has happened by four o'clock in the morning I think we may consider ourselves safe.'

'In any case we only have a local flood to fear now,' Sam put in, 'and as the Ark was built for just such a contingency we haven't got much to worry about.'

'Sure,' nodded Hemmingway. 'But now the gyroscopes have gone we may receive an awful buffeting.'

'Oh, dear! And I shall be so ill,' sighed Margery.

'We shall be far better off than we should be in any other kind of craft,' Gervaise consoled her. 'As the Ark is unsinkable our lives are safe and after drifting for a few hours we are certain to be washed up somewhere.'

Sam went below to try and get the main lighting plant going again. The others settled down to wait. Time dragged interminably. Lavina smoked cigarette after cigarette until the air of the cabin was blue. Just after midnight the full lights came on, and Sam rejoined them. They talked, fell silent, talked again. They tried to keep conversation going but the strain was appalling. One o'clock came, then two. The seismograph showed that the shocks were gradually lessening in intensity. By three o'clock they were incredibly weary but beginning to hope that they would escape the perils of a flood. At four Oliver stood up and reopened the ventilators.

'You think we're pretty well out of the wood now?' Hemmingway asked him.

'Yes. As far as I am in a position to judge.'

At Oliver's pronouncement they all heaved a sigh of relief, and Lavina said suddenly: 'I'm feeling awfully hungry.'

Immediately she had spoken all the others realized that they too were hungry. It was fifteen hours since they had sat down to lunch and even then they had eaten little.

'I'll cook something,' Margery volunteered. 'How about ham and eggs? Would that do?'

'Fine!' Hemmingway laughed. He was thinking how the simple mention of such a good, homely dish seemed to restore things to normal again. They were still alive and there was now every chance that they would go on living.

'I'll give you a hand,' said Sam, following Margery into the kitchen. 'In my younger days I used to be rather a dab at cooking. My old mother taught me when we lived in Bradford, and some time I'll treat you all to some Yorkshire cookies.'

'You're not suggesting we're here for ever, are you?' asked Lavina.

'Good Lord, no, darling!' Sam patted her shoulder. 'But we'll have to make this our headquarters for a day or two; anyhow until we can find out what's going on in the rest of the country. As you're no good in a kitchen, you'd better lay the table. You'd make a splendid Nippy.'

Lavina's white teeth bit into her small, very slightly drooping underlip. She was very glad still to be alive but she had never thought of herself as a Nippy and did not take the suggestion as a compliment. Sam had been brought up in an artisan's home where the women of the family did all the work; but when Lavina had been a child Gervaise had still been able to afford servants at Stapleton. Except for a little assistance at such picnics as she had decorated, Lavina had never waited upon anybody in her life and she saw no reason at all why she should start now. She ignored Sam's suggestion, and, although she hated any form of nursing, declared that, since everybody else seemed to have forgotten him, she was going to have a look at Derek.

When she returned to report that Derek did not appear to have suffered from the upheaval and, although still unconscious, was breathing stertorously, Hemmingway was just finishing laying the table.

Gervaise felt that, having survived the cataclysm, they were all entitled to a glass of wine from the limited stock for which they had been able to spare space in one of the store-rooms and, going down the hatchway, he brought up a couple of bottles of Bollinger.

When the meal was served they had to be careful how they ate it as, now that it was grounded again, tremors shook the Ark every few moments and just as they were finishing there was a moderately severe one which set them afloat for several minutes. But the food and wine did them good and at a quarter-past five they crawled into bed in a more cheerful mood than had been possible all through the long and anxious hours since the previous morning.

Such sleep as they got did little to refresh them as the sheeting rain drummed a tattoo on the top of the steel sphere, and tremors woke them which made them feel sick and queasy. About ten o'clock they forgathered once more in the living-room; a scarecrow crew, the two girls tousled, the men unshaven, Hemmingway with a three-day beard.

The skies were leaden grey and it was still raining, but day-light enabled them to examine the scene of desolation around them. Branches, uprooted bushes and whole trees were floating in the lake; and the meadows, too, were dotted with the debris of the storm. The entire landscape was haggard, dreary and depressing beyond description.

At breakfast, to which they sat down in dressing-gowns, they were rather silent; and, afterwards, Lavina declared that she was going to have a bath. The others voted it a good idea but as it had been her suggestion, they naturally let her have first turn in the bathroom.

After she had been there for half an hour Margery called out to know how much longer she was going to be, but her cheerful treble came back to them:

'What's it matter how long I am? We've got all day before us, haven't we?'

She stayed there for a good hour and then disappeared into the cabin which she shared with Margery. The others took their baths in turn, sat about, read and talked at intervals until lunch-time, while the rain descended without intermission, still further swelling the lake. Margery prepared the meal as usual and the others laid the table. When it was ready they shouted to Lavina.

It was another ten minutes before she appeared and, when she did, they all stared at her in astonishment. Throughout the previous day she had worn the bedraggled garments in which she had spent her captivity and made her escape out of London: her only attempt to restore her appearance having been to comb her hair back flatly on her head in imitation of the Garbo. Now,

H

however, she had selected a girlish summer dress from among the old clothes she had collected at the house before coming aboard the Ark, and had spent the entire morning beautifying her person. Her hair was curled; if not with the art of the professional hair-dresser, at least in a simple and graceful fashion. Her nails were repainted and her make-up as perfect as if she had been going to a Royal Garden Party.

'Well, what are you all looking at?' she asked with supreme self-satisfaction.

'You, of course,' said Sam with a chuckle.

'Oh? What's wrong with me?' she smiled back innocently.

'Why, nothing. It's a joy to see you looking the Princess again. I like that little frock, too. It makes you appear even younger than you really are.'

'Thank you, darling.' She sat down at the table. 'I saw no reason why I should continue to go about looking like something the cat sicked up just because we have to remain cooped up in this thing for a day or two.'

Margery stiffened, and, apparently unable to contain herself, left the table. Dashing into the kitchen she slammed the door behind her.

Lavina looked up wide-eyed. 'What on earth's bitten her?' she inquired, raising her carefully plucked eyebrows.

There was an awkward silence until Gervaise said: 'I fear she took your remark personally.'

'Naturally,' said Sam, with a worried glance at his beautiful young wife. 'Between clearing up after breakfast, looking after Derek, and preparing lunch she hasn't had a moment to tidy herself; whereas you've been gilding the lily the whole morning. I'm sure you didn't mean it, darling, but it was damned tactless of you, and you'd better go and apologize.'

Lavina's eyes snapped. 'Of course I didn't mean it. How absurd! But Margery always was over-sensitive. She imagines that everyone is always thinking about her. I was only expressing a personal opinion as to the best way in which I can keep up my own morale while we have to remain here.'

'Well, you'd better go and tell her so,' said Sam.

'Certainly not. Why should I apologize for something I never said—or, at least, never intended to refer to her?'

'Margery can be very stupid sometimes,' said Gervaise quietly, 'but that's not her fault. I think it would be a gracious act, dearest, to tell her you weren't thinking about her at all, don't you?' He knew his Lavina infinitely better than Sam did, and she rose at once.

'Of course, you old sweet, if you want me to, and I'll offer to set her hair for her this evening into the bargain.'

When the two girls returned from the kitchen everyone began to talk at once, to cover Margery's embarrassment, and Lavina inquired quickly what Gervaise thought of Derek's prospects of recovery.'

'He's still unconscious, as you know,' Gervaise said. 'I had a look at him several times during the night, and this morning we stripped him and washed him all over. He was in a shocking mess with bruises and cuts, but otherwise uninjured, apart from his head.'

'That'll be the packet he got when he was beaten up in Hyde Park,' declared Hemmingway, 'unless he's collected a fresh lot since.'

'I don't think so,' Gervaise shook his grey head. 'All his major injuries were bandaged, so they're almost certainly the ones to which you attended three nights ago. I put fresh lint on them, but until he comes round there's nothing else we can do.'

'I can't think why Roy wasn't with him,' remarked Oliver. 'It's been worrying me all night.'

'But they became separated in Hyde Park. We told you, Oliver, dear,' murmured Lavina, with a warning glance at Hemmingway.

'That's it,' he agreed, 'and Roy may still be quite all right. I expect most people are who had the sense to go underground yesterday, and so avoid the rays of the comet.'

'Well, we can only hope so,' Oliver sighed.

Directly after lunch Lavina set about clearing the things and washing up without making any parade of doing so as, having decided to do it, her one idea was to get through the business as quickly as possible.

During the afternoon the weather cleared a little, but the tremors continued, and they sat about uneasily, disinclined to read as the shocks still made them feel sick and shaky every time they came. At four o'clock the sun broke through the clouds, but

it was a pale, watery disc, quite unlike the splendid giver of light
and life which had been blazing upon them throughout the mid-
June days. Its sinister companion now having rushed from the
heavens to bury itself in the North Pacific, the red radiance had
disappeared, and, removing the coloured mica shades from the
portholes, they looked out once more upon a landscape of
normal colours. The lake was greatly swollen from the hundreds
of tons of water that had rushed into it both from the skies and
down its slopes. The broken trees looked more bedraggled than
ever, and the fields to the south were flooded as far as they could
see.

What with Lavina's incessant smoking, Oliver's cheroots, and
all the others puffing at cigarettes from time to time, the atmosphere of the big room had become so loaded that it was almost
blue. On Margery's remarking on it, Gervaise suggested that
they should get some air and exercise by walking round the circular landing-stage outside the Ark.

The damp, cool air soon cleared their heads, and they began
to feel more cheerful as they followed each other round and
round the narrow platform in single file like, as Sam jokingly
said, a bunch of convicts.

Once a sudden 'quake nearly threw them off their balance, but
they halted in their tracks, and, flattening themselves against the
curving sides of the sphere, hung on by its lifelines until the
tremor was over.

Hemmingway was leading the little procession, and it was just
five o'clock when, having circled the Ark a dozen times, he passed
round its eastern side, and again reached its northern flank. The
second he could see round the curve to westward he gave a shout
of dismay.

'Run! Run!' he cried. 'Get back inside!' And plunging forward himself, he dashed towards the door. It was about forty
feet away, in the section of the Ark that was facing south-south-
west, and, although he was by no means a coward, as he ran his
scalp began to prickle with sheer horror. Some of the others
followed him, the rest turned and headed back the other way; but
a moment later all of them were goggling at the terrifying thing
that he had been the first to see.

To westward, over the burnt-out mansion, something that
looked like a solid black cloud was advancing rapidly. It had

first appeared as a long, low line over the distant trees, but with extraordinary speed its dead flat edge, straight as a ruler, seemed to leap up into the sky. It was denser than any cloud, and at the second glance they realized that it was a huge wall of water; a vast tidal wave, hundreds of feet in height, approaching at the speed of a racing aeroplane and engulfing hills, trees, gardens, as it rushed upon them.

A mighty wind, caused by the air displaced by the oncoming terror, moaned through the trees, its note increasing to a scream. Trees were snapped off short or torn up by the roots and carried high into the air. From a dull, sullen murmur the voice of the rushing waters leapt in a moment to a thunderous roar. The whole earth shook, winced, and writhed, and tormented nature screamed aloud in a hundred tongues as, tumbling over each other, the six humans fell into the Ark, and Sam, who was last in, slammed its door.

Scrambling to their feet, they staggered to the portholes, and Hemmingway was just in time to see the ruined house crumble to pieces as the giant wave crashed against it and roared on.

Next second it had blacked out the whole landscape, and towered above them to the skies.

'Hold on!' yelled Gervaise; and, as they gripped the nearest fixtures, the Ark shot forward like a bullet from a gun, carried away deep in the roaring waters.

For minutes on end they were too terrified even to attempt to think. It was as though some gigantic foot had kicked the ball and sent it spinning. They were flung from side to side and from floor to ceiling like a handful of peas in a tin that is sent rolling down a hillside. Screaming, groaning, their muscles wrenched, their senses reeling, they clung with the strength of desperation to any fixed object they could get a grip on until another twist of the sphere dragged them from it.

At last, the engines and stores in the lower portion of the Ark steadied it and brought the deck almost horizontal again.

Panting, groaning, sobbing, they picked themselves up. As they did so, the Ark began to rise.

The lights had gone out, which added to the confusion, and the portholes showed only as faint, grey patches in the blackness. But as the sphere wobbled upwards they lightened, and it seemed as though a mass of turgid green water was rushing downwards past them with here and there a dark object glimpsed for a second, which might have been a tree trunk or a body.

With unexpected suddenness daylight flashed into the room again. The air the Ark contained had brought it rushing to the surface; its speed had increased as it rose, so that it popped up like a cork, almost leapt clear of the water, splashed back, and settled to a heavy roll.

To add to the discomfort of the shaken and bewildered party, the floor was now awash with nearly a foot of water which had spurted in through the ventilators, Gervaise having had no time to close them. Slowly and painfully they began to pull themselves together.

All of them were bruised, giddy, half-fainting. With the water splashing about them, and the Ark still lurching from side to side, they dragged themselves to sitting positions, and began to examine their injuries. Hemmingway lay still, under the table. At first they feared that he was dead, but Sam crawled over to him, and, raising his head, found that he had only been knocked unconscious. Oliver was moaning with a broken arm, Margery was being violently sick. Lavina, chalk-faced and gasping, was wishing she could die where she lay, her back propped up against a bookcase.

Gervaise had suffered least. He had managed to throw himself down in the small hallway where the other cabins opened into the living-room and, bracing himself with his shoulders against one door and his feet against another, had succeeded in preventing himself from being flung about like the rest.

Standing up, he went over to help Sam with Hemmingway. As they lifted him into a chair Sam groaned from the pain of a wrenched ankle. Lavina pulled Margery to her feet and, half leading, half carrying her, pushed her into another chair; then she flung herself, sobbing, into Sam's arms. He nearly fell. She was heavier than she looked, but he managed to support her and, staggering to the settee which ran round two sides of the dining-table, collapsed upon it, drawing her down beside him.

Gervaise helped his brother to a seat, and, looking round, saw that for the moment no more could be done for any of the shattered party. The first thing was to get the sphere clear of water. Wading through it, he fetched a broom from the kitchen;

then, sloshing back across the living-room, he exerted all his strength and wrenched open the door of the Ark.

So far, he had had no time to think or to realize the full significance of what had happened to them; that they had been spared once again and were all alive seemed the only matter of importance. But, as he opened the door and the water gushed out round his knees, he drew a sharp breath. Using the broom to steady himself, he began to stagger slowly round the platform, gripping the handholds on the sphere's surface with his free hand as he went to prevent himself from being washed overboard.

Far away to the east there was a faint line of whiteness; the foaming crest of the colossal wave as it raced over the country devouring everything before it. He watched it for a few minutes until it had disappeared, fading into the grey of the horizon. Lurching on, he made the full circuit of the sphere.

When he reached the door again he remained there for a moment motionless. They were at sea. The houses, trees, and fields of England lay hundreds of feet below them. On every side, as far as he could see into the grey distance, there lay only the gently heaving waters. They were utterly alone on a huge and desolate ocean.

21

THE GREAT WATERS

After Gervaise had come back into the Ark and swept it clear of water, his next job was to attend to the casualties. With Lavina's help he carried the unconscious Hemmingway into the men's cabin, but directly they entered it their attention was drawn to Derek by low groans issuing from his bunk.

Having hardly recovered their own wits after their frightful tossing, they had not yet had a chance to think of him; but when the Ark had been overwhelmed by the flood he, like themselves, had been thrown up and down like a pea in a box, and the bumping of his head on the upper bunk had brought him back to consciousness.

After the first blow he had instinctively braced himself against the sides of the bunk and so saved himself from being thrown out or from further injury, but during those awful moments when he was being whirled head over heels like a man in a revolving coffin he had not had the faintest idea where he was or what was happening to him.

While Gervaise undressed Hemmingway, Lavina attended to Derek. It was now four days since he had received his beating-up in the Park and three since he had been trampled on while escaping. But during the last twenty-four hours he had had complete rest, so only his major injuries still pained him, and when he regained consciousness he was perfectly clear-headed.

In his delight at seeing Lavina safe and sound he seized both her hands and kissed them. Giving him a quick kiss on the forehead in return she pushed him back into his bunk and, herself still shaken by her recent terrifying experience, asked him how he had come through the upheaval.

'Oh, I'm all right,' he smiled. 'Until you came into the room I thought I was suffering from a nightmare. The great thing is that you're here in the Ark. God! What a time I had trying to find you. But what on earth's been happening?'

In a few brief sentences she told him of what had occurred when the comet had hit the earth and how a giant tidal wave had just carried them away with it; then, remembering Hemmingway's suggestion, she added that they had thought it wise not to tell Oliver of the fate that had befallen Roy.

He nodded. 'Yes, it'd be kinder not to let the old chap know that Roy was killed in a drunken brawl. If he'd been with me in the Park, we might easily have got separated when the prisoners burst out of the enclosure.'

'What happened to you after you left St. James's Square in Hemmingway's car?' she asked. 'He was furious about your taking it, you know.'

'Oh, *damn* Hemmingway! Just because he's got an outsize brain he behaves as though he were the Prime Minister, Chief of the Imperial General Staff and the Archbishop of Canterbury rolled into one. The smug fool! He tried to order me about as though I was a child, and I wasn't having any. Naturally I took his car. I was so darned anxious about you and there was nothing else to get around in.'

'You must have got the note he left, though, saying that he had found me; or didn't you go back to St. James's Square that night as you said you would?'

'No, I couldn't make it. The trouble was, I thought I'd traced you to Tilbury where they were loading a lot of women on to the liners in the Docks. I didn't get there till late afternoon and then the rays of the comet sent everybody berserk. People were doing the most extraordinary things. One chap tried to kill me; and a bank manager, who had opened up his bank and was standing outside it giving money away, insisted on my accepting a ten-pound note. I felt pretty gay myself but I more or less managed to keep my wits because the really urgent matter of finding you was never out of my mind. Getting back to St. James's Square didn't seem particularly important and it wasn't till nearly eleven o'clock that I could get anybody to talk sense. Round about midnight I managed to hire a speedboat and went off to the *Kenilworth Castle* which was lying in the estuary of the Thames. I found the woman I was looking for all right and she was pretty as a picture, but it wasn't you.'

'Poor darling. It was a gallant effort, though.'

'Well, naturally I did my damnedest. But when I got back to Tilbury I found that some A.R.P. people had commandeered Hemmingway's car. I had hell's own job to get it back again and I only succeeded after sun-up, when the whole world had started to go mad. I wasted two hours myself, playing shove-halfpenny with a fellow in the garage, before I suddenly woke up to the fact that I'd got a job of work to do. After that, the whole business was a kind of nightmare. I've no idea what time I got back to St. James's Square, but I read Hemmingway's note and set off again for Stapleton. The scenes I saw on my way down just beggar description and I was driving like a lunatic. I suppose the strain proved too much for me by the time I'd reached the park because everything simply blacked out.'

By this time Gervaise had stripped Hemmingway and got him into a suit of pyjamas. With Lavina's help he bandaged the injured man's head and he came round soon after they had lifted him into one of the bunks on the side of the cabin opposite to Derek. As the cut on his scalp did not appear to be serious they left the cabin to attend to the others.

Sam was hobbling painfully about fetching basins for Margery and trying to comfort her in the frightful bout of sickness from which she was suffering. Oliver sat patiently in a chair nursing his broken arm. They cut his coat-sleeve away and while they were setting the arm in splints he said:

'I've been working out what must have happened. When we built the Ark our purpose was to provide against the possibility of a tidal wave caused by under-sea eruptions in the Atlantic temporarily flooding the lower levels of Britain. But even given the most serious disturbances in that area, no wave of such magnitude as the one which caught us could possibly have been created in that way. Besides, I'm sure that any wave thrown up in the district of the Azores would have reached us long before.'

'What is your theory, then?' Gervaise asked.

'We know that the comet fell in the north-eastern Pacific,' Oliver replied, 'and such a huge body would naturally displace terrific quantities of water. That wave may have been a mile, or even two miles, high when it started. It must have traversed the whole of North America sweeping everything before it, poured into the Atlantic and forced the Atlantic waters up with its momentum so that it was still between a quarter and half a mile high when it leaped right over Britain. If I'm correct, it was travelling at more than 300 miles an hour.

'Then the whole world will be drowned in another deluge,' said Gervaise.

Oliver winced as his brother tightened the bandage. 'The wave, which is still moving east, may exhaust itself by the time it reaches Central Europe; but the effect of the comet must have been like that of a stone thrown into a pond. Australasia will certainly have been overwhelmed and the Far East would have caught the full force of the wave as it moved westward, so the bulk of Asia is certain to be flooded too.'

'India might escape,' suggested Sam, looking up from where he was kneeling by Margery.

'Perhaps. The Himalayas and the highlands of Tibet should certainly be immune; but, even when the waters settle, the comet will have caused a great displacement. The oceans will have risen ten or perhaps twenty feet all over the world with the result that all low-lying lands will be under water. The Sahara will become a lake again and the plains of lower India are sure to be submerged.'

'This is much worse than we bargained for,' said Gervaise gravely. 'You will remember you felt originally that the Rockies would prove a sufficient barrier to any wave the comet might throw up. You thought that only portions of the western coast of America and places like Japan and China would suffer; while we should get off comparatively lightly, with a local wave which would subside in a few hours and leave us safely aground on the mud.'

'Yes,' Oliver confessed. 'This particular aspect of the catastrophe is far more serious than anything I had anticipated. I doubt if there will be a single human being left alive within two or three thousand miles of us by to-morrow morning; and when a deluge of this magnitude is likely to subside it's quite impossible to say.'

Sam gave him an anxious look. 'I suppose the danger now is that when the waters do settle we may have drifted so far that we won't even come down in England?'

'Exactly. We may find ourselves floating in the North Sea or the

Atlantic; but, of course, I shall be able to keep a check on our position as soon as the sun breaks through again and I can take observations.'

'What I can't understand,' Sam went on, 'is why the Ark wasn't crushed like an egg-shell under all that weight of water. We must have been seven or eight hundred feet below its crest when the wave struck us and at that depth the pressure per square foot is simply enormous.'

Gervaise tied a neat knot at the end of the bandage he had been winding round the splints on his brother's arm. 'I think I can answer that. The pressure was mainly behind us and the sphere was free to move forward with the wave. Naturally, the Ark's buoyancy caused it to start moving upwards the second the water covered it. Where we were fortunate was, that it must have been carried up very quickly; otherwise it would have been smashed to pieces against the trees on the far side of the park.'

'Well,' said Lavina cheerfully, 'the great thing is we're still all alive and kicking. Come on, Margery, my dear; although I haven't got a bone left in my body, I'm going to put you to bed.'

Having attended to her sister while Gervaise got the electric light going again, she spent an hour tidying the cabin and generally took charge of all the arrangements in a way that Sam found surprising. As he could cook and she couldn't she made him cook the dinner, but with quiet efficiency she selected what they would have, laid the table herself and, when the meal was cooked, carried trays in for Derek and Hemmingway. None of them felt much like eating as the Ark was now rolling slightly but continuously yet she cajoled and bullied them into eating up the food so that they should preserve their strength. When she was at last able to get to her cabin and undress, she found on her body a dozen great bruises which were already turning a yellowish purple, and her head was splitting with fatigue; but as she crawled into her bunk she had the satisfaction of knowing that she had shirked nothing and gone through with the hideous business as well as any old trouper would have done when called upon to play a similar part on a nightmare film set.

The night passed uneventfully, but in the morning no land was to be seen and it was impossible to take an observation of the sun as the sky was still overcast with thick layers of dull, grey clouds. The compass showed them to be drifting west. It was raining gently and persistently as though it never meant to stop and a sudden change in the weather had made the temperature fall to such a marked extent that it seemed as if they had passed straight from June to October; but Sam coped with the heating plant, which had been thrown out of action, and once he had got it going the temperature in the Ark was soon adjusted.

Derek and Hemmingway both wanted to get up but, having taken charge of them, Lavina insisted that it would be better for them to spend the day in bed as, in any case, there was nothing for them to do and nowhere to go.

With her sister she was less merciful. Margery had passed a miserable night, but Sam's ankle was now swollen and Lavina decreed that he must keep it up; as there was no one else who could do the cooking, Margery would have to bestir herself, for an hour or two at all events, to attend to it. With the air of a martyr Margery obeyed the commands of her imperious younger sister while Lavina, who considered that she had done every-thing that was necessary, employed herself in amusing Hemming-way and Derek.

The two of them had had a brief slanging match after Hem-mingway had come to the previous evening, following which they had agreed to forget the borrowed car; but a definite animo-sity still lingered and Lavina's presence was not calculated to have a soothing effect.

Derek had known her for so long that they had many subjects in common to talk about of which Hemmingway knew nothing. She treated Derek with the familiarity of a brother and now called him 'darling' or 'my sweet' in the same way that she had been accustomed to throw casual endearments about among her friends in the film world. Hemmingway kept on telling himself that he had not a shadow of right to resent their *camaraderie* but he did resent it nevertheless.

On the other hand, Derek had little but his good looks and self-confident manner with which to attract Lavina's attention, whereas Hemmingway had not only an infinitely finer brain but a much quicker tongue, so he was able to offer much better entertainment.

Each would have denied it hotly if anybody had accused him of wishing to arouse Lavina's interest in himself, as they were both only too conscious that being married to Sam placed her out of bounds, but each was wishing secretly that he had her to himself, and cursing the presence of the other.

Lavina was perfectly conscious of the way they felt and, without the least malice, was thoroughly enjoying the situation. As Derek had very little to talk about outside the normal interests of a gentleman-farmer she had no desire at all for a *tête-à-tête* with him but while a heart-to-heart with Hemmingway would have intrigued her a lot she felt that would be too dangerous, in view of the experience through which they had been together.

After cooking lunch Margery retired to bed again, bemoaning the misery which the constant rocking of the sphere caused her. As there was nothing whatever for them to do Gervaise and Oliver decided to take a nap in the men's cabin where the two invalids were also dozing in their bunks. In consequence Sam, who had volunteered to keep a look-out although there was nothing to be seen on the vast expanse of waters which encompassed them, at last got Lavina to himself.

As the wireless was out of action she had just put a selection of records on the gramophone when Sam called her over to him. He was sitting in one arm-chair with his injured foot resting on another and, switching off the gramophone, she sat down in his lap. He petted her a little and then said quietly:

'My sweet, I've been wanting to have a chat with you.'

'Well, now's your chance,' she smiled down at him.

'It's about Margery,' he hesitated. 'You're not being very kind to her, are you?'

'My dear, I never give her a thought. She's just one of those people one doesn't think about. I gave up trying long ago but I certainly haven't been unkind to her.'

'Don't you call it unkind to drag anybody who's feeling ill out of bed to cook lunch?'

'Oh, that!' Lavina lit a cigarette and, tilting her aristocratic profile in the gesture that Sam had so often admired, puffed out the smoke. 'Well, somebody had to cook lunch and you're the only one among us who can cook except Margery. I ought not to have let you cook dinner for us last night with a bad ankle like this and you must keep it up.'

'I know, my dear, but surely you could have knocked up some sort of a meal for us yourself instead of idling away the whole morning with Hemmingway and Derek? There's plenty of cold stuff among the stores; it only meant opening a few tins.'

'Really, Sam, I think you're being rather stupid. Margery's quite all right; only a little sea-sick, that's all. Why should you want me to treat her like a pampered baby?'

'She's a woman like yourself and entitled to consideration. Think of the fuss there'd be if anybody expected you to do a job of work when you were ill.'

'I have, often. Naturally, I like people to fetch and carry for me. Why shouldn't they? They enjoy it. But many's the time I've walked on to a film set feeling like death and gone right through till the small hours of the morning in order not to hold up the rest of the cast.'

'Then I take off my hat to you, darling. But, all the same, I think you've got to take a different view of things from now on. Last week you were Lady Curry, a famous beauty with a million-aire husband, lots of servants and other people, either paid or willing, to run your errands in the sort of life we all knew. Now you're just my darling wife, Lavina, but that's the only thing that hasn't changed.'

'Like hell it is!' broke in Lavina, 'and how does that affect . . .' but, having got into his stride, Sam cut her short and went on:

'What's going to become of us, God knows. But we've plenty of stores so if we're not wrecked in a storm we ought to be able to hang out until we land up somewhere. Whether we do or don't, everything's going to be different from now on. You've got to forget this Princess stuff, become a real woman, and do your share of the work. As you can't cook, the sooner you learn the better. I think you should start in at once as scullery-maid to Margery and when you've got the hang of it a bit you can do the job turn and turn about.'

Lavina removed herself from Sam's lap, stood up, yawned, and stretched gracefully. For the thousandth time he admired the perfect lines of her slim little figure which showed to admir-able advantage in the silk shirt and old bell-bottomed trousers she was wearing that day.

Still with her back to him she said quietly: 'You know, Sam, I've never found you a bore before but this afternoon I don't find you the least amusing. I'm going to read in my bunk,' and without a glance in his direction she left him sitting there.

That evening she provided them with a cold supper for which Derek and Hemmingway, both now more or less recovered, got up. When the meal was finished she said suddenly:

'I've been thinking that we ought to divide up the work of the ship. Gervaise, as Captain, issues the stores and is a father to us all; Oliver's our navigator and looks after the instruments and things; Derek's the engineer, so he'll see to the electric light, the heating plant, and the motors if we have any chance to use them; Margery, quite obviously, was cut out for cook. That leaves Sam, Hemmingway and myself, doesn't it?'

They nodded agreement and she went on:

'Well, I'm easy. Somebody will have to mother you and I'm not at all bad with my needle; so if you loose a button or anything you'll know where to come. Hemmingway can lay the table and do mess-waiter and, as Sam loves pottering about in kitchens, he'd better be scullery-man and help Margery with the washing-up. That's fair division of labour, isn't it?'

'Fine,' Derek and Hemmingway agreed simultaneously while Gervaise, Oliver and Margery smiled their assent. In the face of such a clear majority Sam could do nothing. His clever little devil of a wife had out-manœuvred him completely. She would sew their buttons on. Yes, when they lost them—which would be about once a month—and in the meantime she would lie about smoking and reading while the rest of them did all the work.

He saw her smiling at him beneath lowered lids and twitched his own mouth humorously in reply. He knew that, even if she sat about doing nothing day after day, she would provide them with splendid entertainment and keep their spirits up with constant laughter. That was her natural contribution; to be supremely decorative and delightfully amusing. He readily forgave her the trick she had played him, realizing that he had been a fool ever to suggest that she should use those lovely hands of hers except to stroke his own face.

Again next day the low grey clouds covered the sky as far as they could see in every direction, bearing out any chance of taking the altitude of the sun. To everybody's surprise Lavina appeared shortly after breakfast in an extremely abbreviated swim-suit with the intention, now the waters were calm and only lapping gently round the Ark, of bathing from its circular platform.

The instant Derek saw her he exclaimed: 'By Jove! What a grand idea. I'll be with you in ten secs.'

But by that time Lavina was back again inside the centrally-heated sphere. She loathed the cold and one sniff through her delicately-arched nose at the chill air outside had been quite sufficient to make her abandon all idea of having a swim. Nevertheless she did not change into anything else but lay about all day displaying her admirable limbs.

Hemmingway could hardly keep his eyes off her although he did his level best to expunge from his agitated brain the memories which crowded into it; and Derek fidgeted nervously to such an extent that Gervaise inquired what was the matter with him. He then got down *Mr. Sponge's Sporting Tour* and, turning his back on Lavina, determinedly buried his nose in it.

After lunch there was trouble about the cigarettes. They had a fair supply on board but, with a view to making them last as long as possible, it had been agreed the previous night that they should each be issued with a packet of 20 Virginians per day, except Oliver who smoked only his own long cheroots. In addition, they were to allow themselves one Turkish cigarette each after lunch and dinner; for which purpose a box was to be kept in the drawer with the silver for passing round the table at the end of every meal.

As the first box of a hundred had been opened the previous night at dinner only five cigarettes should have been missing from it for Margery, being ill, had not had one; but a whole additional row was gone.

On opening the box Gervaise noticed the shortage at once and, looking round the table, said quietly:

'I'm afraid somebody's been cheating.'

'I have, darling,' Lavina confessed at once. 'Twenty cigarettes a day isn't half my usual ration. As I ran out last night, I raided the box before I went to bed.'

'Well, you mustn't do that sort of thing, dearest; it's not fair to the rest of us.'

'Now, don't get excited,' she said quickly. 'I only took a couple and I'm not having one after lunch or dinner to-day, to make things even.'

'But, my dear, there's a whole row missing,' he protested.

She shrugged. 'Well then, somebody else has been at the

box besides myself. If I'd taken more than two I should say so.'

Gervaise knew that in many ways Lavina might be spoilt and selfish but quite definitely she was not a liar. She had never told him a deliberate untruth in her life and he would have staked his beloved home, had he still possessed it, on her veracity. He glanced round inquiringly at the others.

They sat there with blank faces and, after a moment, each in turn denied having had any hand in the matter, so the episode was closed. But it left an uncomfortable feeling and, as Lavina was such an inveterate smoker, those who did not know her as well as her father remained under the impression that she had taken a greater number of the cigarettes than she would admit.

She knew what they were thinking but nothing would have induced her to protest her innocence further; and she was extremely intrigued at the thought that the unusual conditions had already produced a sneak-thief and liar among them. Who it was she had no idea but, with the leagues of water on every side of them and no sign of land, she felt that time would show.

22

ADRIFT

The whole of that second day they spent nursing their hurts and recovering from their bouts of sickness. There were many things still to be done to put the Ark ship-shape but they felt too fagged out to give their attention to it and sat about dozing or speculating on what sort of fate the future might hold for them.

On the third morning after the flood it was still cloudy, but as the weather was calm all of them except Sam and Oliver put on their warmest clothes and went outside to get some exercise by walking round the platform. Although they had little hope of seeing a ship or raft with other survivors, they had kept a fruitless watch all through the previous days on the chance that they might sight a piece of high land which was still above the waters. Now as they made the first circuit of the sphere, they strained their eyes once again to peer into the distance by the pale, wintry, morning light, but in every direction the greenish-grey ocean stretched away unbroken to the horizon.

It was a depressing spectacle for, apart from their own utter loneliness, they saw many evidences of the terrible fate which had stricken Britain. As the Ark drifted gently westward on the current the strangest collection of flotsam and jetsam bobbed along beside it, amongst which were great trees, chicken coops, odd pieces of furniture and dead cattle, poultry and human beings. Once they saw a structure which they thought might be another ark with living people in it, but as it drifted closer it proved to be only a wooden barn. At another time they saw an overturned boat and a little later the wreckage of an aeroplane.

After a couple of dozen turns round the sphere the exercisers went inside again except Derek, who declared that he must keep fit somehow and, weather permitting, intended to do at least 500 turns a day; although he found later that he could not yet manage that number because he was still limping from his injured shin and it began to pain him badly.

Under Gervaise's directions they set about giving the contents of the Ark a thorough overhaul, a job they had not previously felt up to, and they spent several hours rearranging cargo that had shifted, fixing cords along the book-shelves and making many other arrangements to ensure that things should not be thrown about quite so readily if the sphere were to receive another buffeting.

It was as well that they had done so as, on the fourth day, a wind got up and from a gentle rocking the motion of the Ark increased to a heavy roll. Margery was ill again and Sam, too, was overcome by sea-sickness. By midday they could not see more than fifty yards from the port-holes as huge waves lashed the Ark, tossing it to and fro while blinding sheets of spray hissed over it. The constant rolling proved a frightful strain upon their nerves, as they could settle to nothing in any comfort but had to cling on to fixtures to prevent themselves from being thrown about.

Hemmingway had been feeling ill all day and lost what little lunch he had eaten. Lavina followed suit but she refused to go to her bunk and made those of the party who were still well enough play 'Consequences' with her.

Margery lay groaning in her cabin; Sam could not trust himself to stand for long on the heaving floor owing to his ankle, which although better was still weak, and none of the others felt like making tea; so Gervaise went below to get a bottle of brandy from their small cellar. When his grey head appeared above the hatch again and he staggered forward to a chair, Lavina noticed that his expression was unusually grave.

Looking round at them he said sternly: 'I should be glad if you would remember that when you elected me Captain of the Ark I stipulated that I should have control of all stores. One of you has had a bottle of brandy out of the wine locker without my authority.'

Everyone denied having taken the bottle and Sam suggested that Gervaise might have miscounted.

He assured Sam that he had not. But Hemmingway went below with him to check the cellar and pointed out that although, allowing for the bottle he had just brought up, there were now only ten out of the original dozen instead of eleven as there should have been, owing to the arrangement of the bins it was quite possible that there had only been eleven bottles there in the first place; and that one might have been found broken in the case when the whole consignment of wines and spirits had been unpacked on arrival from Justerini and Brooks' London cellars. As there was no other explanation Gervaise had to agree that it might have been so but, all the same, he felt quite certain that there had been twelve bottles of brandy there when he had taken a look round the cellar on the day before the comet had struck the earth.

It was pointless to argue further, so the matter was dropped. Their cellar space being limited, Hemmingway had ordered only of the best, and the mellow, sixty-year-old brandy warmed their stomachs; but the waves continued to thud upon the Ark, making the whole sphere shudder. Restless, uneasy and shaken, they made a scratch evening meal of biscuits and then as there seemed no object in remaining up they lurched to their cabins; but the storm continued throughout the night so they spent miserable hours pitching and tossing in their bunks, able to snatch only brief periods of troubled sleep at intervals.

Derek was first up the following morning and he noticed an unpleasant mess at one end of the living-room. When the others, a hollow-eyed, woebegone-looking crew, had assembled for breakfast, he pointed it out to them.

'I don't know who's responsible for that but, whoever it was, if they hadn't time to find a basin to be sick in, they might at least have mopped it up afterwards.'

Everyone looked at everyone else but no one confessed to having been the culprit and they were all so miserable that it hardly seemed worth holding an inquest on the matter. Derek, who was as strong as a horse and had never in his life known what it was like to be seasick, mopped up the mess himself. On Gervaise's then insisting that they should try to eat a little if they could, as it would give their stomachs something to work on, the party sat down to the swaying table and sipped the hot coffee Margery had made for them in spite of her wretchedness.

For the whole of the fifth day the storm continued. Rain sheeted down, obscuring the view from the port-holes. The Ark alternately wallowed in the troughs of the waves or was cast high up on their crests to slide down a farther slope. It never actually turned over, owing to the weight of the stores on its lower deck which acted as ballast, but it pitched about in so terrifying a manner that even those who were not sea-sick were utterly worn out by the evening. Margery, Sam and Hemmingway lay prostrate in their bunks. Lavina was sick again but would not give in and staggered or sat about the living-room, her eyes unnaturally large, and her small face chalk-white.

On the second night of the storm it eased somewhat and the morning of the sixth day after the flood they crawled from their bunks to find that the sea had subsided to an oily swell. During the past few days the rocking of the Ark had been too violent for any of them to have a bath so they employed the best part of the forenoon in that way and by midday were feeling considerably better. The rain had ceased but low clouds still covered the whole sky, so, although they knew from the compass that they were now drifting south they were still unable to calculate their position and had not the faintest idea in which direction or the number of miles that the wind and currents might have carried them. It was still too rough for them to go outside and exercise without danger but by evening they were in normal spirits and had all taken up their allotted duties once more.

Twelve hours later the sea was calm again, but when they looked out of the port-holes they were amazed to see that it had changed colour: it was as black as ink. On going out on to the platform they found the explanation to be that the Ark was now drifting through a great expanse of water which had a foot of sodden black ash floating on its surface.

'This is the result of a terrific volcanic eruption,' said Gervaise. 'The ash has either drifted up here from southern Europe or we have been washed down there by the storm.'

Derek's leg was now all right and, as the sea was now calm he decided to do his five hundred turns round the Ark but it was a raw and bitter morning so the others hurried inside again.

By an adjustment of the ventilators and the heating plant the interior of the Ark could be kept at a pleasantly warm temperature without becoming stuffy, so Lavina changed into an old suit of beach-pyjamas. As her normal high spirits had returned to her and they had now been cooped up in the Ark for over a week, she was becoming extremely bored. Having danced for an hour to the gramophone with Derek she decided to occupy herself by writing a film scenario and cast round among the others for possible assistance.

Sam declared that he was quite useless at that sort of thing. Oliver, who had become a little morose during the last few days, was still automatically busying himself with astronomical calculations which could now be of little value. Gervaise was too interested in the books on folk-lore he was reading. Lavina mentally ruled out Margery as having little imagination and, in any case, being much too busy with her work in the kitchen. That left only Derek and Hemmingway.

Derek was willing enough but, unfortunately, suffered from a complete dearth of ideas. His only contribution, forgetting for the moment the calamity which had overtaken the world, was that there would be a splendid appeal in it if she made her characters hunting people. Hemmingway, although he had failed in his attempts to sell such works of fiction as he had himself produced, at least understood the rudiments of the game and was brim-full of suggestions about types and scenes which might be included in Lavina's *magnum opus*.

During the next three days they worked out the story. Hemmingway thoroughly enjoyed the business but Derek did not. He thought it a silly game and would have thrown in his hand quite early on had it not been that he was not prepared to allow Hemmingway the satisfaction of remaining Lavina's sole collaborator. As it was, he used the gramophone as his ally to distract her with dance records as often as he could and, when she was tired of dancing, sat with them at their story-conferences, making occasional facetious comments which were designed to irritate Hemmingway but which Lavina found amusing.

They had passed out of the area covered with floating ash within eight hours of entering it, since when the weather had remained fairly calm but almost consistently rainy. It was on the tenth day that they woke to find the grey clouds had changed to an angry black. Soon after breakfast a strange rain began which was more like black snow; ash-laden clouds from another volcanic area were releasing their burden and, within an hour, the sea was a blackish-grey from the rain of ash and small pieces of pumice-stone which came down with it. The same day, after lunch, Gervaise looked round the table and said:

'Listen, my friends. As long as the present weather conditions last it is impossible for Oliver to discover our position on the earth's surface. That in itself is not so vitally important; but the fact that we have not sighted land since the coming of the deluge is beginning to worry me. For all we know we may have been swept right out into the middle of the Atlantic Ocean, and may drift there for weeks without coming anywhere near one of the mountain ranges which must still be left standing above the water. We started out with food enough to keep us alive for two months but it certainly will not last that length of time if one of you continues to steal it.'

Varying expressions of amazement greeted his remark, and Sam said at once: 'Are you suggesting that somebody has been raiding the stores the whole time?'

'I wouldn't go as far as that,' Gervaise replied quietly, 'as it was only three days ago that I first noticed a shortage; but I've kept a careful check on things since and there is no question about it, one of you is going below at night and helping yourselves to additional rations.'

They all shook their heads and there was a chorus of denials but Gervaise went on insistently:

'It wouldn't matter so much if any of you felt you weren't getting enough to eat and asked for a little extra. Or, if the guilty party feels that would be an exhibition of greed, it wouldn't affect us very seriously if they confined themselves to taking an additional handful of biscuits or a tin of salmon or something of that kind. The trouble is that whoever is making these raids upon our stores cannot possibly eat all that they are taking. In the last three days enough food has disappeared to have fed the lot of us during that time. Goodness knows what the person who takes it does with the balance after he's had his midnight meal. But there it is.'

'How very extraordinary,' murmured Lavina.

'It's mighty serious,' Hemmingway said quickly. 'If the same amount of food that we use for our rations each day is disappearing every night, the stores will only last one month instead of two; and, including the two days before the flood that we spent in the Ark, we've been here getting on for a fortnight already.'

In vain they argued and speculated. While several of them had secretly believed that Lavina had been responsible for the shortage of Turkish cigarettes they nearly all suspected now that it was Derek who had been at the food. He was far the heartiest eater among them and had complained on several occasions of what he called the 'messy trifles' that Margery served up at some of their meals. Yet there was not the least evidence against him any more than against any of the others.

On the following day Gervaise found that another half-dozen tins of food had disappeared and, when he opened a fresh case of cigarettes, he discovered that somebody had been there before him and removed a good half of its contents.

That afternoon Sam got Hemmingway on his own for the moment and said: 'I've been thinking a lot about these raids on the stores and I'm sure I know who it is.'

'Who?' asked Hemmingway.

'Derek,' whispered Sam. 'It's certainly not Gervaise or he would never have raised the matter at all; it can't be Oliver because he couldn't open cases with one of his arms still in a sling. You can count the two girls out; I haven't done it; and I know you much too well to imagine that you'd ever do a rotten thing like that—so it must be Derek.'

'Perhaps,' Hemmingway agreed. 'He's always talking about good, square meals and what he'd give to see an underdone steak again. But what I can't understand is, why he should take so much more than he requires each time?'

'Can't you?' Sam smiled a little grimly. 'I've got a theory about that. You know how badly he was beaten up before he escaped from London; then he had concussion just before we got him into the sphere. I believe that's affected his brain, not badly, but enough to make him irresponsible. He may even have blank periods when he doesn't know what he's doing. I'll tell you another thing that makes me think he's got a screw loose—the way he's always staring at Lavina.'

Hemmingway suppressed a smile. One did not have to be mad in order to derive a pleasure from looking at Sam's young wife. But although he had had ample opportunity to observe for himself the way in which Derek was always following Lavina with his eyes he did not think that any useful purpose could be served by admitting it and possibly aggravating the jealousy which the easy-going Sam was now showing for the first time.

'I can't say I've noticed it,' he shrugged. 'Derek and Lavina are pretty thick, of course, but that's quite natural because they've been friends for so long. You may be right about the food, though. Anyhow, we might keep watch to-night and see if he sneaks out of the cabin when he thinks we're all asleep.'

The alternate watches that they agreed upon proved, after all, to be quite unnecessary for the simple reason that when Derek failed to appear at dinner that evening Gervaise went below to look for him and found him lying face downwards, unconscious, on the engine-room floor, and by the time they had got him up through the trap-door and tucked up in his bunk it was quite clear that, even if he wished to, he would not be in a condition to do any raiding that night.

He had a nasty cut on the back of his head. When they had bathed it, bandaged it, and brought him round, Gervaise sent everybody else out of the cabin and began questioning him.

Derek's story was that he had gone down to clean the heating apparatus at about six o'clock and had nearly finished working on it when he had heard the sound of footfalls behind him. He had been just about to turn when somebody had rushed at him and struck him on the back of the head, knocking him out. As he had not even glimpsed his attacker he could not possibly give any account of him and, as Sam, Hemmingway and Gervaise himself had all been below decks on various errands between seven and seven-thirty, it might have been any one of them.

Although he would not say so, Gervaise thought that Sam must be the culprit. No one knew better than her father the extraordinary fascination which Lavina exercised over men. Hemmingway, as far as he could see, appeared to be immune from it as, although he was friendly, it was with a detached friendliness and he never went out of his way to amuse or intrigue her. But Derek had been in love with her and she with him three years ago. That Derek was still in love with her Gervaise was quite certain, and his shrewd old eyes had not missed the fact that Sam was perfectly well aware of Derek's passion.

Sam was a very even-tempered man so, at first sight, it hardly seemed likely that he would have made this murderous attack on Derek. But the conditions under which they had been living for the last fortnight were so far outside the normal that they were calculated to upset the balance of any but the most stable brain, and even the fact that they were all living right on top of each other was enough to fray the strongest nerves. If Sam really

resented Derek's attention to his wife and had been bottling up
his feelings for some days, the sight of them constantly together
could easily have driven him to such a state of suppressed fury
that, when he had gone below that evening, he might have given
way to a sudden temptation and have struck Derek down on the
spur of the moment.

The next day Derek was feeling better and as he loathed staying in bed he wanted to get up, but Lavina insisted that, as there
was a risk that delayed concussion might set in, he must be good
and remain lying down for the day. But she sugared the pill by
promising to come and talk to him.

After lunch, when the others were dozing or reading in the
lounge, she settled herself in a chair beside his bunk. Having
exchanged a few of their usual flippancies, she asked:

'Derek, who'd you really think attacked you? You must have
some idea?'

'I don't *think*. I know,' said Derek angrily, 'it was Hemmingway.'

'But how can you be certain if you didn't see him?'

'Isn't it obvious? He knows I'm in love with you and he's
jealous—jealous as hell—because you hardly look at him;
whereas you call me "darling" and it's me you turn to whenever
you want to dance or play the fool.'

'Oh,' she shrugged, 'that's nothing. We've ragged about
together since we were children. What makes you think that he's
in love with me, though? He doesn't show any signs of it as far
as I can see.'

'No, he doesn't show it. In fact, one would almost think that
he dislikes you, at times. But I'll bet he's in love with you, all the
same.'

'I haven't even tried to flirt with him; so why should he
be?'

'Why not?' Derek demanded. '"Still waters"—all that sort
of thing. How could any man who was shut up with you in this
bally tin tub day after day *help* falling in love with you? It's all
I can do to keep my hands off you when you're strutting round
showing yourself off. He must have seen that and made up his
mind to try and out me first and Sam afterwards in order to get
you for himself.'

Lavina shook her head. 'No, Derek, I simply don't believe

it; but, as you've raised the matter, you have been rather over-doing things yourself. Sam hasn't said anything because he knows quite well that he can trust me; but he's been awfully grumpy lately and I'm sure it's owing to the way you look at me. You really must try and control yourself a bit more.'

'God knows, I try; but whose fault is it that I get so het up? I've been meaning to talk to you about it as soon as I got a chance. For God's sake stop wandering about the place in swim-suits. It isn't decent and it's calculated to send any man off his rocker.'

'Really! You amaze me. I quite thought the excitement of seeing a girl's legs had gone out with the Gaiety Chorus and opera hats. Do you seriously suggest that I'm less attractive in trousers?'

Derek sighed. 'No. Not really. That's just the trouble. You get me boiled up whatever you're wearing.'

'I'm sorry, my dear; honestly, I don't mean to. It's frightful that you should feel the way you do about me, because I am terribly fond of you, but I do beg you to do your damnedest not to show it quite so plainly; otherwise it may lead to the most blood-some row, and we simply *must* avoid anything like that.'

'All right,' Derek agreed reluctantly. 'I'll do my best. But, all the same, I'm certain it was on your account that Hemmingway tried to murder me.'

It was not until after breakfast the following morning that Lavina managed to get Hemmingway alone. Knowing the others would be busy for a few moments, she said in a low voice: 'Listen, I want to talk to you.'

'Go ahead,' he murmured.

'That was a queer business about Derek being attacked, and I feel that it's up to any of us who have ideas about it to get to the bottom of the matter so that we can try and prevent anything of the sort happening again. D'you agree?'

'Certainly.'

'All right, then. I know I shouldn't ask you this, but—are you in love with me?'

'No,' said Hemmingway, looking her straight in the eyes.

'That's good,' she nodded. 'I didn't think you were.'

'Why do you ask?'

'Because Derek believes it was you who attacked him; and that you meant to murder him first and Sam afterwards.'

'What utter nonsense! You know how I feel about Sam. Is it likely that I'd . . .'

Lavina held up her hand. 'Derek's theory is that you're in love with me and that you intended to eliminate any possible rivals in order to get me for yourself. On the face of it that may sound fantastic, but men have done queerer things for love, you know.'

His strange eyes held hers and it was only with his mouth that he smiled, before he said: 'Derek is a fool. He's in love with you himself and so jealous of your every glance that he's allowed his imagination to get the better of his common-sense. I give you my word that it was not I who attacked him. As for the rest, I know you think that every man you even sit around with is in love with you, but it just happens that I'm not.'

'All right, I accept that,' replied Lavina gravely. 'But, just in case there was anything in Derek's theory, I thought I ought to let you know that if any "accident" *did* befall the others I'd shoot anyone I believed to be responsible and, as you may remember, when I do shoot, I shoot to kill!'

Suddenly Hemmingway laughed. 'You're a grand person, Lavina. If you like, I'll lend you my gun.'

Lavina laughed, too. 'Don't bother. I don't think I'll need one; but if I do, I can always borrow Gervaise's.'

The sea remained placid, the clouds showed no signs of breaking, and the Ark drifted onwards among the debris which had floated to the surface from the flooded world. For two days there was no further incident to disturb their dull routine although they all continued to be nervy and suspicious of each other. Derek was up and about again; Oliver's arm was slowly mending. The raids upon the food had ceased, so Gervaise, who had a theory that the thief and Derek's attacker were one and the same, had begun to hope that whoever had been responsible had taken a hold upon themselves through fright at discovering that they had nearly committed a murder, and that he would be faced with no more unsolved mysteries.

It was, therefore, with an appalling shock that, on coming out of his cabin on the fifteenth morning of the flood, he found his brother lying dead on the living-room floor.

Before he could warn the others Margery had come out of the women's cabin. Her piercing scream brought the rest of the party running; and in a horrified group they stood staring at

Oliver's dead body. The back of his head had been smashed to pulp. There could be no doubt that he had been murdered.

His face drawn and anxious, Gervaise looked slowly round. 'There is only one explanation for this,' he said huskily, 'and since there is no possibility of any of us leaving the Ark it is a terrible thing to have to face. One of us is a homicidal maniac.'

23

THE MANIAC

The full horror of their situation slowly dawned upon them. There was no escape from the Ark. They must remain living cheek by jowl in its narrow confines; yet the brain of one of them had been turned by their terrible experiences and, whoever that person was, while appearing normal for the greater part of the time, he was afflicted with occasional periods of hideous aberration in which he was capable of murder.

With a nervy gesture Gervaise passed a hand over his white hair. 'You see, it all ties up,' he went on gravely. 'I know most of you think it was Lavina who took the cigarettes but I'll swear that she would never lie to me if she had done so while in her senses. The bottle of brandy might have been taken by any of us; or perhaps that twelfth bottle was never there. I believed that it was Derek who had been at the food because he is the heartiest eater among us; but that doesn't explain the fact that much more food has disappeared than any one person could have eaten. Sam, Hemmingway and myself, all had an opportunity to attack Derek and it is plain, to me at least, that the other two had a possible motive; but neither of them had the least reason to kill poor Oliver. These acts are those of a madman and the lives of us all now depend upon finding out which of us suffers from these terrible fits of lunacy.

Each one of them was quite convinced that it was not themselves and regarded the others with reluctant suspicion. It was a frightful thing for them to think that from now onwards, if ever they remained alone for a few minutes with one of the others, that other's mind might suddenly go blank and they would find themseves fighting with a maniac; or that one of their friends might steal upon them in the dark and strike them down, as had happened to Derek and Oliver.

'Well, there are six of us now,' said the practical Sam, voicing the thoughts of them all, 'and the best precaution we can take is that never less than three of us should remain alone together.'

'How about at night?' asked Margery. 'Lavina and I must continue to share a cabin.'

'I don't mind that, if you don't,' Lavina said promptly. 'We'll lock our door, and if I see you walking in your sleep, I shall scream the Ark down.'

Margery shrugged. 'I don't mind, either. It can't be you, because you're not strong enough to have delivered those terrible blows on the back of Uncle Oliver's head.'

'I don't know so much. They say that maniacs have super-human strength.'

Sam shook his head. 'No, it isn't either of you girls. The fact that Derek was attacked when he was below rules both of you out. It's one of us men; either Gervaise, Hemmingway or myself.'

Sadly they set about preparing Oliver for burial. Margery washed his body while Lavina sewed up a sheet to be his shroud and weights into its lower end. It was only after they had finished that the relief of tears came; and both girls sobbed as Gervaise read the Burial Service over his brother's body. The door of the Ark was opened and the shrouded figure consigned to the cold, grey waves.

The dreary grey skies still stretched low overhead from horizon to horizon. Although it was only mid-July the temperature was that of November and it seemed to be growing colder day by day. A slight but chill wind was blowing and the waves lapped hungrily at the landing platform of the Ark; the only thing showing above the waters in all that vast desolation.

When the Funeral Service was over and they had again returned, shivering, to the warmth, none of them felt like talking. An uneasy silence brooded over the living-room as they sat about doing nothing or making a pretence of trying to read. The minds of all of them were filled with dark suspicion of their neighbours and horrid, fruitless speculation as to when and upon whom the murderer would make his next attack.

Lunch was a gloomy meal and after it, as had become their habit, they retired to their cabins for an afternoon sleep.

It was about half-past three when Derek, waking from a doze, noticed that Hemmingway was no longer in the bunk opposite him. Instantly he roused Gervaise and Sam and, slipping from his bunk, muttered quickly:

'It's Hemmingway. I felt sure it was. Look! His bunk's empty. He must have tiptoed out of the cabin while we were asleep. Come on! Arm yourselves with anything that's handy; we'll probably have to knock him out.'

At that moment there was a muffled shriek. Gervaise wrenched a sheet out of his bunk to tie the maniac, Sam grabbed a clothes-brush for a club, and Derek a heavy ruler which still lay where Oliver had left it by the side of his now empty bunk.

As they dashed out of the cabin the screams came again. For a moment they had assumed that one of the girls was the new victim; but in the tiny hallway they ran full-tilt into them, for they also had been roused and were leaving their cabin to find out who was screaming.

The trap-door in the living-room, which led to the lower deck, was open. Rushing towards it, Sam cried:

'He's down there! The poor chap must know he's the maniac and be trying to commit suicide—or else he's got caught up in the machinery.'

In his anxiety to save his friend from further injury Sam dropped the twelve feet to the lower deck straight through the trap. Derek and Gervaise followed by the ladder. A yell of 'Help! Help!' came from a storeroom where the seeds and bulbs were kept.

Picking himself up Sam sprang through the open doorway, the others hard on his heels. In the dimmish light of the single electric globe they saw that a desperate struggle was in progress. Rolling on the floor Hemmingway was at death-grips with another man.

The other three flung themselves upon the struggling couple and succeeded in wrenching Hemmingway's attacker away from him. Their opponent fought with all the strength of a madman, but between them they managed to pinion his arms and feet and roll him over on his back. As the light struck his face Sam gasped:

'Good God! It's Finkie!'

Fink-Drummond's chin was covered with a fortnight's beard, his hair was matted, his clothes indescribably dirty. He was

I

slavering at the mouth and his eyes shone with a maniacal hatred. Few of his old colleagues would have recognized the ex-Cabinet Minister but Sam had known him, after a moment, by his long, pointed nose.

Having bound their captive with the sheet that Gervaise had brought from his bunk, they hoisted him up to the living-room and sat him down in a chair. Out of pity for his state Lavina brought him a glass of water to drink but, with a violent jerk of his head, he knocked it out of her hand. All their efforts to make him speak were quite unavailing. He was stark, staring mad.

Gervaise went below to investigate and, returning after a few moments, said to the others:

'I think he must have been still sane when he came on board, because he chose for his hiding place the one storeroom that none of us were likely to go into until the Ark touched land. By rearranging a lot of the cases of seeds and bulbs he'd hollowed out a six-foot tunnel and in it, I'm glad to say, I found most of the missing food. I imagine he took as much as he could reach each time because he was afraid we might make some new arrangement of the stores so that he wouldn't be able to get at them again later on.'

'But how on earth did he get aboard in the first place?' Sam inquired.

'Roy,' said Margery. 'Roy used to sit with him when he was a prisoner at Stapleton, if you remember, and they became quite friendly. Roy must have told him about the Ark and, after he was free, he must have decided that he'd stand a better chance of saving himself by stowing away on board it than by any other means. It would have been quite easy for him to have got into it and made his arrangements on the night Roy went to London, while we were all asleep in the house.'

'That's about it,' Derek agreed. 'And during that terrible time we had those first few days, being cooped up there in the dark while the Ark was thrown all over the place must have sent him mad. God knows, it was bad enough for us; but just think what the poor devil must have suffered with all those cases sliding about or being flung on top of him in the darkness. Light as most of them are, it's a miracle they didn't kill him. But how did you find him, Hemmingway?'

Hemmingway smiled. 'I've read quite a lot about insanity at

one time and another and I felt fairly certain that none of us was mad; the only other explanation was a stowaway. I remembered then that whenever I've passed the seed room lately there's been a very unpleasant smell. I thought some of the roots in there were going bad, but after lunch to-day it occurred to me that it might be something else. As my idea seemed a bit far-fetched, I didn't like to tell the rest of you about it in case you thought that I might be the madman myself, so when you were all asleep I took my loaded crop and went down to investigate. But Finkie was on me before I could get a blow in and he was near murdering me by the time you chaps came on the scene.'

Gervaise nodded his grey head. 'Well, I do congratulate you. Having found him explains everything and relieves all our minds of an intolerable burden. It was plucky of you, too, to risk taking on a madman on your own.'

'What're you going to do with him?' Lavina asked, staring nervously at the wild-eyed figure in the chair.

'We can't leave him loose about the Ark,' said Gervaise, decisively. 'We'll shift the cases round a bit to make things more comfortable, keep his hands tied so that he can't attack who-ever brings him his food, and put him back where he came from.'

Fink-Drummond was held while Gervaise gave him a morphia injection; they then rearranged the stores and, when he had gone off, they carried him down to his prison. Having put looped cords over his head, hands and ankles, they knotted these behind his back so that he could sit or lie in reasonable comfort but could not free himself and would choke if he attempted any violent movements. There was a risk that in a frenzy he might strangle himself while they were all up in the living-room or asleep in their bunks but that risk had to be taken as there was no other way in which they could ensure his not attacking whoever acted as his gaoler. They eliminated the chance as far as possible by padding the cord that went round his neck, and made up a bed for him with the mattress and bed-clothes from the spare bunk in the men's cabin that Roy was to have occupied.

After the discovery of the maniac-stowaway life in the Ark became normal. Day after day it tossed or drifted on the bosom of the grim, uncharted seas, first in one direction then in another. Gervaise was now convinced that they must be somewhere out

in the North Atlantic. The ever-increasing cold was a clear indication that they were being swept a long way north, while had they
been floating over the old countries within a few hundred miles
of Stapleton it was almost certain that they would by this time
have sighted some of the European mountain chains; the tops of
which must still be above water.

All of them were now used to the constant rocking of the
sphere, but at times a strong wind got up upon which the waves
set the Ark rolling and lurching most uncomfortably; and for
two days in the latter part of July they suffered again the terrors
of another storm.

Margery and Sam had renewed bouts of sea-sickness whenever the weather was rough, and partly on account of the fact
that they shared the same distressing weakness a strong sympathy
developed between them; but other things also contributed to
their cordial friendship. Margery was a serious-minded person
and had always admired Sam for his sense of responsibility and
decisive, straight-thinking mind; while, from having at first been
sorry for her as Lavina's less lovely sister, he came to realize
that she had many sterling qualities that Lavina lacked.

All of them had now begun to worry in secret as to whether
they would ever see land again. With the rediscovery of the bulk
of the food that Finkie had stolen they still had ample provisions
for some weeks, but the flood had proved so much vaster in its
extent than even Oliver's most gloomy forebodings had led them
to expect, that horrid doubts as to if they would survive had
returned to nag their minds and they now feared that they might
be washed up and down the Atlantic until they died of starvation.

Margery, quite naturally, took refuge from her fears in the
consolations of her stereotyped religion; frequently reading her
Bible and the numerous sacred works which the library of the
Ark contained. The others were not irreligious but thought of
spiritual things in a somewhat different way. Only Sam, who was
fundamentally a Christian but had neglected his religion for many
years, observed the great comfort that Margery derived from her
faith and began to join her in discussions which drew them still
more closely together.

At times Lavina still plumped herself down on Sam's lap, gave
him quick kisses and played with his greying hair. But Sir

Samuel Curry, millionaire, with his host of friends and hangers-on, was one thing; the middle-aged, kind but somewhat ponderous man in the Ark, rather another. He seemed to have lost his sense of humour and the lightness of touch which was so essential in dealing with the moods of a flame-like creature like herself. She never questioned the fact that she still loved him but there were times when he bored her to distraction, and she began to rely more and more for her entertainment on Derek and Hemmingway.

Derek was much the more satisfactory in that respect as he never seemed to have anything on hand to occupy his attention for any length of time and so was always at her beck and call. It was Derek who turned on her bath in the morning; Derek who fetched her cigarettes when she had left them a few yards away in her cabin; Derek who, after every meal, brought her handbag from the table to the arm-chair which she had chosen to decorate with her graceful limbs; and Derek who changed the records on the gramophone according to her instructions whenever it was played.

Besides, Derek was really very nice to look at. His handsome face had lost none of its bronze during their month of drifting on the bleak, cold seas. His crisp, brown hair was good to touch and in fooling with him she often ruffled it. True, he had few subjects outside huntin', shootin', fishin' and farmin' upon which he could discourse intelligently, but he was a ready listener, his hearty laugh was a certain echo to every sally that she made and he jumped at the chance of dancing with her whenever she told him to clear the rugs at one end of the living-room.

Hemmingway, on the other hand, had many interests of his own. He read a great deal, often played chess with Gervaise or six-pack Bezique with Sam, and sometimes he did not even glance in Lavina's direction for hours at a stretch. When he did he was friendly enough and he was always willing to discuss the development of her film scenario with her when he was not otherwise occupied.

His behaviour puzzled her extremely. During their first few days in the Ark she had been quite convinced that he had fallen for her but was keeping a tight hold on himself through loyalty to Sam and from a desire not to take advantage of the experience they had been through together during their flight from London.

Yet when she had frankly challenged him, after Derek had been knocked out, he had categorically denied having any feeling other than friendship for her and as the days wore on she had become convinced that he had been speaking the truth.

Whether she was glad or sorry about that she was unable to make up her mind. She was quite sure that she was not in love with him and she had all her work cut out to handle Derek, so she was really rather glad that Hemmingway was not likely to provide a further complication in her relations with Sam. But at the same time it was a sad blow to her vanity that Hemmingway should remain immune from her fascination.

She made no attempt to attract him but she felt that the mere fact of her constant presence should have been enough; and she could never resist the temptation to watch him covertly whenever he was reading to see if he was watching her. But he always appeared to be completely absorbed in whatever he was doing and after a time she became conscious of a queer reaction in her feelings for him. From having considered him, when they had first really got to know each other, as rather a charming and amusing person she reverted to her first opinion that he was a cold, monkish intellectual; and by the time they had been in the Ark a month she was thinking of him as dispassionately as she did of Gervaise or her sister.

Gervaise had taken over Oliver's job with the instruments as well as carrying on with his own work of writing up the journal of the Ark and issuing the stores. But there had still been no opportunity to use the sextant and take the altitude of the sun, moon or stars, as day after day, night after night, the dense banks of low cloud remained unbroken overhead.

The general level of their spirits sank as the days dragged by. Whenever the weather was too rough for Derek to get his morning exercise he became grumpy with everyone except Lavina. She turned on the gramophone so frequently that they were almost tortured by the incessant repetition of her favourite dance tunes. Margery discovered that Sam had never been confirmed and was taking him stage by stage through the catechism.

On July 24th Gervaise called a conference. Over half their edible supplies had been consumed and he suggested that they should make a reduction in their daily rations. They agreed unanimously, but the fact that they had to do so sounded a warning note. Their nerves deteriorated and, under the constant strain of watching for the land which never appeared above the grey horizons, they began to be terse with each other and apt to have high words over trifles. Only Gervaise remained calm and secure in his spiritual fastness, the outcome of a lifetime's study of the great philosophies, and ever ready to restore good feeling between the others with a well chosen word.

Sam, Derek, and Hemmingway took it in turns to look after their mad prisoner. On the day following his capture they brought him up and gave him a very badly needed bath, after which they fitted him out in a suit from one of the bags that Roy had never reached the Ark to claim. He had occasional screaming fits when he would throw himself about, but otherwise gave no trouble, as Gervaise kept him on a low diet and mixed sedatives with his food. With the welding implements, which were among the large collection of such things that had been stored in the Ark, Derek succeeded in forging the ends of a length of chain into two anklets, so that they were able to hobble Fink-Drummond and release him from his other bonds; after which he was able to move freely about his narrow prison but unable to separate his feet more than twelve inches, which rendered him incapable of exerting his full strength in any attack. He made no attempt to escape, however, but became increasingly lethargic rather like a wild beast that has been doped, as he remained obdurately silent although on many occasions they tried to persuade him to talk.

In the latter days of July they had several severe hail-storms during which bits of ice as big as pigeon's eggs drummed on the outer sphere of the Ark like bullets, making a deafening but harmless din, and on the first of August they saw their first snow.

For thirty hours the fast-falling flakes blotted out the monotonous seascape, but when the snow ceased on the second day they were overjoyed to see that at long last the clouds had broken, revealing the sun. For over five weeks it had remained hidden by the dense clouds which had accumulated as a result of the deluge.

Gervaise quickly got out Oliver's sextant and took an observation; a very simple matter as it consists only of bringing an image of the sun in a mirror to a point on the sextant's arc where the rim of the image just touches the rim of the sun itself seen through a smoked glass. Hemmingway, meanwhile, stood by to take the time on the chronometers which, although probably inaccurate now from the buffeting the Ark had received, could not be far out as they had never stopped.

The two of them then worked out the easy sum which gave the Ark's latitude, and it proved to be 71° 17′ north.

Finding their longitude was a different matter, as neither of them knew more than the rudiments of nautical astronomy, but they hoped that they would be able to do so if they could get observations of some of the stars.

The discovery that they had drifted so far north was extremely perturbing as, following the 70th parallel of north latitude on the map, they saw that it ran from Baffin Land, across the middle of Greenland, past the North Cape, and through the Arctic Ocean to Siberia.

Gervaise and Hemmingway both felt convinced that their calculation had been correct but hoped, as did the whole party, that it had been wrong. Even if they sighted land now it looked as if they would be faced with the grim prospect of fending for themselves in some desolate region of the Arctic.

Yet the weather seemed to confirm the reckoning, as they had more snow and sleet in the days that followed, and when the sun broke through again for a brief period on the 5th of August further observations gave their latitude as 71° 20′ N., which established the fact that they were still drifting in a northerly direction.

It was on the 7th of August that Sam, going into the kitchen first thing in the morning to help prepare breakfast, found Margery lying there motionless, face downwards on the floor.

His first thought was that Fink-Drummond had escaped during the night and was responsible for this new outrage. His second, that she was dead and that he had lost her. Only then did he realize how much her companionship had meant to him through all these desperate weeks.

It was not that he no longer loved Lavina; her grace and beauty still played havoc with his senses, but her youthful vitality, her insistence that they must always be doing something even though they were shut up in the narrow confines of the Ark, and her insatiable craving for amusement had proved a great strain on him lately, in spite of the fact that Derek and Hemmingway occupied a good part of her time.

Sam was a strong man, but from his first youthful struggles in Bradford he had worked himself unmercifully and he was now getting on for fifty. He had been young for his age when he went on his honeymoon with Lavina but the strain of the last seven weeks had told upon him and he now looked, and felt, even older than his years. The holocaust which had swept all his worldly possessions away had revived something primitive in him. Gone was the veneer which had so long overlaid his simple inbred habits. Even his voice had changed, the vowels broadening as he reverted to his childhood tongue.

He wanted a peace and repose that Lavina could never give him, but that Margery could. Lavina's finer qualities, her courage, her independence, her sense of fair play and her real integrity were so masked by her apparent irresponsibility that Sam was only faintly conscious of them, whereas Margery's straightforwardness, thoughtfulness for others and unselfishness had stood out all the more by comparison because she lacked the glamour of her younger sister.

As the mistress of his great house in St. James's Square Lavina could have been unsurpassable, but Margery would have made a real home for her man and her children anywhere; and now that money, position and power had all been swept away from him, Sam knew that he would never miss them in the least if the future held a simple home for him like that which he had known with his mother in Bradford.

While these thoughts raced through his brain, Margery stirred. In an instant he was on his knees beside her and had taken her in his arms. Her eyes opened; his heart began to hammer in his chest. Before he knew what he was doing he was kissing her feverishly and pressing her to him.

'Sam—oh, Sam,' she murmured, leaning her cheek against his. Then, as realization dawned upon her, she pushed him back, exclaiming, 'Oh, what are we doing? We're mad! You mustn't, Sam!'

'I—I couldn't help it—in my relief at finding you weren't dead,' he stammered. 'I love you, Margery. I love you.'

'So that—is that,' said a quiet voice from the doorway, and, swinging round, Sam saw Lavina standing there, a cigarette dangling from her lips.

24

DOMESTIC UPHEAVAL

'Margery fainted and I—I—' Sam stuttered, coming slowly to his feet.

'No need to explain,' said Lavina, with dangerous quietness. 'I understand the situation perfectly,' and, swinging on her heel, she slammed the door.

'Oh, God!' groaned Sam, 'what a hellish mess! I'm sorry, Margery—most terribly sorry—to have let you in for this.'

But Margery was smiling. It was her hour, her triumph, her vindication as a woman. She had loved Sam from the moment that he had kissed her in the cloakroom at Stapleton on his wedding-day. His strength, his kindness and his uprightness of purpose made him all that she had ever wanted in a man. She had not consciously gone out to get him because he was her sister's husband, and her code forbade that; but all her scruples had gone overboard the moment she had come round to find herself in his arms. Morality was man-made; she was woman, aching to be loved. And, joy piled on joy, after Lavina had casually taken every man that had come into their ken, the final victory lay with her, for she, without even scheming to do so, had taken Lavina's own husband.

With an enormous effort of will she forced herself not to show the incredible happiness she was feeling. Sam must be played quietly now. He would become remorseful and she would lose him if she followed her burning impulse to fling her arms round his neck.

'It's all right, Sam,' she said, as she scrambled to her feet. 'If you feel that way you couldn't have helped it; so you're not to blame. I would have done just the same if I had found you lying on the floor and thought you were dead.'

'You would?' he exclaimed, seizing one of her hands.

She quickly withdrew it. 'Of course. You can never know what our friendship has meant to me. I haven't had a very happy life and when you walked into it you were Lavina's fiancé. I know I ought to have forced myself not to think of you but I simply couldn't help doing that. Perhaps we poor women are made weak with a purpose. But it wouldn't have been right for me to show you that I loved you.'

'Oh, Margery—Margery!' He passed a hand over his eyes. 'I'm not worthy. This is a terrible thing that I've done.'

'No, Sam. A Providence that sees into all our hearts willed that we should at least have the joy of knowing of each other's love.' Margery was playing her part superbly and she knew it. All the old clichés rolled automatically off her tongue and she could see that for Sam they were the words of the perfect woman. She wondered if she dared risk saying, 'We must forget this— never, never think of it again,' but decided that she had better not chance it. Sam might take her at her word, and that was the last thing she wanted. Instead, she went on: 'We have our duty; we must think of others, not of ourselves. I leave myself in your hands, Sam dear, knowing that whatever you decide will be right.'

Sam hardly knew what to reply to this. Margery was perfectly right, of course. They must think of Lavina, not of themselves. They must not let their guilty passions blind them to their sense of duty. How like her it was to voice those high ideals. The fact that during his long bachelorhood Sam had from time to time kept numerous young women in very comfortable flats did not stand him in any stead now. They had been invariably beautiful and usually empty-headed little gold-diggers without any moral principles, but they had served the purpose of providing him with light recreation during the few hours of leisure he was able to snatch from his preoccupation with big business. Now, for the first time in his life, he was up against something totally different; a woman with ideals, a good woman such as his mother had been; and he felt the enormous responsibility that the declaration of her love had laid upon him. But, for the life of him, he could not see what decision could be taken.

There had been no misconduct. Such a thing was almost unthinkable in connection with Margery. So, in a normal world, Lavina would have had no grounds for divorce, but matters might have been arranged so that he could have persuaded her to give him his freedom; whereas here, in the Ark, how could he possibly even suggest casting off his young wife with a view to marrying her elder sister? In any case, there was no one to divorce or re-marry him, unless the father of the two girls could be considered to have special powers as Captain of the Ark; and the fact of Gervaise being with them seemed to make the position even more impossible. Yet Margery obviously expected him to do some-thing about it.

After a moment, the habit of years reasserted itself and, using the same technique as that which he had applied on innumerable occasions when difficult problems had arisen at board meetings, he said firmly:

'Leave this to me. We mustn't hurry things. But after a little thought I'm sure I shall find a way.'

Margery was equally puzzled as to what step could next be taken, but that, she thought, was Sam's affair and, in the mean-time, he had definitely committed himself, which was all that really mattered.

'Of course we mustn't rush things,' she agreed. 'I'm perfectly content to wait. Your love will give me the strength and courage to do that.'

Sam knew that he would have to do some pretty hectic think-ing and had just decided that he would take refuge at once in one of the storerooms so as to be by himself when he suddenly recalled the state in which he had found Margery ten minutes earlier. Turning at the door, he said:

'By Jove! I'd entirely forgotten to ask what happened to you. I thought Finkie must have escaped and attacked you; but it seems you'd only fainted. Whatever caused you to do that?'

Margery's mouth dropped open and her eyes almost popped with excitement. 'Of course, I haven't told you,' she cried, grab-bing him by the arm. 'When I came in here to make breakfast I looked out of the port-hole and I saw land, Sam. Land!'

'Good God!' In two strides Sam was across the kitchen staring eagerly out of the port; and there, no more than five miles distant, was that for which they had watched in vain through so many dreary weeks.

'The sight of land after all this time came as such a shock to me that I fainted,' Margery murmured.

'Yes, yes,' Sam breathed, gazing enraptured at the low, green shore. 'But come on! We must tell the others.'

Running from the kitchen with excited shouts they broke the news to the rest of the party. The land was not visible from the port-holes of the living-room so they crowded about those in the cabins on the other side of the Ark; all of them wildly thrilled by this new hope of release from their prison and a real chance, at last, that they might live out their lives to their allotted span instead of slowly starving to death on the empty ocean.

They had naturally anticipated that when they did sight land it would be the top of a mountain chain; some snowy peaks and a jagged, rocky shore; but this was totally different. Before them in the distance spread a low, greenish landscape of trees and meadows splashed here and there with white patches which they knew must be half-melted snow.

Gervaise and Hemmingway had dashed into the men's cabin and, after a moment, Gervaise remarked:

'It's surprising that we didn't see it when we were dressing.'

'I don't think so,' Hemmingway replied. 'It's quite a long time now since we used to look out hopefully each morning. Anyhow, we'd better not waste any time in getting the engines going, otherwise a storm might get up and blow us away from it again.'

'You're right,' Gervaise agreed, and leaving the cabin he called to Derek, who, as their Engineer, hurried below at once.

They were by now so used to the silence of the Ark and its gentle rolling, that it was a queer sensation to hear the pulse of its engines and feel it chugging slowly forward in a given direction. Fortunately the weather was calm, so, in spite of its un-wieldy shape, its big drop-keel and rudder kept it from revolving, and although its pace was less than that of a rowing-boat it made steady progress towards the shore. While it was slowly forging ahead Sam and Hemmingway got up from the stores the parts of a collapsible canvas boat, which they unpacked and assembled. An hour and a half after the engines had been got going the Ark jolted slightly as its keel cut into earth, and came to rest in shallow water about fifty yards from land.

Opening the door, they went out on to the platform to survey this domain that the gods had decreed for them. On closer inspection it was by no means so attractive. A great number of its trees had been uprooted and broken branches dangled from the others giving them a pathetic, woebegone appearance. In some places the grass was mired by great patches of mud or snow, a dead horse lay on the foreshore, and for as far as they could see, the land was sprinkled with the debris of the flood.

It was bitterly cold upon the platform after the warmth of the Ark, so, having seen Sam and Hemmingway launch their canvas boat and set off in it to row ashore for a brief exploration, the others hurried inside again.

By lunch time the explorers were back to report that they had been unable to penetrate inland more than a few hundred yards in any direction. The whole earth was so sodden that they had got bogged wherever they went. They had seen a small, square, grey stone house in the distance and come across some drowned cattle but had discovered no indication as to what country they might be in.

'We may be in northern Norway, Iceland or Greenland,' said Gervaise sadly, 'but it's impossible to say which.'

'I'm quite sure it's not Norway,' Hemmingway volunteered. 'This is low meadow-country, not unlike England, and if we were in Norway we should certainly be able to see mountains in the distance.'

'True,' Gervaise agreed. 'For the same reason I doubt if we are in Greenland, unless we've landed somewhere on the high table-land of its interior. I should think Iceland is the most probable; but, of course, we may have drifted very much farther than we thought, either west to Canada or east into Northern Russia.'

'But the country doesn't look like that,' Lavina objected. 'It's too green and friendly.'

Gervaise smiled. 'It's a big mistake to imagine that countries bordering on the Arctic are always lands of snow, dearest. The most beautiful wild flowers in the world grow in the meadows of Siberia and it's greener there during the short Arctic summers than it is in England. Now that it's August their winter is approaching and soon they will be buried deep in snow; but we're seeing one of them just before the long Arctic night sets in.'

'It is neither Canada nor Russia,' Hemmingway said decisively, 'otherwise the trees would be mostly larch and pine. Besides, the country is too much cut up into small fields. I should say the betting is a hundred to one on our having fetched up in Iceland.'

'Anyhow, there's one comfort,' Sam added. 'The flood is definitely subsiding. This is typical low, wooded country so we can't be very far above sea-level and everything is so drenched that it's quite obvious that the whole of this area was still under water not more than two or three days ago. There are no snow patches within five hundred yards of the shore either, which indicates that the water must have gone down that much since the early hours of the morning.'

That Sam was right about the flood subsiding was evidenced an hour later. Unnoticed by them the waters had seeped away from under the landing-platform, but they realized it only when the Ark gave a sudden lurch, flinging everything off the table and most of them to the floor. Its keel, stuck deep in the mud, had kept them upright since the sphere had grounded, but with the lessening support of the waters it had given way. They were floating again now, with the deck at a sharp angle.

Picking themselves up, Derek and Gervaise scrambled down to the engine-room, and operating the levers, drew in the keel and rudder; upon which the Ark righted itself, bobbing gently.

'We'd best tow her in as far as possible,' Hemmingway suggested. 'Then, as we lost our anchors, we'll throw out some kedges made of weighty objects we've got among the stores.'

Having fixed a tow-rope, Sam and Hemmingway got into the collapsible boat again and laboured manfully for half an hour to bring the sphere nearer to land. They got it to within ten feet of the shore-line, where it grounded again, but kedge-anchors were found to be unnecessary as the water was going down with the quickness of an outgoing tide.

When Hemmingway and Sam came aboard again their hands were blue with cold and they were both shivering. By four o'clock it had started to snow, blotting out most of the landscape, and the big white flakes continued to fall softly and persistently until darkness hid them from view.

The joy of finding land again was marred for Sam by his domestic contretemps. The scene in which he had participated early that morning had never since been absent from his mind. Margery seemed normal, and even cheerful, while Lavina gave no indication that anything unusual had occurred. But Sam was so nervy that he could not sit still happily for five minutes together. In an agony of suspense he waited for bedtime, wondering if Lavina would give him her usual good-night kiss.

His torture was prolonged by the fact that they stayed up much later than usual as Gervaise had brought up some bottles of wine and spirits to celebrate their having survived the flood, and for a couple of hours after dinner they speculated uselessly but garrulously as to what the future might hold in store for them.

At last Lavina said, 'Well, it's been an exciting day but I'm going to bed,' and stood up.

The others followed her example and Sam watched on tenter-hooks to see what she would do. She kissed her father, smiled round at the others and, apparently forgetting him, went towards her cabin.

'Lavina,' he called after her, with a tremor in his voice, 'if you don't mind, I'd like a word with you before you turn in.'

'Right you are,' she answered, without turning her head. 'I'll come back again in my dressing-gown.'

It was Lavina's habit to take a long time preparing herself for bed. Sam had never quite discovered why it was necessary for her to sit so long in front of her mirror after she had brushed her hair, but she never spent less than three-quarters of an hour tinkering with her face. To-night she deliberately took nearly double that time, then strolled out of her cabin with a cigarette dangling from her newly carmined lips. The others had all retired so husband and wife had the living-room to themselves.

'Well?' said Lavina, sitting down in an armchair and crossing her well-formed legs.

Now that the moment had come, Sam's nervousness had dis-appeared. He went into action just as he would have done if faced with any other tricky situation.

'About this morning,' he began. 'You saw me kissing Margery. First of all, I'd like to assure you that there's been nothing else between us. We haven't been having any private sessions below deck of the kind you and I used to have during our first weeks in the Ark, or anything of that sort.'

Lavina smiled. 'Knowing Margery, I didn't suppose for one moment that you had. She's in love with you, of course; has been for a long time. Any woman could see that. But Margery's the sort who would demand marriage before she went to bed, and I can hardly see her playing slap-and-tickle with you among the packing-cases. Are you in love with her?'

'Yes.'

'Then you're not in love with me any longer?'

'I wouldn't exactly say that.'

'Hell! You can't have it both ways.'

'I didn't say I could, but it's quite possible to be in love with two people at the same time.'

'It all depends on what you call love.'

'I mean that I love you both in different ways.'

'What you mean, Sam, is that you don't *love* me any longer but you still desire me; whereas you do love Margery—for her worthiness, and all that. But you've no particular desire to sleep with her.'

'On the contrary. I think one thing goes with the other; anyhow, for a man like myself. And most people would consider Margery darned good-looking if you didn't happen to be about.

'Yes, she's only twenty-six, and decidedly attractive in a saintly sort of way. I suppose what's got you down is that you've been a casual bad-hat all your life but never before run into a good-looking woman who goes about clad in woollens and a halo. But that's beside the point. What I imagine you're trying to tell me is that if we were living in a normal way you'd ask me to divorce you so that you could marry her?'

'Oh, God!' Sam groaned. 'This is simply frightful. We've only been married ourselves just under three months.'

'I know. But having been cooped up for so long in this thing, where we haven't been out of each other's sight except when asleep, has made all the difference, and that has come practically on top of our five weeks' honeymoon when we hardly saw a soul. We've spent more hours together since our marriage than most married people do in a couple of years. Besides, life in the Ark is so totally unlike the sort of life we'd be living if the comet had never appeared. This sort of existence has brought out all my very worst points. I'm lazy, thoughtless, unpractical, and very easily get bored; whereas Màrgery, being the perfect *hausfrau*, has had a marvellous opportunity to do her stuff. Naturally, by comparison, she appears as a shining example of what a good woman should be. I'm not a good woman, Sam, and I've never pretended to be, but I would never willingly have let you down.'

Sam knew that every word she spoke was true, and he marvelled at the cold logic with which she summed up the situation. 'It's my fault entirely,' he admitted unhappily. 'You've got qualities that Margery hasn't, but you've had little chance to show them in the last few weeks; whereas she's had all the opportunities she could possibly wish for to show hers. That doesn't excuse me, I know, but it is a fact; and I'm desperately worried as to what to do about the future. You see, I want to be fair to both of you, but I don't see how it's possible.'

Lavina smiled a little bitterly. 'As far as I can see, the future isn't going to be very different from the past few weeks. The whole world has been drowned; so there's no prospect of our getting anywhere, and very little of our meeting any other people. We'll have to pig it in some collection of ruins, I suppose, and I shall be no more use to anybody than I am now. But Margery could run a derelict cottage for you perfectly, cook your meals, clean your house, put your slippers by the fire to warm, and all the rest of it; while you cultivated a bit of land with some of the seeds and things we've got. Besides, she could give you children, and you'd like children—wouldn't you, Sam?'

'Yes,' he nodded.

'Well, I'm not playing. I might have, if I could have had a Harley Street gynaecologist to look after me and all the usual comforts; but I'm damned if I'm going to have a baby like a peasant girl in a cow-shed, and work myself to death bringing the brat up.'

'No. I shouldn't ask you to. You weren't made for that sort of thing; nor, for that matter, to slave in any workaday world. You were born to be served, and to reward men for their service only with your beauty. Where you're unfortunate is that, our civilization having gone down the drain, it looks as if we'll have to live out the rest of our lives in primitive conditions; and in primitive societies there is not much call for idle women however decorative they may be. But what do you suggest?'

'Well, as it happens, Sam, I'm rather fond of you and, as I *am* your wife, I have first claim to your protection and support in this lousy dead world that is all that's left to us. You took me on knowing my qualities and I'm still good entertainment. I suppose you agree that by all the laws of God and man, and all the decencies, it's still up to you to fend for me even if I refuse to do a hand's turn?'

'Yes, I quite agree about that.'

'Then I think we'd better leave things for a month. During that time I can make up my mind as to whether I want to keep you; and, since you say you *do* still love me, you'll have a chance to decide if that's really true. You'll be able to say definitely by then if Margery's good-womanishness and Victorian morality are quite enough compensation for all you'd lose if you lost me.'

'That's very sound,' Sam agreed, 'and damned decent of you. I think you've behaved frightfully well about this and I'm more grateful than I can say; but then, you never were a mean-spirited person. I don't think you've ever done a mean thing in your life.'

'Thanks,' said Lavina calmly, standing up. 'Anyhow, we know where we are now and I'll let you know my decision on the 7th of September. In the meantime, though, I shall consider myself perfectly free to amuse myself, if I wish, with Derek—or Hemmingway.'

She had already turned her back as she uttered the last words, and before Sam could say anything further, she had closed her cabin door behind her.

25

CALAMITY

As Sam moved over to the table to mix himself a drink, he was thinking that Lavina had really behaved very fairly. The interview that he had been dreading so much all day was over and there had been no fireworks or bitter recriminations. But then, he had been unjust to Lavina in even thinking that there might be. In any emotional crisis she could always be counted upon to preserve her dignity, which was one of the reasons why her father referred to her as The Princess.

How damnably attractive she looked, Sam thought, in that old dressing-gown she had dug out before leaving Stapleton Court. He had long ago decided, in fact, that she was even more bewitching in the oddest garments than when wearing the most expensive clothes; with the exception, perhaps, of evening dress, in which she became breath-takingly lovely.

He dismissed her mention of Hemmingway without a second thought but her statement that she would consider herself free to amuse herself with Derek gave him much food for uneasy speculation. Although he had always tried to regard their casual intimacy as the natural outcome of a very old friendship he had never like it, and now, here was Lavina threatening to 'amuse' herself with Derek. What sort of amusement could Lavina have in mind in which she did not already indulge with her good-looking friend? Too late, Sam saw that, owing to his own action, he had put himself in a situation in which he could no longer complain about their friendship. Margery, of course, was a wonderful woman but Lavina had a lot of things that no other woman he'd ever met had got, and he had not yet entirely lost her. By the time he went to bed the wretched Sam was as miserable as he had been an hour earlier, and hopelessly undecided as to which of the two sisters he wanted to have as his constant companion for the rest of his life.

When morning came the snow was still falling, the sphere

was high and dry and the edge of the flood had receded a mile or more southwards. The whole landscape was now a wintry scene of ice and snow.

The change in the weather provided them with one advantage: they would no longer have to plod about in ankle-deep mud as Sam and Hemmingway had had to on the previous day. The land was now frozen, so after breakfast, having wrapped themselves in their warmest garments, the whole party were able to walk across it with comparative ease as they set out to explore the surrounding country.

On the other hand the snow limited their range of vision, and although they spent the whole morning trying to find the grey stone house that had been sighted on the previous day, they were unable to locate it. By midday they had decided to give up the search and turned back along their tracks in the snow towards the Ark.

It seemed, however, that in their attempts to find the house they had covered more country than they remembered. The tracks meandered all over the place and gradually became fainter until, after half an hour's walk, they gave out altogether, having become filled up with fresh snow. This placed them in an extremely serious predicament as it meant that if they could not find the Ark they would have to remain out all night. Their only indication of the Ark's direction was that it must lie on lower ground, so they trudged down a slope hoping eventually to come to the water, which would give them the line of the shore. But the slope ended in a valley-bottom which rose to a steeper hillside, so, now silent and anxious, they turned back and tried the other way.

Lavina, who loathed the cold, was feeling absolutely desperate and cursed herself for having allowed her curiosity to overcome her reluctance to accompany the others on the expedition. But she knew no good purpose could be served by worrying the men, who were doing their best to find the way, so she said nothing. It was Margery who began to complain and irritated the others by nagging at them until Gervaise abruptly told her that she would do better to save her strength for further walking than to dissipate it in pointless criticisms.

For three hours they wandered, first in one direction and then in another, their spirits sinking lower and lower, until at last Hemmingway stumbled over the dead horse. They knew from its colour and position that it was the one which they had seen on first landing, so the Ark could not be very far away. While the rest remained near the horse, Derek set off at a brisk walk down the gentle gradient and kept in touch with the others by yodelling to them every few minutes. His first cast took him too far to the right; but when he felt that he must have passed his objective he turned back and began to move in a constantly increasing spiral, until he eventually came upon the giant snow-ball that the sphere had become in their absence. He then returned to the others and led them in along his last tracks.

It was past four in the afternoon when they wearily dragged themselves up to the door of the Ark, and as they had left it at nine o'clock in the morning they had been out in the snow for over seven hours, walking nearly the whole time; and for four of those hours they had been lost. In consequence they were frozen to the marrow, ill-tempered and thoroughly tired out. It was not until they had drunk some hot tea laced with rum that any return of cheerfulness manifested itself among them and they all agreed that never again would they leave the Ark during a snow-storm.

Even the tea and rum failed to warm Lavina. She sat shivering in a chair, her small face pinched and miserable until Derek, who thought of little else but her well-being, suggested that he should get her some hot bottles and that she should go to bed.

She thanked him with a pale smile and agreed that would be best; but she had a bad night and was feverish when she woke the following morning, having caught a nasty chill.

Gervaise doctored her and said that she had better stay in bed until she felt all right again, so she did not get up for the next three days; but she did not miss anything by remaining in her cabin as the snow continued to fall without interruption and the others did not leave the Ark except to stretch their limbs in its immediate vicinity.

The fact that they were now able to get away from each other by going outside their steel home enabled Sam and Margery to have some long talks while walking up and down in the snow. Sam reported the conversation he had had with Lavina and Margery derived much secret satisfaction from the way things had gone. She was surprised and pleased that Lavina had made so little trouble but gave her sister little credit for the fact that it was her direct mind and generosity which really formed the basis of the agreement.

In Margery's eyes, Sam had done the right and manly thing in tackling Lavina without delay, and she felt sure that it must have been Sam's own firmness which had carried the tricky interview through to a successful conclusion. The very fact that Sam insisted on giving Lavina full marks only made Margery admire him the more for his strength and modesty, and she felt that her sister, although impetuous and self-willed, must be a weak creature underneath to have surrendered her man with hardly a struggle. Margery had no doubts in her own mind that with Lavina nominally out of the way she could now safely count on having Sam to herself; but then, she did not really know Lavina.

Being able to leave the sphere made a great difference to Derek as he was able to get as much exercise as he wanted without being dependent on the weather, and whenever he was not engaged trying to amuse the sick Lavina in her cabin, or asleep in his own, he was out in the frosty, snow-filled air which he thoroughly enjoyed.

As he soon grew tired of walking up and down within sight of the Ark he decided to employ himself in banking the snow up under its platform and cutting a set of steps in the bank up to its door. Some of the others helped him in his shovelling from time to time and the business was completed by the end of the second day of Lavina's indisposition.

It then occurred to him that it would be a good thing for Fink-Drummond, too, to have some exercise, so he brought the mad-man up from his prison, muffled him in a warm coat and, taking him outside, walked him up and down. As he could only take very short paces, owing to the chain which linked his ankles, the experiment did not prove very successful and such slow-going was anything but pleasant with the thermometer well below zero.

It was a long time now since Fink-Drummond had had one of his fits of insanity, although he still remained apparently dumb; so, having decided that there was little risk of trouble as long as he was in this quiet mood, Derek borrowed Hemmingway's loaded crop in order to defend himself if he was attacked and undid the padlock which secured the chain round the prisoner's legs. The result justified his humane gesture as the lunatic seemed delighted at the chance to stretch himself properly, and behaved quite perfectly, even when he was led back to his cell afterwards and had the chains replaced on his feet.

It was on the fifth day after they had been lost that the snow at last ceased falling. White clouds heavy with it still lingered overhead, but once again they were able to see the surrounding country. To the south of them the great flood had disappeared but the five days' fall of snow had been so heavy that it was impossible to pick out the characteristics of the landscape in detail. On every side they could see long, rolling slopes of snow running into other slopes until these gradually faded into the distance, while in the foreground the universal whiteness was broken here and there by a hedge or coppice that had not been completely covered. They had just decided to set out on another expedition to try and find the grey stone house when the clouds parted and a pale sun shone through.

It was ten days since Gervaise had had a chance to shoot the sun so he immediately got out his sextant, and so eager were the others to know in what country they had come to earth that all thought of the expedition was abandoned while he took an observation and worked out their position. At last he said:

'Our latitude is now 71 degrees 26 minutes north.'

'Then we're still right up in the Arctic Circle,' Hemmingway said at once, 'and much farther north than Iceland.'

'I think we must be in Greenland,' Gervaise replied, 'although I'd never imagined that its scenery looked anything like that which we saw here on the day we were washed ashore.'

'I hadn't, either,' Hemmingway agreed, 'but the scenery of the world doesn't vary quite as much as most people are apt to think. I've seen photographs of parts of semi-tropical Africa which look very like England; and in winter, when there's plenty of snow on the mountains, distant views of Greece might be mistaken for Norway later in the year. Still, if only the sky keeps clear you'll be able to get some altitudes of the stars to-night and fix our longitude; then we'll really know where we are.'

As the weather remained good, Sam and Hemmingway made an expedition that afternoon to try and find the house, but the snow had obliterated such features of the landscape as they remembered so they had to return without having had any success. Derek, meanwhile, exercised Finkie, this being his third outing, and he continued to behave like a model prisoner.

At sundown they watched the sky anxiously but luck was with them. A large section of it remained unclouded, so Gervaise was able to take another observation of the sun at its setting, and an hour later he took the altitudes of some of the principal stars which they were able to identify from their celestial charts. After a couple of hours' work with Oliver's books of logarithms Gervaise gave them their exact position on the earth's surface. It proved to be 71 degrees 25 minutes north and 9 degrees 10 minutes west.

'That settles it,' said Hemmingway, pointing to a spot on the map. 'We're on Jan Mayen Island, up on the edge of the Ice Barrier—about 280 miles east of the coast of Greenland.'

'The hell we are!' exclaimed Lavina, who was with them, having now recovered from her chill.

'Not a very jolly prospect,' agreed Sam. 'I don't suppose the place was ever inhabited except by a few fisher-folk; and we won't find much to start life with again in any of their cottages. It would have been a much better outlook if the Ark had beached itself somewhere within reasonable distance of the great cities.'

Gervaise had been looking over Hemmingway's shoulder at the map. 'I suppose you're right about our being on Jan Mayen, as it's the only land anywhere within several hundred miles of the position I worked out. But, actually, the most northern point of the island barely touches the 71st parallel and we're 25 minutes north of that.'

'I know,' Hemmingway nodded. 'But you must remember that the chronometers may be a little out.'

'Anyway, there's plenty of timber,' remarked Derek. 'If we put our backs into it we could build a seaworthy boat, get down to Iceland, re-fit, and make our way by easy stages through the Hebrides to Scotland and so to London.'

'Easy stages!' echoed Lavina. 'Hundreds of miles in an open boat! No thank you, Handsome, not for this child—at least, not till next summer anyway.'.

'There's no point in trying to get to London,' Margery put in. 'Everyone will have been drowned and the place will be a shambles. The land here looked good for cultivation and I can see no reason why happy homes could not be made here for those of us who're prepared to work.'

'I don't think we have much choice,' Gervaise announced dryly. 'Now the flood has subsided, all the dead bodies of animals and humans will be decaying farther south, and the air will be full of pestilence within a week. Even if we could make a seaworthy boat, as Derek suggests, I wouldn't dream of leading you there until the cold of another winter has killed off the bacilli. Here, we'll at least be safe from plague, as the ice and snow will prevent the corpses rotting. I'm, er—not a religious man, as you know, but it almost seems as if a merciful Providence had ordained that we should land in a place where we could live without fear of being stricken down by some terrible fever.'

'I suppose half a loaf's better than no bread, dearest,' sighed Lavina, 'but I think it's a pretty mean kind of Providence, all the same. Just think what we'll have to go through stuck here during an Arctic winter.'

The thoughts of darkness, cold and discomfort which her words called up were so grim that none of them cared to discuss the prospect further and soon afterwards they went to bed.

The next morning it was a cold but sunny day again; so they decided to make another expedition towards the higher ground. Derek had now formed the conclusion that Finkie was no longer dangerous and, being fond of all dumb beasts, had come to regard him as a sort of tame animal. In consequence he insisted, rather against the wishes of the others, that instead of the imbecile being left a prisoner all day, he should be taken with them. When the whole party set out from the Ark soon after breakfast, therefore, Finkie shuffled along at Derek's side like a morose Caliban.

The going was not easy because the snow was thick, they had no snow-shoes and they occasionally came into heavy drifts which delayed their progress; so they covered barely a mile an hour. Hedges and woods barring their paths at intervals also necessitated considerable detours and it was eleven o'clock before they came upon any other sign that the land had been inhabited by human before the flood.

This was an unnatural hump rising in a corner of one of the fields, and when Derek had knocked some of the snow off it with one of the spades they had brought, they discovered it to be a motor-tractor. The fact that it had been made in England, as they saw by the manufacturer's plate, gave them a strange sense of comfort, and, as Gervaise remarked, since they still had a good supply of petrol left in the Ark, the tractor might come in very useful to them later on.

It had taken them ten minutes or more to clear the snow away and it was only when they had finished that Derek suddenly said: 'Where's Finkie?'

Swinging round they saw that Fink-Drummond had disappeared.

Behind them in the snow his tracks showed that he had padded to the nearest bank, and the black small-wood and leaves of a hedge could be seen through the snow, marking the place where he had scrambled over it.

Derek and Hemmingway ran to the hedge and looked over, but Finkie was nowhere to be seen and his track led towards a small wood in which, if he had decided to hide from them, it was going to be very difficult to find him.

'I shouldn't worry,' Gervaise called to them. 'He'll make his way back to the Ark as soon as he's cold and hungry.' So, for the moment, they abandoned any thought of trying to recapture him and continued their exploration of the country.

Scrambling up a smooth bank of snow an hour later Gervaise suddenly tripped and fell; burying his arms, which he had thrown out to save himself, in the snow up to his elbows. Picking himself up he began to kick round with his feet and soon discovered that the satin-smooth snow surface concealed something unusual.

'This isn't earth below here,' he said, 'it's something jagged and uneven.' Stooping down he pulled out a yellow brick; upon which they set to work clearing the snow in various places and soon found that the mound concealed the ruins of a modern cottage.

'It was probably only a jerry-built place,' Sam remarked, 'and that's why the flood bowled it over.' His idea was confirmed a moment later when Margery gave a cry of dismay. In moving some bricks she had uncovered the sole of a boot and, on pulling at it, had suddenly realized that it had a dead foot inside it which was still attached to a leg and body buried deeper in the debris.

They covered the foot up again, left the mound and went on, still looking for the grey stone house; but they could not find it and at one o'clock sat down to the picnic lunch they had brought with them.

It was hard work ploughing through the heavy snow so they
were a little tired after their ramble and, as sundown came far
earlier in this high latitude than in mid-August in England,
Gervaise suggested that when they had finished their picnic they
should abandon their exploration for that day and return to the
Ark.

On the way back they reverted to their discussion of the
previous night about the hardships of being compelled to winter
in the Arctic; but both Gervaise and Hemmingway were comparatively cheerful about it.

Gervaise pointed out that if they could not find better accommodation they still had the Ark in which to live. That would
mean that they would have to continue living in rather cramped
quarters but, in the Ark, they would have every reasonable comfort and would suffer no more from being thrown about in rough
weather. As they had used hardly any of their petrol for propelling the sphere they still had the bulk of their supply which, used
economically, should be sufficient to run the electric-light and
heating plants through the winter. They would have to cut down
their rations of food but there were ways in which these could be
supplemented. The dead cattle they had come across had already
decayed to such a degree through their forty-three days' submergence in the flood waters that, although now frozen meat,
they were no longer fit for human consumption. But there would
be nuts on the trees, edible roots in the ground and seeds which
could be crushed for life-giving substances.

Hemmingway took up the theme to add that if the supply of
food looked like giving out before the spring came round they
could eke out their tinned goods with stews of seeds and roots
from their own stores of these, many of which were edible. Moreover, the fact that they had discovered a motor tractor that morning showed that the land was farmable; so, although it would
mean hard work to clear the snow, there was no reason why they
should not sow some patches of cereals and root-crops during
the next few weeks before the land had frozen solid and the real
Artic winter set in.

For the hundredth time they congratulated themselves on
their forethought in stocking the Ark with so many items and
implements which would now prove more valuable than gold
and ensure their being able to maintain themselves even in such

a terrible climate. The Ark and its contents were their fortress and their salvation.

It was four o'clock when they came over the last crest and sighted it; a huge snowball in a flat field half a mile away. They were still a quarter of a mile off when a sudden cry of dismay burst from the whole party. A great tongue of flame, red, fierce and curling, had leapt from the doorway of the sphere, lighting up the snow all round with a lurid glare.

Instantly they began to run towards it. They had not covered a dozen yards when a human figure appeared right in the centre of the flame. It was Fink-Drummond. With a piercing scream he leapt down the snow-steps and raced away across the field.

His clothes were on fire and his shrieks of agony could have been heard a mile away as he floundered down the slope away from them.

Derek, who was leading the party, turned a little in his stride and raced after him while the others ran straight on towards the Ark. When they reached it they drew to an abrupt halt and stood there panting, their faces expressing every shade of fear, horror and distress.

Either deliberately in a fit of lunacy, or through some accident, Fink-Drummond must have set light to the petrol tanks in the bilge of the Ark. Its interior was now a white-hot furnace. There was no way in which they could enter it, except by the door, and that was a roaring sheet of flame so fierce that they had to stand twenty yards away to prevent themselves being scorched.

There was nothing whatever that they could do. They were compelled to stand there in helpless misery, watching while the angry fire devoured all their possessions and all those stores which meant their very hope of life.

Five minutes later, Derek came panting back to them. 'He's dead,' he gasped. 'He fell before I caught up with him. If only the poor fool had had the sense to roll in the snow instead of running away like that he might have saved himself; but every stitch he had on was burnt to a cinder. The shock must have killed him.'

The flames issuing from the Ark gradually grew less fierce. After a time they died down to a flicker and Gervaise, mounting the snow-bank which had only partially melted, peered over the charred platform into the Ark's interior. The deck was gone, the partitions had disappeared; all that was left was a heap of glowing ashes. He stumbled down the bank again and joined the others.

They were still standing there half an hour later, robbed of initiative, utterly stricken by this appalling catastrophe. The brief wintry afternoon was nearly over; night was approaching. They had nothing but the clothes they stood up in and they were alone, friendless, foodless, fireless, in the grim, snowbound Arctic.

26

THE FROZEN WORLD

They were at their wit's end to know what to do. All Hemming-way's academic knowledge was now completely useless. Sam's flair for dealing with obstreperous shareholders of company meetings and shaking world markets left him with no more idea than a child how to cope with the situation. Derek's knowledge of the countryside at home in England could not help him to maintain the party in this totally different climate. Margery could cook but she was helpless without food and fire. Even Lavina, whose presence would have cheered most people who were temporarily stranded, had not the power to raise their spirits now that it seemed that they were condemned to die there. It was Gervaise who showed his natural capacity for leadership.

'Come,' he said, rousing at last, 'it's no good our remaining here. We must seek shelter for the night.'

Margery shrugged despairingly. 'What shelter is there? We've spent two days looking for the house Sam and Hemmingway saw when we first arrived here, but we haven't found it; so we certainly shan't be able to in the darkness.'

'I didn't suppose we could,' Gervaise replied shortly; 'but we still have an hour's twilight and we've got to find shelter somewhere from this wind, even if it's only under a hedge.'

Turning on his heel, he led them back towards the higher ground and selected a place half a mile from the burnt-out Ark where two snow-banks, covering high hedges, met at right-angles in the corner of a field. Derek and Hemmingway still had the spades so he set them to dig out the snow from the drift and pack it into a third wall. He then sent Sam and the two girls off to collect any broken branches or brushwood they could find by turning up the snow under the nearest large trees.

As they brought it in he arranged it just outside the opening of the three-sided pen which the two younger men were forming. Soon there was a big enough pile and he managed to light some dead twigs from some old papers they had in their pockets and a petrol lighter. Even when the bonfire blazed up he would not allow the party to rest, but made them continue gathering wood so that they should have a sufficient supply to keep the fire going throughout the night.

Except for the wind, from which they were protected in their pen, the weather was clement. Darkness fell and the stars came out overhead, but Gervaise was still not satisfied. He made them strip the half-decayed leaves from the branches that had been brought in until they had two big piles apiece; one to use as a pillow on the snow-ledge that Hemmingway had fashioned, and the other, a much larger one, in which to bury their feet.

He then ordered them to take off their outer coats. Margery's, Lavina's and his own he spread on the ground, after which he said that they must lie down in a row as close as they could get to one another, spread the remaining three coats over them and pile up the heaps of leaves over their feet and ankles. Derek and Hemmingway took the two outside places in the row, as they had volunteered to watch alternately and keep the fire going through the night with fresh supplies of fuel. Gervaise and Sam came next, with the two girls in the centre.

As they had hollowed out places for their hips they were not uncomfortable and, crowded close together, they were surprised at the warmth they obtained from each other's bodies when they were lying at full length under the shelter of the hedges and the wall.

Once they had time to think, their thoughts were chaotic. Nightmarish speculations about their impending fate through cold or starvation flickered through their brains. Unless they could find some human habitation it did not seem possible that they could manage to exist for long under such terrible conditions, and, even if they could find a house, where were they to get food with which to support themselves through the long Arctic winter? But they were very tired after their long day's tramp, the shock of seeing their refuge and all it contained destroyed, and their recent labours, and, one by one, they dropped off to sleep.

When morning dawned the fire was still burning brightly.

Derek and Hemmingway had fulfilled their task and, waking each other at intervals, had kept it going. Having warmed themselves at it they decided to set off at once, as they had nothing to pack and only the two spades to carry with them. Every moment was precious as, if they failed to discover some place that they could make a permanent headquarters while they devoted their energies to searching for food, it was certain that cold and hunger would put an end to them within the next few days. Since they had not succeeded in locating the grey stone house on two previous expeditions it seemed foolish to expend further time in looking for it; yet they had no idea which direction would give them the best prospect of coming upon some distant habitation.

'I think our best plan,' Gervaise announced, 'is to make for the highest ground we can see. Jan Mayen Island is about forty miles long but only five to ten miles broad. If we can reach a spot where we can get a good view in several directions we should be able to see the sea. Once we've done that, we must head for it and follow the coast-line until we find a village, as it's certain that in an island like this nearly all the inhabitants would live down by the shore.'

For an hour they trudged slowly but determinedly on, plodding through the crisp snow up the gentle slopes towards the higher ground to the north. Crossing a high bank they came down into a broad, snowy bottom. They followed it for some distance until they arrived at a place where it was intersected by another shallower valley, the sides of which were less than 20 feet in height and were, in fact, only banks crowned by buried hedges.

It was Hemmingway who suddenly pointed to one of the corners of the intersection and began to run towards it. Almost at the same second the others also noticed that the top of a signpost was protruding some feet above the snow. They followed his lead and, coming to a halt, stood there spellbound with amazement.

The signpost had two arms, one of which read: 'WOODSIDE PLACE 1 Mile,' and the other 'LONDON 19 Miles.'

Lavina began to laugh. To find such a thing in the Arctic Circle was positively fantastic and, quite obviously, beyond the bounds of possibility. Throwing her arms round her father's neck, she cried:

K

'You darling old silly, with your funny calculations! You were right off the map, my sweet—right off the map. We're still in England.'

It was impossible to believe that she was not right. The signpost stared them in the face and forbade all argument; yet Gervaise remained utterly bewildered.

He had taken two observations on each occasion that he had shot the sun and had taken the altitude of half a dozen stars as well. It was inconceivable that those could all be wrong and every one of them had worked out to show that their position was within a few minutes of 71 degrees 25 minutes north.

Hemmingway, who had checked his sums, supported him in his assertion that his calculations had been correct, but the fact that the country with its meadows, little woods and small fields was so like England bore out the message of the signpost.

As they set out to explore a little farther, taking the wider of the two valleys which they now had reason to believe was a road, Lavina said:

'I wonder what part of England we're in? I've never heard of Woodside Place. Have any of you?'

'No,' murmured the others, and Sam added:

'Wherever it is it's only nineteen miles from London.'

'Perhaps,' said Gervaise, 'but I wouldn't be too certain of that. There's just a chance that some mad Englishman may have settled on Jan Mayen Island and put the signpost up for a joke. The sun and the stars can't lie, you know, and it's very easy to take accurate observations with a sextant; in fact, if you've once learnt how, as I did many years ago, it's impossible to make a mistake.'

For a time they trudged on in silence, depressed again by the thought that his theory of the mad Englishman might conceivably be right, but twenty minutes later they came to another cross-roads which also had a signpost. It had three arms which read respectively: 'WOODHILL ½ Mile', 'LONDON 18 Miles', 'HATFIELD 3 Miles'.

That settled the question. Not only were they in England, but they were on the northern outskirts of London in the county of Hertfordshire.

At last they were able to give rein to their feelings. The hunger they had been beginning to feel from having had neither supper

THE FROZEN WORLD 291

nor breakfast, the cold, and the loss of all their possessions were all forgotten as they joyfully took the road south, to London. But Gervaise was still extremely puzzled about his calculations being so many hundreds of miles out, and as they marched along he began to postulate a theory which might account for it.

'You may remember,' he said, 'how Oliver mentioned on one occasion that some scientists believe the South Sea Islands to be the remnants of another great comet which hit the earth many millenniums ago. There is a theory about the axis of the earth which ties up with that. Most of the planets revolve with the plane of their equators horizontal to the sun so that there are no seasons and the climate on different parts of their surface remains the same the whole year round. The theory is that our earth was like that originally, but when this first great comet hit it in the South Pacific the blow was so terrific that it threw it right off its axis, shifting the North Pole from a spot about 7½ degrees north of Scotland to its present position—or rather, to that which we know it to have occupied before the new comet hit us; and that instead of swinging back again the earth, from then on, revolved round a new axis at a tilt of 23½ degrees to the sun.'

'The business of the mammoths supports that,' said Hemmingway. 'Their remains are found in Siberia and in the Andes at high altitudes where the climate of the world as we knew it would have made it quite impossible for such animals to live.'

'How about the ice ages, though?' Lavina inquired. 'The ice caps shifted up and down, didn't they? So for long periods when there wasn't much ice Siberia might have been quite warm enough for them to live in.'

'That doesn't explain the mammoths in the Andes. There is a high plateau in Peru which is not more than 10 degrees south of the equator, and the southern ice cap certainly never got as far north as that. On the plateau there are the bones of hundreds and hundreds of mammoths. The only explanation for their all being found together is that the place must have once been a mammoths' feeding-ground, and the fact that they could not possibly have lived at such a height, owing to its low temperature, proves that they were all wiped out by some sudden and drastic change of climate before they had time to migrate to pastures nearer the sea level. No one has been able to explain what could have caused such a change; but Gervaise's theory of the shifting of the axis of the earth would certainly do so.'

'Exactly!' agreed Gervaise quickly. 'And I suggest that since our comet hit the earth in the Northern Pacific, it threw the earth back again practically on to its original axis. We know, too, that the impact occurred in longitude 165 degrees west so, if I'm right, the new North Pole must be some 20 degrees farther south on the 15th parallel of longitude east, which would place it approximately on the coast of north-western Norway. In consequence, Britain would be well up within the Arctic Circle.'

The others agreed that his reasoning offered the only possible explanation which tallied with the two established facts that they were only about twenty miles north of London and yet their latitude was 71 degrees north. But, after a moment, Lavina said gloomily:

'In that case we'll still have to spend the rest of our lives like Eskimos, so it doesn't seem that we're much better off than we were before.'

'Oh, yes, we are,' Sam hastened to reassure her. 'All London is ours for the taking. Houses, food, furs, jewels. Why, you'll be able to sleep in the Queen's bed at Buckingham Palace for the rest of your life, if you want to.'

'That would be rather fun,' she admitted. 'I hadn't thought of it quite that way. The whole idea of London being a city of the dead is so terrible, but I suppose we'll get used to that, and once we do there'll be all sorts of queer ways in which we can amuse ourselves.'

'I think I shall make my headquarters in the British Museum,' said Gervaise thoughtfully. 'Some of the manuscripts may have been damaged by the water, which is tragic, but being packed side by side on their shelves the volumes can't have suffered very much. It's a little awe-inspiring, though, for a bibliophile like myself suddenly to find that the greatest library in the world is his for the taking.'

Suddenly Hemmingway began to laugh, and on Sam's asking what had bitten him, he replied: 'All our lives long we've been striving to make money. You and I, Sam, have been pretty successful. Gervaise and Derek haven't striven so hard but a few months ago both of them would have found a few thousands apiece very useful. Now, all of us are billionaires—multi-billionaires. The jewels in the Tower of London, the gold in the Bank of England, the script and securities of the greatest city in the world are all ours if we like to go and collect them. But we shan't, because they're utterly useless to us.'

'Not quite,' said Lavina. 'The Koh-i-noor, or whatever the big diamond is in the top of the crown, would have a much more appropriate setting if I wore it in my hair.'

'That's all very well,' grunted Derek, 'but d'you realize that there's not a horse left alive; and there's not a partidge or a pheasant, nor even any eggs to restock the coverts.'

'You'll still be able to fish,' Hemmingway consoled him. 'Cut a nice hole in the ice of the Thames and put a light down it as the Eskimos do. That attracts the fish, then you can spear them.'

Derek gave him a supercilious smile. 'Evidently you're not a fisherman, or you'd know that that sort of thing isn't fishing.'

Margery brought them all down to earth by suddenly remarking: 'It's all very well for you to talk about fun and jewels and living in Buckingham Palace or the British Museum and things like that, but you're not being very practical. What we have to find are a few small houses which can be easily run so that there's not too far to carry the food from their kitchens.'

'That's right,' Sam nodded. 'And, after all, what more do we want as long as we've got food and fire and comfortable beds to sleep in? I'm afraid we've rather overlooked the fact, too, that we've still got the best part of twenty miles to walk to London.'

'Now we're on the main road we'll find plenty of houses to rest in,' said Gervaise. 'A great many of the jerry-built places outside London will have been demolished by the flood, like those cottages we came upon the other day, but I should think that most of the better built places will still be standing.'

He had hardly spoken when they came round a bend in the road and saw a good-sized house among some trees a quarter of a mile ahead. It was a two-storeyed building and a snowdrift, almost as high as the house, buried one wall. The roof was heavily covered and the only patches of mellow red brick which showed through the snow were under the front windows; but with a sense of fresh excitement they hurried forward, scrambled over the banked-up snow which hid a hedge, and approached the front door.

All the windows of the house had given under the pressure

of the water and stared at them blank and foreboding like the eye-sockets in a skull. The door had swollen from the wet so they had some difficulty in getting it open and, as Derek and Hemmingway forced it with their united weight, a mass of snow slid down from the porch upon the others. Shaking it off, they went inside.

There was a thin coating of ice on the floor of the hallway which crunched under their feet as they advanced and, just as they entered the first room on the right, Derek slipped and fell. The whole floor of the room was covered with a three-inch-thick layer of glassy ice from the flood water which had failed to drain away and stuck fast in it, at all sorts of odd angles, were its furnishings, which looked as though they had been hurled about by a typhoon. Actually, the flood water had only swept the ornaments from their places and floated the lighter pieces of furniture up to the ceiling until, on its receding, they had been left scattered about the floor. Long icicles hung from the ceiling and the walls had a satin-like sheen from the frost rime that covered them.

It was a sitting-room equipped with pieces typical of middle-class England during the last three generations. Lavina sat down on the sofa, which had remained upright, but she promptly stood up again, as its appearance was extraordinarily deceptive. With its rather worn cretonne cover it did not outwardly appear very different from any other sofa, but the whole thing had been water-logged during the flood and frozen afterwards so that it was now as solid as a piece of iron.

Margery had gone straight through to the back of the house and she called to them from the kitchen. When they joined her they found her in the larder. It contained the half of a cold chicken, some eggs, fruit and other oddments. The discolouration of the fruit showed that it had gone bad, although it was now frozen solid. The eggs were encased in a solid pack of ice as the flood water, which had filled the bowl in which they were, had had no means of draining away; while several broken plates and odd items of food lay half buried in the ice on the floor where they had been swept when the waters had gushed through the larder window.

They were all now ravenously hungry and Derek immediately suggested: 'How about a meal before we go any farther?'

'That's just what I was thinking,' Margery laughed, laying hold of the dish on which the chicken reposed to wrench it up from its bed of ice.

'Don't bother with that chicken,' said Gervaise quickly. 'It was submerged in the flood for forty-three days at least and it must have gone bad long before it became frozen. The eggs will be bad too. We must see if we can find any food in tins.'

In a kitchen cupboard they found some tins of sweet-corn and salmon; also some pots of jam, although there were no bread or biscuits with which to eat it. They were so cold that they badly needed a hot meal, so Margery said:

'There won't be any gas or electricity but I could heat up the sweet-corn and salmon if some of you will get a fire going in the sitting-room.'

Instead of going outside to see if there was a supply of coal or wood in a nearby shed, Derek, having found a chopper, returned to the front room and began to hack some of the lighter furniture to pieces: remarking as he did so that, as they would have the whole stock of Harrod's, Maple's and Hampton's from which to choose at their leisure, they could well afford to use the stuff in their temporary quarters for firewood. Hemmingway, who had joined him and was busily applying the poker to a hideous Victorian cabinet, replied:

'You can have all the furniture shops and Mr. Drage's plain vans as well. I intend to furnish my flat with some of the pieces from the South Kensington Museum. As for this hideous muck, I derive a peculiar joy from smashing it.'

Lighting a fire was not as easy as they had imagined. The wood lit all right but huge clouds of smoke bellowed out from the fireplace and it was soon apparent that the chimney was blocked, probably by ice or snow. After an equally fruitless attempt in the grate of the dining-room, which lay on the other side of the hall, they carried their remaining supplies of broken wood back to the kitchen on Gervaise's suggesting that their only course was now to light a fire on its stone floor.

The mess of sweet-corn and salmon was eventually cooked, but only after the greatest difficulties. And, as the bonfire filled the room with smoke and melted the ice on the floor and the icicles which hung from the ceiling, they ate in considerable discomfort.

After this unsatisfactory experiment they again took the road to London. A hundred yards along it they came to a big mound in its middle which, on examination, proved to be a buried car that had overturned and still had its frozen passengers in it. Farther on they found other humps concealing more wrecked cars, vans and lorries. It was past midday when they left the house, and trudging through the snow was heavy work so it was half past one by the time they entered Potters Bar.

Since finding the first house, where they had cooked their meal, they had seen others almost constantly along the sides of the highway; some standing back from the road in their own gardens, others in rows; but most of the rows had been demolished by the flood and were now only indicated by long, snow-covered humps at the roadside. Many of the single houses, too, had collapsed and in those which remained every window had been broken.

At three o'clock they were passing through Monken Hadley, where the buildings became more numerous, and half an hour later, in the middle of Barnet, they came to a place where the road disappeared, being completely blocked. At first they wondered what the snow-covered eminence in their path might be but as they mounted it the uneven surface beneath the snow soon showed them that they were walking on heaped-up bricks. A whole block of shops and flats had collapsed and been swept by the flood right into the middle of the highway. Here and there things projected from it; the top of a lamp-post, a broken wireless mast with a tangled aerial still attached and a stout pole, from the top of which dangled a cord with some snow-whitened lumps which proved on investigation to be frozen articles of clothing still pegged on to a washing line.

The light of the short, wintry afternoon was fading so when they had passed over the great mound they set about looking for a suitable place in which to pass the night. Now that twilight was falling the snow made it difficult to pick out from a distance the houses that were still standing, as only an occasional slab of wall or tree trunk from which the snow had fallen relieved the blank whiteness of the landscape.

After a little they came to a flat-roofed building on a corner where two roads crossed. Its door stood wide open and, on going in, they found it to be a road-house. Great heaps of snow had drifted in through the open doorway and half filled the lounge, partially covering many of the brightly painted tables and chairs which had been thrown into heaps by the flood.

Forcing open a door at one side of the lounge they found it led to an office. The hideously swollen figure of a drowned man, now frozen stiff, was set fast in three inches of ice through which they could still see the carpet. They shut the door quickly and tried another on the far side of the lounge.

It opened into a bar where most of the bottles had been swept from the shelves by the inrush of the waters, their broken fragments frozen into the glassy surface of the floor making it as dangerous to walk on as the top of a park wall. Red-topped stools were scattered about in confusion and the till on the counter stood open.

Picking their way carefully through the broken glass they looked at the labels of the unbroken bottles, selected one of Cherry Brandy which was almost full, and had a couple of rounds of extremely welcome drinks. The liqueur warmed them up and they set about exploring the small hotel with renewed vigour.

It was getting dark now but they found some candles in the kitchen and, when several of them were lit, the place looked like some weird, fairy cavern as the light glinted on the icicles, the frozen floor and the snow which had drifted in through the windows, turning them to rainbow hues. There was a fair supply of food, all of which had gone bad before it had been frozen; but in a cupboard they found some tins of soup, sardines, vegetables and fruit as well as some bottles of coffee essence. Delighted with their find, which ensured them of several future meals, they hurried upstairs.

Each room had to be broken into as the doors had first swollen and then been frozen. In one room they came upon three more corpses; one, that of a woman, having been left by the receding waters dangling grotesquely from the top of a wardrobe. The sight of the poor drowned bodies made them feel slightly sick so they quickly left them and busied themselves choosing other rooms in which to sleep.

They were tired now after their long day and very cold. All of them were longing for a quick evening meal to warm them up and the joy of crawling between the sheets of comfortable beds immediately afterwards to sink into a long deep sleep.

But suddenly they realized that they were faced with a horrid problem. As with the sofa upon which Lavina had sat down in the house where they had had their midday meal, all the beds and bedding were frozen solid. How could they possibly unfreeze and dry them again so that they could be used that night?

27

LIFE MUST GO ON

For a few moments they dejectedly discussed various methods of setting to work. The sheets and blankets could not be pulled off the beds as they were frozen to the mattresses and to have endeavoured to hack them off would have torn them in pieces. The only solution seemed to be to thaw out each set of bedding at one operation and as no ordinary fire would give out enough heat for such a proceeding Gervaise said that they must light a super bonfire.

Through the broken window of the back bedroom in which they were talking they could see a smaller building only about a hundred yards away across the garden and, going downstairs, they walked over to it. The place was a fair-sized cottage, evidently much older than the inn as it was half-timbered and had no electric fittings.

'Our luck is in,' said Gervaise. 'This place will suit us admirably, and as the people here used oil lamps there must be a drum of paraffin about somewhere.'

In the kitchen they found one two-thirds full, so returning with it to the living-room they smashed up the lighter furniture, piled the heavier pieces on top of it, sprinkled the whole heap with the paraffin and, touching the oil off with a match, ran out of the cottage.

For some moments Gervaise was anxious as to whether his plan would work. He feared that the snow in the room and the ice that saturated the furnishings would prevent the fire getting a good hold as they thawed and sputtered down into it. But, with an angry hissing, the flames licked at the beams which spanned the ceiling and the fire was soon eating through the floor boards of the room above.

The next job was to get the beds down into the garden. When one of them had been hacked free of the frozen floor it was found that owing to the weight of the ice with which it was laden it was

299

much too heavy to carry downstairs, so the men of the party heaved it out of a window and others after it; then laboriously dragged them through the snow over to the cottage, from the sitting-room window of which big flames were now spurting.

It was a tiring, muscle-wrenching business and darkness had long fallen by the time they had got six beds set up on end in a row before the glowing pile of red-hot logs and bricks; but the fire also served to revitalize them with its heat after their long day in this new and terrible frozen world.

Margery, meanwhile, had thawed out some of the tinned food and boiled some snow on a small fire that Lavina had made in a brick surround on the concrete floor of a garage which adjoined the kitchen of the inn. They fed round the fire and having washed the meal down with some drinks from the bar they re-crossed the garden to see whether their beds had thawed.

The sheets and blankets had fallen away from the sodden mattresses and, now wringing with water, were lying in heaps on the wet ground. Having wrung them out as well as they could they hung them up on a wire fence which the melting snow had disclosed at the side of the cottage. While the men turned the mattresses and prevented the clothes from scorching, the girls made a tour of the hotel bedrooms and collected such items as they could find which might prove useful and brought these too down to be thawed at the roaring blaze.

It was past one in the morning before the mattresses were thoroughly dry and fit to sleep on without fear of chills or rheumatism. Carrying them back to the inn they laid them out on the billiards-tables of a big games-room next to the lounge. Still in their clothes they drew the blankets over them and fell asleep, utterly exhausted.

When they were awakened by the pale morning light it was snowing again with that same gentle persistence which had marked the previous five-day blizzard, and Gervaise said he thought it would be inadvisable to attempt to go farther until the fall had ceased. After breakfast, as it seemed that the snow might keep them there for another night, they set to work trying to make the place as habitable as possible.

The cottage across the garden was now a pile of blackened embers, smoking and hissing as the snow drifted down on to it. By turning up the crust of ash with their spades they were able

to warm themselves at the red embers which still glowed underneath and to thaw several pairs of curtains for nailing up across
the broken windows of the rooms they were occupying, to keep
out the snow and wind. Hemmingway had wandered off on his
own and when they got back they found that he had collected
three buckets from the garage. He was busy knocking holes in
them with a hammer and spike, as he said:

'If we set these up on bricks we can turn them into braziers
and thaw the rooms properly. There's plenty of coke in the
boiler house although one of us will have to hack it out with a
pickaxe.'

Derek volunteered for the job and in half an hour they had
the braziers going in the kitchen. Water dripped from the ceiling
and sweated from the walls, temporarily making the place
extremely uncomfortable, but Sam found a broom with which
to sweep away the slush from the floor while Gervaise nailed
the curtains across the windows. By midday they had at least
made the room habitable.

It was now over two days since they had left their comfortable
quarters in the Ark, and ever since it had been burnt out there
had been so many vital things to do, if they were to keep the life
in their bodies, that they had had no opportunity to clean themselves up at all. The men's faces had an ugly stubble and the
girls' hair was limp and bedraggled. Even Lavina could not bear
to look at herself in a glass any more. One hasty glance in the
bar-room mirror when they had arrived at the inn had shocked
her beyond belief. Her hair was straight and wispy and her cheeks
sunken so that her high cheek-bones had an unusual prominence
in her thin little face. Beneath her eyes there were black shadows
and the tiny, blue veins in her eyelids were swollen, giving them
the appearance of having been heavily mascaraed, but she had
actually been much too weary to do anything about herself.

After the midday meal, being a little restored by warmth and
food, they boiled some snow on the braziers and began to clean
themselves; the men using the shaving gear, etc., of the dead
hotel proprietor and the girls the toilet articles which they discovered in some of the bedrooms.

That evening they discussed their future plans. Gervaise
pointed out that if they remained where they were the small
stock of tinned food which they had found in the road-house

would soon become exhausted. They would then have to forage for further supplies, a tin here and a tin there, in the houses in the neighbourhood. At the rate the snow was settling it looked as though they might be snowed up before long. If that occurred their forays for food would become more and more difficult as on each they would have to go farther afield. It was essential therefore that they should get to London with the least possible delay and find a new refuge, with abundant stocks of food, which they could use as a permanent headquarters.

Hemmingway agreed, and added that now they were on a main road, which had houses on both sides for most of the way, there was little chance of their losing their direction; so there was no reason why they should not move on the following day, even if it was snowing, providing that it was not blowing an absolute blizzard.

Sam put up the objection that wherever they halted next they would be faced with the same appalling conditions. That meant that they would only be able to do a short stage each morning and must devote every afternoon to the grim labour of preparing a refuge for the night. Surely it would be better, therefore, to wait for a fine day when they would have a reasonable chance of covering the ten or twelve miles to London, and work all night if need be, when they had arrived, to make themselves the beginnings of permanent quarters there.

The argument was settled for them by the weather, as next day dawned clear again. The snow clouds had discharged their cargo and the sun was brighter than they had yet seen it. Having had the best part of a day's rest and an early night, they were able to set off a little after eight o'clock.

Although the sun was shining there were no signs of a permanent thaw. They estimated the general depth of the snow to be about six feet deep, but in places it had piled up in drifts that were as much as fifteen feet in height. The temperature was still far below zero and the previous day's snow had frozen solid making a hard crust which, apart from occasional pitfalls, made fairly easy going.

In order to save themselves the labour of thawing out fresh bedding they took their blankets and sheets with them, tied round their bodies like bandoliers. Derek, Sam and Hemmingway each carried in addition one of the bucket-braziers, into which they had packed the remainder of the unused tinned foods from the inn, some bottles of drink, and various oddments such as the chopper, candles, razors, soap etc., which would come in useful.

As they advanced they came upon many hummocks in and alongside the roadway, which concealed abandoned cars and lorries. When they rested for a little at 9.15, on the slope of another great, snow-covered mound of rubble which blocked the highway, Sam, who knew the road well, was able to tell them that the debris had formed part of Whetstone.

Soon afterwards the road divided and they took the right-hand fork, reaching Finchley by half-past ten. After another rest they pressed on again, arriving just after midday at Golders Green, where they sat down to lunch off some of the cold food they had brought. There was no possibility of mistaking the point at which they had arrived as Sam, Hemmingway, Lavina and Derek were all able to identify the clock tower, near which they ate their lunch, and the long snow-covered roof of the station on the far side of the open square. Part of the station roof had fallen in, as had several of the houses, but most of the blocks were still standing. Further out of London the silence had not seemed unnatural, but here, while they sat eating their picnic lunch on a site that most of them had seen filled with the bustle of modern life, it seemed extraordinary and rather frightening.

By half-past twelve they were on their way again, passing between big banks of snow along the roadsides which partially obscured the low houses set back amid their gardens. As they trudged on the going became more difficult. The sunshine was melting the upper crust of snow, and walking in overcoats with blankets tied round them made warm work. Coming down the Finchley Road past the eastern portion of Hampstead the trek became more laborious still, as most of the way had been lined with big blocks of buildings and many of these had fallen in so that at times the road entirely disappeared.

To their right, as they went downhill, they could get a view of London between the piles of snow-covered ruins, but in spite of the sunshine it was difficult to get a clear impression of the great metropolis. Every roof and spire was snow-covered, which blurred the outlines, and, except for buildings in the foreground, the countless thousands of houses, innumerable big blocks and well-known landmarks all merged into an uneven carpet of white which stretched as far as the eye could see.

It was three o'clock before they reached the easily distinguishable road junctions at Swiss Cottage, after which the way proved better for a little while as they were once more passing through an area where the houses stood back from the road, but soon the way was again choked by debris where several large blocks of flats had been swept away. By the time they had got to St. John's Wood Church, where they paused for another snack and a welcome go at the liqueurs, they were all very tired, and the two girls were thoroughly fagged out.

Their thickest clothes, in which they had left the Ark, were only English winter weight and much too light to protect them properly from the rigours of this frozen world. Each time they halted there seemed to creep up their limbs a deathly chill which they could check only by flailing their arms and stamping their feet. Their faces tingled and their eyes smarted from the snow-glare.

Sam suggested that they should shelter in Lord's cricket pavilion for the night, but as there was still an hour or more to go before sunset Gervaise insisted that they should not lose the balance of the day's good weather now when, by a last effort, they could cover the remaining two miles into Central London.

At four o'clock they started off once more. The sun had lost its power and all traces of the temporary thaw which had set in at midday had disappeared. The snow crust had frozen solid again but, owing to the partial thaw, it was now treacherously glassy, which made walking hazardous.

The half mile south from St. John's Wood Church was not so bad, as for a good part of the way they had Regent's Park on their left but when they entered the north end of Baker Street their real troubles began. The Abbey Road Building Society's block still reared its tower to the sky, but great numbers of the shops and flats had been demolished by the flood. Instead of a broad thoroughfare Baker Street was an uneven mass of snow-covered debris from ten to thirty feet in height.

At half-past five they were still only half way along it, plodding and scrambling wearily from mound to mound of concealed bricks, beams and girders. Then, from the top of a high mound near the Telephone Exchange they sighted Selfridge's in the distance and all agreed that, somehow, they must reach it, as there they would be certain of finding everything they could want, as well as shelter for the night.

Soon afterwards it began to snow again, blotting out both the sinking sun and also the Selfridge building, which caused them extreme anxiety as they might now lose their way among the unidentifiable piles of demolished houses and shops. The next hour was a nightmare. Darkness fell, which added further to their difficulties; their extremities ached with the cold, their legs were giving under them and they were no longer certain that they were moving in the right direction as they dragged themselves wearily through the falling snow from one heap of rubble to another.

A little before seven they stumbled into a level space that Sam and Hemmingway felt reasonably certain must be Portman Square. The girls were now almost fainting with fatigue but the men half-pulled, half-carried them for a further ten minutes up and down a fresh chaos of slopes and valleys until, to their unutterable relief, the great Selfridge building loomed up before them.

As soon as Sam was able to get his bearings he led the stumbling group back a little along Orchard Street to the annexe in which the Provision Department was situated. Its windows were shattered and snow was piled up eight feet deep on the pavement, half-filling the empty frames. They scrambled over it and down into the store. It was dark in there but they lit some of the precious candle-ends they had brought from Barnet and staggered forward.

The floor was slippery with ice and jagged with broken glass. Some of the counters must have floated about in the flood waters as they were piled up at all sorts of odd angles and, as at first the weary party could see no food, they thought that the place had been completely looted; but soon they discovered that most of the remaining stocks had been swept by the water to one side of the gloomy cavern that they were exploring and had been frozen into a solid mass against the wall.

A brief examination of this glassy bank revealed it to be composed entirely of fruit and vegetables, so they turned through an opening into the next department. The same scene of havoc was shown as far as the flickering light of the candles penetrated, but to their relief they found there a considerable quantity of groceries among which were many tins and bottles, lying in scattered heaps about the frozen floor.

'The first thing to do is to get a fire going and warm ourselves,' said Gervaise after an effort to stop his teeth from chattering.

Lavina was almost crying with the cold. The tips of her ears and of her nose were smarting and her fingers ached so much that she thought they were going to drop off. 'Yes, for goodness' sake, get one going quickly!' she stuttered. 'Even if you have to burn down the whole building.'

'No need for that,' Derek grunted. 'Everything here's so frozen up it'd take a week to melt it.'

As he spoke he produced the chopper which he had brought with him and started hacking pieces off one of the wooden show-cases. Shaking with cold they worked until they had their three braziers going in a clear space near the middle of the department, then stood about them trying to restore some warmth to their chapped hands and half-frozen limbs.

'We'll have to make do as well as we can here to-night,' said Gervaise. 'It would take us hours to thaw out mattresses.'

'The carpet section is only above the next entrance so we might get down some piles of rugs,' Lavina suggested.

Taking the spades and a couple of candle-ends Sam and Hemmingway made their way along and up the ice-covered stone stairs. They found some woolly lamb-skin rugs and bashed at them till they fell apart, each a stiff, solid slab. As the rugs would have taken too long to thaw and dry they beat them. The ice among the springy wool was like spun glass and, once broken into powder, could be shaken out.

By the time they got downstairs with these makeshift mat-tresses the others had dug into the frozen piles of provisions and set some tins of soup on the fires to warm. Having drunk the soup they spread the rugs on some of the counters, converted their overcoats into pillows and, wrapping their blankets round them, did their best to get to sleep. The counters made hard beds but they were so exhausted that, one by one, they dropped off with the firelight still glowing and flickering on the strange scene about them.

Although it was late when they woke, only a gloomy half-light filtered through the gutted ground floor windows of the store as these were now almost filled with snow and the snow was still falling. Having breakfasted off a tinned tongue and some *café au lait*, which they mixed with snow and heated over one of the braziers, they prepared for the day's activities.

It was clear that with the vast resources of the great store at their disposal they could not find a better place for their permanent headquarters and their first business was to select a more comfortable spot in which to settle themselves. Putting out the fires they cooled the braziers with snow so that they could use them to transport the oddments they had accumulated. Then they climbed over the snow bank in one of the windows, made their way to the main block and entered it by a window that gave on to the Tobacco Department.

Deep snow which had drifted in covered the wrecked cases near the windows, but farther in cigar cabinets, tobacco jars, pouches and lighters littered the place in incredible confusion; yet Lavina gave a little sigh of relief as she saw the tumbled piles of cigarettes. Many of them were in tins and the others might still be good for smoking after they had been dried out. Passing into the Book Department they saw that although thousands of volumes lay heaped on its floors most of the shelves were still full, as the weight of the books had kept them from shifting. Scrambling over the piles of books to a back staircase they made their way upstairs.

Owing to the store's huge bulk its central departments had suffered comparatively little. The flood wave had been less violent when it reached them, and although show-cases and goods had been washed about and left in considerable confusion on the icy floors, no snow had swept so far in through the broken windows.

Beds were the first consideration and going to the Furniture Department on the first floor they took their choice. As the Department abutted on the big windows overlooking Oxford Street they moved the beds back behind the shelter of a row of lifts and decided to screen off this small section of the store. Derek and Hemmingway smashed up some of the surplus beds and relit the braziers while the rest went off to find bedding, screens and other items that they required. To their relief they did not come across any dead bodies but if any of them was alone for a few minutes they found the eerie silence of the place unnerving. It seemed to be peopled by the ghosts of countless dead shoppers, but the many jobs to be done left them little time to grow morbid. They all worked hard, contenting themselves with snatching a cold lunch, and by mid-afternoon had thawed out mattresses and pillows, provided themselves with screens, tables and chairs, and broken up a good stock of wood to keep their fires going.

While Lavina settled down to warm her feet at the blaze, Gervaise, Hemmingway and Derek returned to the Provision Department. Out in the street another blizzard was raging, but that worried them no longer as they had not far to go and, having buffeted their way through it, they pried a good variety of tinned stores from the icy piles, and several unbroken bottles of wine; all of which they carried back to their new quarters.

In the meantime Margery had taken Sam with her across to the Turnery Department, where she selected an oil stove and such cooking utensils as she would need. Later, it took Sam an hour's roaming round the store before he found a drum of paraffin, but by six o'clock they were all gathered together with food, drink, warmth and bedding. For the first time in four days their immediate anxieties were relieved and they were able to speculate on the future with some cheerfulness, Lavina becoming her old self again and keeping them in fits of laughter until they turned in for the night.

On their second morning at Selfridge's it was still snowing, so they set about improving their circumstances by collecting a canteen of silver, chinaware, glasses, rugs for the floor, games, a clock, candlesticks, books and all sorts of other items. But a little after eleven the snow stopped and Gervaise said to Hemmingway:

'I'm still extraordinarily puzzled by this amazing change of climate. To-day is only the 19th of August yet we might be in Moscow in mid-winter. I believe my theory that the axis of the earth has been tilted by the comet must be right and that my observations in the Ark *were* correct. Now the sun has come out I'm going to try to find some instruments to check them.'

'We ought to be able to find a sextant in the Optical Department,' Hemmingway declared, 'and logarithm tables among the books. Let's get down to the ground floor and see.'

Amongst the piles of smashed glass and wreckage they found several sextants, undamaged in their plush-lined cases. Having selected one they took also two pairs of powerful binoculars. At the inner end of the Book Department, where the maps and other geographical matter were kept, they succeeded in finding the tables they wanted; then, crossing the small intervening street to the other building, they helped themselves to paper, rubbers, pencils and a set of geometrical instruments.

With this gear they mounted the stairs of the main block and, as the proper exit was hopelessly blocked, climbed out to the roof through a broken skylight. Before taking the altitude of the sun they mounted the iron staircase to the top of the two-storey tower overlooking the roof gardens for a good look over London through their binoculars. They were amazed to see, in the clear, frosty air, that towards the south a huge section of the city had been entirely blotted out. In the near distance they could see the tops of Grosvenor House and the Dorchester to their right, and the Air Force Headquarters in Berkeley Square to their left. Farther off, the modern tower of Westminster Cathedral was still standing, but Big Ben and the dome of St. Paul's had disappeared, evidently having been overthrown. The queer thing was, however, that about a mile away in each direction, towards the curve of the river, the roof-tops of the medium-sized houses merged into a flat plain of snow.

'It looks to me as if the river is still flooded to a depth of from sixty to a hundred feet,' said Gervaise.

'Surely the water all over the world couldn't have risen as much as that,' Hemmingway murmured doubtfully.

'One would hardly think so, but the water in the Thames Valley may have frozen over before the flood had time to seep away to a permanent level. There may be several feet of solid ice out there which is supported by the houses. But by this time an air cavity might have been created below it as the flood water runs out into the sea which must still remain unfrozen a few hundred miles farther south.'

'That's about it,' Hemmingway agreed. 'Anyhow, as it's just on midday, let's shoot the sun.'

The simple operation was soon completed and there was no question that the latitude of London was now 71 degrees 14 minutes north instead of 51 degrees 30 minutes north as it had been before the deluge. The city was nearly 20 degrees nearer to the North Pole.

'All the same, you were wrong about our longitude,' Hemmingway remarked. 'Must have been, as we know that London is on 0 and you made us 9 degrees west.'

Gervaise smiled. 'But if the earth has been thrown off its old axis, as we are now quite certain that it has been, the longitude of London would have altered too.'

'No. Latitude is calculated from the Equator to the Poles so, if they shift, the latitude of every place on the earth shifts too; but longitude is calculated from London so, however cockeyed the earth becomes, London is still neither east nor west, but dead on zero.'

'Theoretically, yes; but, in practice, surely all the astronomical tables would be thrown out by an alteration in the point of rising of the sun? I don't know sufficient about astronomy to prove my point, but one thing is beyond doubt. We are now right up in the new Arctic Circle.'

'Sure,' Hemmingway agreed, 'and it's one hell of a nasty thought.'

When they went below they found that Sam was preparing to set out on a visit to St. James's Square. The others thought it rather pointless, as everything which had remained unruined by the flood was available in the store, but he said that he preferred his own clothes to ready-made ones and intended to collect a bag full. Hemmingway volunteered to accompany him so they had an early lunch and the two friends started out at a quarter past one.

As snow began to fall again in the mid-afternoon the others became extremely anxious about them, but they got back after a three-hours' absence and had a strange story to tell of the changed face of London. Where the streets and squares still remained unblocked by rubble they were now twelve feet deep in snow, but the queer part about it was that where the surface should have sloped downwards in Berkeley Square it no longer did so. The little valley at the bottom of Hay Hill had been filled up so that, in passing it, they were on the level of the second-floor windows. The same thing had occurred on the far side of Piccadilly where the road level should again have sloped south and west. Urged by curiosity to see more of this odd change, they had turned left towards the Ritz and found that the whole of the Green Park was buried under many feet of snow and ice, and that only the top storey of Buckingham Palace showed above it in the distance.

Turning back they had reached St. James's Square, which was submerged to its second-floor windows but before going into the house they had penetrated south-west as far as Trafalgar Square. Nelson's column was broken off short and the square was submerged to a depth of over thirty feet, while the roofs of the buildings at the lower end of Whitehall only just appeared, like a row of bungalows, above the snow line.

They returned with a couple of heavy bags containing clothes for themselves and a certain number of things for Lavina but their journey back had been difficult. At half-past three a bitter wind had started to blow, and with it had come the snow, driving so thick and fast they could see no more than a dozen yards ahead and had constantly had to check their bearings.

On Lavina's inquiring how the house had fared, Sam told her that it had been impossible to descend to the downstairs rooms as they were full of ice, while the upper ones were in the usual state of chaos and part of the roof had fallen in owing to the weight of snow. Before packing the clothes they had had to get a small fire going to thaw them partially; a process which they set about completing on their return.

Fortunately the others had made and lit additional braziers in their absence, as they had been selecting entirely new outfits of clothes that afternoon, all of which had to be thawed. Lavina had also had a grand time in the Jewellery and Perfumery Departments, while Gervaise and Derek were transporting a supply of cigarettes and, at her special request, a ping-pong table upon which they played after dinner that night.

The blizzard continued the following day and the snow level in Oxford Street had now risen to fifteen feet, bringing it up to the sills of the first-floor windows of the store.

On the previous evening Derek had noticed some canvas baths in the Camping Department so he brought them down after breakfast and, having boiled a number of kettles of water on the braziers, they were all able to enjoy the luxury of a warm tub.

When they had dressed again it seemed to most of them that during the last twenty-four hours their prospects had assumed a much more roseate hue but they were soon to be sadly dis-

illusioned as Gervaise, who had been watching the snow most of
the morning with a worried look on his fine, lined face, called a
conference after lunch.

'I'm afraid,' he said, 'that as leader of our party it falls to me
to put forward a proposal which some of you may not regard
at all favourably; but I have been considering it for the past two
days and it's only right that I should place the facts before you.

'As you know, London is now situated in the same latitude
as that of Greenland before the deluge. I checked that quite
definitely with Hemmingway yesterday. Mercifully we have been
spared the horror of seeing the thousands of drowned and muti-
lated bodies which must lie all about us under the snow; but the
thing which concerns us is that London must now for ever remain
a city of the dead.

'The Arctic winter is only just setting in. You have seen for
yourselves how the level of the snow has risen in these last few
days. Blizzards will continue for many weeks to come, so that
long before the winter is over the whole city will be buried in
snow and ice. During the flood walls, roofs, floors all became
saturated. As water expands when it freezes every structure
beneath the snow line is now cracked and would fall to pieces if
it were not for the ice which still binds it. When the spring comes
a thaw will set in. Everything, even the strongest buildings, will
crash in heaps of ruins; then, after a brief Siberian summer, they
will be buried deep in snow and ice again.

'We might drag out a miserable existence through the winter,
like cave-dwellers, living many feet under the surface of the snow
and moving to other places when our stores here are exhausted;
but, when the thaw comes, the thousands of dead bodies will be
exposed again and pestilence will set in. It is unthinkable that we
could live through next summer with rotting bodies in every
house and street. I know we've made ourselves comfortable here;
that we seem to have everything that any reasonable person
placed in our strange situation could want, and that for a little
time we are apparently secure from every hardship and danger.
But it is only a temporary security. That is why, however much
we may dislike the idea, we have to go on the march again and
leave this City of Death behind us.'

'Leave London!' gasped Lavina.

'Yes. And at once. Every day we delay will make things harder for us as places along the road where we can get supplies will become more difficult to break into. And if we wait until the spring it will be impossible to break into them at all before the thaw comes; because they will be buried too deep. We would be caught too, before we had gone fifty miles, by the plague that will sweep right over England. That is why we must go now.'

'But where can we go?' asked Sam in a low, worried voice.

'To a part of the world that is not frozen. The Equator is now twenty degrees farther south; but conditions there must be much the same as they were in the old equatorial belt. Therefore, there are still semi-tropical lands below the new ice-caps which are forming so rapidly. I know I'm asking you to face incredible hardships but somehow we *must* make the journey out of this land of death to a country beyond the ice-caps where we can dig the soil and make food grow.

'To live like animals in a burrow, feeding on such tinned food as we can find, until we're overtaken by pestilence and die a miserable death is no fitting end for people of spirit. It may be that we are the last survivors of the human race. Whatever your beliefs, have any of you the temerity to suggest that among all these countless thousands of the dead we have not been spared for a purpose? Life is in our keeping, and Life must go on. Whatever the dangers and difficulties, we must cross the frozen Channel into France and march south to the Mediterranean.'

'I can't!' wailed Margery suddenly. 'I can't! I can't!'

'You will,' Gervaise said firmly. 'I am determined that we shall live or die in an attempt to preserve that thing which makes us different from the animals. To-morrow we take the Dover Road.'

There was no argument. They all knew that Gervaise was right.
If they were to die it would be better to do so soon, numbed into
sleep, after a gallant failure, by the coldness of the snow than to
cling on for a few brief months tortured by the thought of being
stricken down by plague in the coming spring. It was now clear,
too, that their one hope of escaping that agonizing death lay in
starting at once while they would still have easy access to the
houses on their route.

That afternoon, very silent and subdued, they made their
preparations; visiting many departments of the store and collecting every item they could think of which might make their trek
across the snowy world a little easier.

From the sports rooms they carried down a fair-sized sledge,
snow-shoes, snow goggles, ski-sticks and three folding tents,
each six feet long by four wide by four high, as these would be
simpler to erect than one large one. Hemmingway collected maps
and instruments while Gervaise selected the food, which had to
be easily portable and highly nutritive and stimulating. Such
items as glucose, Brand's Essence, Horlicks Malted Milk Tablets,
Oxo cubes and tins of Bantam coffee figured largely in his choice.
To eliminate the possibility of breakages he filled a number of
silver flasks with brandy while for light and fuel he took candles,
two Primus stoves, methylated spirit and a drum of paraffin.

Then all of them went in search of clothes suitable for their
journey, selecting fur coats with big collars, fur gloves, fur-lined
boots, baggy trousers that could be tucked into the tops of thick
socks, loose jerkins and light, woollen underclothes of which
three sets could be worn one on top of the other as a better
protection against the cold than a single, thicker garment. All
of these had to be thawed out and dried, after which they sewed
the collars of the fur coats into hoods and a number of fur rugs

into sleeping-bags. They put in eight hours' hard work with only a short break for dinner, but by ten o'clock their preparations were completed. Still overawed by the vastness of the adventure before them they went to bed wondering when they would spend a night in comfort again.

It seemed to them a good omen that when they woke pale sunlight was filtering through the windows of the store. Gervaise was anxious that they should not lose a moment of it as getting out of London seemed likely to be one of the most difficult parts of their journey. Immediately they had breakfasted they dressed in their furs and looking like six Eskimos pulled the already loaded sledge out of the first-floor window onto the snow which now buried Oxford Street to a depth of nearly sixteen feet.

They would have given a lot for a team of dogs to drag the sledge but there was no alternative to pulling it themselves. It was not very heavy and two of the men could draw it easily, but they knew that hours of hauling it behind them, up hill and down dale, were certain to add considerably to the strain of their journey. Gervaise and Derek formed the first team, strapping the harness round them, while Sam and Hemmingway were to steady the sledge behind and help to lug it over obstructions; it being understood that the parts played by the two teams would be reversed after the halt for rest which they intended to make every hour.

Lavina and Margery shared the task of guiding the party. Margery had no bump of location and was of little use in finding the way, so her function was to walk no more than twenty yards ahead of the sledge, signalling to the men to show the places where the snow lay smoothest. Lavina acted as advance guard. She knew her London better and was less likely to lose her way when it might seem best to make detours down side-streets to avoid dragging the sledge up the hills of snow which covered buildings that had fallen into the roadway.

Gervaise had given her a map of London and pointed out the route he wished them to follow; down Regent Street, Piccadilly Circus, Leicester Square, Trafalgar Square, Charing Cross, and the Strand, over the river where the frozen ice covered Waterloo Bridge, and thence into South-East London. There they would try to pick up the Old Kent Road where it emerged from the frozen, flooded area. But Lavina had other ideas. It was certain that the broad thoroughfares were less likely to be blocked than the narrower turnings off Piccadilly Circus and Leicester Square, so she decided to lead them straight along Oxford Street to Holborn, then down Kingsway to the river; and when they reached Oxford Circus she sent back by Margery a message to that effect.

From their appalling experience in Baker Street four nights before, they had anticipated great difficulty in getting the sledge even as far as the river, but much snow had fallen since so they were no longer faced with lumpy obstructions like buried cars or the wickedly difficult surface formed by debris under a moderate crust of snow. The recent falls had increased the thickness of the snow-layer to such an extent that the way was now smooth except for gentle undulations here and there where vehicles or piles of fallen bricks and mortar lay buried deep under the surface.

By ten o'clock they had passed the Holborn Restaurant and turned south down Kingsway. The top of Bush House still protruded high above the snow at the bottom of the broad thoroughfare but the snow-covered road seemed to run uphill towards it as the buildings at its southern end were buried considerably more deeply than those at its entrance from Holborn. As they advanced they now entered the area where the flood waters had become frozen before they could recede from the lower levels of the city. Only the upper storeys of the tall buildings in the Aldwych still showed above the snow and those in the Strand were buried to their roof-tops. As soon as Lavina had passed them she saw that a great open plain of snow stretched on either hand and far away to her front where, with very few exceptions, the buildings on the south side of the river lay buried. No chimney-stacks, towers or spires broke the vista, so these had evidently been overthrown by the rush of the flood-waters.

She waited, somewhere above the northern end of Waterloo Bridge, for the others to come up to her, then proposed a new and better plan. The open plain of the flooded river offered much better going than they would find when they had crossed it and had reached the higher ground in South-East London, where the buildings were still above the ice-level and where they might get themselves hopelessly lost in trying to pick up the Old Kent Road. It would be much easier, she suggested, to strike a course east over the flat, flooded area, then turn inland towards the Dover Road farther on.

Gervaise agreed at once, and after taking a compass bearing for her guidance, they set off down-river.

The great, arched roof of Cannon Street station had fallen in, as had the dome of St. Paul's, although its main structure still stood out high above the stricken city. The bulk of the Tower of London was submerged but the top of the White Tower with its four turrets showed the position of the ancient fortress. One of the towers of Tower Bridge had been swept away but the other still reared its pinnacles to the cold, blue sky.

By mid-afternoon they were somewhere over the London Docks and the wide plain became broken and hilly. At first they failed to identify the hillocks by their shape, but they soon realized that the mounds were made by the funnels and super-structures of wrecked shipping.

As snow had begun to fall and evening was approaching, Gervaise decided that they would camp for the night in the lee of one of these great hummocks which concealed a stricken ship. He reckoned that they had covered between seven and eight miles of their journey and considered that to be excellent for their first day's trek. They pitched the three small tents so as to form three sides of a square, the open side of which faced to leeward. One was to be shared by Gervaise and Derek, one by Sam and Hemmingway and one by the two girls. The sleigh was unpacked and Margery cooked their evening meal on the primus. It was bitterly cold and to-night they had to do without a fire, so they turned in immediately they had eaten.

On the second day they again followed the course of the river, identifying a snow-covered hill on their right as Greenwich Park and the hump on top of it as the Observatory. At their next halt Gervaise gave Lavina a new compass bearing, south by east over Woolwich Marshes, in order to cut off the big bend of the river.

No buildings of any kind now broke the skyline, but by com-pass and map bearings they reckoned that they were approxi-mately over Erith when they halted that afternoon; again having covered eight miles during the day. They still had to do without a fire but they had ample supplies of food, warm furs and com-fortable fur bags in which to sleep.

On the third day they moved south-east, parallel with the river;

then, cutting off another bend, south by east to Tilbury, accomplishing another eight miles. The whole of Tilbury was under the ice-bank so once more they fed from their stores.

The trek had not, so far, proved too arduous. Gervaise knew that it was absolutely essential to conserve the strength of his party so he gave them frequent halts and never pressed them to a longer day's march than they could manage with reasonable ease. They had been lucky with the weather as snow had fallen only in the late afternoons and during the nights. All of them were in good health and as they were warmly wrapped in furs the intense cold did not seriously affect them. As they marched they often sang and Lavina, having once made up her mind that she must face the journey, had become her old, gay self. She still bullied the others into doing things for her and poked fun at them, but it was kindly fun, and nothing pleased her better than when by accident or design the laugh was turned against herself. At every halt her spontaneous chuckles echoed through the deadly silence of the snow waste and they adored her for the gallant spirit which made light of the labours of their journey.

On the fourth day they left the course of the river, moving south-east again but now striking inland. By midday they reached the edge of the frozen plain where it rose on their right to higher ground. Tree-tops broke the surface of the snow here and there, although their upper leaves and branches were so powdered that they were only recognizable from close quarters, and now and then they saw the upper storeys of houses that were still standing. An hour later, having crossed a spur, they were in the valley of the River Medway, the lower part of which had been flooded to the same level as the Thames.

Snow started to fall at half-past three, but as Gervaise was anxious to make Rochester or Chatham that night they pressed on through it for another hour and a half and were rewarded at last by the sight of Rochester Castle. Bishop Odo's great Norman tower had survived the deluge, but its upper sections were all that stood out above the plain of snow; the city below it was entirely buried.

Gervaise had thought that would probably be the case, but as it was now four days since they had known the joy of a fire he had hoped that if Rochester Castle had not been overthrown they might get inside it and spend the night in greater comfort than on the open plain. Unfortunately, his plan proved impracticable because the entrances to the castle were deep under the ice and its arrow-slit windows much too narrow for them to get through. But they were able to pitch camp under the lee of the great keep, which protected them from the wind, and had the satisfaction of knowing that they had made a record by covering ten miles since the morning.

They were now on the Dover Road, or rather, from eighty to a hundred feet above it, and their next concern was to advance south-east again until the road rose out of the ice-pack, so that they could identify and follow it. Next morning, passing over submerged Chatham, from which the ground rose steeply to their right, they pushed on in the direction of Sittingbourne. It was not until reaching Rainham that they found the road and although they had covered only five miles as the crow flies, having spent a considerable time that day zigzagging across the now uneven country trying to locate the highway, they decided to halt there for the night.

The buildings in the village were almost buried, but picking a fair-sized house, they climbed into a servant's bedroom through a broken window in its top storey. The room was two feet deep in snow that had drifted in but the landing was clear, and lighting some candles they proceeded downstairs. It was an eerie experience to descend into the bowels of the buried house and on entering a first-floor bedroom, the door of which stood open, they came upon a group of frozen corpses.

The bloated, partially decayed faces seemed to take on a horrid life when glimpsed only by the light of guttering candles. Margery screamed and fled in terror to the pale daylight of the top storey. Sam followed to quiet and comfort her. The others wrenched-to the door, shutting in the dead occupants of their new refuge, and went down to the ground floor.

Having smashed up some of the lighter furniture they took it upstairs and got a brazier going in another bedroom, at the back of the house, into which comparatively little snow had drifted. The warmth of the fire cheered them and the prospect of finding innumerable other such houses in which they could shelter, now that they had passed out of the great ice-plain, gave them fresh confidence in the eventual success of their mad journey.

After cooking a meal they explored the house, but there was little in it of any value to them. Two tins of pork-and-beans, a few candles, and half a bottle of methylated spirit which would come in handy for the primus, were all the place yielded.

On the sixth day they were able to follow the road; but only with some difficulty. The houses along it were the best indication of its position, but in the places where it passed through open country these were comparatively few and far between. In such stretches the road was no more than a very shallow depression which at times disappeared altogether, merging into the slopes of the hillsides, when their only guide was the top of an occasional telegraph pole which had been left standing. By comparison the great plain of the flooded river-valley had been easy going, as that had at least been level, whereas they now had to drag the sledge up steep inclines whenever the road wound over a hill. Although they had only done six miles it was late in the afternoon when they reached the outskirts of Sittingbourne and chose a roof-top which looked as though it had once sheltered a prosperous family under which to spend the night.

They selected a big playroom under the eaves in which to light their fires and, on exploring the depths of the house, had the good fortune to discover that, in addition to quite a considerable stock of tinned goods which a careful housewife had laid in, it contained a well-chosen cellar of wines. That night they all got very jolly and slept like tops after partaking liberally of some excellent mulled claret which Gervaise made for them.

Their happening upon such well-equipped quarters proved particularly fortunate because when they woke the next morning a blizzard was raging and Gervaise decided that it was quite impossible for them to proceed further until it had ceased. Ever since leaving London their luck with the weather had held and on only two occasions had they had to press on through snow for the last hour or so before halting for the night. But the driven flakes which obscured everything more than ten feet distant from the broken upper windows of the house showed them the sort of peril which they might have to face if they were caught in a storm later on their journey.

Bathing was out of the question and they had long since given up worrying themselves about the lack of such an amenity; but they boiled some kettles of water over their braziers, and the men were able to rid themselves of their seven days' growth of beard while the girls washed their hair and generally made themselves a little more presentable.

As there was nothing to do except feed the fires, Derek amused himself by setting out a fine collection of toy soldiers which he found in a cupboard in the playroom. Having thawed out the ice-logged boxes of troops, guns and wagons he arranged them all and was as delighted as a child while crawling round the floor to play at battles.

Lavina soon got bored with helping him as she was not particularly interested in soldiers and she did not care for crawling about on her hands and knees on the board floor which, although thawed out by the fire, was still damp; so she suggested to Hemmingway that they should have another look round the house together.

Taking candles with them they descended to the ground floor and spent a little time exploring the rooms; but the jumbled furniture was frozen too hard where it lay for them to move it without effort, and trying to wrench open cupboards was difficult as long as they kept their thick gloves on and chilly work if they took them off. When they reached a small library which had a couple of armchairs in it Lavina proposed that they should sit down and talk instead of exploring further.

To anyone not fully acquainted with their circumstances it would have seemed a mad idea to think of sitting in the cold down there when they could equally well have sat upstairs in the warmth of the braziers, but Hemmingway did not consider her suggestion at all strange. For many days now the whole party had been compelled to remain together, and from necessity the conversation had been entirely general. Every topic that could be discussed with interest by all concerned had long ago been exhausted and they were beginning to find the repetitions of each other's opening gambits or the long silences which often occurred among them equally nerve-racking. For two of them to get away from the rest for a little was almost an adventure and, although the chairs were frozen hard and the temperature of the room was well below zero, they were not cold because they were muffled to the eyes in their thick furs.

When they had put their candles on the mantel and settled themselves in the chairs Lavina said:

L

'What d'you think our chances are of coming through?'

'At least fifty-fifty,' Hemmingway smiled. 'Unless we're hung up permanently by a blizzard during the next fortnight, we ought to make it.'

'You really think that? You're not just saying it to keep me cheerful?'

'No. I honestly believe it. We're all fit, we haven't suffered severely from the cold, we've got plenty of stores to go on with, and there are lots of places along the road where we can pick up more.'

She shivered. 'Don't run away with the idea that I don't suffer from the cold because I'm not always moaning about it. At times I could scream, it makes me so miserable, and we seem to have been trudging through the snow for half a lifetime already.'

'In six days we've covered over forty miles.'

'Hell! What's forty miles? It's at least a thousand to the straits of "Gib", and Gervaise admits that we'll have to go much farther south than that before we strike a really decent winter climate.'

'Now don't be despondent,' he chid her gently. 'Once we're over the Channel and start moving south the weather will improve with every stage we make. We'll be able to travel faster then and do a hundred miles a week. We've got a rotten month or two ahead of us but once we're past the snow line we'll be able to pick up bicycles and with luck we'll be in North Africa before November's out.'

'You seem pretty confident, I must say.'

'I am. If we can once get across to France I think the odds are ten to one on our reaching a place where we can settle and start our lives afresh in reasonable safety and comfort.'

'In that case I've got to do some pretty hectic thinking.' Lavina paused and went on after a moment: 'D'you believe it's possible for anyone to be in love with two people at the same time, Hemmingway?'

'I should say,' he replied slowly, 'that one can be extremely attracted to quite a number of people but, faced with the old proposition of being able to rescue only one if all of them were swimming round in the sea, one would never have any real hesitation about which of them one meant to save. I can't conceive ever being in love with two people at the same time myself; but why d'you ask?'

'Sam says that although he's still in love with me he's now fallen head-over-heels in love with Margery.'

Hemmingway nodded. 'I guessed that something was boiling up between them long before we left the Ark. What d'you propose to do about it?'

'I don't quite know.'

'I'm sorry. That's rotten for you. When faced with a choice of ways everything becomes comparatively easy once one has formed a decision. It's trying to make up one's mind which is such an ordeal. I can quite understand what's happened to Sam, though.'

'You can?' she exclaimed, opening wide her eyes.

He laughed. 'Don't look so surprised, or take what I said as a personal insult. I'm not inferring that Margery's more attractive than yourself; only that you're completely different types. When you married Sam you honestly intended to make a go of it if you possibly could, didn't you?'

'I did,' Lavina agreed.

'Well, I think you might have succeeded in the sort of world we knew before the deluge. There, you would both have been protected from ever getting to know each other too well by a sort of veneer, or, if you like, a series of screens provided, by the many outside activities which would have occupied such a large portion of both your minds. But, as things are, you've been thrown too much together and you've seen each other much too clearly. You're a very complex person and, for all your apparent faults, you're spiritually on a far higher level than Sam. He's a very simple person, really; so he naturally gravitates towards Margery who is his own type.'

Lavina regarded him thoughtfully for a moment from beneath eyelashes that half-veiled her eyes. 'What you say is very interesting, Hemmingway, but why do you consider that I'm on a higher spiritual level than Sam or Margery? She's a much more saintly person than I am.'

'Not necessarily. She just accepts the dogmas she's been taught; whereas you have your own code and never allow yourself to be influenced by accepted standards or by what other people may think. By that I don't mean to imply that either of you is *better* than the other; only that if one regarded life as a school you would have to sit for your exams in a much higher form.'

'How do you account for that?'

'Because you're what Buddhists call a "twice-born". Sam and Margery are bound only by the conventions of the time in which they live; the simple rulings of the lower school. But the sub-conscious memory of past lives compels you to base your judg-ments on a broader yet more fearful conception of the Law. Their path is easy compared to yours because they only have to play the game as the modern world understands it; whereas you must sometimes appear to do wrong in order to do what you know inside yourself to be right. You either do the right thing regardless of opinion, or if you do the other you do it consci-ously, knowing quite well that sooner or later you'll have to pay for your weakness.'

'You certainly know a lot about me,' she admitted; 'because I am like that. But I've never had anyone tell me so before. Are you a "twice-born" too?'

'Yes, I've lived many times before. I know that from having recognized places and people that I'd never seen before in this life. In some of those lives we must have met, too, because I felt that I knew you through and through the very moment I set eyes on you.'

'It's queer you should say that, because I felt something, too. When Sam introduced us and we stood looking at each other in your room at St. James's Square it seemed as though time had ceased to exist for a moment and as though Sam and the room and everything were no longer there. I didn't recognize you as anyone I'd ever met, but it was like a sudden warning that we had been brought together for some hidden purpose which might be supremely good or incredibly evil.'

'That was probably a forewarning of the night we were to spend together on Burgh Heath under the influence of the comet. Both of us succumbed to evil then because both of us betrayed a trust and, although you may not realize it, that's contributed very largely to breaking up your marriage with Sam.'

'I don't see that; since he doesn't know anything about it.'

'No. But it affected you to such an extent that it was weeks before you could get it out of your mind. Am I right?'

'Yes.'

'I tried to help you all I could, and you fought desperately hard to behave as though nothing had happened. Your acting was good enough to prevent Sam from suspecting anything but you didn't dare to remain alone with him for a moment longer than you had to; and in order to keep up an appearance of gaiety you let yourself go much more than you should have done with Derek.'

She laughed a little ruefully. 'And I thought I'd hidden it all so cleverly. I think you must be the devil himself from the way you seem to have read my every thought. God! How I dreaded those little petting-parties with Sam down in the storeroom during the first weeks we were in the Ark. But go on. Now the butterfly is under the microscope, tell me a little more.'

'There isn't very much more to tell. If there had never been anything between us you would have continued to feel, as well as act, perfectly naturally. You would have sought Sam's company instead of instinctively avoiding it. You would have made him, instead of Derek, fetch and carry for you and he would have enjoyed it. You would have occupied his mind to such an extent that he would never even have looked at Margery. So you were right in your premonition that meeting me might bring evil to you. Unfortunately there was no way in which I could repair the damage that I'd done.'

'It wasn't your fault any more than it was mine.'

'It was my fault to the extent that, although I lied about it afterwards to make things easier for us both, the comet never really caused me to lose consciousness of what I was doing. I knew quite well that I could have brought you to your senses by slapping your face and that I ought to have done so; but I didn't.'

'Well, I lied, too, for the same reason. I don't mind telling you now. I was never out of my senses and I knew all the time that by one word I could have stopped you; but there came a point when I felt that, whatever happened afterwards, it was worth it, so I deliberately let myself go.'

He nodded. 'It was just the same with me.'

'I get the same feeling sometimes with Derek,' she confessed.

'That's hardly surprising. Your guilty conscience built up in your mind a complex adverse to Sam. Derek's a good-looking chap, and propinquity can play the very devil with their feelings when two attractive, healthy people are thrown together a great deal. D'you think you would be happy with him?'

'Yes; for a time, at least. Perhaps for a long time. But how does that square with your theory of types? Derek is even less complex than Sam or Margery.'

'Perhaps. But in such a tie-up you would be the dominating partner. You know him so intimately that you could play on his every mood, like a pianist on the keyboard of a piano. It's the easy way, and such unions are often very happy. There's practically no mental strain at all, you see, because the senior partner runs the whole outfit, and providing they don't hanker after spiritual companionship they get everything else they want with very little effort.'

'It might not be a bad thing, then?' said Lavina.

He laughed. 'As you're bone-lazy it might be a very good one!'

'Am I lazy—in the real sense?' she smiled.

'No. You have one of the most active minds I've ever met, but, physically, you'd like a man who'd be prepared to wait on you hand and foot, wouldn't you?'

'I suppose I should.'

'And Derek fills that bill admirably.'

'Yes, but I'm not quite certain yet that I want him to. You see, life with Derek could be grand for a bit but he's still to some extent an unknown quantity; whereas I know Sam's worst points and his best. I can't make up my mind whether to take a gamble on a new deal turning up trumps or to stick to something very fine; because, of course, I only have to lift my little finger to get Sam back.'

'Yes,' Hemmingway agreed, 'and perhaps that might suit you best.'

29

INTO THE BLIZZARD

Lavina remained silent for a moment. Suddenly she shivered. Sitting there motionless had caused her to become very cold although she had not noticed it while they had been talking. She shook herself and stood up. 'All you've said has been terribly interesting and it's helped me a lot, much more than even you can realize. But I'm simply frozen. Let's get upstairs now and warm ourselves by the fires.

That night she was unusually silent, but even Hemmingway, who guessed that she was preoccupied with their conversation of earlier in the day, could not tell whether her inclination was veering towards a definite understanding with Derek or a determination to recapture Sam.

On the eighth morning the blizzard had ceased, so they took to the road again. Their enforced rest had made them the more eager to push on and after they had passed the roof-tops of Sittingbourne they made good going on a long, straight stretch of road, covering six miles before they halted at the village of Ospringe. They put up there for the night in the straw-filled loft of a high barn, there being no necessity for them to look for a house which might contain stores as they had renewed their supplies from the mansion outside Sittingbourne.

The next was a harder day as they lost their way while passing Faversham; but they found it again and accomplished another five miles, arriving late in the afternoon at Broughton Street. Snow had fallen again during the preceding night, and with that of the blizzard which had held them up for a day, it now buried all but the tallest houses to near their roofs; while the cottages and two-storeyed buildings were entirely submerged, only their gables being indicated by hillocks in the snow.

From Broughton Street they proceeded towards Canterbury, which was easily discernible in the distance as its Cathedral tower could still be seen dominating the almost buried city. When they were within a mile of it Gervaise called to Lavina to incline right, so that instead of entering its maze of roof-tops they would by-pass the city and pick up the road again on its south-eastern side.

His idea very nearly proved their undoing as, half a mile farther on, Lavina led the party up a slope on to a flat plateau which appeared to consist of firm snow. It bore her weight and that of Margery who followed; but the sledge party had not advanced more than ten yards on to it before the crust of snow gave way.

The sledge plunged downwards and the men with it, who were buried up to their arm-pits. The plateau of snow concealed a closely planted orchard where air-pockets still remained beneath the branches of the trees. Fortunately none of them was injured and they soon scrambled out, but the heavy sledge was in a hole eight feet deep, and when they had succeeded in scraping away the snow that had fallen on it they found that its weight was too great for them to drag it out. They had to unpack most of their gear before they could lighten the sledge sufficiently to pull it up, and the misadventure delayed them for over an hour.

They were now so far from the highway that it seemed better to go on than to go back; but for the next half-mile, until they reached a row of roof-tops which indicated another road, Lavina had to test the snow-crust every few yards of the way by jumping on it with her ski-sticks. Once they got above the road again they were happier, and picking out their way between the lines of chimney-pots on the south-eastern outskirts of Canterbury they eventually succeeded in locating the Dover road once more.

Darkness was falling when they halted for their tenth night after leaving London, but their short cut had enabled them to place another seven miles of the way behind them. They slept in the attic of a road-side inn and, by combing the place, managed to add a few items to their stores.

On the eleventh day they again did well—seven more miles— but night and snow caught them on the open road, which was now so difficult to follow that, fearing to lose it, they were forced to bivouac in the open; and, although she kept face before the others, Lavina's limbs ached so with the cold that once in her fur bag she cried herself to sleep.

The twelfth day was the worst they had so far experienced as the road was now almost untraceable and snow fell at intervals further delaying their progress. Although Lavina did her utmost to keep to the track there were many occasions when she led the party off it and the heavy sledge got ditched in the treacherous drifts which concealed deep culverts by the road-side. Half the day was spent in pulling the sledge out of holes and, although the whole party were exhausted when twilight came, they had only managed to do four miles. But they had good quarters for the night as Lavina led them to another inn which was standing at a crossroads with its slate roof still showing above the surface.

The thirteenth day was even worse. They lost the road entirely and the scattered houses along it gave no indication, from a distance, where it lay, as they were now snowed up to their chimney-pots. All the natural features of the land except its general contours had disappeared. Even tall trees, pylons and woods were concealed beneath one vast, white blanket which stretched away in a series of rolling slopes as far as the eye could see in every direction.

Sweating in their furs, pulling and shoving, the men laboured on, while the girls sought in vain for any landmark which might guide them. But at two o'clock in the afternoon Lavina gave a cry of joy and pointed ahead.

Following the direction she gave them they saw, rising to their left front, a steep hill crowned by a large white knob. In that locality, even in such a waste of snow, it could only be Dover Castle.

It was a long pull up the hill. With aching muscles the men dragged the sledge from snow-drift to snow-drift, but two hours later they were among the chimney-pots in the higher quarter of the town. No sign of its lower part remained, as the sea had risen to the same level as the Thames, burying its main street, harbour and dockyard deep below the icy surface.

They chose a row of chimney-pots on the slope above the town and, digging away the snow from round about them, soon discovered a broken skylight through which they were able to climb down into one of the houses. Utterly tired out, they forced themselves to break wood and get their braziers going. After they had made some coffee and eaten a little cold meat they crawled into their fur bags and fell into an exhausted sleep.

On exploring the house next morning they discovered it to be a fair-sized villa so they had reason to assume that the other buildings in the row were the same; and it was decided to break into all of them in order to collect as many stores as possible before attempting what must prove the most hazardous part of their expedition—the crossing of the Channel.

They were faced with twenty-one miles of frozen sea which they had to cross before they could hope to secure fresh supplies in Calais, and although they said nothing of their fears, they were dreading the journey.

Derek voiced a doubt that had occurred to them all when he suggested that with the ever-increasing depth of the snow all the houses in France might be so deeply buried when they got there that they would not be able to locate them, and that the wiser plan therefore might be to remain in Dover.

But Gervaise was unshakeable in his determination that they must push on. When the thaw came pestilence would strike Dover as well as London. It was vital, he said, that while there was breath left in their bodies they should continue their march until they reached not only the edge of the ice-pack but a land well beyond it to which the plague could not be wafted by the winds in the springtime.

'But there will be dead bodies there as well,' Derek argued. 'I hadn't thought of that before, but, now I have, it seems to me that our risk of dying from some ghastly infection will be just as great when we get there.'

'No,' Gervaise shook his grey head. 'The bodies of the people in those lands are rotting in the sunshine as we sit here now, and the pestilence which they germinate will have been dissipated by the winds and flood waters long before we reach a suitable spot far from all risk of contamination in which to settle.'

That morning they divided themselves into couples and searched the whole row of villas, entering them, as they had the first, through their skylights. It was a grim and horrible business, as they found many drowned bodies of men, women and children who had remained cowering in their homes in preference to rushing out into the streets during those last moments in which the deluge had swept down upon them. But the foray resulted in a hoard of fresh supplies sufficient for Gervaise to decide that they might attempt to start the Channel crossing on the following day.

In the afternoon they rested in order that they should be fresh and fit, when morning came, for their hazardous undertaking.

It had been decided to make an early start so as to take advantage of every moment of daylight, and at seven o'clock on the morning of September 3rd they set out from Dover. Behind them the great cliffs still stood out high above the ice-pack; before them stretched an apparently limitless plain of snow. The weather was favourable although intensely cold. Only a mild wind was blowing and the sun shone overhead in a blue sky.

Hour after hour they pressed forward, the men bending their backs to the weight of the sledge as they ploughed along on their broad snow-shoes, the girls cold but uncomplaining and determined. All topics of general conversation had been exhausted by now. During the last few days they had ceased singing on their marches; even Lavina's joyous treble no longer quavered, small but tuneful, across the snow flats. Every breath was needed for the great effort they were making. They knew that if they could reach Calais a new lease of life would be granted to them, but if they were caught by a blizzard in mid-Channel their chances of survival would be very slender. Once in France they could lie up and rest if need be, but until they reached the coast they dared not spare themselves.

When they halted that night and set up their camp Gervaise was more than satisfied. Over the flat surface they had been able to make far better progress than in the preceding days and he estimated that they must have covered a good twelve miles. They spoke little over their evening meal, as they were very tired, but when they turned in they were immensely comforted by the thought that over half the crossing was accomplished.

The second day proved equally satisfactory until the early afternoon, when, having covered six miles, they came upon broken ground. That it was not land was certain, as they could see the cliffs to the south of Calais, now only about three miles distant. Hemmingway and Gervaise decided that the uneven surface was due to a strong wind having got up when the ice had been only partially formed in that area, and great chunks of it having been piled up on top of one another by the heaving sea.

After their splendid start in the morning Gervaise had hoped to camp above French soil that night but they were not destined to do so. To add to the difficulties of the broken terrain a strong wind began to blow, whirling from every eminence great puffs of powdered snow which loaded their clothing and penetrated the openings of their hoods until their faces were almost blue with cold. Margery had to have Sam's help to stagger onward and the tears froze on Lavina's cheeks as they ran from under her snow-goggles.

A halt was called when they judged themselves to be still about two miles from the French coast, but they could no longer see it as the evening was drawing in and the nightly snowfall now obscured everything more than a few yards distant.

Next morning they crawled out of their tents to find that their camp was half-buried in a drift and that it was still snowing. As Gervaise had taken a compass bearing of the French cliffs the previous afternoon they were able to continue their journey, but they had to pause every hundred yards to restore their circulation by flapping their arms and stamping their feet or taking a sip of brandy.

They could not see more than ten yards ahead, and lugging the sledge over mounds of snow sometimes fifteen or twenty feet in height was desperate, gruelling work. At midday Sam suggested that they should camp again and hope that the next day would bring better weather; but Gervaise would not hear of it. The blizzard might last for days, and unless they could reach a place within the next twenty-four hours where there were materials to make a fire so that they could again warm themselves thoroughly, he felt that there was a serious danger that they might die of cold and exhaustion.

It was shortly after they had moved on again that a major catastrophe befell them. The weight of the two girls, who were plodding on together a few yards ahead, was not sufficient to test the snow-crust and it suddenly gave way under the sledge. Sam and Hemmingway, who were drawing it at the time, were nearly jerked off their feet by the pull of the harness as the front of the sledge tilted up and the back end disappeared into the mouth of a deep crevasse. There was a loud report as one of the cords which secured their stores to the sledge snapped under the strain. Next moment the things upon which their very lives depended were slipping and falling into the icy crack.

In a desperate effort to stop them Derek and Gervaise, who were walking behind, flung themselves on their knees and, leaning over the narrow gulf, grabbed at the slipping packages just as Sam and Hemmingway gave a terrific heave and hauled the sledge into safety.

Panting with anxiety they hurriedly examined the remaining contents of the load and peered down the fissure in the frozen snow to see what they had lost. It was about four feet wide at the top but some twenty feet in depth and narrowed till the sides met at its bottom; so many of the packages had stuck about half-way down.

Their tents were safe, as these were stacked on the forepart of the sledge, and so were three of the sleeping-bags, but the others had fallen into the crevasse. Gervaise had caught their drum of paraffin as it fell and Derek one of the primus stoves; but all their stores, medicines and scientific instruments were gone; and many of the cases having burst on hitting the sides of the cleft, most of their contents were now scattered right at its bottom.

It was vital that they should retrieve everything possible so Derek was lowered on a rope. He managed to fish up the sleeping-bags, a case of maps, and a brazier bucket into which were packed candles and some food; but he could not get far enough down to reach the tins and flasks or their picks and shovels, and half a ton of snow suddenly failing in a few feet farther along the top of the crevasse buried the rest of the goods beyond hope of recovery.

Almost overwhelmed by this stroke of evil fortune they examined the contents of the brazier. In addition to candles it contained salt and some tins of Camp coffee but barely enough food to suffice for a full day's ration for the six of them. From standing about inactive while the men endeavoured to salvage the stores the girls had become half-frozen. As they clung together the biting wind tore at their clothing, the snow stung their faces and their lips were blue. Neither of them were fit to go further yet they knew that they must force themselves to another effort.

It had now become imperative that they reach Calais or they would surely die, so the party staggered on again, making a little better progress owing to the decreased load which the sledge now carried. But a few moments later they became aware of another bitter blow which their recent accident had caused them. As Gervaise had flung himself forward to save the drum of paraffin his prismatic compass had been jerked out of the small leather case in which he carried it on his belt.

They returned to look for it but after a quarter of an hour they gave up the search, concluding that it had fallen into the crevasse; and as the spare compass was buried there with their other instruments they had now no means of finding their direction.

As they knew that they must now be very near, if not actually on, the coast of France and would certainly be able to see it once the snow-storm ceased, they decided that it would be better to camp where they were in the hope that the next day would bring clear weather, rather than risk losing themselves and, perhaps, marching out to sea again. Pitching their camp in miserable silence they ate a small evening meal from their now incredibly precious stock of provisions, and turned in to an uneasy sleep harassed by fears of what fresh trials of their endurance the morrow might bring.

Peering fearfully from their tents when they woke they saw with sinking hearts that the blizzard was still raging. But they had to go on now, or die. Calais, the Mecca of their nightmares, could not possibly be more than a morning's trek distant, yet they only had food for two more snack meals, or three if they cut themselves down to starvation rations. They decided to do without breakfast and, unrefreshed by their troubled sleep, set off once more.

The cold was so intense that it seared their lungs with every breath they drew as they fought their way through the blinding curtain of whiteness which seemed to dance before their eyes. They were now chilled to the marrow and felt that they would never get properly warmed through again. Even their furs could not protect them from the icy wind which drove the snow against them and pierced their clothing, making their limbs ache with every step they took; but with clenched teeth and straining muscles they forced themselves forward from sheer desperation.

Two hours after they set out they got clear of the broken surface, which cheered them a little, but by that time Margery was so done that she broke down and declared she could not go any farther. Sam gave her the last mouthfuls of brandy from a private flask he was carrying and Gervaise said that, as they dared not stop, she must ride on the sledge. They tied her on it a sobbing, unprotesting bundle and again lurched forward.

It seemed by this time that unless they were moving in circles they positively must be over the French coast. The cliffs they had seen before the blizzard had not been high ones, as the new level of the sea and twenty feet of snow had concealed their base; so it was possible that they had passed through a gap in the cliffs without knowing that they had done so.

At midday, after they had eaten another small portion of the remaining food and drank some coffee that Sam had made for them, Gervaise decided that they should take a new direction. Feeling certain that they must now be above French soil and knowing that Calais lay a little to the north of the cliffs for which they had been making, they now headed left.

Heartened a little by their few mouthfuls of food and the coffee, they trudged on looking like snow-men from the flakes that clung to their clothing. Even the small portions of their faces which they had to leave exposed, in order to see their way, were powdered with it. Their snow-goggles were rimed with frost as their steamy breath turned to ice almost as they exhaled it, and although they constantly rubbed them their noses ached intolerably.

Lavina was no longer strong enough to concentrate on finding the easiest track for them so Sam led the party. Margery, half-comatose, still lay on the sledge. After half an hour Lavina began to lag behind. Gervaise took her arm and urged her to get on the sledge beside her sister, but she mutely shook her head so he tied round her waist a cord which was attached to the sledge and, jerked along by it, she managed to blunder onward.

In the mid-afternoon Sam gave a sudden cry of warning. He had almost stumbled over a forty-foot precipice. The party halted and joined him to examine it, walking some way in each direction along its brink. But the fall was sheer and there was no way down. They knew then that they must have crossed the coast-line earlier in the day or the previous afternoon and had since made a semicircle, returning to it on higher ground, as the place where they were standing could only be the summit of the cliffs of France.

It was now a gamble as to whether Calais was on their left or on their right as they stood looking out through the whirling snow towards the frozen sea. If they chose rightly there was still a chance that they might save themselves, but if their choice was wrong there were only fishing villages along the coast and by this time these would be buried in the snow-pack.

Gervaise decided to turn right, but his heart was sinking. The ground had become uneven again and their progress was intolerably slow, so he feared now that, even if they managed to find Calais with so little food left and no shovels, they might be too exhausted to dig round until they struck the roof of one of the snow-covered houses.

At four o'clock they could lurch no farther so they started to pitch their camp about sixty yards from the cliff edge. While they were struggling with half-frozen fingers to erect the tents in the usual three-sided 'square' Derek missed Lavina and, looking round, found her sitting in the snow a little apart from the rest. Her head was bowed and she was weeping bitterly.

Sitting down beside her he put an arm round her shoulders and drew her muffled head on to his chest.

'Oh, Derek darling,' she sobbed, 'I've stuck it all day but I'm so cold; so cold I think I'm going to die.'

'Nonsense,' he whispered, with his lips beside her ice-cold cheek. 'We'll make Calais yet—if only the food hangs out.'

'That's just it,' she moaned. 'If we had another day's rations we'd do it, but now we've lost the spades we'll have to dig down to the houses with our hands, and mine are frost-bitten already, I think.'

Quickly he undid his coat, jerkin and shirt, then drawing off her gloves, placed her frozen hands flat against his chest so that they might receive the warmth of his body.

'That's sweet of you,' she smiled up at him in the semi-darkness. 'But it's no good, my dear. You couldn't warm my body even if you stripped to do it, as long as this wind lasts. There's not much of me and I'm chilled all through.'

'You'll be all right again once the tents are up and you've had some coffee.'

'Yes, I'll be better then, and through the night I'll be warm enough in my sleeping-bag. But to-morrow! Some of you may get through but I won't. I'm the weakest and I'll never be able to stick another day of it without a decent meal to keep up my strength.'

Derek was hungry too, yet he would gladly have given his share of the remaining food to Lavina. The trouble was that he knew she could never be persuaded to take it. He knew, too, that she had never once complained in the whole grim journey so now that she had at last broken down she must really be at the end of her tether, and that the flame of her life would flicker out unless she had enough food to sustain her next day during their last desperate bid to find Calais.

That the rest of them, with Margery riding on the sledge, could reach Calais he did not doubt. If the snow ceased they would probably wake to see its remaining spires within an hour's march and, even if the blizzard continued, now that they had the line of the cliff-top to guide them they could hardly fail to strike it if only they had chosen the right direction. He thought of carrying Lavina to conserve her ebbing strength when they set off next morning, but knew that he could not do so for any distance. With frequent halts he might have done so for a mile or two over firm ground but even the strongest man cannot carry a woman any distance over snow.

'You must ride on the sledge with Margery,' he said suddenly.

Rather disconcertingly, Lavina laughed, and withdrawing her hands, put on her gloves again. 'Thanks for my hands,' she said. 'They won't go bad on me until to-morrow now. But you can't pull two of us with this blizzard raging. No, Derek, no. I was in the dumps just now but there's no need to worry about me. I'll manage somehow.'

'I'll see you do,' he said slowly. 'You're more than life to me. You know that. Even if all of us don't reach Calais you've got to.'

'Why me?'

'Because you're the best of us. I can't tell you why I know that, but I do. It's not just because I'm nuts about you, and your beauty is only a sort of bodily expression of it. There's a kind of spirit in you which I can't define, but it's something that's the salt of the earth and the champagne too. God knows, humanity's suffered a bad enough set-back but there are probably countries that escaped the flood and other little groups of survivors like ourselves. Life's darned hard to kill, you know, and it will struggle on somehow but it can't afford to lose its finest elements. That's why you owe it to yourself, and to us, to reach Calais and keep the old chin up until you can find a better land to live in.'

'A better land,' echoed Lavina. 'That's it, with sunshine and flowers and things. I'll get there, darling, but I'm worried about you.'

'Oh, I'm a tough guy,' Derek laughed.

'I know, but I do worry,' she sighed. 'You've been so marvellous all this time. You'd melt a heart of stone, and mine's only flesh and blood. Take me in your arms a moment.'

He put his arms round her and they sat there silent for a little time in the snow.

She lifted her face and kissed him, then drew away as she said: 'Look, they've got the tents up; let's get inside.'

All of them crawled into one of the tents and lay for an hour huddled together in their sleeping-bags, until their mutual warmth had restored their circulation. Margery, who was the least fatigued of the party from having ridden most of the day, then got up and crossing to her own tent began to heat some coffee on the primus. As they had been so economical with their remaining food they had enough left for a small evening meal and for one more on the following day.

A few minutes later Lavina entered the tent carrying her sleeping-bag. She got one of the maps, crawled into the bag, and turning over on her tummy, began to write in pencil on its back. When she had done, she took some items out of the pockets of her coat and folded the map round them. They were a one-pound tin of marching chocolate, two small bottles of Brand's Beef Essence and a good-sized flask of brandy. She had selected them herself before they left Selfridge's and carried them with her through the whole journey as an emergency-ration in case she got separated from the party at any time and was temporarily lost.

Having made up her package she turned over and said to Margery: 'Do you know what to-day is?'

Margery looked up quickly. 'Yes, it's the 7th of September.'

'I expect Sam told you,' Lavina went on, 'that I promised to give him a decision on the 7th about our matrimonial tangle.'

'Yes, he told me that,' Margery replied, trying to still the sudden beating of her heart. 'But hadn't we better leave things now until we, er—well, you know what I mean?'

'No, I made a promise so I'm sticking to it. Whether any of us will live to cross the Straits of Gibraltar is pretty uncertain, but I see no reason why those of us who survive the next forty-eight hours shouldn't do so. This blizzard has been raging for over two days now and it can't go on for ever. Once it lifts, we'll be able to see a church tower or something sticking up out of the snow which will show us where Calais lies; and once the party's restocked from the food that must be in the houses there, it can begin the long trek south. Things should improve from then on with every stage of the journey, and even if some of the villages are buried completely it shouldn't be difficult to identify others from towers and gasometers, so there's quite a decent chance of getting through.'

'Yes, I feel that too,' Margery nodded. 'If only we can hang out for another forty-eight hours; but can we? With no fires, no brandy, and so little food?'

'Well, whether we can or not; as to-day's the 7th I'll tell you my decision. I believe you think that you're a better woman than I am because Sam's fallen for you; but that isn't true. You may be a very good cook and housewife but don't kid yourself that those things make you so very marvellous.

'You've never earned a penny in your life. If we were back in normal surroundings you couldn't hold down a job at more than a couple of pounds a week, however hard you tried; whereas I am an artist. People who know have even said that I'm near-great as an actress and you can't achieve that sort of thing without working for it. While you sat at home I slaved in the studios to make a career for myself. It isn't easy to do that and keep your self-respect, if you happen to be good-looking, in a game where all the strings are pulled by men; but I did it, and I did it by sheer hard work. When I threw up my job to marry Sam I was earning as much money as a Cabinet Minister, and I did that without any help or favours from anybody.

'What's more, you threw your hand in to-day but I didn't; and as woman for woman, you wouldn't stand an earthly chance against me. If I wished, I could get Sam back from you before to-night is out. But, as it is, I'm very fond of Sam and I believe that he'll be happier with you than he would with me.'

Margery's hands trembled and she drew a sharp breath as Lavina went on quietly:

'And I'm not thinking only of Sam. Although we've never been great friends I'm fond of you in my own way, because you *are* my sister and I haven't forgotten the good times we had together as children. We've grown apart a lot, but now we're up against it those sort of memories come back. It wasn't always my fault that every man we knew always fell for me, but I'd like to make it up to you a bit, now I have the chance.

'As there're no Law Courts or clergymen or anything left in the world, we'll have to go back to primitive conditions and look on Gervaise as our law-giver and priest. By his word, in the presence of the party, we must consider that he has formally divorced myself and Sam. Then he can read the marriage service over Sam and you. I hope, darling, that you'll be very happy.'

'Oh, Lavina!' Margery suddenly burst into tears and flung her arms about her younger sister. 'You don't know what this means to me. You can't. You've had so many people in love with you; but I've never known the joy of the love of a fine man before. If only we can get to Calais you've opened the gates of Heaven for me.'

For a little she sobbed, and then she said: 'But what about you, darling? What are *you* going to do?'

Lavina gently disengaged herself from Margery's embrace, picked up her package, and stood up. 'Oh, you needn't worry about me,' she smiled. 'I've still got a string to my bow.'

Pulling her furs round her, she added as she left the tent: 'I'll send Sam to you.'

The four men were still huddled in the tent which was shared by Sam and Hemmingway. Lavina undid the flap, poked in her head, and calling Sam out led him to the third tent, which at the moment was empty.

'Sam,' she said, as they crouched together in the confined space, 'I've just left Margery. I suppose you feel the same as you did when we talked things over a month ago?'

He nodded. 'Yes. I hate to hurt you, but I'm still in love with her—in fact I love her more than ever.'

Lavina smiled. 'I felt quite sure you did because I've been watching both of you very carefully.'

'To-day's the 7th, isn't it? What have you decided?'

'That I love you a great deal, Sam dear.'

As she paused she saw by the light of the candles that his face went white and that he was biting his lip, so she went on quickly: 'Therefore, I'm going to give you up. Just give me one kiss before you go to her.'

Sam took her in his arms and kissed her cold little face, muttering his thanks; then, feeling an utter brute, he turned and left her.

Sam had felt all along that Lavina would release him and he knew now beyond a shadow of doubt that he loved Margery best. Their perfect understanding of each other all through the long hours they had spent together during the last terrible month had proved that to him. As he entered the tent she lifted a face radiant, transfigured, beautiful, to his, and said:

'I didn't think Lavina would say anything until we were really safe again but I've just realized why she insisted on telling us now.'

Sam smiled as he knelt down and gently drew her to him. 'Why, it's the 7th and Lavina always keeps her promises. What other reason could she have had?'

'She wouldn't have waited till the 7th if we'd been in such desperate straits before. She wanted to give us to-night, Sam; and afterwards—well, I'm not going to mind half so much if we do have to die.'

'But we're not going to,' he said firmly. 'I have a hunch we're coming through. I don't get such hunches often but when I do I'm never wrong.'

Ten minutes later the coffee was boiling and Margery called out to the others. The three men came out of their huddle and as they crossed the few feet of open space between the tents Gervaise exclaimed:

'Hullo! The wind's dropped. Thank God for that at least.'

'It did last night,' said Hemmingway, 'but it didn't stop snowing.'

'Anyhow, it'll make it easier for me to do a little job I have in mind,' remarked Derek. 'There's a biggish hump about fifty yards inland. I noticed it while we were pitching the tents but I was too cold to go and examine it then. There's just a chance that it might conceal the roof of a cottage and it would be a godsend if we could shelter there for the night. Ask Margery to keep my coffee hot for me, will you, while I go and see?'

'Where's Lavina?' Gervaise asked as he and Hemmingway joined Margery and Sam.

'She's in your tent,' Sam replied at once. 'I left her there about a quarter of an hour ago.'

They called her loudly but she did not come, so Gervaise stepped outside, crossed the yard of snow, and lifting the flap of his own tent looked into it. Lavina was not there, but by the light of a candle he saw the big flask of brandy. Scrambling inside, he picked it up, then the chocolate, the Brand's Essence and then the map. Turning the map over, he saw writing on it that was addressed to him and, his hands trembling so that he could hardly hold it, he began to read.

Dearest, if the rest of you can hang out for forty-eight hours I'm sure you will find Calais; and, once you've done that, there'll be a really sporting chance for you all. But you'll never stick another two days of this without fires and with so little food. My share won't amount to very much between the five of you, but it'll help a little; and I've been carrying my own emergency-rations. The beef essence, the chocolate and the brandy will keep the warmth in you for just that extra day you need.

You're such a clever old sweet that I expect you guessed long ago how the wind was blowing between Margery and Sam. They love each other and I want them to be happy. I've released Sam and told Margery that you'd divorce him and me, but that won't be necessary now because I love you all so much that I'm going to leave you.

You mustn't worry about me because I'm not a bit frightened. It all seems quite natural and the reasonable thing to do. I'm the most useless member of the party and physically the weakest and, anyhow, I wouldn't be able to stick it out for another day.

It's no good your rushing out and trying to follow me. I know you will, but I'm going to cheat you there. I'm going to walk straight over the cliff edge, just to prevent your doing anything silly out of your dear love for me.

It's agony not to see you again before I go but I daren't risk any of you guessing what I mean to do, and I must go before the meal otherwise I'd have to eat my ration with the rest of you.

Give my love to them all but keep my fondest love for your own dear self. Lots of luck, and remember that I'm quite happy because I'm certain that, somehow, you'll pull through.

Your own Princess.

While Gervaise had been reading Lavina's scrawl Sam and Hemmingway, their suspicions aroused by his continued silence, had entered the tent behind him. One glance at the things Lavina had left, and another at Gervaise's stricken face, was enough to tell them what had happened.

Without a word the three men turned and went out into the snow. Outside the circle of the tiny encampment the broad tracks made by Lavina's snow-shoes showed plainly leading towards the cliff. Had she been gone one minute, two minutes, or ten, was the thought that leapt into all their minds. It would take her a good five minutes to cover the sixty yards of snow to the precipice. If she had been gone less than that time they still might save her.

Shouting her name at the tops of their voices, all three of them dashed forward along her tracks, but there came no answer to their shouting and at the cliff edge the tracks ceased.

A gap in the line of snow which fringed the precipice showed where Lavina had gone over. They had no means of descending and as they halted, staring blindly out into the still falling snow, they knew that their brave, self-willed little companion, who had brought them so much joy by her gaiety and beauty, must now lie dead upon the ice-pack forty feet below.

30

ONE MUST DIE

Before leaving Gervaise's tent Lavina had taken a good swig at
the flask of brandy to give herself strength for what she meant
to do, but she had no intention of throwing herself over the
precipice. She had said that she meant to in her letter because she
knew that that was the only possible way to prevent her friends
from following her and, once having abandoned their camp, all
dying of exposure that night.

Moreover, ever since she had been a little girl she had been in
love with her own body. It was such a perfect thing that she would
gaze at it in her long mirror for hours before going to bed at
night; and one of her favourite pastimes as a girl had been to
dance naked before that mirror for her own amusement. If she
ever bruised herself she felt the pain far less than the distress of
having temporarily marred that beautiful thing which was herself. Her skin was so fine and her blood so healthy that she rarely
suffered from a spot on the face, but if one ever appeared it
caused her greater agony of mind than a gnawing toothache, and
she would cheerfully have worked all through her school holidays
if by so doing she could have escaped such childhood ailments as
chickenpox and measles. Therefore, nothing could ever have
induced her wilfully to smash this thing that she had tended for
so long and with such loving care.

To fool the others she had walked straight to the cliff edge,
pushed a great lump of snow over, taken her snow-shoes off and,
jumping as far as she could from the place where her track ended,
set off along the cliff-top in her fur-lined boots, only putting the
snow-shoes on again when she had covered about fifty yards. In
the uncertain light it was extremely unlikely that any of the others
would notice the break in the snow at the place to which she had
jumped; and from there on she had taken the longest strides that
she could manage, so she was quite confident that none of her
friends would find out what she had done.

By the time she had covered a quarter of a mile the effect of her rest and the brandy had worn off. She was very tired again and began to stumble as she cast about for a sheltered place in which she could lie down. Two humps of snow with a shallow valley between them provided a likely-looking spot, so scooping up the snow with her gloved hands she blocked the far end of the little valley with a wall about two feet high. Then, making a pillow of snow, she sank down in the valley-bottom.

She knew, as does every British schoolchild, the epic story of that very gallant gentleman, Captain Oates, who walked out into a blizzard in the Antarctic, sacrificing himself in order that his fellow-explorers might have a better chance of surviving from being able to use his share of the remaining food; and perhaps that courageous act had subconsciously inspired her, but she herself did not feel any sense of heroism.

Although she was very young to die she had had a good life; beauty, success, many friends, even a happy marriage, before the comet had come to wreck everything. But now there seemed very little left to live for. Even if the others succeeded in reaching Calais there was the incredible hardship of the journey south still to be faced. The intense cold would wrinkle her beautiful face, frost-bite might strike at her any day. Her delicate shoulders were already assuming a permanent stoop from slogging forward through the snow. The journey would age her prematurely and she would be only a caricature of her former self by the time they had covered the thousand miles south to a warmer climate.

She had told the truth when she had written that she was not afraid. She had feared any risk in which she might be maimed all her life, but not death itself; and death would come gently to her as her limbs gradually numbed and she fell asleep in the snow. The cold was creeping up her limbs and she felt drowsy already as she surrendered to it now and thought fondly of her friends.

Gervaise would be heartbroken; poor Sam most terribly upset. Margery would persuade herself and the others that she felt the loss of her sister, but deep down she would not really be sorry because that loss would prevent any possibility of Sam's starting to hanker after his first wife again. Derek would be like a wounded animal nursing his grief in silence.

Dear Derek; what a good and faithful friend he had been.

And he was not so stupid that he could not also see how things had been going between Sam and Margery; yet he had played the game to the last and had never traded on his knowledge, as most men in his situation would have done, to try and draw her further from her husband.

And Hemmingway. Even in the blizzard he would hold his head high to-morrow, because he would be so proud. He loved her utterly. She knew that now; she had known it all along. He had loved her from the very moment he had first seen her, but how strong he had been in concealing it while they were in the Ark; and he had kept up that iron control over himself even when she had deliberately told him that she and Sam were on the point of parting, and given him a chance to come out into the open, that afternoon when they had sat together in the freezing downstairs room of the house at Sittingbourne.

She loved him, too, with all her body, with all her mind, with all her spirit. If only she had been a little stronger, strong enough to go on for another few days, everything would have come right. Directly he had known that she was free he would have claimed her. But that would only have made things worse for both of them when she died from exhaustion while they were still searching for Calais. The way that she had chosen was better, and it gave all her friends a good chance. The hardest thing of all had been for her to leave the camp without telling him that she loved him; but then, of course, he knew it. They had both known that they loved each other from the very beginning. She would have bartered her glorious golden hair for one half hour in which he could take her in his arms again. Her whole body ached for him. Then, as she lay thinking of him he came to her out of the blinding snowstorm.

Kneeling down beside her, he peered close into her face, and seeing that her eyes were open, smiled as he said simply: 'So here you are. I knew I'd find you.'

'How did you guess that I hadn't gone over the cliff?' she asked in a low voice.

'No one with a spirit such as yours could ever commit suicide. Waiting for death to take one in a case like this is quite different. I had to wait for a bit until I could slip away from the others before I could follow you, but I soon found the tracks of your feet in the snow.'

'I'm not going back,' she announced quietly, 'and I shall only run away again during the night if you try to carry me.'

'I know,' he said.

'Then why did you come?' she smiled, knowing the answer to her question even before she asked it.

'Because I prefer to die with you than live without you.'

'Dear Hemmingway.'

'My sweet Lavina. We've had a hard deal, haven't we? But our troubles are over now. You've given Sam his freedom, as I knew you would, and it's me you love, not Derek. There's nothing to separate us any longer and we'll spend the last hours of our lives together.'

She drew his head down to hers and kissed him, first gently then fiercely, crushing her mouth against his. As she released him she sighed. 'Yes, it's you I love. And you love me. How blessed we are in that we shall have such a happy death. But now you've come I don't want to die just yet.'

Hemmingway had brought with him his fur sleeping-bag. Stretching it out on the ground he laid her on it and chafed her hands and feet; then the two of them crawled into it and lay tightly embraced. Soon she was quite warm again. It was not until a quarter of an hour later that they even noticed in their sheltered little valley that the snow had ceased falling.

'Oh, thank God!' Lavina exclaimed. 'The blizzard's over at last. Now it's quite certain the others will find Calais to-morrow.'

'Yes. And they can eat a good meal now,' Hemmingway smiled. 'With only three of them left they can afford to have a proper breakfast.'

'Three of them?'

'Yes, I was just going to tell you. About the time you left the camp Derek left too. He said he was going to explore a hummock of snow that might conceal a cottage; but he didn't take his furs, and he didn't come back. After we had failed to find you we went out to look for him, but he'd abandoned his snow-shoes about thirty yards from the camp and his footprints were covered with fresh snow. When we got back we found he'd left a note. It simply said "*This is my last will and testament. I leave my share of the remaining food to Lavina and a wealth of good wishes to you all.*"'

'Dear, splendid Derek. How like him. But how I wish that he

could have the happy end that ours will be. Without furs he'll
die very quickly; he may be dead by now.' Lavina's voice
quavered but she steadied it and asked after a moment: 'How
long d'you think we've got, darling?'

'Until to-morrow, I should think. We may not wake up after
we go to sleep to-night, but if we do wake we'll remain lying here;
and once we start to get numb from inaction the end will come
quite peacefully.'

They talked far into the night in the great silence of the snow
that lay all about them, while the stars twinkled overhead in a
cold, frosty sky. They no longer felt any tiredness, and the dawn
was near breaking when they kissed for the last time and sank
into a peaceful slumber.

It was mid-morning when they woke. The warmth from each
other's bodies, their fur clothes and the fur sleeping-bag had
prevented them from freezing, and although they felt a little
empty from having had such short rations the day before, they
were overjoyed to know that they would have another day
together. The sun was shining so they knew that the odds were
all in favour of the others.

'We can change our minds if you wish, my sweet,' said Hemmingway. 'It'll be hard going on empty tummies but now the
blizzard's over we might find the town.'

She shook her head. 'No, darling, I'm too weak. I couldn't
manage another mile and when the others get to Calais they'll
only have their hands and the tent pegs to dig with. The houses
must be so deeply buried that they won't be able to break into
one until to-morrow; and then they may not find food until
they've tried several.'

As Hemmingway nodded she went on: 'It may be two or three
days yet before they find more than a few odd tins to keep them
going, and it wouldn't be fair to jeopardize the lives of the others,
even if we could rejoin them, now.'

'I know,' he smiled. 'That's just how I feel.'

For a long time they lay curled up in their bag talking softly
and caressing each other. Gradually they grew colder and their
lower limbs began to get numb. Time drifted on, and unnoticed
by them the sun passed the meridian. They became drowsy and
Lavina was half-asleep when, as in a dream, a tiny, insistent
sound caught her ear, breaking the great silence. Suddenly start-

ing up, wide awake, she wrenched herself out of Hemmingway's arms.

'What's that?' she cried. 'What's that?'

A faint, high, whining note came from the distance, gradually increasing to a roar.

'God!' shouted Hemmingway, struggling out of the bag. 'It's a plane! A plane!'

Next moment they saw it, flying at about 2,000 feet; a great, silver monoplane soaring through the blue sky southward down the Channel.

As it approached they stood on the cliff-top waving and shouting wildly. The plane passed almost overhead and they feared that its pilot had failed to see them but suddenly it curved out to sea, and, turning, came back towards them. It rose again, banked steeply, and turning into the wind, came gracefully down on to the flat surface of the hard-frozen snow at the base of the cliffs.

Frantic with excitement Lavina and Hemmingway waved to the occupants of the plane, who waved back to them from one of its windows. Stumbling from numbness but given new strength by their intense mental exhilaration they lurched along hand in hand seeking a way down to the sea-level.

After a twenty minutes they found a gap in the cliff and scrambled down it. Lavina fell, staggered up, and fell again; she could go no farther. Hemmingway picked her up in his arms and stumbled across the snow towards two people who had got out of the plane to come and meet them. To their joy and utter amazement they recognized the man and woman as Rupert Brand and Conchita del Serilla.

Half-fainting Lavina collapsed in Conchita's arms the moment Hemmingway set her down, while the two men crushed each other's hands as though they meant to break every bone in each other's fingers.

'Lord knows what happened when the comet hit the world!' said Rupert when their first greetings were over and the brandy from his flask was coursing through Lavina's and Hemmingway's veins, bringing them new life. 'We decided to face the business in my stratosphere record-breaker just as I'd planned half-jokingly at that lunch-party of Sam's where we first discussed the comet. We started out from central Spain, of course, and I took her up to

30,000; then just ran her round in wide circles. At the moment of impact we were chucked about as though the plane was a piece of paper in a high wind, but I managed to pull her out of it at about 9,000, and when we went down below the clouds to see what had happened we found that Spain had disappeared and we were in the middle of the ocean. I turned her then and headed her eastwards, but we had to fly nearly 400 miles before we came down and I landed her on a grassy plateau without having the faintest idea where we'd got to. After walking a few miles we struck a village and, would you believe it, I'm damned if we weren't in Norway!'

Hemmingway explained Gervaise's theory of the world having been thrown right off its axis, which would have flung Spain twenty degrees farther south while the plane had been bucketing in the air, and Rupert went on:

'By the mercy of God I decided to fly home to England the following afternoon, so we were in the air again when that huge wave came crashing along but I succeeded in finding a high stretch of land that the deluge hadn't submerged, somewhere up in the highlands of Scotland. It was only an island, but it was enough, and with the stores in the plane, some mountain-sheep that had escaped the deluge, and a crofter's potato-field we were lucky enough to find, we managed to exist somehow until the flood went down. After that the problem was petrol, and for the last month we've had one hell of a time scouring frozen villages, getting a tin here and a tin there until we could collect enough to fly the plane down to a decent climate.'

He had hardly finished speaking when Gervaise, Sam and Margery appeared in the distance. From Calais, which they had found that morning, they had seen the plane come down and had hurried out across the frozen sea towards it.

Ten minutes later they were all taking off their furs in the glorious warmth of the big, engine-heated cabin of the plane. Sam and Hemmingway were smiling at each other unable to find words to express their joy at their reunion. Gervaise only stopped hugging his cherished Lavina to spread out a map on her lap so that they could choose an oasis on the coast of equatorial Africa where they would be able to live on fish and dates until the plague from the dead bodies of men and animals in the towns of the equatorial belt had abated.

Rupert wheeled the big plane and taxied it across the hard snow. With its burden of three gloriously happy pairs of lovers and the gentle, elderly man who had led those he loved out of the land of death towards a new beginning, it rose gracefully into the clear, bright sky and sped south—south—south—to the Sunshine.

ALSO IN ARROW BOOKS BY DENNIS WHEATLEY...

THE DUKE DE RICHLEAU SERIES
The Prisoner in the Mask
Vendetta in Spain
The Second Seal
Three Inquisitive People
The Forbidden Territory
The Devil Rides Out
The Golden Spaniard
Strange Conflict
Codeword—Golden Fleece

THE JULIAN DAY STORIES
The Quest of Julian Day
Sword of Fate

ROGER BROOK ADVENTURES
The Launching of Roger Brook
The Shadow of Tyburn Tree
The Rising Storm
The Man Who Killed the King
The Dark Secret of Josephine
The Rape of Venice
The Sultan's Daughter

OTHER DENNIS WHEATLEY BESTSELLERS NOW IN ARROW EDITIONS...

Stranger Than Fiction
Star of Ill Omen
Curtain of Fear
Sixty Days to Live
The Fabulous Valley
They Found Atlantis
The Eunuch of Stamboul
Mediterranean Nights
The Man Who Missed the War
Gunmen, Gallants and Ghosts
Uncharted Seas
The Secret War
Such Power is Dangerous
Mayhem in Greece

GREGORY SALLUST STORIES BY DENNIS WHEATLEY

Black August
Contraband
The Scarlet Impostor
Faked Passports
The Black Baroness
V for Vengeance
Come Into My Parlour
Traitors' Gate
The Island Where Time Stands Still
They Used Dark Forces

BLACK MAGIC NOVELS BY DENNIS WHEATLEY

The Satanist
The Devil Rides Out
To the Devil—a Daughter
The Haunting of Toby Jugg
Strange Conflict
The Ka of Gifford Hillary

If you would like a full list of Arrow books
please send a postcard to
Arrow Books Ltd, 178-202 Great Portland Street, London W1